"RANNE...
RARE LIBRARY PROGRAM

He wa...
Scotlan...
bourne...
running...
in love...
fiery s...
woman who holds his heart, but revealing his heritage now would condemn them both. Yet as the mysterious Raven, an outlaw who defies the English and protects the people, Alec could be Leitis's noble hero again—even as he risks a traitor's death.

. . . But He Knew Her Heart Was His

Leitis MacRae thought the English could do nothing more to her clan, but that was before Colonel Alec Landers came to reside where the MacRaes once ruled. Now, to save the only family she has left, Leitis agrees to be a prisoner in her uncle's place, willing to face even an English colonel to spare his life. But Alec, with his soldier's strength and strange compassion, is an unwelcome surprise. Soon Leitis cannot help the traitorous feelings she has when he's near . . . nor the strange sensation that she's known him once before. And as danger and passion lead them to love, will their bond survive Alec's unmasking? Or will Leitis decide to scorn her beloved enemy?

KAREN RANNEY

BOOK ONE OF THE HIGHLAND LORDS

One Man's Love

An Avon Romantic Treasure

AVON BOOKS
An Imprint of HarperCollinsPublishers

This is a work of fiction. Names, characters, places, and incidents are products of the author's imagination or are used fictitiously and are not to be construed as real. Any resemblance to actual events, locales, organizations, or persons, living or dead, is entirely coincidental.

AVON BOOKS
An Imprint of HarperCollins*Publishers*
10 East 53rd Street
New York, New York 10022-5299

First Avon Books paperback printing: April 2001

Avon Trademark Reg. U.S. Pat. Off. and in Other Countries, Marca Registrada, Hecho en U.S.A.
HarperCollins® is a trademark of HarperCollins Publishers Inc.

Printed in the U.S.A.

10 9 8 7 6 5 4 3 2 1

To Lee Narek

Prologue

On his eleventh birthday, Ian kissed Leitis MacRae. She retaliated by slapping him. Hard.

He rubbed his cheek while glancing around quickly to see if anyone had witnessed either act.

The courtyard of Gilmuir was blessedly empty. No groom stood with a horse on the glittering white stone that covered the ground. Not one of the wagons that made its way daily across the land bridge from the glen was standing in the corner waiting to be unloaded. There wasn't a maid, cook, or blacksmith waiting patiently to see the laird. The massive iron-banded oak door remained fully closed, no amused face peering around it.

Ian sighed in relief, even as he prudently stepped away from Leitis.

"Don't ever do that again!" she shouted, glaring at him and scrubbing her hand over her mouth.

"It was only a kiss," Ian said, even as he realized it might well have been a mistake to act on impulse. But he had been thinking about kissing her for days now.

She was unlike any girl he'd ever known. Not that he met many, living in England at Brandidge Hall for most of the year. But it was summer, and he was in Scotland.

Every year he and his mother came to the Highlands. For two months no one told him to straighten his jacket or button his waistcoat. His tutor was left behind in England and Ian was not scolded once that he was acting like a ruffian. His mother only laughed when she saw him running through the stronghold that was his grandfather's home, as if she knew the feeling of freedom that thrummed in his blood.

Even his name was different, bestowed on him during his first visit to Scotland when he was six.

"Ian means John in the Gaelic and your middle name is John, am I right?" his grandfather had asked.

"Alec John Landers, sir," he said, nodding his head.

"A proper English name," his grandfather said, frowning. He had large bushy brown eyebrows and a wrinkled face as weathered as the cliffs of Gilmuir. "You'll be Ian MacRae here. I'll not hear the name of Landers."

And so it happened. No one ever knew his English name in Scotland, a testament to his grandfather's power. Niall MacRae had the ability to decree a thing done and it was.

Ian sometimes wondered at the cause of the enmity between the laird and his father. His parents had met in France when his mother was visiting relatives and his father was on his Grand Tour. Moira MacRae

had asked only one thing of the earl she married—
that any children they might have could learn first-
hand of their Scots heritage.

He was their only child, but that fact didn't stop
his father from allowing him to come to Scotland.
Every summer Ian and his mother came back to
Gilmuir, and each time he viewed Ben Haeglish in the
distance, he felt himself changing. By the time the
coach stopped in front of the old castle, the buttons of
his coat were half undone and his heart racing with
eagerness to see his friends Fergus and James. For the
last two years, however, he'd been just as anxious to
meet Leitis again.

She could fish as well as any boy, knew the forests
surrounding Gilmuir better than anyone. Bugs didn't
bother her and she could run faster than all three
boys.

"It's only a kiss," he said again, wondering if she'd
ever forgive him.

"Well, you shouldn't have done it!" she yelled.
"It's disgusting!" She stomped away, leaving him to
gaze helplessly after her.

"She has a right temper, does our Leitis," a voice
said.

Ian felt his face warming as he glanced over his
shoulder. Fergus and James stood there, both of them
looking somber. James was the elder by two years,
but he was shorter than Fergus. Their features
marked them as brothers, their red hair darker than
Leitis's.

"How could you kiss her?" Fergus asked in wonder. "It's Leitis."

"Are you angry?" Ian half expected it, and braced
his feet apart the way his grandfather had taught him.
He and Fergus had tested each other over the years,
with Ian winning a fight as many times as he lost.

Fergus shook his head. "Now, Mary I could understand. Or even Sarah. But Leitis?"

"She'll never let you forget it," James said soberly. "She has a long memory."

"And she'll tell the laird, too," Fergus offered with a grin.

Ian felt his stomach drop.

As laird, Niall MacRae could do more than change a name. He had the power of life and death over the entire clan, a group that numbered well over three hundred. His word was law and his dictates final. He often had a twinkle in his eye and a smile that said he didn't take himself that seriously, for all his authority. But he was fierce about protecting the people of Gilmuir.

What would he do after hearing Leitis's complaint?

"I don't know why you did it," James said, still staring after his sister. "It's not that she's all that pretty."

Incredulous, Ian stared at her two brothers.

She had red hair as bright as the dawn sun trailing down her back. Once, he'd had the temerity to touch it, wondering if the color would burn him. She'd jerked away and nearly coshed him for his daring. Her fair skin had only the smallest dotting of freckles across her nose. Her eyes were such a light blue that they reminded him of windows. He wanted to simply gaze into them, wondering if he could see all the way inside to her soul.

"Ian's daft, Jamie," Fergus said. "That's why he kissed Leitis. Is it from being half Sassenach, do you think?"

Ian felt the same flush of embarrassment each time his heritage was mentioned.

"I'd live here all the time if I could," he said, feeling a pang of disloyalty to his father even as he spoke the words.

"But then I'd miss you too much." A gentle laugh made him turn his head. His mother stood there, dressed for riding. Her habit of dark blue had a divided skirt, unlike anything she wore home in England. But here in the Highlands she chose to ride astride, not in the fashionable saddle his father decreed proper.

Both his friends fell silent at his mother's approach. Not simply because she was a countess, he thought, or the laird's daughter. She was so pretty that men sometimes stopped talking simply to gape at her.

Her black hair fell below her shoulders in tumbling curls that smelled like lavender. Her eyes were a piercing blue, the same shade as the laird's. People always wanted to be around her, as if sensing that there was something special about Moira MacRae. His mother found the smallest things fascinating, like the delicacy of a spider web or a pattern of ice on the window.

She extended her hand and ruffled Ian's hair. He ducked beneath her touch, embarrassed at the display of affection in front of his friends. She smiled understandingly and he grinned back at her. In private he didn't mind her sitting with her arm around his shoulders, or smoothing the hair back from his forehead. It was only with other people that he thought it important to look manlier.

He stood beside his mother as her horse was brought around, watching as she effortlessly mounted the big bay. "Will you be taking a few men with you?" he asked, remembering his grandfather's recent edict. The Drummonds were raiding again and no one was to leave Gilmuir without an escort.

It was one thing he'd never become accustomed to, the countless battles between the clans. In England a feud was resolved with a carefully worded note or even a request through a solicitor.

"Barbaric," his father said, often enough. "The damn Scots are all damn barbaric." But then the earl's gaze would fall on his wife's amused expression and he would smile and be silenced.

Here in Scotland it was almost commonplace to wake to his grandfather's shouts of anger at the news of another raid. He'd watched many times as the laird led his own men across the land bridge, the moonlight illuminating their kilted figures.

"No one can keep up with me," his mother said, smiling at him. "Besides, if the Drummonds raid," she said with a little laugh, "they'll be taking the cattle grazing in the glen or our sheep, not a woman on horseback."

She bent low over the saddle and whispered to Ian, "You should be less worried about me, my son, and more concerned about your birthday surprise," she said, smiling. "I'll give it to you when I return."

She gave her horse its head, racing across the bridge of land that connected Gilmuir to the glen. Once there, she halted and waved at him. She rode better than anyone he knew, even his father, and she'd become a common sight on these summer mornings, flying over the grass with her hair flowing behind her.

He waved back and then turned to his friends, impatient to be gone from the courtyard. It would be better, he decided, not to see Leitis yet. He'd give her temper a time to cool first.

"Are we fishing today?" he asked.

"No, I've another idea," Fergus said, grinning. "A secret."

"The staircase?" James asked, giving Fergus a quick, remonstrative look.

"What staircase?"

James punched his brother in the side sharply with his elbow. "We aren't supposed to tell. The laird made us promise."

"But Ian is his grandson," Fergus protested.

Ian looked at one brother, then the other. "What staircase?" he asked again.

The two boys fell silent, each glaring at the other.

"If we get into trouble, I'll say it was my idea," Fergus offered finally.

"You know what he'll say to that," James said, his eyes narrowing. "He'll say a man must weigh his temptations and consider the price he pays for every sin."

"We'll make Ian swear an oath," Fergus said, turning to Ian. "Hand me your dirk, James," Fergus said, commanding his older brother with the ease of much practice.

"Where's yours?"

"In the rain barrel," he admitted. "I used it for target practice and I couldn't free the blasted thing."

James shook his head and reluctantly handed him the knife, hilt first.

Ian stretched out his hand palm up toward his friend, knowing what Fergus planned. It was Fergus's version of the MacRae oath, binding once blood had been spilled.

"Swear on all that's holy to the MacRaes that you'll not tell anyone what we're about to show you," Fergus said solemnly, his words a mere whisper.

"I'll not," Ian said, and nodded to accentuate his pledge. Both James and Fergus nodded, satisfied with his curt vow.

Ian told himself not to flinch, even as the other boy

made a small cut in the fleshy part of his hand beneath his thumb. It was surprisingly painful, but he tried to ignore it, dropping his hand to his side and letting the blood drip onto the stone.

Fergus handed the dirk back to his brother and led the way through the courtyard.

Gilmuir, the ancestral home of the MacRae clan, stretched upward three floors to a high-pitched roof. The exterior walls had darkened over the years until the fortress appeared part of the earth itself. The castle was perched upon an elevated promontory jutting out into Loch Euliss. Bordered by cliffs on three sides, a wide bridge of land was the only passage to the glen.

The squat buildings clustered around Gilmuir housed the various occupations designed to support the clan. The carpenter's hut sat beside the forge, with the tanning shed and stables nearby.

They were all well-known places to the three boys. Fergus was to be a smithy, while James was training to be a carpenter. But during those weeks when Ian was in Scotland, they were released from their apprenticeships and given no more onerous task than being companions to the laird's grandson.

Fergus headed, not to one of the outbuildings, but to the priory instead. The structure was reputed to have been built long before the first MacRae made his home here nearly three hundred years before. The island was reputed to have been the refuge of a saint and a sacred site of pilgrimage.

Over the years, the MacRaes had shored up the brickwork of the priory and replaced the roof. Shutters had been built to enclose the stone arches. On fair days, like today, they were left open and sunlight spilled inside, illuminating the cavernous space.

Today the wind from the loch careened through the arches, sounding low and fierce, almost as if it growled at him in displeasure.

The two brothers moved to either side of the room, quietly closing the shutters until the room was encased in shadows.

Fergus halted in the center of the room. James walked a few steps farther, staring down at the slate floor.

"What are you looking for?" Ian asked. Neither boy answered him, so he waited in silence.

A moment later James spoke. "Here," he said, pointing to a spot in front of him.

"There's a hidden staircase here?" Ian asked, reasoning it aloud.

Fergus nodded.

"Where does it go?"

"I don't know," Fergus said, his grin broad and white in the gloom. "But I mean to find out."

"You don't know? Then how did you find it?" Ian asked, kneeling beside his friend. Fergus removed the top stone to reveal another square piece of slate, an iron ring embedded in the center of it.

Fergus's face changed, his grin fading as James frowned at him before reluctantly nodding. Ian had the impression that the older boy would just as soon be anywhere but here at the moment.

"Go ahead, tell him. We can't be in any more trouble than we are right now."

"We saw the laird come here one day," Fergus admitted.

"And we came to talk to him," James added.

"But he'd disappeared," Fergus said. "Then all of a sudden he popped up from the floor," he added, grinning broadly again.

"So did my heart out of my chest," James said. "I think he was as surprised as we were."

Fergus nodded. "But he wasn't pleased, that's for sure. And swore us to secrecy."

"Then we shouldn't go down there," Ian said, even as he peered into the hole. Although he wanted to explore it, his conscience whispered that his grandfather was not to be disobeyed.

"Ian's right," James said, moving to his side.

"What's the harm? The stone's already been moved, and you already know the secret." Fergus braced his forearms on either side of the space and a moment later disappeared into the darkness.

"What are you doing?" James asked as Ian sat and dangled his legs over the side.

"He shouldn't go down there alone," Ian said, the lure of the unknown proving to be irresistible.

His foot slipped before he found the first step. He reached out with both hands, feeling his way. The walls of the staircase were narrow and damp, the air heavy with moisture.

Ian heard James behind him, knew the other boy followed. A moment later Ian heard the sound of the stone being moved across the opening.

"Why didn't you bring a lantern?" he asked only a few feet below the surface.

"And what excuse would I have given for that?" Fergus asked derisively. "My ma wouldn't have let me out of the house without an explanation, not to mention what the laird would have said, to see us with one."

"He would have known we meant to disobey him," James said from behind Ian.

It was darker than night, oddly disorienting, the only reference point being either boy's voice.

The stench became even more intense as they traveled farther. He hoped it was only lichen clinging to the walls. Something equally slimy coated the steps, making them slippery. Twice he almost lost his footing.

The staircase finally widened. Gratefully, Ian stepped out of the darkness and into a domed cave, only to stop and stare at the space around him.

The morning sun illuminated the paintings on the tan-colored walls and ceiling. What the artist lacked in talent he made up for in perseverance. Each successive rendering of a woman's portrait was more skilled than before, until Ian stood transfixed at the beauty of the final painting. Here the woman was attired in a pale yellow dress adorned with trailing sleeves and a coronet of daisies in her hair. Her winsome smile and soft green eyes had been so perfectly executed that it seemed as if he could hear her breathe.

"Who do you think it is?" Fergus whispered beside him.

Ian only shook his head.

"It's Ionis's lady," James said, emerging from the staircase.

Ian looked at him questioningly.

"Ionis? The saint?" He glanced above him again. He'd heard the stories about Ionis from his grandfather and had thought them only MacRae lore. Now it seemed as if they were real after all.

Slowly, Ian followed the two boys out of the cave, his boots crunching on the pebbles. Ahead of him was a cove he'd never before seen. The deep blue water was surrounded on three sides by cliffs. Where Loch Euliss should be was a series of massive stones emerging from the bottom of the loch like the blackened teeth of some great monster.

Tipping his head back, Ian stared upward, expecting to see the priory above. Instead, there was only the steep wall of an overhanging cliff. He walked along the shoreline, his attention riveted on the last of the rocks in the chain. He circled the shoreline until his perspective was better. There was an opening between the chain of rocks large enough for a ship to pass.

The cove, Ian realized suddenly, was the true secret, not the staircase. It was Gilmuir's one vulnerability.

"We should leave," he said, his hand throbbing as if to remind him of his honor. Ian pushed past Fergus and entered the cave again. All he wanted to do now was leave this place, seal up the staircase, and pretend that he had never learned the secret.

"Where are you going?" Fergus asked.

He spun around, frowned at his friend. "The laird will not be happy," Ian cautioned. "And being his grandson won't matter if he learns I was here." In fact, his birthright might well make the punishment more severe.

He retraced his steps, ascending the staircase in half the time of the original journey.

It was with a sense of doom that he emerged from beneath the stone, saw the boots, then let his gaze travel upward. There was a woman in the clan who had the Sight, and claimed to feel the burden of the future. At that moment, Ian MacRae, born Alec John Landers, felt the same.

Most of the time there was a twinkle in his grandfather's blue eyes, but now they appeared icy.

"Come with me, Ian," the laird said, his voice echoing in the priory. "It's a man you'll be this day, and I'm sorry for it."

"Yes, sir," he said, forcing himself to look up into his grandfather's face and accept his punishment with bravery.

Ian hoped that his courage would not fail him. But his grandfather did not stop in the clan hall, nor retreat to the laird's chamber. Instead, he led the way through the archway and into Gilmuir's courtyard.

His grandmother stood in the courtyard, her apron over her face, weeping uncontrollably. "Moira, Moira," she moaned, rocking back and forth on her heels.

Ian felt a sense of dread so strong that it almost made him ill.

His mother's horse stood there, tied to the end of a wagon. His sides were lathered, his eyes rolling as he pulled away from the groom who attempted to calm him. Surrounding the wagon were several men, none of whom Ian recognized.

But it wasn't the strangers that caught his attention, nor his grandmother's weeping. He stepped forward, forced to by a feeling he could not name. A sense that after this moment there would never be the childish innocence and delight he'd felt at Gilmuir.

He walked closer to the wagon thinking that he truly wasn't here but in the midst of a strange waking dream. He was exploring in the cove below with Fergus and James.

The Drummonds had killed his mother, his beautiful laughing mother.

He wanted to be sick. Or cry. Or throw himself into his grandmother's waiting arms.

"The women will prepare her," someone said, laying a supportive hand on his shoulder. He glanced up to see his grandfather looking down at him, a look of pity in his eyes. Ian shook his head, determined to remain with her.

They took his mother to her chamber, the weeping women trailing behind. Ian also followed, silent and determined. When they washed her body, he turned away, but he would not leave her, and he did not speak.

"They raped her to death," one woman whispered in horror while his grandmother wept, inconsolable. Ian closed his eyes, his fists clenched at his sides to contain all of the rage and grief he felt.

He sat beside his mother's bier all night, watching for the moment when her eyelids would open, and she would smile and rise up, laughing in that merry way of hers. *Only a jest, my dearest,* she would say, and her eyes would sparkle with amusement. He stared so long that his eyes burned, barely blinking in case he missed that first halting breath. But her lids remained shut and her face was still and white in the light of the thick white candles at her head and feet.

His grandfather sat beside him, their chairs only a foot apart. But there was no talk during the lykewake, only a watchfulness maintained in order to guard the body and soul of the departed.

At dawn his grandfather stood as several members of the clan entered the room, signaling an end to this ceremony and the beginning of another. His mother would be laid to rest beneath the hills of Gilmuir.

He would never see her again.

James and Fergus, attired in their dress kilts, came to stand at his side, but Ian wished, suddenly, that they would leave. He was perilously close to crying and he would not do so in front of the two brothers.

Leitis emerged from the crowd, her hair tamed by a ribbon, her eyes brimming with tears. Her cheeks were flushed, her mouth red and swollen. He glanced at her and wondered why it felt as if a thousand years had passed since he'd been daring enough to kiss her.

Leitis came closer to him, stood on tiptoe, and kissed his cheek. Hours ago he would have been overjoyed at her gesture. Now he felt nothing.

She stepped back, and handed something to him. He cradled it in his palm. She'd wound a length of black wool tightly around a thistle and formed it into a circle.

"It's a remembrance," she said softly. "So that you'll not forget this day."

He glanced over at her, studying her as if he'd never seen her before this moment. How could she think that he would ever forget?

He deliberately dropped her gift, ground it beneath his boot.

"God wills," his grandfather said, placing his arm around Ian's shoulders. He looked up at the laird, his eyes dry and gritty. "We learn that as Scots, my boy. There's no need to punish someone else for what fate has brought us."

He stepped away from all of them, distancing himself from the clan, feeling an instant and overwhelming aversion to anything Scots. He was Alec John Landers, not Ian MacRae, and he stood clinging desperately to that thought in order not to cry.

"I am not a Scot," he said stiffly. "I will never be one. I'm English and I hate all of you."

Chapter 1

*I'm giving you a command, Colonel, one almost as vital
as your mission. Stamp out this damnable insurrection. Execute every one of those miscreants if you must, but
deliver the Highlands to me in peace.*

The Duke of Cumberland's words echoed in Alec
Landers's mind as he neared Fort William. Behind
him rode five handpicked men who'd accompanied
him from Inverness. Their conversation mingled with
the jangle of harness, the clop of horses' hooves on the
thick grass, and the moan of wind, forming a backdrop for his thoughts.

On the crest of a hill not far from his new post, he

stopped and raised his hand. His men halted, remaining in position. Not one of them questioned his delay or why he dismounted and walked a few feet to the edge of the road. It would never have occurred to them to do so.

He stood staring down at the scene before him, memory furnishing the quiet moment with details.

For six years, from the time he was five until his eleventh birthday, their coach had stopped in exactly the same place. His mother would lean out of the window beside him in order to view her childhood home. Gilmuir sat like a welcoming beacon, a wondrous world that might have been created solely to grant her every wish. She would begin to smile in a different way than she did in England, as if she, too, threw off all constraints.

What would his mother think now, all these years later, to discover that Fate, or a vengeful God, had sent him back to her native country? A foolish question to ask because he'd never know the answer.

For most of the year this land was covered by a stark, inhospitable grayness, a monochromatic hue that announced it was Scotland. But now heather and thistles and wildflowers bloomed riotously over the hillsides, casting shadows among the green grass and clover. Loch Euliss was deeply blue, surface waves stirred by the sudden fierce wind.

A storm loomed, as if to greet him. The sunlight, diffused through the curtain of clouds, bathed the castle in an otherworldly light. It was a strange welcome to this place of memory.

The promontory was a place ideally suited to repel invaders. But the builders of the castle had not been prescient about English cannon or the anger of the Empire as they extracted revenge against the recalcitrant and rebellious Scots. Gilmuir had evidently been bombarded into submission and now nothing more than a roofless shell.

Will Gilmuir last forever, Grandfather?

As long as the sea, Ian. As long as the sea.

But it hadn't. Instead, it had fallen and now lay broken and shattered, a skeletal companion to the newly constructed Fort William.

Cumberland himself had chosen Alec among the cadre of officers in Flanders to accompany him back to Scotland to quell the rebellion. For his ability to stay alive in battle and for his greater capacity to remain silent and obedient, Alec had been given command of Fort William.

He'd wanted to protest, to give the duke some rational refusal of the post, but it would not be wise to tell Cumberland of either his heritage or his reluctance. The first could get him hanged; the second would only result in the duke's displeasure.

A mist was blurring the horizon, tinting the mountains blue. The glen was heavily forested on the western side, but on the east was cropped as cleanly as if sheep grazed on the grass. Below him, in a secluded corner of the glen, was the village he knew almost as well as Gilmuir. A clachan, the Scots called it. He had been a visitor to many of those houses, almost a third son in the place Fergus and James called home.

The stones of the cottages were tinged with green, moss having added its own hue over the years. Each was alike, a long rectangular structure intersected in the middle by a door and flanked by two tall windows. The thatching on the roofs had matted over the years until they appeared like crisp brown crusts on freshly baked bread loaves.

Yet another place of memory, one he would do well to avoid.

He mounted again, gave the signal, and began to ride toward Gilmuir, banishing all thoughts of the past. It was easier to concentrate upon his task, and the duty given him.

The sky was darkening even as the wind increased, the gusts blowing bits of leaves and grasses past the open door of her cottage. Leitis glanced outside. A beam of light suddenly speared a menacing cloud, brushing its outline in gold as if announcing the presence of God in the oncoming storm. Sadness seemed to linger in the air as if the earth prepared to weep.

Leitis closed her eyes, hearing the murmur of the threads beneath her fingers. The sounds became, in her longing mind, teasing conversation between her brothers. The wind, laden with the scent of rain, was not unlike the subdued laughter between her parents. The gentle kiss near her ear was not the air brushing a tendril of her hair, but a touch from Marcus as he bent close and whispered endearments.

Above the sound of the oncoming storm she could almost hear the music of the pipes. The tune pierced her heart, reminding her of times of welcome. In her mind, her younger brother Fergus waved to her from a nearby hill. Beside him, her older brother James grinned, glad to be home once more. Marcus, the man she was to marry this spring, walked with them, as did her father. He made a jest and all four men laughed, their heads tipped back, the sound of their merriment lost in the sound of the wailing pipes.

Spirits. All of them nothing more than spirits, summoned to her on this storm-filled summer day to wet her eyes once more.

The loom was a comfort. She had learned this skill when she'd been barely tall enough to sit on the

carved bench. All of the memories of her life were entwined with the acts of her fingers and the touch of
the threads. She'd been weaving when news had
come of the prince landing at Loch nan Uamh. She'd
finished a plaid just in time to drape over her father's
shoulders as he led his sons off to bring Scotland's
rightful king to the throne. Here, too, she'd been occupied when word had come of Culloden and the loss
of life there.

The cottage had never seemed as large as it had
this past year. The interior rock walls had been white-
washed years ago, the earthen floor tamped down by
generations of feet until it was smooth as stone. The
furniture was simple but built for wear—a large table
of oaken boards surrounded by six chairs, a tall bureau that held her mother's treasure, a fine porcelain
ewer, and a basin adorned with a pattern of purple
flowers. In the corner, beyond the two partitions built
by her father, was her parents' bed, and farther still
her own. Her brothers had slept in the space above,
reached by a ladder propped in the corner.

She was the only occupant of the cottage now. Her
father, Fergus, James, Marcus, all gone. Her mother
had died almost in relief only weeks after her sons
and her husband had been lost.

The sound of the pipes grew, punctuating the far-
off sound of the thunder. The MacRae Lament
swelled, the music seeping into her bones and her
very soul. She blinked open her eyes, suddenly realizing that the melody was too clear to be a memory. Too
dangerous to be anything but foolish.

Not Hamish again.

She abruptly stood, pushing the bench beneath the
loom. Walking to the open door of her cottage, she
stopped for a moment, one hand upon the frame, the
other tightened into a fist and resting in the folds of

her skirt. The sound was not a dream, nor a fancy, but her uncle daring the English.

Perhaps the soldiers had not heard, and the people of Gilmuir would be safe from the consequences of Hamish's defiance. Even as she had the thought, she chided herself for the foolishness of it. The music of the pipes carried well over glen and hill.

Reaching for the shawl hung on a peg by the door, she covered her head and walked quickly from the cottage, cutting in front of Malcolm's puny garden and up the cleft created between two gentle mounds of earth. A well-worn footpath led to the hills above her, a journey she knew well.

The wind pressed her dress against her body and blew her hair back. Nature was a lover in that moment, caressing her ankles and wrists and throat, bathing her in a kiss that tasted of moisture and sunlight in one.

A flash of lightning taunted her, reminding her that it was not the wisest thing to be climbing a hill in a thunderstorm. Still, there was less to fear from nature when mankind was loose on the earth. A lesson she had learned this past year.

She climbed up the rolling earth, past the gathering of flowers. The primrose with its yellow center and bright pink blossoms bobbed in the gusting breeze as if welcoming her. The thistles were proud things, tall and spiky, their large-headed blooms a bright yellow or purple. The harebell had a delicate stem and pale blue nodding blooms and was her favorite of all the flowers. It was hardy and thrived despite its fragile appearance.

The glen was bordered on one side by dense forests, thick pines crowning a knoll that provided a commanding view of the countryside. It was there she sought out her uncle, knowing that it was a favorite spot of his. She followed the path upward, ducking beneath low-hanging limbs and pushing her way through the undergrowth.

The hillock was bared of trees like a bald man's pate. Once, a giant pine had stood here, sentinel for the forest. But it had been struck by lightning years before and had fallen to the ground so hard that the earth had shuddered.

To her right was Gilmuir. Veiled in the morning mist, it looked whole again, and if she squinted, she could almost pretend that smoke emerged from its four chimneys and the courtyard was filled with people all going about their business. Lively ghosts crafted by her wishes.

The squat fort beside it could not be ignored, no matter how much she wished it away.

To her left the forest stretched up over rounded hills, then undulated down into a neighboring glen. Ahead was the loch, and beyond it the firth leading to the sea. A vast place, she'd been told, where a ship might travel for weeks without viewing land. But the reward was the sight of places that sounded mystical and almost frightening—Constantinople, China, Marseilles.

She pushed a few branches out of the way to see Hamish standing there defiantly, dressed in his kilt. Nestled in his armpit was the deflated bladder of his bagpipes. His back was to the newly constructed Fort William. A mischievous breeze blew the rear of his kilt up, but he didn't appear at all concerned that he bared his arse to the English.

"It is a foolishness you do, Uncle," she said with asperity.

He frowned at her, his fierce expression reinforced by the fact that his brows, white and furry like overfed caterpillars, grew together over the bridge of his nose.

"I'll not be scolded by a slip of a girl," he said fiercely. "Especially not about the pipes."

"I've not been a slip of a girl all these many years, Uncle, and you know it," she said. Placing her fists on her hips, she glared at him. "And playing the pipes is outlawed now, or have you forgotten that?"

"An English law. Not mine." He drew himself up to his full height and stared up at her.

It was difficult to see him at that moment. Once a broad bull of a man, he'd shrunk in the last two years. His beard had whitened to match his hair. But he still bore a look of stubbornness about him.

"There are young ones in the clachan, Uncle, who do not deserve to suffer." The English would enforce their laws despite Hamish's defiance and bluster. The soldiers at Fort William were never going away, a fact she regrettably understood, but one Hamish did not yet comprehend.

"Come away," she said kindly, reaching out for his arm. But he had ceased to listen to her. Instead, he had turned and begun to play his pipes again. She glanced at him, then beyond to Fort William. The soldiers spilled out of the fortress like a determined column of red ants. A foolish wish, indeed, to hope that he had not been heard.

"The English are coming," she said, resigned to another visit from Major Sedgewick. Another threat, another act of cruelty. What would he do today? Take away their livestock? It was gone, all the cattle and sheep. Trample their crops? Already done. Take their possessions? He'd already stripped the village of all those valuables not concealed in the neighboring caves.

"You should hide the pipes," she said, biting back a more severe retort. It was worthless to be angry with him. In some ways he still lived in the past, when the

MacRaes had been kings of this land. "Hide yourself as well, Hamish," she cautioned.

She left him without turning to see if he took her advice. Hamish would do as he wished, regardless of what she said.

By the time she'd descended the hill, the English soldiers had reached the village. Those people who were not quick enough to gather were roughly pulled from their cottages. Twenty-seven of them left, where once there had been over three hundred. But that had been in her youth, when the only English troops in Scotland had been General Wade with his eternal road-building.

She walked swiftly to the gathering place in the middle of the village. Major Sedgewick sat upon his horse, his officers similarly mounted and surrounding him. He was dressed in his usual fashion in a square-cut red coat, the lapels pinned back. His breeches were blue, his boots and belt of buff leather. His hair, golden and clubbed in the back, was lit by a last gleam of sunlight spearing through dark, boiling clouds.

She reached up with one hand and gripped her shawl tightly, engaging in a tug-of-war with the fierce wind, feeling a chill that had nothing to do with the weather. Instead, it was the look in Sedgewick's eyes as his gaze rested on her.

"What will they do, Leitis?" Dora asked from beside her. The older woman's face was tight with worry. Leitis only shook her head, uncertain.

"What else can they do?" Angus asked. He leaned heavily on his cane and frowned at the English soldiers.

The major reminded her of a rat, with his narrow face and pointed teeth. He had carried out his orders with great zeal. A lesson, then, about the English notion of victory. Keep people hungry and they will have no will to rebel. Watch as they bury first the old and then the young, and soon enough they will obey without question.

She kept her gaze upon the ground, wishing that he would look away. She took care to avoid the attention of the English. Every woman in the clan knew the danger that faced her with one hundred soldiers at Fort William.

"One of you is guilty of disobeying the Disarming Act again," the major announced. At their silence, he smiled thinly. "Where is your piper?" he demanded.

It was not the first time Hamish had angered the English. Nor, she suspected, would his defiance end today. But not one person spoke up to betray him. Despite their common knowledge that it would cost them all, they remained mute.

The major dismounted, stood before them, his face twisted by anger.

"Have you nothing to say?" he asked, coming up to Angus. "If I promised you a full meal and a pint of ale, old man, would you speak?"

"I'm an old man, Major," Angus wheezed. "My hearing is not as good as yours is. I heard nothing."

Sedgewick studied the old man's face for a long moment before he moved on, stopping in front of Mary. She cradled her child, born after her husband's death. "And you, madam?"

Mary shook her head, then pressed her cheek against Robbie's downy hair. "I was tending to my child," she said softly. "And heard nothing."

Sedgewick strode through their group, studying each face, his expression growing increasingly angrier when no one spoke up to denounce Hamish.

Leitis saw his boots as he approached her. "What about you? Were you occupied with other duties?" he asked in a low tone.

She said nothing, only shook her head, wishing he would move away.

"Where is the piper?" Sedgewick demanded, turning and addressing the clan.

No one spoke.

"Bring me a torch," he said. One of the soldiers hurried to obey him, returning with a length of thatch torn from a nearby roof and twisted into a sheaf. Sedgewick waited until it was lit, then grabbed it and held it aloft.

"How much is your loyalty worth?" he asked them. "Your homes? Your lives? We shall have to see."

He moved to the nearest cottage and put the torch to the low-hanging roof. It immediately burst into flame, the fire fueled by the winds of the coming storm.

The cottage was blessedly empty, its occupant having died the summer before.

Sedgewick moved on to the next structure. Leitis watched in silence as her own home was set ablaze.

Her thoughts were her own, and as long as she held them tight within, she could not be punished for them. She stared at the ground, unable to witness the destruction of her home. At that moment her hatred of all things English grew so strong that it threatened to choke her. But her anger would not aid Hamish and it would not stop Sedgewick.

The major moved on to the next cottage, watching with some satisfaction as another roof erupted in a blaze. His intent was all too obvious. He would not stop until their entire village was on fire.

It wasn't enough that she had lost her loved ones. But now all her memories were to be destroyed, too.

The pottery her mother loved with the faint blue pattern upon it, the plaid she'd hidden below a mattress, the loom that occupied her days.

The black storm clouds mimicked her mood, crowding out the last hint of blue sky and rendering the day nearly dark.

"Tell me where he is," Major Sedgewick said, approaching Leitis once more.

"You English will not be happy until there is no trace of a Scot in Scotland, will you?" she asked unwisely. But she was suddenly weary of remaining docile when it brought nothing but more cruelty. "Are we not dying fast enough for you?"

He struck her, so hard that she fell to her knees. He stood above her, waiting for her to stand, no doubt, so that he could strike her again.

"I would rid this place of its vermin," he bit out. "Perhaps you will be the first."

Lightning answered him, streaking suddenly from cloud to earth, the flash so brilliant that it blinded her for a moment. The thunder following a second later was loud enough to be the voice of God. In that next moment, all Leitis could hear was emptiness, an echo of her own heartbeat, fast and panicked.

She pressed her hands against her eyes, then blinked rapidly in order to regain her sight. The air smelled like fire, as if the earth had opened up in that moment and the creature she saw emerging from the white glare had ascended to earth on Satan's mission.

He was outlined in the next flash of lightning, an image limned in black. His black hair, like the other men's, was tied back with a ribbon. His coat was crimson, his waistcoat beige and bearing an ornate badge on one lapel and an insignia on the other. His breeches were also beige, topped with a white shirt ruffled on the chest and cuffs.

He wasn't an illusion or a demon after all, only an Englishman. A red-coated officer not as richly outfitted as the major. There were fewer buttons on his waistcoat, and they appeared to be made of bone, not gold.

She wished, improvidently, that she might see his face.

He ignored the lightning flashing around him as if it were no more than a minor inconvenience. His left hand rose and the men who followed him slowed. A man accustomed to authority, if the way he controlled his restive horse was any indication. He held the reins loosely in his right hand, his left hand now resting on a muscled thigh.

Major Sedgewick cursed softly, moved away from her.

"Colonel," he said, standing stiffly at attention. "I did not expect you until next week."

The other man said nothing, his gaze fixed sternly on Sedgewick. Leitis had the sudden thought that she would not like to be the focus of his anger. As if he heard her, the stranger looked over at her. Her breath was captured on an indrawn gasp.

His face was square, his jaw accentuated by the tightness of his expression. The look in his eyes was so direct that Leitis felt as if he stripped her bare in that moment, learned her secrets, and divined her silent rebellion. His cheekbones were high and well defined, his mouth now thinned by rage.

A dangerous man.

She took one step back, away from Sedgewick. A moment later the stranger granted her unspoken wish by looking away. Only then did she dare to breathe.

Chapter 2

L eitis.

·His recognition of her was instantaneous, even though he had deliberately not thought of her on the journey from Inverness, telling himself that she would have married and moved away from the village long ago.

Riding to her side, he dismounted quickly. She flinched when he bent and placed his hands on her arms and helped her to rise. He frowned as he noted the swelling on the side of her jaw. Sedgewick's blow would leave a mark.

"Are you all right?" he said softly.

She nodded, averted her head, staring instead at the troops encircling the village.

Her mouth was full, her cheeks pink with color.

The years had darkened her hair until it was not bright red as much as a muted auburn, but it still curled around her shoulders, tied back with a ribbon just as she'd worn it as a child. Her eyes, those surprising light blue eyes, marked her as the girl he'd known.

"You will have a bruise," he said gently, studying her face.

She turned her head and looked directly at him. There was no doubt as to her feelings at that instant. Her eyes were filled with hatred and her mouth thinned in anger. "I've known worse, Colonel."

Time had not softened her daring. But perhaps she'd had need of it in the past year. The weak had not survived.

Alec turned, surveyed the soldiers. "Who's in command here?" he demanded.

"I am, sir. Major Matthew Sedgewick," one man said, stepping forward.

"Explain yourself, Major," Alec said, his voice low with fury.

"She is a Scot, sir," Sedgewick said tightly. "One who does not know her place."

"Striking a woman is more the act of a coward than an officer," Alec responded.

The major's face darkened, but he said nothing.

"Is there a reason you've set fire to this village, Major Sedgewick?" Alec asked. "Or did you do so simply because it's Scottish?"

Sedgewick's brows drew together. "These people are guilty of sedition, sir. After numerous warnings, they continue to shield a man known to encourage rebellion. A piper, sir."

Alec glanced over at the huddled villagers. There was not one able-bodied man among them. Mostly women and children in the company of a few old men.

Where were James and Fergus? Had they perished, as well as other members of the clan he'd known as a child?

"Would it not be more worthwhile to find the miscreant, Major?" he asked. He gestured for his adjutant. Harrison dismounted, walked to his side.

"Get those men into a fire brigade and have them find whatever they can to carry water," he said, pointing in the direction of the stream that fed the glen. "I want a trench dug between the cottages that are ablaze and those that have not yet caught fire."

Harrison nodded and left to convey his orders.

"I am charged with controlling the Highlands, sir," Sedgewick said testily. "These barbaric Scots do not deserve any clemency. Cumberland himself decreed that any man who gave aid to the enemy was to be hanged."

"I'm well aware of the duke's words, Sedgewick," Alec said curtly. "Are you presuming to remind me of my duty?"

Sedgewick wisely remained silent.

"I apologize for the actions of this man," Alec said to Leitis. An errant wish made him want to smooth his fingers over her cheek, spare her the pain of the blow.

She looked startled at his words, but she remained silent. So as not to anger him? He felt a surge of anger toward Sedgewick once again.

The men began to form a line from the stream. As they realized what the soldiers were doing, the villagers began to move. They retrieved buckets, bottles, basins, pitchers—anything that could hold water from their own homes in an attempt to save their friends' cottages. Alec watched as Leitis joined the procession, glancing back at him once before looking away.

The lightning flickered across the darkened sky, the thunder drowning out the noise of the flames. It was a curious sensation, Alec thought, to be so aware of the moment that it seemed to slow. Leitis's hand reached up and, in a delicate motion, brushed a tendril of hair from her cheek. Turning, she took a bucket from the man behind her and relayed it to the person ahead of her, the movement swirling her skirt, revealing an ankle and the feminine sway of a hip.

Her eyes, however, were downcast, her attention directed on her chore. He had the feeling that she deliberately didn't look in his direction, and her effortless repudiation stung. He had recognized her easily enough, but she did not look past the crimson of his uniform.

The rain began at that moment, hard and punishing, as if to summon Alec back to himself.

Black smoke from the fire curled into the sky like wet ribbons. The rain-soaked air carried with it the smell of burning thatch, acrid and choking.

Hamish MacRae stood on the crest of the hill and watched the conflagration, feeling a sense of pride so powerful that it nearly knocked him to his knees. Not one person had spoken out to denounce him.

He readjusted the bladder beneath his arm, straightened his sporran. He wore the MacRae plaid, another sin according to the English.

There was no choice, after all. He must surrender himself. Either that or allow the village to be burned to the ground.

He left the knoll, strangely exuberant as he followed the path that wound through the forest. Perhaps he should have been afraid, but he wasn't. And that might have been the most foolish thing of all.

He tucked the bag into place, the plaid sticky with the honey that rendered the bag airtight. Three pipes rested on his shoulder as he blew into the blowstick and fingered the chanter.

The pipes were designed to be played in the open air, with God listening above the bowl of sky. Hamish hoped that God was indeed listening now, and began to play.

The thunder finally eased as if nature had tired of its noisy tantrum. But the air was still white with rain.

In moments her dress was sodden, the hem dragging in the mud. Her hair hung in wet tendrils down her back. Her eyes smarted from the smoke.

It was only too obvious that there was no chance of saving her cottage, but Leitis passed a bucket filled with water to Angus and forced a smile to her face when he glanced over his shoulder at her.

As the blaze grew hotter, glass and pottery began to burst from the heat. Every sound affected Leitis like a cannon shot.

There was, in the end, nothing to be done. It was, perhaps, a lesson in the strength of hope that she did not stop working even long after the others began to slow and step aside.

Finally, Angus touched her shoulder in wordless comfort, his eyes filled with pity. She nodded, moving out of the line. Walking to the ruins of her cottage, she stared inside the doorway. The moss-covered stones still stood; the mortar only grayed by the smoke. But the interior was blackened, every item reduced to ash or a glittering puddle of melted glass. The raindrops hissed as they struck the heated objects, the sounds almost like the whispers of grief.

Her home was gone.

She heard the thought, knew it was true, but for some reason she couldn't feel anything. She stared at the destruction, unable to understand.

A movement to her side made her turn her head. The English officer stood there, his face and hair slick with rain.

His presence, oddly enough, rendered the devastation real. The sudden pain she felt was almost unbearable.

He said nothing to her, still studying her in a way that was unsettling. His face was oddly arresting, as if she recognized it somehow. But she had never before seen him. If she had, she surely would have remembered.

"I will send some men to help you salvage what you can," he said.

She glanced inside the cottage once more. "Will you replace the porcelain that my mother was left from her mother?" she asked, the words coming fast and without thought. "Or the silver bracelet that was my dowry? And my loom? Will you replace that, too?"

For a moment he simply stared at her, giving her time to wonder at the consequences of her words. What could he take from her now? Her life? What was left of it? Sleeping when dreams did not come. Eating when she could find something edible. Everything else of value had been taken from her, and the last of it, those possessions and trinkets that had recalled a more joyous time, were now unrecognizable smoldering lumps.

To make the moment even worse, Hamish began to play the pipes. The tune was not a lament, which might have been more appropriate at this moment, but the MacRae March, used in past years to summon the clan to Gilmuir.

Now she was going to lose her last relative. She glared at her uncle, but Hamish blithely ignored her, piping himself to his death.

Chapter 3

A t the first sounds of the pipes, grating and harsh, Alec spun around.

A man, attired in a kilt of red, black, and white MacRae plaid, stood halfway up the hill. On his shoulder was a set of pipes, the sound coalescing into a tune of sorts. The last time Alec had heard the bagpipes had been at Culloden, and that memory was never voluntarily recalled. Now the glen echoed with the music as if the hills and rocks magnified the sound.

The face was older, the body more bowed and stunted as if age itself weighed heavily on him. But Alec recognized the man from his childhood. Hamish MacRae.

Several of the English soldiers moved to intercept

the Scot, but he didn't attempt to elude them. Instead, he continued to walk stiffly down the hill, defiantly playing.

"He has courage," Harrison said quietly from beside him.

"There's a fine line between bravado and bravery," Alec said dryly.

"Restrain him!" Major Sedgewick called out. As the soldiers grabbed the piper, the tune abruptly ended, the dying notes high-pitched and whining.

Alec strode to where Sedgewick stood surveying the prisoner.

"Take him to the gaol," the major said, then glanced over his shoulder at Alec. "Unless you would like to question him here, Colonel," he said.

Alec shook his head.

Hamish focused his attention on Sedgewick. "It's me you want," he said. "Not them. Unless the English only choose to wage war on women and children."

Alec deliberately stepped between Hamish and Sedgewick. If the major would strike a woman, nothing would make him hesitate in harming an old man. From the look on Sedgewick's face, he was close to doing so.

"Perhaps it would be better if you returned to the fort, Major," Alec said curtly. "I will attend to the prisoner."

For a moment he thought the major was going to protest. His unspoken words seemed to choke him. But Alec had been battle-hardened since he'd left home at the age of eighteen, trading his paternal grandmother's legacy for a commission in the army. He was well prepared to handle a recalcitrant officer.

Sedgewick finally nodded before striding away, his anger evident in the stiffness of his shoulders. Alec watched as he mounted and rode toward Fort William.

He turned to two of the men who'd accompanied him from Inverness. "Keep the men here until you are certain the blaze is extinguished," he said, "then take the prisoner to the gaol."

"I believe you have made an enemy there, sir," Harrison said, joining him a moment later. He nodded in Sedgewick's direction.

Alec glanced at his adjutant.

Thomas Harrison was the most sober of his officers, rarely speaking when a gesture could suffice. Alec had relied on Harrison's discretion from the moment they met in Flanders. Only his adjutant and his aide, Sergeant Tanner, knew all of the secrets of his past.

Harrison, for all his attributes, had a remarkably unappealing face. His nose was broad and his chin pointed. Deep-set hazel eyes peered out at the world with a steady and watchful expression.

If there was only formality between them, it was because of Alec's reserve. He was conscious of his command and the fact that it was not wise to grow close to the men he sent into battle. Yet there were times, such as now, when their relationship slipped into friendship.

"It was to be expected that he would resent my presence here. After all, he was in charge of the garrison before my arrival," Alec admitted.

"It will not be an easy task you've been given, Colonel," Harrison said.

"Cumberland's dictates have never been particularly effortless," Alec said.

Without glancing at Leitis again, he mounted, turning toward Fort William, Harrison at his side.

Constructed of red sandstone, Fort William sat to one side of Gilmuir, its back to the sea. The structure was built in the shape of an open square, the front facing the land bridge.

"It's ugly," his adjutant said without apology.

"It's utilitarian," Alec countered, smiling.

He noted the details of construction, similar to other English fortifications in Scotland. Ten cannon portals faced the glen, the slope of the facade attesting to the fact that the guns were surrounded by inner and outer walls with a layer of earth between to act as a barrier for both fire and noise. If the rest of the building proved true to similar fortifications, the seaward side would have cannon as well.

He would need to hold inspection, be introduced to the troops, and ascertain the duties of the men under his command. But he glanced, instead, at the ruins of the structure located to the right of the fort.

Harrison's gaze followed his. "Castle Gloom," he said with a smile.

"Gilmuir," Alec corrected him.

He rode closer, feeling as if he were being inexplicably drawn to the castle by memory.

"How long did it take to destroy it?" Harrison asked, surveying the ruins.

Alec only shook his head in response. It was evident from the patchwork nature of the fort that Major Sedgewick and his men had run out of sandstone and used the bricks and stones from Gilmuir to complete the fort. Piles of rubble still remained where the courtyard had once been. The outbuildings had been destroyed, any trace of the structures vanished.

He dismounted, stared up at the castle. The roof was gone, the tall front wall only half its original size. A year of rain and cold had already made its presence known. The interior bricks were no longer a warm ochre, but tinted with green as moss grew in nooks and crannies.

He strode inside what he had known as the clan hall. The rain pattered against the battered floor timbers, adding to the air of melancholy.

The shields and the claymores that had once adorned the west wall were gone. As a child he'd thought them both terrifying and wondrous. There, in that empty space, had been the large banded chest where his grandfather kept his plaids, the hunting tartan, and the dress kilt. And at the head of the hall was where the laird had sat to keep counsel, in a carved chair that looked to Alec's young eyes to be a throne. It was gone now, only a light square remaining where it had once stood.

A surge of memory came with each footfall, each step across broken bricks and shards of wood. Harrison followed him a few feet behind, as if he recognized that these moments were difficult.

Gilmuir was built in the shape of an H, the castle and priory backing up to each other and connected by an archway now partially open to the rain.

He entered the priory with caution. Not in fear that the remnants of the roof or walls might fall. They looked sturdy enough. It was the bombardment of memory he dreaded, and just as he'd expected, it soared through him.

He was suddenly eight years old again.

"Stop squirming, Alec," his mother whispered. She leaned over him and brushed her hand over the top of his head. She was always doing things like that, brushing back his hair, tapping his cheek with a finger, holding his shoulder. Today she had a bit of lace scarf on her head and a smile like the statue of the Madonna not far from where they sat.

"But Fergus is going to show me how to tickle a fish," he whispered back. "And we've already been here so long."

She'd smiled and shook her head, wordless remonstrance. He'd sighed like the impatient child he'd been and resigned himself to another hour of prayers.

Alec bent now and picked up a board lying in the bricks, brushed it free of dirt. It appeared to be a carved piece of the altar facade. He looked south, but only a pile of bricks remained where the altar had stood. He let the fragment fall to the floor.

The shutters were gone, now only shards of wood. Only four of the arches remained instead of the original seven. They framed the view of the loch and the dimpled surface of the lake as the rain continued to fall.

Bits of brick and mortar crunched beneath his boots as he walked back through the archway and the clan hall.

On the other side of the castle, at a point farthest from Fort William, were the sleeping quarters. Alec pushed open the door to the laird's chamber, kicking at it to dislodge the debris on the floor. Finally it creaked open and he stood on the threshold, surprised. It was almost as if his grandfather's will had overcome days of English bombardment.

Although faded and filthy, the room was still intact. On the walls was the heavily embossed paper his grandfather had ordered from France to surprise his wife. Alec ran his finger over one small cream and gold rose, remembering the last time he'd been in this room.

He was leaving for England, the coach prepared and waiting for him. He'd reluctantly followed his grandfather here. They'd rarely spoken in the week since his mother had been killed because Alec had locked himself away in his chamber and refused to emerge.

"I've something to give you, Ian," his grandfather had said on that day. He'd handed him a small silk-covered wooden box, the top of which was heavily embroidered. He recognized his mother's work in the depiction of the tiny thistles.

He had stared at it with dread, knowing that it was his birthday gift, the one she promised to give him after her ride.

Cautiously, he opened it, to find the MacRae clan brooch nestled inside. Made of gold, it gleamed brightly in the morning light. Above a clenched fist holding a sword was the MacRae motto, *fortitudine*, with fortitude.

He would have handed it back to his grandfather and wordlessly left the room, but it was a gift from his mother. Oddly enough, the clan brooch had become a talisman over the years. It was his habit to keep it with him, tucked into his waistcoat pocket especially on those days he went into battle.

He looked at the ceiling above him, the plaster-work done by a master from Italy. The cornice work was unblemished, a repeating pattern of thistle and sword, symbols from the MacRae banner.

His grandfather may have ridden like a banshee from hell, been able to throw a dirk with such precision that it pierced a spider's eye, and capable of drinking more than any man in his clan, but he also possessed an innate love of beauty.

A fireplace dominated one wall of the room and Alec wondered if it was damaged or still drew well. A door in the south wall led to a short hallway and the privy chamber.

Against one wall was the massive bed that had seen the birth of countless generations of MacRaes and the deaths of more than a few. The counterpane was full of holes, mice-ridden, no doubt. He pressed his hands down on the sagging mattress. The ropes were sound and the mattress could easily be restuffed.

This bed would be a hedonistic luxury compared to the Spartan military cots he had become used to over the years. For the first time in years his feet would not dangle over the end of his bed. And when he awoke in the morning it wouldn't be to find his hands braced on either side of the cot as if to keep himself from falling.

"I'll quarter here," he told his adjutant.

Harrison frowned at the bed, the filth on the floor. "Naught but mice, sir."

"See the bigger picture, Harrison," Alec said, smiling. "Not as it is, but as it should be."

Alec left the room, retracing his steps through the clan hall, stepping easily over the rubble before heading toward Fort William.

The English had indeed conquered this place. But the Scots had peopled it with memories. He had thought it might be difficult to return to Gilmuir. Until this moment he had not realized how painful it would be.

His heritage, however, must remain a closely guarded secret. No one must know that the Butcher of Inverness was half Scot.

Chapter 4

"**W**e have to do something," Leitis said, "or they will kill him."

The members of the clan were crowded together in Hamish's cottage. It was surprisingly neat and tidy, for the home of a man who had lived alone these past years. None of the furniture, from the benches to the shelves built against one wall, showed any signs of dust. The dishes were stacked on the shelf above the table, and the bed was neatly made.

In a vase on the windowsill were a few flowers, a common sight in the spring and summer. Leitis had always thought the bouquet was her uncle's way of remembering his wife, since she had often done the same.

The people who faced her now might have refused

to betray Hamish to the English, but they were in no mood to forgive him. It wasn't only Leitis's cottage that had burned today. Malcolm was now homeless, as well as Mary and her son.

"Hamish made the choice to surrender to the English," Malcolm said bluntly. "And now you want us to rescue him."

"Would you leave him to be hanged, Malcolm?" she asked quietly.

She studied the faces of these people she'd known all her life. They had all suffered a loss in the past year, had known privation and hardship. "Not one more person should die," she said softly. "Not even if he was foolish."

"Sedgewick will not listen to us," Dora said. "Have you forgotten what he did to you?" She stared pointedly at the bruise that covered half of Leitis's face. Dora had been like a second mother to her. But that did not mean that their relationship was always easy.

"Perhaps the colonel would listen," Leitis said coaxingly.

"Why should he? He's just another Englishman," Malcolm said, looking as skeptical as Dora.

"He saved the village," Leitis said.

Malcolm fell silent at that comment.

"He would have to listen if we all went together," she said, desperate to convince them.

"All that would do," Alisdair said, "would be to get the lot of us killed."

"Very well," she said, pressing her suddenly damp hands against her skirt. "I will go alone." A bluff that she hoped would sway them. But instead of an argument, she was greeted with stunned silence. A moment later, protesting voices filled the cottage.

"You cannot be that foolish, Leitis," Dora said.

"A lone woman with all those Englishmen? Are

you daft, Leitis?" Peter asked. "Send you to the sea
and you'll not get salt water."

Leitis glanced at him. Peter had a saying for every
occasion, and it mattered little to the old man if any of
them made sense. Most of the clan had learned to ignore him.

"Hamish would not be pleased for you to sacrifice
yourself in order to save him," Alisdair said.

"I'm aware of the danger," she said quietly. "But
there is no other choice."

Dora moved closer, her look intent. "Do you think
the English will simply release him because you ask
it?"

"Should I not try, Dora, because it will be difficult?" she asked, returning the other woman's gaze.
"It's a pity our men did not learn that lesson before
they marched off to follow the prince."

Dora looked away.

"Will none of you come with me? Have we become
such cowards?" Her question silenced them.

"Don't empty your own mouth to shame others,
Leitis MacRae."

She turned and stared at Peter. "It's an honest
question I've asked, Peter. Have we all lost our
courage?"

"Not every shoe fits every foot," he replied.

Leitis frowned at him. His pronouncements were
growing wearisome.

Mary stepped forward. Her husband had been
killed at Falkirk. The child in her arms was the
youngest in their clan, born after his father's death.
She came and stood beside Leitis. "I'll go with you,"
she said calmly.

"And I," Malcolm said surprisingly. He walked to
stand beside Leitis, one hand fingering his beard.

Snow-white, it came to a point halfway to his waist and marked him as one of the oldest men in the clan.

"You're all fools, then," Peter said. "Just like Hamish." He left the cottage without another word. Most of the clan followed him a moment later, although more than one person looked back regretfully.

Leitis surveyed those who remained. Ada's swollen and knotted joints pained her greatly on damp days like today, but she smiled her cooperation, and Malcolm had lost the use of his left arm a few years earlier from palsy.

Mary stepped up to Dora, placed her sleeping child in her arms. "Will you care for my son until I return, then?" she asked, bending and placing a soft kiss on her child's cheek.

"And if you don't come back?" Dora asked sharply.

Mary tilted her head up proudly. "Then tell him that I was as brave as his father."

"I'll care for him," Dora said grudgingly. "As if he's my own." She glanced above the child's sleeping form to Leitis. "Your family would counsel you against this, Leitis," she said, narrow-eyed. A final remonstration, one that had the power to hurt.

Leitis took a deep breath, wishing she felt more courageous. "Hamish *is* my family, Dora," she said softly. With a forced smile, she left the cottage.

Patricia Anne Landers, Countess of Sherbourne, sat beside her husband, his hand held warmly between hers.

His bedchamber was a shadowed place against the bright afternoon sun. The day was fair, with not a hint of clouds in the deep blue of the sky. A faint breeze, laden with the heady scent of flowers, coaxed the thickly leafed branches of the home woods to trembling.

She had ordered the curtains and windows opened so that Gerald might enjoy the sight of Brandidge Hall in summer for one last time. But it should be a day of gloom and rain, one of wild winds and chill, because her husband was dying.

The Sherbourne estate was a splendid place, a tribute to Gerald's love of antiquity. This room was the same, a relic of another time, a life he'd lived with his first wife, Moira.

Burgundy silk covered the walls; plaster cornices painted a soft ivory adorned the ceiling. The floor was the color of roasted chestnuts and heavily polished, reflecting the elaborately carved legs of the French furniture. A delicate-looking table, heavily inlaid, sat on one side of the room, an armoire crowned with an ornately carved design of flowers on the other. Gerald's bed with thick columns and soaring headboard dominated the room, however.

A picture was mounted on the wall beside the bed, the scene one her husband had commissioned on his last visit to the continent. It depicted a series of gray and dusky steps descending down to a riverbank. The landscape held some significance for Gerald, she believed. But he'd never told her and she'd never asked. Some things were not mentioned between them.

Such as the portrait hanging above the mantel.

She glanced at it now, as she often had in the past hours. When she had first married Gerald, she'd not objected to its presence, having agreed to be his wife for reasons of property more than fondness. His estate had bordered her father's land, and his wealth had greatly exceeded her family's own dwindling coffers.

But what had begun as a marriage of convenience had altered over the years to become more, at least for her.

Gerald, however, had been a distant husband, one who insisted upon his own activities. He preferred to live in London several months of the year, or visit another one of his properties for the change of scenery. As if to placate her for his paucity of presence, he was overly generous, providing her with a large allowance and encouraging her to spend it on activities that would bring her pleasure.

As if money could ever replace the love she craved.

If he could not love her, at least he had given her David, the child of her heart.

Gerald's breathing was growing worse, and they had added camphor pots to the room and a mustard plaster to his chest. He'd only pulled it off, complaining that it burned him. His illness had come upon him suddenly, so quickly that she had no time to prepare for the eventuality of his death.

"You should sleep, my love," she said, standing and pressing a kiss upon his forehead. It was coldly damp, as if the fever were passing. Taking a cloth from the table, she blotted his face gently. "When you've rested, I'll call David."

Gerald opened his eyes and turned his head slowly to the side, his smile fleeting and weak. Tenderly, Patricia placed her palm against his cheek. Time was short, that much she knew from the waxen color of his face.

"Rest, Gerald," she said gently.

"Alec," he said, the name only a breath.

"I would send word to him, Gerald, but I don't know where he is."

He shook his head feebly. "There's not enough time," he wheezed, the effort of talking taxing his fading strength. "Tell him . . ."

"That you love him," she interjected. "That you've always been proud of him," she added.

He nodded weakly.

A few moments later, he spoke again. She bent close so that she could hear his words. "Tell him to care for David," he whispered.

She nodded, pressed her fingers against his cool lips. "I shall," she said, in an effort to reassure him.

Alec was under no constraints to provide for his half-brother. The Sherbourne fortune was inexorably tied to the entailed properties left to Alec as heir. A second son was expected to make his own way in the world.

Once more she glanced at the portrait. Even now she could not hate the woman seated there. Instead, she envied her. Moira MacRae Landers had been a beautiful woman, one whose vivacity shone through her blue eyes. She was depicted sitting on a carpet of green, not in a dress, as was more proper, but in a sapphire-blue riding habit. Her hand was resting on her son's shoulder while Alec's brown eyes were brimming with happiness.

Patricia bowed her head at her husband's side. Her prayers had ceased to be for his recovery, since it was so obvious that he would not live. Now she only prayed that he felt no pain.

His lips were nearly blue, and there were deep gray circles beneath his eyes. The handsome Gerald she'd once known had become an old man in the last week. She stroked the back of his hand, leaned down, and placed her cheek upon it.

"Moira," he suddenly said, rising up from the pillows, his voice strong and filled with joy. He looked at the far side of the bed where the hangings were drawn, a blinding smile on his face. Trembling, he stretched out his hand. Then he sighed, deeply and heavily, before collapsing back on the bed.

It took a moment for her to realize that he had died, left her in that instant with no more a farewell than a simple gasp. The surge of grief was so strong that Patricia felt it pressing against her chest like a giant fist.

Slowly she reached up and closed his eyes. Only then did she place her hands over her face and succumb to her tears.

As a leader of men, Alec had to be able to judge character quickly and accurately. In the case of Major Matthew Sedgewick, his initial impression did not improve as the hours passed.

The major proved to be reluctant to divulge information, contentious when questioned, and generally sullen. Alec was not accustomed to tolerating such belligerence. Yet Sedgewick posed a difficult problem.

Alec understood the major's sense of betrayal at being passed over for command. He had accomplished a great deal in the last year by constructing Fort William using unseasoned troops. His current behavior, however, was not furthering his career in an army that was growing increasingly political. Instead of simply accepting the situation as it was, he was choosing, instead, to let his resentment fester.

But then, this was a man who had struck a woman. Indication enough of the deficiencies in Sedgewick's character.

Pushing his personal feelings aside, Alec concentrated on the task at hand, a surprise inspection of a few of the soldiers' quarters.

In larger garrisons one wife was normally allowed for every hundred soldiers. Preference was given to those women who'd been on campaign before and were used to the harsh conditions, including the fact that she must share a rough cot with her husband in a chamber that housed eight men.

Each room boasted a fireplace used both for warmth as well as cooking. From the lingering odor, the inhabitants of this particular chamber preferred their rations scorched.

He opened the chest at the end of each bed. White dress gaiters lay on the bottom, covered by waist and pouch belts. An extra blanket, two lengths of toweling, and sheeting comprised a man's essentials. What other personal articles a soldier possessed were not to occupy more than a hand's width and be stored at the bottom of his chest.

A few minutes later Alec left the room, followed by Sedgewick and Harrison. The sighs of relief from the occupants of the room were premature. The soldiers stationed at Fort William were about to undergo a radical change in their duties come morning.

Alec had already completed his inspection of the magazine, ordinance, and provision stores. As he had originally suspected, Fort William was not appreciably different from other English fortifications. It was built to be self-sustaining in that it boasted a brewhouse and a bakery. But he had never before seen a stable where the horses were outnumbered by the pigs and cows. The assorted grunts, lowing, and neighing rendered speech nearly impossible.

He stared at the animal stalls. Sedgewick's talents obviously did not extend to animal husbandry. The condition of the enclosures was as slovenly as that of the soldiers he'd seen.

"We've had to import the livestock, sir. As well as the grains," Sedgewick grudgingly explained.

He didn't need to elaborate. The emaciated condition of the inhabitants of the village attested to their near starvation. It was the same all over Scotland. Cumberland's orders were severe and designed to punish the vanquished Highlanders.

Alec was grateful he'd chosen to quarter at Gilmuir. The stench of men and livestock wafted through the barracks, remaining long after the three men left the courtyard.

"Have the men been treated for lice?" he asked. Each soldier in his command was required to maintain a certain order about his uniform and person. Another detail on which Sedgewick was obviously lax. The men in the courtyard had not impressed him with either their cleanliness or their discipline.

His troops could be fighting in mire that day, but before they bedded down, time would be spent cleaning their weapons, polishing their brass, and shining their boots. He had discovered years ago that discipline in the details made for better soldiers. Consequently, the men in his command were more concerned about passing morning inspection than in worrying whether or not they would survive the next battle.

"Lice?" Sedgewick asked, an answer couched in the question.

"Have them bathe in vinegar and water," Alec said. "Beginning immediately."

Sedgewick frowned but did not respond.

"I want to meet with your commanders tomorrow morning after inspection," Alec said as they walked down the narrow hallway leading to the front wall.

"Commanders, sir?"

"What is your objection now, Sedgewick?" he asked impatiently, glancing over his shoulder.

"I have had no need to delegate, sir," Sedgewick said rigidly. "I oversee the details of this command myself."

"Not an adequate way to manage a great many men, Major," Alec said sharply.

He turned to Harrison, quietly following them. "I want a staff meeting in the morning," he said.

His adjutant nodded.

"Let's see about these cannon, Major," Alec said, anxious to finish the inspection and rid himself of the other man's company.

An hour later he left Sedgewick nursing his own petulance and gratefully returned to the chamber in Gilmuir. Removing his coat, he hung it carefully on the peg beside the door. There was no armoire in this room, nothing of the studied comfort of his home in England. But then, there hadn't been for many years. Strange, how coming to Scotland had initiated in him a longing for all those things he had once set aside with such ease. Or perhaps it was not so much Scotland as it was the fact that he was weary of war and campaigning.

He hadn't realized how tired he was until this last year.

He went to the fire, stood staring down at the remnants of cold ashes. How long had they been here? Years?

His aide, Donald, had already made his presence known. In addition to moving Alec's dispatch case in here, along with a small round table and two chairs, the rubble that had littered the floor had been brushed away. The counterpane had been removed along with the mattress. In addition, Donald had placed two lanterns and a variety of stubby candles on the mantel and a thick candle in the middle of the table. Signs of progress, then, and habitation.

He sat at the table, opened his case, and retrieved his maps. His adult mind sketched in details his memory of childhood had forgotten. He divided his territory into quadrants and assigned a schedule of patrols. Beginning tomorrow, he would begin to ascertain the degree of rebellion in this section of Scotland. He doubted, frankly, that the Highlanders would ever challenge England again, so thoroughly had they been defeated.

The schedule finished, he began his report to General Wescott, his immediate superior. He carefully worded his overall impressions, along with his proposed changes in command. But he did not mention the fire or his opinion that Major Sedgewick was unfit for any type of command. Criticism of the man after only one day of observation would be seen as impulsive and rash.

But he had struck Leitis, an act Alec could not forgive.

He leaned back in his chair and surrendered to memory only hours old. Her coloring was too vibrant for her to be considered attractive in England, where a pallid appearance was all the rage. But she fit this land of sharp cliffs and rolling glens. She was taller than he had thought she would be, and too slender.

What had life been like for her since that day when the carriage had taken him home to England? Improvident thoughts, almost childish ones, as if his boyish self had escaped from the box where he'd been carefully stored all these years.

I am Ian. Words he could not speak to her. *I am the boy you knew so long ago.* Time had changed both of them.

He concentrated on his letter again, pushing Leitis's face from his mind with difficulty.

He sealed the dispatch and left it on the table for Donald to take to the messenger. A nicety of his rank, a courier when he wished it. As a lowly lieutenant he had not been so fortunate. Even so, his correspondence to his family had dwindled and finally stopped years ago. He couldn't remember why, now. It had simply become a habit not to write. An attrition of caring, perhaps, aided by the fact that he had not seen any of them for years.

His father had never been the same after his mother had died. Gone was the Earl of Sherbourne who had once laughed with abandon, who rode with his son and showed him the best fishing places along the River Brye. The man who'd taken his place was somber and stern, and had little time for the pursuit of pleasure just for the sake of it.

He'd married again, to a woman who had been sweet and kind to him. Patricia, Alec remembered, had sided with him when he had wanted to purchase his commission.

There had been, after all, few options open to the son of an earl. Either fritter his time away waiting for his father to conveniently die, or manage the properties soon to be left him. His nature despised indolence and his father's factors left the earl well informed and ably served. Alec had never regretted his choice to serve in the military.

What would the earl say to see his current accommodations? Or even better, he thought wryly, to witness his pleasure at such Spartan conditions?

He surprised himself by pulling another piece of paper closer, dipping his quill in the inkwell, and beginning a letter to his father.

The only residual signs of the storm were the puddles in the gravel and the slow drip from the water barrels. The air was clear, as it was after a storm, but it still tasted sourly of smoke.

The journey across the land bridge was slow out of deference to the age of two of her companions.

Leitis had not been to Gilmuir since the day the English came. That afternoon she had stood upon a high hill and watched as the castle was systematically destroyed. The cannon had sounded like thunder; the fist of God knocking the old fortress to the ground, brick by brick. It had taken two days for it to finally crumble, and she had watched the destruction of the MacRae stronghold in a bitter kind of joy.

A shameful admission, but at the time she had been grieving for Marcus and for her family. It had seemed a right and proper thing that Gilmuir should be razed. She had been so filled with rage and pain that she had wanted others to suffer as well. It appeared as if she had gotten her wish after all. All of Scotland now wept.

Fort William loomed like a squat monster on the landscape. A stark red from the distance, it appeared even uglier up close.

She gathered her courage into little parcels, tying it together with a net made of sheer bluster. She didn't pretend that their errand would be easily accomplished. But Hamish did not deserve to die for his foolishness.

She pulled down on her sleeves, a nervous gesture, but no amount of tugging would make them come below her elbows. Of pale blue, this was the least favorite and the most ill-fitting of her four dresses. Now it was the only garment she owned.

"There's no door," Ada said, staring at the front of the fort. "Only those windows."

"They're for cannon," Malcolm said, squinting at the wall.

"How do we get in?" Mary asked.

"Perhaps we should walk around to the rear," Leitis suggested.

"They have no guards about," Malcolm said.

"We don't pose much of a threat," Leitis replied.

"Still and all, I'm not in a mood to be shot because I'm skulking around an English fort."

Leitis frowned at him, led the way down the end of one long wall, only to find a courtyard, one filled with soldiers and animals. For a moment Leitis could only blink in amazement at the scene.

In the corner a man was stirring a huge wooden wash pot with a long-handled pole. And in another corner men bathed in what looked like troughs, splashing each other and yelling as an odor reminiscent of brine wafted in the air, vying with the animal smells.

"Dear Saint Columba," Mary whispered, "they're all naked as the day they were born."

"Not quite," Ada said with a chuckle. "They're a bit larger than bairns."

Malcolm sent Ada a fierce look, but she only wiggled her eyebrows back at him.

"We've come at wash day," Leitis said, startled.

"And not simply sheeting and clothes, either," Mary said.

"You'd think the lot of you had never seen a naked man before," Malcolm muttered.

"I've never seen an Englishman," Mary said, moving closer to Leitis. The four of them huddled in the corner, pressed together so tightly that they could feel each other breathe.

"What do we do now?" Ada asked.

"Find the colonel," Malcolm offered. "Unless he's bathing, too."

"Do you suppose it's some sort of English ritual?" Mary asked, peering over Leitis's shoulder.

"If it is," Leitis said, "I doubt it's repeated in winter."

"They'd freeze their . . ." After a quick look at Malcolm's frown, Ada's words stuttered to a halt.

"Well, we have to do something," Leitis said. "We can't simply stand here gaping."

"I'd rethink my words, lass," Malcolm said, frowning. "It's the three of you who are acting all ninny-like."

Leitis squared her shoulders, took a deep breath, stepped forward before she could lose her nerve. A man walking across the courtyard halted and stared at her. He approached her slowly, as if he feared she was only a vision.

"I need to speak with the colonel," she said resolutely. Her hands were clasped tightly in front of her, her chin tilted up.

"You want to see the Butcher?" His accent was difficult for her to understand; the look in his eyes was not.

He had a thin, almost wolfish face, his grin revealing childlike nubbins of teeth and gums that were red and inflamed. His white shirt was stained and gaped open to reveal a hairy chest. It was evident he had not yet taken advantage of the bath.

"The Butcher?" she asked faintly.

"The Butcher of Inverness. The new commander."

"No, the colonel," she said, shaking her head. The man who saved the village could not be the Butcher of Inverness.

"That's the one," he said, nodding. He looked, she thought dully, pleased at her shock.

The Butcher of Inverness. They had all heard tales of the man. Those Scots who had escaped the slaughter of Culloden had been imprisoned at Inverness, only to be sent to their deaths on a whim. It was said that the Butcher would spare a prisoner because it amused him, or send him to the gallows because of the look in a man's eye.

The Butcher of Inverness? Her stomach clenched, and Leitis felt as if she might be ill.

The knock on the door was not unexpected, nor was Donald's face. His words, however, were a surprise.

"Begging your pardon, sir, but we've got trouble."

Donald had been with him ever since Flanders, having joined the army filled with dreams of grandeur and far-off battles. At first his light blond hair, rosy cheeks, and eagerness to please had marked him as barely out of boyhood. But in the past year Donald had been promoted to sergeant and lost the last of his innocence. There were times when his smile was a bit too forced and his laughter had an edge to it. The effect of Inverness, no doubt.

"What is it?" Alec asked.

Donald stepped inside the room. "Sir, there's a group of Scots in the courtyard, and there are women among them. It's almost a riot."

By the time Donald had finished his sentence, Alec was putting on his coat and out the door.

Four Scots stood surrounded by at least thirty men in various stages of undress. One elderly woman was holding her hands clenched to her chest and one old man looked ready for a fight. But it was the younger women the crowd was concentrating on, and one of those women was Leitis.

She took a few steps back to avoid one man's touch, only to bump into another man behind her. The man laughed as he pulled both her arms backward.

"Please," she said, "let us go."

"Give me a kiss and maybe I will," the man in front of her said.

"Evidently you have a great deal of time on your hands, Sergeant," Alec said curtly. "However, I can think of a number of tasks to occupy your time, none of which includes terrorizing women."

The soldiers surrounding Leitis and the other woman stepped back quickly when they realized that they had been overheard.

"Begging your pardon, Colonel," the sergeant said. "But she's a Scot."

It had been a long day; he had been in the saddle since dawn. Surely that was the only reason for the anger that nearly overpowered him then. It was too much like the emotion he felt on the battlefield, a visceral rage that masked his will to survive.

"What exactly does that mean, Sergeant, that she's a Scot?" he asked carefully, expunging from his voice any hint of emotion.

"Well, you know how they are, sir," the man said. "They'd do anything for a bit of bread and such." He grinned at Alec, an expression no doubt meant to convey masculine understanding. It had the effect of making Alec wish he were wearing his sword.

Leitis turned and faced him. Her face was pale, except for the mark of Sedgewick's blow darkening her skin. He frowned at it, suddenly irritated by her foolishness.

"The men stationed here haven't seen a woman for months," he said sharply. "Did you give no thought to your safety?"

She didn't answer his question, only asked one of her own. "Are you the new commander of Fort William?" she asked, her voice little more than a whisper. "The Butcher of Inverness?"

He nodded once.

She took a deep breath. "I am Leitis MacRae," she said. "You have my uncle here," she said. "I have come to ask for his release."

"Have you?"

She still possessed the devil's own arrogance. Who else would demand of him concessions when a hundred men surrounded her and her puny group of rescuers?

He spun around and led the way through Gilmuir, more in an effort to organize his thoughts than a wish to have privacy for their meeting.

The four of them followed him, glancing occasionally at the ruins of Gilmuir and whispering among themselves. Did they mourn the old castle's death, or did they simply condemn the invaders?

A blue and ebony horizon loomed, touched only here and there with a tinge of pink. Night came with reluctance to this land of sweeping shadows. But then, dawn was birthed with as much difficulty.

A stubborn land, one that mirrored its people well.

He stood with his back to them, ostensibly looking out over Loch Euliss where it flowed into Coneagh Firth. In actuality, he was thinking of the girl he had known, of five summers in which he had been first shy and then daring around her.

He turned and surveyed them.

Leitis stood in front of the group, her face carefully expressionless. So as not to anger the Butcher of Inverness?

"My uncle is an old man," she said. "Hamish sometimes forgets what year it is."

"Or the fact that Scotland lost its rebellion?" he asked dryly.

"Yes," she said simply.

The others aligned themselves behind her, as if

they looked to her for guidance. She should not be here at all, let alone leading a misfit group.

"So I am to pity an old man," he said. "What are you offering in exchange?"

"We have nothing," she said shortly. "Your soldiers have slaughtered our cattle and trampled our crops."

He folded his arms over his chest and leaned back against the half wall.

"Therefore, you are relying solely on my compassion."

"Isn't that the definition of it?" she asked. "To give without thought of recompense?"

"I am the Butcher of Inverness," he said. "Am I supposed to have such sensibilities?"

She looked away, then glanced back. "Perhaps you should," she said firmly, her mouth in a thin line. As if, he thought, she were scolding him.

"I promise that he will never play the pipes again," she said in the silence.

"I could achieve that guarantee with his hanging," he said bluntly. "Do you also pledge obedience?"

"Mine," she said, nodding.

"And that of your clan?"

Her lips thinned as she looked down at the gravel path. "I have no right to speak for anyone else," she said reluctantly. "But I can promise that I will not disobey English laws."

"For this paltry promise you wish your uncle's safe return?"

"No," she said, looking up. "I also want the safety of my village guaranteed."

He faced Loch Euliss again. As a boy he'd stood here many times marveling at the view before him. Below Gilmuir the loch was narrow, surrounded by blue-tinged hills. In the distance, Loch Euliss widened into the firth, flowing beneath towering cliffs before meeting the sea.

Alec unfolded his arms, turned, and walked slowly toward her. He didn't answer her, merely studied the bruising on her jaw. The blow angered him still; so much that he mentally rearranged the major's duty schedule. A protracted patrol would not be amiss.

He suddenly wanted, unwisely perhaps, to protect her, keep her safe from the consequences of her own courage and from those who would think nothing of harming her.

Alec told himself it was because she was a link to his past, even as he realized the discord of that thought. His finger reached out and traced the line of bruising on her jaw.

His hand was slapped away by the old man at her side. "The bargain doesn't include touching our women," he said fiercely, his wrinkled face twisted by anger.

Although he could not recall his name, Alec remembered him from his childhood. Back then, he'd thought him ancient. The intervening years had not marked his face further, but the old man was trembling badly either from disease or fear. A brave man, to challenge Alec with words when he had no other weapons.

He inclined his head, conceding the inappropriateness of the gesture. "You should not have come," he said. "Send your laird to me and I'll bargain with him."

"There are so few of us left, there is no need for a leader," the old man said.

Alec wanted to ask Leitis the fate of the others, to know for certain what had happened to the laughing Fergus and the solemn James, and her father, who had always been kind to him. But he did not ask the question, preferring the ignorance of the moment to the bluntness of the truth.

"My uncle is all the family I have left," she said, as if she'd heard his thoughts. Her chin tilted up and her lips firmed into a thin line.

They exchanged a glance. He could not ease her pain and she should not know his sudden, bitter regret.

"Return to your village," he said, addressing the group. "I will release Hamish shortly."

An old woman spoke up. "Why?" He didn't recognize her. Either she had changed so much in the past years or he had simply not known her as a boy.

"You beg me for my compassion, then question it?" he asked wryly.

"An Englishman always has a price for his generosity," she said, narrowing her eyes at him.

"Because I have a hostage for his good behavior," he said, reaching out and encircling Leitis's wrist. He knew the second she understood.

"No!" she said angrily, attempting to pull away. He held her easily.

"Leave now," he said to the others, "and I'll guarantee you safe passage. Linger, and you'll be prisoners."

The others moved away, looking back as if they challenged their own courage in doing so. They'd come to rescue one of their own and lost another.

Perhaps it would teach them that it would not be wise to act so precipitously in the future.

After all, he was the Butcher of Inverness, a soldier given that sobriquet by the Scots themselves. A man of fearsome reputation and deadly intent.

He smiled and began to walk toward the laird's chamber.

Chapter 5

The Butcher signaled with his free hand and a man emerged from the shadows. His face was unnaturally lean, both his chin and nose pointed. He fell into step behind them as they moved through the archway and what was left of the clan hall. The Butcher was relentless in his grip, but his hold on her was not painful all the same.

She could almost hear the voices of her brothers admonishing her for her foolishness, the soft wails of her mother, her father's angry remonstrances. Other voices, too, but not so recognizable. The Butcher's previous victims?

What had she done?

He opened a door, stood aside motioning for her to

enter before turning to the other man. "I want you to guard my guest, Harrison," the Butcher said.

The other man nodded and moved into position in front of the door.

"I have a piper to release," he said, glancing down at her.

"Are you truly going to let him go?" she asked, surprised.

His smile startled her. "I am a man of my word," he said, and waited for her retort.

She did not give him the satisfaction of responding. But the words seemed to linger in the air between them. *No Englishman is a man of honor.*

He stepped back, closed the door, leaving her alone. She looked around the room in desperation. She had helped to tend the dying laird herself and therefore knew this chamber well.

She opened the door to the clan hall again. Harrison was still there, leaning against the doorframe with his back to her.

"You'll stay put, miss," he said calmly as if he could see her. Perhaps he only sensed her panic.

"He can't keep me here," she announced, a bit of bravado in the face of her very real fear.

He glanced over his shoulder at her, his face oddly less attractive when he smiled. "Can't he? He's the colonel of the regiment. He can do anything he pleases," he said, then reached over and pulled the door shut in her face.

She turned and surveyed her prison. Against the wall was a curious-looking chest equipped with a series of drawers restrained by a brown leather strap. Well worn, it looked to be something the Butcher carried with him on his travels.

The Butcher had evidently chosen this room to be his.

Was she to be his hostage or his whore?

She walked around the table and stood looking down at the Butcher's maps. The loch's perimeter was carefully delineated. She had never thought that it was so large. It led to the firth, that much she knew, ebbing and flowing with its own tides. Each tiny mark upon the map appeared to be a village, just as a larger symbol must indicate another fort. Another blight upon the landscape. An irrefutable piece of evidence that the English were here to stay.

A knock on the door preceded the arrival of a young man, his head nearly buried beneath the doubled mattress he carried. She watched as he heaved it onto the bed frame, then stepped back and smiled shyly at her.

"I'll not share that with him," she said, stepping away until her back was against the wall.

"I don't know about that, miss," he said, his cheeks flushing a bright red. "I'm just here to settle the colonel's quarters."

He bent and arranged the mattress until it was square on the frame, then tested its plumpness by pressing on it with both palms. "I would have stuffed it with hay," he said, addressing his comments to the bed, "but it smelled of horse and other things."

She said nothing, only watched him as he walked around the side of the bed closer to her. She backed away, but he didn't notice, being so concerned about the placement of the mattress.

"I used grass and pine needles instead," he said, as if she'd asked. "But I put a few flowers in it," he confided, glancing over at her. Unexpectedly, he grinned, and the smile reminded her oddly enough of Fergus and his occasional misdeeds. That sudden memory

sobered her enough to look away rather than be
charmed by a young English soldier.

"I'll be bringing you the evening meal, then, miss,"
he said, walking to the door. "Is there anything else I
can fetch for you?"

"Is it customary to ask for a prisoner's prefer-
ences?" she asked, rankled by his good cheer.

"Oh, you're not a prisoner, miss," he said earnestly.
"You're the colonel's guest."

She was left without a word to say as he closed the
door behind him.

The fact that he'd decided to keep Leitis with him
disturbed Alec on a visceral level. *A foolish thing to
do, to hold Leitis MacRae hostage,* a warning whispered
in a voice that sounded like his long-dead grandfather.

The gaol was located not far from the chapel and
Alec wondered if the architect had planned this irony.
The room was the size of one of the barracks chambers, the only concessions to its function the series of
manacles mounted high in the wall and the bars over
the window.

A gaol was a necessity in a fort this size. Al-
lowances had to be made for those who did not easily
accustom themselves to military life. Disobedience
was severely punished in His Majesty's Army. But
most of the discipline meted out was for other infractions. Men who were systematically trained to kill, as
soldiers were, did not easily discard that fierceness of
temper after battle.

The prisoner he visited was not, however, a private
who had taken a bottle to his roommate or a captain
who had challenged another man to a duel for the
honor of a lady. Instead, it was a grizzled Scot with a
glower that could melt the bars of his cell. A slim man

of short stature, his wrists were manacled to the wall a few inches above his head.

Alec could almost feel the hatred directed at him, Hamish's eyes were so filled with it.

He glanced over his shoulder at the guard stationed inside the door.

"Give me the keys," he said sharply, then frowned at the look of surprise on the other man's face. As a lowly lieutenant, he'd had to obey any order given him with quickness, respect, and above all obedience. It appeared, however, that both Sedgewick and the men under his command had not yet learned that lesson.

"Do you have a problem obeying me, Sergeant?" he asked curtly.

"No, sir," the other man said, handing the ring to Alec.

Alec heard the door of the gaol close behind him as he stared at Hamish MacRae. Hamish had been kind to the young boy he'd been, had taught Alec the basics of the bagpipes. But it had been James with the talent and the wind for the instrument.

Hamish looked at him contemptuously, a glance at odds with his current pose of being manacled to the wall.

"So you're the new commander of this eyesore," he said.

"I am," Alec said sharply, walking closer to the old man.

"Have you come to gloat, then? If so, you've found a poor target for it. I'm an old man and I've seen too much to regret my passing."

Alec raised an eyebrow at Hamish. "Is it a trait of the Scots, this eagerness to martyr yourselves?"

"Is it a trait of the English, to push us toward it?" Hamish glared at him from beneath bushy eyebrows, not unlike a trapped badger.

"If I let you go, will you promise to obey the law? Or is it your story that you don't know about the Disarming Act?"

"That English law? About as worthless as anything else you English have given us."

"That's the problem with martyrs," Alec said, disgusted. "They only see themselves and their ideals. They rarely care about those who must pay the price for their martyrdom."

"You English have taken my country and my kin. You'll not have my pride."

Alec reached up and unlocked the manacles from the old man's wrists before stepping back. Hamish lowered his arms, rubbing his wrists while he glared at Alec.

"You've a hostage to your obedience, Hamish MacRae of the Clan MacRae," Alec said curtly. "I've made a trade for you."

"I'll not agree to a trade," Hamish muttered.

Alec ignored him. "Your pipes will be destroyed, and I suggest you find more acceptable attire," he said, glancing down at Hamish's kilt. "Your hostage's safety depends upon your willingness to obey."

"I'll not go," Hamish said stubbornly.

"You haven't a choice," Alec said.

"Who have you taken?"

"Leitis," he said, tensing for the old man's reaction. But Hamish only closed his eyes for a moment. When he opened them a moment later, he turned his head and spit on the floor. "That's what I think of an Englishman's threat."

Not one word of concern for Leitis. Not one thought for his own niece.

Alec called out for the guard. When he entered the room, Alec motioned to Hamish with a jerk of his head. "Get the old fool out of here," he said, "before I change my mind."

Chapter 6

Alec entered his chamber, the wooden door easing shut behind him with a muffled groan. He
strode to the table and, pulling open the tinderbox, lit
the candle sitting there.

Leitis was standing with her back against the
wall, her arms folded in front of her. Her chin was
tilted up and her eyes were staring at him impassively.

"Were you content to remain in the dark, then?"

"I do not believe my contentment mattered," she
said coolly.

He shrugged out of his coat and hung it on the
peg beside the door, then removed his waistcoat until he was attired only in shirt and breeches. When
he turned and walked toward her she didn't glance

away, almost as if she dared him to approach her. Her gaze was direct, the contempt in her eyes a challenge.

He reached out one hand and touched a tendril of her hair. It had darkened over the years, but there was still a hint of the unruly girl she'd been, Leitis of the flying orange curls and infectious laugh.

He trailed his hands from her shoulders to her wrists, feeling the coarse weave of her dress. With a fingertip, he marked the places on her sleeves where the fire had burned small holes. She had no other clothes, no other belongings. She stood devoid of all earthly possessions except for her character, improvident, rash, and impossibly courageous.

"I won't be your whore, Butcher," she said, her voice trembling faintly, enough that he suddenly understood that the anger was merely bravado.

"Is that why you think I've brought you here?" he asked softly.

"Yes." An answer tightly voiced. He had heard men shouting out their crimes to him and it affected him no less than this reluctant admission.

"I believe your post as hostage does not require that sacrifice," he said wryly.

She looked skeptical. "Englishmen are like any other men," she said, taking a step away from him. "They're like stallions, always wanting the act."

He raised one eyebrow and gazed at her. "And have you been someone's mare, Leitis?"

"No," she said, meeting his look resolutely.

He knew in that moment that she lied. "Who was he?" he asked, fighting back a sense of possessiveness so strong it baffled him.

She looked equally startled by his question, or perhaps the tone of it. He was surprised when she answered him. But her look was defiant as she did so.

"There was a man," she said proudly. "I loved him and he was going off to battle."

"So you lay with him," Alec said, congratulating himself on the even nature of his voice. He walked to the fireplace, staring down into the cold ashes.

"Yes," she admitted softly. "I lay with him."

He had not seen her for years. She was, despite his memories of her, little more than a stranger. What did he care of her experience? Calm and rational thoughts, but they did not ease his surprising anger.

"Where is he now?" he asked finally, the question itself too intrusive.

"Marcus was killed at Culloden."

He closed his eyes, the battlefield recalled with ease, not simply because of the atrocities that occurred there but because of his nightly recollections of it. He was never spared the sight of Culloden in his dreams. He had the sudden unwanted thought that he might have killed her Marcus himself, or watched as it was done.

He turned and glanced at her. There was color high on her cheeks. She wrapped her arms around herself, but did not look away.

A knock on the door interrupted the painful silence between them. Alec called out a greeting and Donald entered carrying a tray. He placed it on the table, arranging the dishes.

"I brought you roast beef, Colonel," Donald said, glancing over at Leitis with a smile.

"Have you met our guest?" Alec asked. "Leitis MacRae, hostage; Donald Tanner, sergeant and aide."

Donald smiled at her coaxingly. Leitis didn't smile in return, but the look in her eyes changed a little. Not as much caution there as a moment ago. Donald was not without his female admirers. Women, for some reason, wanted to cosset him.

"Shall I bring your bath, sir?" Donald asked, and Alec nodded.

A moment later the door shut behind him and they were alone again. Alec walked to the table, sat with his legs stretched out before him. He removed his boots slowly, waiting for her next barb. It would come, he was certain of it. Leitis had never been comfortable with silence.

"Now you'll convince yourself that since I've known the touch of a man, it would not be rape," she said suddenly.

He glanced at her, shaking his head. "Don't you realize that I could give orders to raze your village and it would be done without a word spoken in protest? Or that I could have each one of your clansmen killed and no doubt receive a commendation for it?"

"The English reward cruelty, then," she answered fiercely. "Not courage."

"Yet with all that, you keep slinging mud at me," he said, ignoring her comment.

"It would be dung, Butcher, but I can't find any at the moment."

He bit back his smile, knowing Leitis would not be pleased at his amusement. But she was so foolishly fierce at the moment.

"Is it difficult being an instrument of death?" she asked quietly.

She'd meant the words as an insult, but he chose to answer her honestly. "It is difficult to send men into battle, knowing that they may die. I do not doubt your leaders felt the same."

"I hope they did," she said surprisingly. "It should cost a man something to order another's death. Even if the cause is worth dying for."

"The more death you witness," he said bluntly, "the more you question causes."

She turned away, staring through the window as if the view of the night were new to her.

"You hate well, Leitis," he said quietly.

"I have reason to," she said icily, narrowing her eyes. "The English killed my family and the man I loved."

He abruptly stood, walked to his dispatch case. Pulling open the top drawer, he retrieved a sheet of paper, a quill, and a pot of ink. She frowned as he returned to the table and calmly cleared a place on which to write. The scratching of the quill was grating in the silence.

He stood, walked to her side, and handed her the list.

"What is this?" she asked, reaching out to take it.

"All those men I knew who died at the hands of the Scots. It's only fair that we keep score, isn't it?"

Instead of answering him, she scanned the list he'd written.

Lieutenant Thomas
Captain Hastings
Sergeant Roberts
Lieutenant Hanson
Major Robison

A list of twenty names, all English, and all good soldiers and decent men who had not deserved the fate meted out to them.

"What?" he asked. "No biting remark, Leitis? No comment that a dead Englishman is the only bearable one?"

She stared at the names. "They all had mothers," she said softly. "And wives or sweethearts. It would be cruel to wish them dead."

"But they were Englishmen," he said tightly. "Shouldn't you rejoice at their deaths?"

She glanced up at him. "Do you rejoice each time a Scot dies?" she asked, the words tinged with an odd kind of sadness.

At one time he had, a confession he'd made to God but would not voice to her.

"Kings should have to fight a war, and no one else," she said in the wake of his silence.

"You would have King George and your pretender wage battle in a field somewhere?" he asked, startled at her comment.

"But it isn't just kings and princes, is it?" she asked, glancing at him. "It's men who would make war a game. Not for peace, but for other reasons. Greed, for example."

"Greed?" He smiled tightly. "Colonels into generals and privates into sergeants?"

"To obtain land or castles or power," she corrected, handing him the list before turning and staring out into the night.

"The world has always been that way, Leitis," he said softly.

"It does not mean," she said, shaking her head, "that it's right."

"And how would you have the world?"

"As it was," she said faintly. "But then I didn't know what I had. Peace now seems so simple to wish for and so difficult to obtain."

"For all of us," he said somberly.

"Where is your world, Butcher?"

He smiled at the effortless insult of her tone, but answered her question easily enough. "Where is any soldier's home? Where his commander has sent him. Where his dispatch case is, or his cot."

"It is not here in Scotland," she said acerbically.

"I'm afraid it is," he replied, speaking the truth in a soft voice. Her shoulders were rigid, her stance stiff and unyielding. She ignored his words, even his presence. A deft repudiation, effective for all its silence.

A knock on the door preceded his aide's entrance. The young man was bent low beneath the weight of a large copper vessel.

"Where did you find that?" the Butcher asked, surprised.

"Major Sedgewick ordered it from London," Donald said, lowering the tub to the floor. The tall back was embossed with carved flowers and a tree. Peering out from behind the spring foliage were several scantily clad nymphs.

"The major likes a bit of elegance," Donald said. "Fancies himself, I think." He flushed, then ducked his head. "Begging your pardon, sir. I meant no disrespect to a senior officer."

"I heard nothing," the Butcher said, exchanging an amused look with his sergeant. "Did you ask if he had any French-milled soap?" he asked sardonically, finally moving away from her to stare down at the copper vessel.

Donald shook his head regretfully. "All I've got is that sorry excuse for barracks soap, sir."

"It will do well enough. I'm used to my skin stinging."

"Do you bathe often?" she asked, a bit of curiosity she could not forestall.

"It's a ritual I observe after spending a day in the saddle," he said dryly. "I haven't the fortitude of the Scots who ride bare-arsed on a woolen blanket for days and don't notice either the rash or the smell."

She turned away to hide her unexpected amusement. There had been too many times when she'd

wished her brothers had taken more than an occasional dip in the loch.

Donald placed the toweling next to the bath before
leaving the room. Leitis wished he had stayed in
those next moments. The silence between the two of
them seemed too loud, almost expectant.

She clasped her hands together, tipped her head
back to look up at him. The flickering light favored
his face, creating shadows and highlighting the sharp
line of jaw and nose. A man of authority, blessed by
Fate, and given power over all the Scots of Gilmuir.

He waved his hand in the direction of the tub. "The
gentlemanly thing to do is to offer you first privi-
leges," he said bowing in her direction.

She would not show fear in front of this man, nor
allow him to see her tremble. "I've no intention of
bathing in your tub. Or in your presence, for that matter," she said crisply.

"I would leave you in privacy," he promised softly.
"My word."

"What is an Englishman's word, Butcher?" she
asked.

"That sounds too much like your uncle, Leitis," he
said curtly.

He took a step toward her and she stiffened in anticipation. But he halted before he reached her, as if
he'd seen the aversion in her eyes.

"Why are you Highlanders so stubborn? Is it something in the climate?" He waved his hand in the air as
if to measure the mountains, indicate the glens. "Is it
the mist? It's forever raining in this misbegotten
place; perhaps it's soaked into your brains."

"You would have me accede to your demands
without a protest, Butcher? Then you have, indeed,
chosen the wrong hostage." She clasped her hands together so tightly that her knuckles hurt. "I am Leitis

MacRae of Gilmuir and I do not do as an Englishman wills simply because he wishes it."

For a moment he simply stared at her, then a smile began to curve his lips. She frowned at him, but it had no effect on his amusement.

"Very well," he said, almost casually. "Then at least share my meal. Or are you too proud to eat English food?" he asked sardonically.

"I'm not a fool," she said, irritated. "Food is food, and I doubt it has a nationality."

She walked to the table, stood looking down at the meal his aide had brought. There were thick slices of roast beef piled high next to a bowl of gravy, a round loaf of crusty bread, its top glistening with butter. A slab of blue-veined cheese sat on a separate plate, its odor so strong that the scent of it wafted up from the tray. Two flacons of ale sat in the middle of the table, the sides of the earthenware containers dotted with moisture.

There was more food here than she had seen in months, enough to feed three people.

She sat and began to eat slowly. During the last year she'd not had more than one meal a day, and those had been paltry next to this feast.

He continued to undress, hanging each garment on a peg. The Butcher was neat and orderly, but then she supposed soldiers were. His disregard for her presence was disconcerting, however.

Leitis glanced over at him once, only to meet his gaze. His fingers stilled in the act of unfastening his shirt; his face was expressionless. She looked away and heard him move again.

She stared down at the thick candle in the middle of the table, its cream color so pale as to be almost translucent. Wax slowly dripped down its side, puddling at the base of the silver candle holder. Even the innocuous candle revealed the differences between them. Her cottage had been illuminated by twisted ta-pers soaked in fat. They always smelled and smoked when lit. This one had a scent of something sharp and aromatic that hinted at faraway places.

Donald entered the room again a short time later, followed by two men carrying buckets filled with steaming water. They bobbed their heads nervously in the Butcher's direction as they finished their chore and left the room again.

"Why did you save the village?" she asked abruptly.

He hesitated for a moment before speaking. "Sedgewick's actions were tantamount to taking an axe to a fly. Why burn a village when I would just have to rebuild it?"

"That's your excuse?" she asked, angered. She glanced in his direction, her words sputtering to a halt as she stared.

There was only so much man the copper tub could hold. He had not looked quite so large in his uniform. His arms, sprinkled with black hair, rested on the sides of the tub, while his knees, bent in order for his long legs to fit, reached his chin.

As she watched, he squeezed the cloth against his shoulder, rinsing it. Soapy water ran down his chest as he lathered it, his hand moving in slow, almost en-thralling circles before flattening against his stomach.

She thought, for a moment, that he might have been anyone. A Scot. A warrior. Yet the look in his eyes, level and imperious, was that of someone who expected obedience to his word and his wishes. That labeled him a victor in any era.

She was neither a maiden nor an innocent. Then why was she staring at a naked man with such rapt attention? She told herself to glance away or say something cutting to him, words that would prove she was not tongue-tied and witless.

In a thoroughly unwelcome and unbidden thought, she realized that the Butcher of Inverness was a handsome man. She stared down at the plate in front of her, horrified by that traitorous thought more than by his nakedness.

"I did not mean to embarrass you," he said casually, as if the silence between them had not been stretched thin.

"I've seen naked men before," she said, willing her voice to steady.

"Your Marcus?"

She nodded, although it was not the truth. Their one and only coupling had been done in haste and she'd kept her eyes tightly shut from the beginning. But she'd helped to tend the sick and bury the dead, and more than once a wrestling match between two kilted men had resulted in bare backsides and fronts being exhibited for the entire world to see.

He said nothing further, the stillness interrupted only by the sounds of his bathing, a splash of water, droplets falling back into the tub in a slow trickle that recalled a spring rain, the scrape of soap being placed back into its container, the hollow note as the edge of the copper bath was lightly tapped.

She stood and walked to the window once more, carefully averting her eyes from his side of the room. Fort William's lanterns had been lit, the chain of lights defense against the night. Beyond was the land bridge, the small torch carried by the newly dispatched sentry bobbing as he walked his post. There would be no escape there.

"Have you never once wished to be quit of this place?" he asked.

"It might be easier to leave," she conceded. "It's

difficult when everything around you only brings back memories."

"The memories will follow you wherever you go," he said.

"As yours do?"

"Yes, but then, Scotland has been the source of most of my recollections."

Inverness, no doubt. She had heard tales of his atrocities, of the helpless prisoners whose only crime had been to love their country. That is what she should think about, not the fact that he was a man of disarming charm and a curiosity that surprised her.

"Gilmuir is my home," she said, "for all that I've not been here since the laird died."

He said nothing for a long moment. Finally, he spoke again. "I thought you had no leader," he said soberly.

"No one in the clan could replace Niall MacRae. And after the war, there was no need. There are only a handful of MacRaes left."

"Did your laird counsel rebellion?" he asked quietly.

"Yes," she said, "but did not live to see it. He would have led his men into battle against the English, if for no other reason to avenge his daughter's death."

"What do you mean?" he asked, and his voice sounded cautious, almost hesitant. "The Scots killed her."

She shook her head. "It was the English who brought murder to Gilmuir."

"You lie," he said quietly, his voice laced with a dangerous emotion, one she could not discern.

She whirled, angered by his attempt to intimidate her.

He was standing, his foot raised to leave the tub,

one hand reaching for the toweling. The candlelight gleamed on his flesh, the water droplets accentuating the plate of his chest, a flank, the muscled beauty of a limb.

He stepped out of the bath making no move to cover himself, the toweling bunched in one hand and held at his side.

She looked away from him.

"Tell me what you mean, Leitis," he said, his voice grating. A quick sideways glance revealed that he had wrapped the linen around his waist and was walking toward her.

"The laird's daughter was killed by the English," she said, tensing as he came closer. He stood beside her, the heat from his body so great that she felt warmed by it.

"Moira MacRae was married to one of you," she said, folding her arms, her palms cupping her elbows. "But she suffered greatly for it, for all that she was a countess. General Wade's troops didn't care that she was titled. All that was necessary was that she was a woman and alone."

His hands gripped her shoulders. Slowly, resolutely, he turned her until she faced him. His hands inched down her arms until his thumbs were gently resting against her inner wrist.

"I've heard it was the Drummonds who killed her," he said tightly.

It seemed as if he held himself motionless, naked but for a strip of cloth, barely drawing a breath. She had the sudden, surprising notion that he was enraged.

She wished he would move away. Or perhaps she might. *Take a step, Leitis. One tiny step so that you do not feel him so close.*

It seemed as if the moments ticked by sluggishly as

she stared at him. She felt herself warming again when his fingers trailed along the inside of her wrist. As if he tested the truth of her words by measuring the beat of her blood.

"What do you care, Butcher?" she said finally, uncomfortable with his silence and her own reaction to him. "It's an old tale. A tragedy for us, not the English." She stepped back even farther. "They killed her, just as you killed the Scots in Inverness."

Chapter 7

Alec stared at her, unable to deflect her sudden rage or shield himself from the look of contempt in her eyes. She protected herself with anger, a ploy that had not worked successfully until this moment.

Walking to the table, he glanced down at the meal Donald had brought him. He rarely ate with the other officers unless he was on campaign. Instead, he chose to remain aloof, a habit that had begun at Flanders. It was difficult to form friendships among his troops, only to have to order them into battle and possibly to their deaths. But at this moment he doubted he could eat; breathing was difficult enough.

He traced the lip of a plate, feeling the curve of it, and the blue and white raised pattern beneath his fingertips. "Are you certain of this, Leitis?"

"Yes," she said shortly. "Ask anyone in the glen, if you don't believe me."

Alec nodded, as if reluctantly accepting the truth, but slowly, so that he might tolerate the rawness of it.

He sat, pressing the heels of both hands against his closed eyes, hearing Donald entering the room as if summoned by his confusion. His aide began to fill the buckets from the tub, a chore he'd evidently chosen to perform alone.

"Why does it matter to you?" she asked curiously once he'd gone.

Alec didn't answer her. What could he say? That he had based a lifetime's worth of hatred on a falsehood?

He had become a different person the day his mother had died, the journey back to England solidifying the change from laughing boy to angry young man. He'd known that those halcyon days of his childhood were over.

He glanced over at her. Leitis stood with her back against the wall, her eyes wary, her arms crossed. Not the pose of a penitent or a reluctant hostage.

He wanted to tell her that he was not as loathsome as she thought, that his actions in Inverness should count for something. Instead, he remained silent, reticence being safer than revelation.

An hour passed; her eyelids began to droop and twice Leitis almost fell.

"Do you intend to stand there all night?" he asked.

"Yes," she said shortly.

Finally, she sat cautiously on the edge of the bed, leaning one shoulder against the carved oak headboard garnished with the MacRae crest. He continued to sit where he was, legs stretched out before him as he stared into the black bricks of the fireplace as if it were a doorway to a secret room, a place to escape from his thoughts.

The wind was sighing around Gilmuir, brushing against the thick blown glass of the windows, rushing around the ruined walls. It was a mournful sound, an eerie accompaniment to the other noises in the night. Somewhere a timber creaked, a floorboard popped. A brick fell to join its companions. It was as if the old castle were moving around them slowly, coming back to life in the darkness.

When Alec stood, Leitis jerked awake, the scrape of his chair against the floorboards evidently warning her. He threw the towel toward the bath and watched her eyes widen as she stood and backed to the wall, instantly wary. He donned his breeches and walked out of the room, leaving the door open behind him.

Night enshrouded the old castle, the roofless clan hall bared to the elements. The moon was an egg-shaped glow in the sky. He tilted his head back, staring up at the stars. They seemed to wink at him, in commiseration, perhaps. Or were they weeping, instead, and every blink was another tear shed?

Darkness was kind to Gilmuir, filling in walls that had been destroyed in the bombardment, giving the shadows life until it was possible to believe that he was not the only being of substance in this chamber.

He was not a man given to flights of fancy or one to believe in specters and phantoms. It was simply that his thoughts were on the past more than the present. His memory furnished the picture of his grandfather, seated in his thronelike chair, presiding over judgments with more ease than Alec had ever felt. But then, the laird's pronouncements had been for minor infractions and rarely meant a man's death.

He could remember sitting here beside his mother's bier. She'd been dressed in her finest gown, a blue linen that made her look like a princess. A wooden platter had been placed upon her chest. On it his grandmother carefully piled a mound of earth and one of salt. Any object that could reflect an image had been removed from Gilmuir, the dirks and shields in the hall covered with the MacRae plaid.

The clan was in mourning, and the wind was transformed into the wails of women. It seemed as if they brushed by him like grief-stricken ghosts, their vaporous hands outstretched as if to commiserate with him in his self-imposed vigil.

The five pipers of the MacRae clan lined up one after the other to give tribute to the laird's daughter. They played the MacRae Lament, a tune of indescribable sorrow. He had hated the sound of the pipes that dawn morning. But then, he'd hated everything about Scotland from that day forward, the savagery, the barbarity, the cruelty of this place.

The stars were suddenly veiled in the nighttime mist, a not-uncommon occurrence at Gilmuir. The MacRae March swirled around him, a celestial choir of high-pitched notes; a tune that brought back memories both joyful and sad.

Reason came to him at that moment. It was neither a dream nor an apparition, but only Hamish defying his edict. That stubborn fool.

He spun around and returned to the room. Leitis was standing in the doorway, her expression one of confusion rather than contempt.

She stiffened as he moved closer until her back was pressed against the open door. He placed his hands on either side of her head, pressed his thumbs below her jaw, and tilted her face up, studying her in the soft yellow candlelight.

His fingers trailed over her face softly and without haste as if he sought the child in the woman's features. Her only response was to close her eyes and remain immobile beneath his touch. But she trembled beneath his fingers, evoking a surge of tenderness so strong that it startled him. Pulling back, he dropped his hands and stepped away from her.

"Where did Hamish get the pipes, Leitis?" he asked.

"Do you think I would tell you, Butcher?" she asked, blinking open her eyes.

"I should have hanged the old fool," he said, placing both of his hands on her waist and pulling her gently to him. He backed her up to the bed, the lone candle illuminating the strange dance between them. She landed on the wide mattress in a flurry of skirts and flailing limbs.

He lifted her hair, pressed his lips against her bare throat. Her blood seemed to race, even as she angled her head aside.

"No," she said, the word both a protest and a command.

Slowly he rose over her.

What else had he expected? He almost spoke the words. *Leitis, I knew your brothers. I knew you. You are my fondest playmate and my first love.*

But he knew he wasn't going to divulge his true identity. He didn't want her memory of him tarnished by what he had become. Just as he held an image of her in his mind, he wanted the boy named Ian to always live in hers, forever young and innocent and untainted by war or labels.

He moved to her side, placing his hand at her waist, feeling the movement of her chest beneath his palm.

Leitis turned her head and stared at him, her eyes turbulent and filled with loathing. Even so, she was warmth and loveliness. Comfort and welcome. Perhaps not for him, but for this one moment he could pretend. In his mind, fogged by too many memories, it was another time, another place. Not Scotland battered by war. Not this woman scarred by sorrow. Not him, the Butcher of Inverness.

She would not show her fear, not even if he raped her.

But as the moments passed and his breathing slowed, it was evident that the Butcher of Inverness was falling asleep.

His hand lay flat against her waist as if claiming her. His grip was not punishing as much as it was a restrictive one.

Leitis waited a few moments longer until she was certain that he was asleep, then began to slowly move to the edge of the bed. Her left foot slid soundlessly to the floor, and then her right. Cautiously, she moved beneath his arm, lifting his hand, finger by finger, from her waist.

She stood, only to feel her skirt being tugged. He rose up, gripped her arm, and pulled her until she fell heavily on the mattress.

"I sleep lightly, Leitis," he said softly.

"Let me go," she said desperately, but he held her tightly against him. Her cheek lay against his bare chest. His skin was tight with muscle, his chest dusted with curling hair that tickled her nose.

"Sleep, Leitis," he commanded wearily, wrapping his arms around her again.

"I want to go home," she whispered. A bit of weakness whispered against his skin. But he startled her by easing his grip, pulling back, and placing the most tender of kisses on her forehead.

"So do I," he said surprisingly.

His sleep deepened as the moments passed, but each time she tried to slip away, his grip tightened reflexively. He was a formidable enemy, but not in the way she'd imagined. Yes, he wielded power, but he had the oddest ability to strip the breath from her and escalate the beat of her heart. Even worse, he amused her until she had forgotten, for a moment, exactly who he was.

She should spend less time thinking of his eyes, darkly brown and brimming with secrets. Or his mouth, squared and resolute in duty yet hinting at a smile. Instead, she should be feeling compassion for his victims.

The curiosity she felt was unwelcome. But he had stood in the clan hall, staring into the shadows as if he saw ghosts there. What had he sought from the darkness of Gilmuir?

She lay pressed against him, hoping that sleep would capture him so that she could at least move away. But he seemed restless; his breathing altered and the beating of his heart increased.

She pulled back and glanced up at him. His face was contorted in a grimace as he began to speak, the words mumbled and unclear.

A dream, and a troubling one, at that. A man named Butcher must sleep ill indeed.

Suddenly he flung out his arm, his hand balled in a threatening fist. He twisted on the bed, allowing her to move. He gripped the pillow with both hands, holding on to it as if it were his salvation.

No ordinary dream, but one that was born in his soul.

She stretched out her fingers tentatively, touching his forehead. He turned in her direction like a child reassured. Although it was awkward ministering to the Butcher of Inverness, she didn't move away, perhaps because he appeared so helpless at the moment.

She reached out and placed her palm on his cheek. "It's only a dream," she softly said, a reassurance she might have made to a child.

"All dead," he said softly. For a moment she thought him awake, so clear and reasonable was his voice. His eyes, however, were closed and his face rigid, the muscles in his jaw prominent. She pulled back her hand, a hollow feeling in her chest as if her heart were waiting a long agonizing moment before beginning to beat again.

"All dead," he said again, his voice oddly expressionless.

"Who is dead?" she whispered.

He turned away, his hands clenched into fists at his side. The words he began to speak were an unintelligible murmur, each utterance followed by an interval of silence. After several moments of listening closely, she realized that it was a roll call of names he repeated. Men he'd ordered into battle? Or those he'd killed?

Troubled, she moved to the edge of the bed, but his hand reached out and gripped her waist, pulling her back. A moment later he buried his face against her bodice.

Her hand wavered in the air above him before she finally lowered it, stroking back the hair from his damp face. "It's only a dream," she murmured, confused by her sudden wish to comfort him. "Go to sleep," she said softly.

What battle did he relive? What horrors did he see in his mind? She would never ask him. An Englishman's memories were not those she wished to plumb.

It was a childhood verse she repeated, something that her mother had sung to lull her to sleep. The poem, in the Gaelic, was a lyrical comfort:

Hush, little one, you are safe in your bed.
Hush, my darling, and rest your sweet head.
All the world is asleep, and the night is still
I'll stay with you and guard you from ill.

He no longer spoke, but from time to time he shuddered, as if returning with difficulty from a land of ghosts and graves. His breathing began to ease as he calmed.

Fort William settled down for an uneasy sleep. Somewhere her uncle was, no doubt, playing his pipes. The villagers were probably talking of her and of Hamish, having finished their communal evening meal. And she, Leitis MacRae, was crooning softly to her enemy.

Chapter 8

The smoke-laden air made it difficult to breathe. But Alec blessed the cannon fire and the powder. It masked the stench of death.

The earth was so saturated with blood that his boots sank into the ground. But the Scots kept coming, even after they'd been fired on. The men in the front ranks fell and the others simply walked over them, their faces stoic, their earlier battle cries muted now in the face of their defeat. They fell, dying, and a moment later rose again.

Cumberland shouted over the melee, his face contorted by an unearthly grin. His white stallion pawed the air and the duke laughed. "Kill them all, Landers!" he shouted. "Let not one man leave this place alive."

He heard himself speak words of protest. Cumberland ignored him as he gave instructions for a poor hut to be fired.

"Dear merciful God," he whispered, and the sound of his prayer strangely slowed the carnage. Men, English and Scot alike, frowned at him, as if to challenge his charity.

"There is no God in this place, Landers," the Duke of Cumberland said, riding close to him. Suddenly the other man glanced up as a radiance spread over the battlefield.

"It's all right," the angel said, startling him. There had never been the presence of an angel in this place of hell. Iridescence surrounded her, blessedly obscuring the rest of the battlefield and banishing the sight of Cumberland.

Her warm and loving touch eased his mind. A gentle voice soothed him, promised him solace. He wanted to thank her for her kindness, for the compassion she so effortlessly granted him in banishing the sight of Culloden. But then, she was an angel and ordained to grant pity to sinners.

His mind focused on her, noting the solemn expression on her face. Did she represent all those prisoners who had been condemned, then? Was she the angel of righteousness, the one who spoke out for the Scots?

Her silence mocked him.

His fingers threaded through her hair. Each individual curl seemed to reach out and snare his hand. She was so warm, and he was so very cold. Even her scalp felt heated where his palms rested. He moved closer, feeling the angel stiffen as if she became marble in that moment.

Vignettes of memory marched through his mind, reminded him of those acts performed in the heat of battle when survival mattered more than kindness. A litany of transgressions he felt duty-bound to reveal to her. But she only placed her warm hand on his brow to silence him. The tips of her fingers were callused, as if she'd performed countless acts of charity in the past.

He wanted to seek forgiveness in the sanctity of her touch, be healed deep inside where grief, sharp enough to cut, lingered.

She bent forward, arching over him in protection. Did tutelary spirits speak in voices as soft as a breeze? This one did. A celestial trick, then, to assuage his fear at an angel's presence.

Alec wrapped his arms gently around her in case she took flight. She was possessed of womanly curves that fitted against his body perfectly. An angel crafted only for him, then. His personal guardian.

She pushed against him, a soft fluttering of wings. But her strength was no match for his. He bent and kissed her mouth, softly, so as not to frighten her. But her lips thinned as if she were enraged.

It was not wise, perhaps, to anger an angel.

His thumbs brushed beneath her chin, tilting her head so that he might deepen the kiss. Her mouth felt mortal, warm and full, a pillow for his lips. Did he transgress against heaven with such an act?

She murmured something and he deepened the kiss to silence her protest. In a moment she would disappear, leaving him only a memory of a dream so sweet that it had pulled him from carnage into carnality. He felt himself swell, desire overpowering the lingering aftertaste of his nightmare. His hand cupped her cheek, fingers splaying to hold her still. But lightly, so carefully that she could not claim to an ethereal tribunal that it had been coercion.

But the angel struggled, her wings slapping at him,

her head tossing from side to side. He held her pinned beneath him, desperate to convince her to remain. He kissed her, deeply, completely, feeling as if she were a well and he a man dying of thirst. Again, and she began to quiet. Once more, and she lay quiescent beneath him, her lips slack beneath his.

"Is Moira MacRae's fate to be mine, then, Butcher?" she asked curtly.

Were angels granted the ability to wound with words? To speak in a bitter tone to audacious mortals? He kissed her once more, but she only lay rigidly beneath him.

"Hurry, then. Rape me and be done with it."

The angel's face began to change, the strange luminescence altering to become reddened lips, pink cheeks, and flashing eyes the color of a pale dawn sky.

A spirit garbed not in ethereal raiments, but those of a temporal world. She was not the living instrument of his forgiveness, but a woman enraged.

No angel, then, but Leitis.

He was atop her, his hands gripping her arms tightly over her head. He stared down into her face as sleep vanished in that instant. She turned her head on the pillow, the resignation in her eyes painful to see.

Pulling away from her, he stood, stumbling away from the bed. His words of contrition were halted by the fixed and immobile look on her face.

He was, suddenly, desperate to leave her. Donning his shirt and boots quickly, he left the room in silence.

It was a lonely night, one that was empty of nature's sounds. Not one bird called or squirrel chittered. Not one single forest creature squawked or screamed, remaining mute as if they knew his plans and the significance of his solitary journey.

Nodding absently to the sentry on duty, Alec began to cross the land bridge, following a worn path up to the north end of the glen. To the one place in all of Scotland that he dreaded visiting.

He climbed over several large boulders, up past the other cairn stones that marked the burial place of the MacRaes. A venerable pine, shadowed by night, stretched its branches against the sky and marked her resting place. She lay alone here in a place of honor, her eternal view the loch and Gilmuir below. The gentle winds carried the scent of summer to this place. And here the bitter cold of winter would linger.

The marker he'd made for her as a boy was still intact, surrounded by a larger stone that looked to have been placed there only to protect his childish efforts. He didn't need to read the words to remember them. He'd done the painstaking carving, locked in his chamber so that no one could see his tears.

It was the English who brought murder to Gilmuir. He knew Leitis's words were the truth. All these years he'd learned to hate, only to discover that his enemy was innocent. Where did he put that anger now? Where did that rage go?

What was happening to him?

He felt himself changing in a way he could feel but not articulate. Perhaps it was the various burdens he felt pressing down on his shoulders—the millstone of command, the secret of his heritage, and his acts in Inverness. Or it could be that this past year had sickened him to what he was and what his countrymen had done.

Here, in this lonely place, he prayed silently. Not to God, who had often heard his pleas in the midst of battle, but to his mother, the one person in the world who had seen only goodness in him and who had granted him love and enduring understanding.

If there was a sound in the night, it was only the

soft wind soughing around the cairn stones. But in his mind his mother whispered to him.

Forgive, my darling son. Be forgiven.

For almost an hour Leitis sat on the edge of the bed and stared at the door, waiting for him to reappear.

He hadn't upended her skirts and entered her quickly as Marcus had, so intent on the deed that he had not noticed her pain. She had been prepared for the act to be even more unpleasant with the Butcher. Instead, he had looked shocked at his own actions.

It was not until she had pushed him away that she'd realized he had still been in the throes of a dream. His look of stunned horror upon awakening had been too real to be feigned.

She didn't want him to be bound by honor, gentle with her, or even repelled by his own frailty. It contradicted all she'd thought of him, made him someone she didn't understand. The degree of curiosity she felt about him was unwise. As foolish as the memory of his dream-induced kiss.

She stood, walked to the window. There was no moon to shine a light inside the window, nor fire to cast an orange glow. Only the candle burning silently on the table, its faint glow no match for the darkness that encapsulated Gilmuir.

She walked to the door and opened it slowly, half expecting to see Donald on guard. But there was no one there. An invitation, perhaps, to escape. But it was too dangerous to take the cliff path in the dark and she doubted if she could get past the sentry stationed at the land bridge.

Instead, she walked toward the priory. The large, open chamber lay in solemn silence. A strange feeling of loneliness crept over her, as if the whole world slept comforted and safe on this night, but for her.

She stepped into the middle of an arch, stretching out her arms as if to capture the warm night breeze from the loch. The moon was tucked behind a cloud and there was no light to differentiate the darkness of the water from the horizon. As a result, it appeared like an impenetrable black curtain stretching as far as the eye could see.

Even Gilmuir seemed nestled in shadow, a great black bulwark silhouetted against the night. Within its walls were voices and laughter, the footfalls of children, the grumbling from old men, the giggles of young girls. All the sounds layered from generation to generation.

This was how she would always think of the old castle, even if it crumbled to nothing but dust. Here, there was the history of Gilmuir and the memory of proud people not yet defeated.

"Forgive me," he said.

She whirled to see the Butcher approaching her, a dark shadow in a place filled with them. Cautiously, she backed up until she felt a brick pillar behind her.

"Forgive me," he said again, halting a few feet away. "My actions have no justification, so I cannot offer you excuses," he added stiffly. "All I can say is that such behavior will never happen again. I will sleep at Fort William in the future."

She said nothing in response, silenced by surprise.

Without another word, he turned and left her, leaving her to stare after him until he disappeared into the darkness.

Chapter 9

Alec stood in Fort William's courtyard, oblivious to the cacophony around him. He'd given orders that they would begin patrols this morning and the troops were scrambling in preparation. An irritant, since they should have been ready at a moment's notice.

But his attention was not directed at the horses being led from their stalls, or the furtive looks sent his way. Instead, he stared at Gilmuir as if he could see through the walls. He wanted to go to her, to tell her who he was and what he had done. But he doubted she would listen to him, especially after his actions of last night.

He'd bunked with Harrison, his adjutant's surprise at being awakened abruptly quickly hidden. Instead of sleeping, however, Alec had spent the hours staring up at the ceiling engaged in thought.

He had believed, for most of his life, in the barbarity of the Scots, only to witness more cruelty by the English in the past year. He'd been trained to obey, yet he'd spent the last few months actively disobeying his commander's orders. He'd always thought of himself as a man of honor, but a dream had almost lured him to force himself on Leitis.

Alec felt as if he were being split in two. The man he had been vying with the man he was becoming. Only he was not certain of this new identity. It was more Scot than English, more rebellious than obedient.

Turning, he walked through the courtyard and into the regimental hall. The men he'd requested for this meeting had all assembled. He sat at the head of one of the dining hall tables, the room emptied but for himself and the six other officers.

The large room was similar to the clan hall, a meeting place with flags hanging from the walls in a display of nationalism. In the case of Gilmuir, the walls had been festooned with banners and weapons.

Present were Captains Wilmot and Monroe, along with Lieutenant Castleton, all of whom had accompanied him from Inverness. In addition, Sedgewick was in attendance, as well as his adjutant, an officious lieutenant by the name of William Armstrong who was now in the process of staring down Harrison.

"It is my place you've assumed, sir," Lieutenant Armstrong said.

Harrison merely smiled, his face unchanged by such an expression. In fact, Alec thought, it might be that the other man appeared more genial when he did not smile at all. As if his face, ill favored as it was, was not suited for amiability.

"My adjutant always occupies the position to my

right, Armstrong," Alec said, impatient with the maneuvers that occurred at such functions. The arrival of a new commander was always a cause for celebration for some and panic for others.

Armstrong sat, his face twisted in an expression of annoyance the mirror of Sedgewick's expression. Alec had little tolerance for either of them.

"This meeting is for one purpose, to outline the changes that are in effect immediately." He nodded across the table, acknowledging his officers. "Captains Wilmot and Monroe will each be responsible for approximately fifty men." They would browbeat them, lecture them, coddle them if necessary, but in a few weeks each soldier would understand what was required in Alec's command.

"Lieutenant Castleton will oversee ancillary functions such as the bakery and the stores. And the barnyard," he added dryly. "Do something with that, Castleton, before we're all dead of the stench."

"And my duties, Colonel?" Sedgewick asked stiffly.

"You are going to be on patrol," he said bluntly. He nodded to Harrison, who passed Sedgewick a map. Sedgewick wasted no time unrolling it. A moment later, he passed the map to Armstrong.

"My patrol area is almost to the Irish Sea," he said resentfully, making no effort to disguise his disgust at the assignment.

"I'm aware of the area, Sedgewick," Alec said crisply. "Just as I am of the fact that you are challenging my orders."

Sedgewick's mouth tightened, the look he gave Alec without even a pretense of respect or compliance. It was obvious he was furious, so much so that the control over his temper and his words was hard-won.

The moment lengthened as the two men stared at each other.

"May I take any of my men with me?" Sedgewick asked finally, "or shall I patrol half of Scotland by myself, Colonel?"

If Alec had used that sarcastic tone with any of his commanders, he would have been whisked away in chains. But if he put Sedgewick in gaol, it would not rid him of the major's presence. Sending him on patrol was the best recourse.

Alec wanted Sedgewick gone from Fort William. The reason was simple. It wasn't because of his posturing, nor for his barely veiled insubordination, but for his character. And his ability to accept any act no matter how vile under the aegis of duty.

There were limits that men created in the secrecy of their own minds, lines they drew between obedience and their conscience. He had reached his in Inverness, discovered it was a barrier as firm and solid as a wall of brick. He wondered, however, if Sedgewick would ever know that his own line existed.

"You'll have twenty men," Alec said, determined that any man who'd been labeled a laggard or troublemaker would accompany Sedgewick.

Sedgewick stood, the bench scraping against the wood. "Then if you will excuse me, sir," he said, standing at attention stiffly, "I'll be preparing for my departure in the morning."

"I will not, Major," Alec said, also standing. "You'll have plenty of time to ready for your patrol when we return. Right now, you'll accompany me on a tour of the vicinity." He wasn't about to leave Sedgewick at the fort with only Donald to guard Leitis.

"Then I'll give the orders to move out," Sedgewick said.

"Have the men pack provisions for one day," Alec ordered, watching as Sedgewick left the room.

When the door closed behind the major, he felt only relief.

Armstrong spoke up as Alec dismissed the men. "The supply wagons need repairing, sir," he said. "And the smithy's anvil cracked."

"Tell the man in charge," Alec said, glancing down at the lieutenant. "Lieutenant Castleton, in this case."

"But you're the colonel, sir," Armstrong said, looking confused.

It would be unwise to judge Armstrong because of his association with Sedgewick. But it was obvious that the major's style of leadership differed greatly from his own.

"Every man at this table, Armstrong," he said patiently, "is capable of having his own command. The reason for that is that they have learned to govern. The officer who refuses to give his men practice in responsibility only thinks of himself and not his regiment. My duty is to see that the Crown's mission is accomplished in the Highlands, and that will not be done with my attention being directed toward anvils and wagons."

"Yes, sir," Armstrong said, chagrined. With any luck there was promise to the lieutenant. Alec would keep him at the fort and ascertain whether his loyalty was reserved for Sedgewick or the regiment.

The meeting completed, his next priority was finding Hamish. The old fool couldn't be allowed to flaunt his disdain for English authority so publicly. If he continued with his nightly serenades within hearing distance of Fort William, the men in his command would wonder why Alec did not punish his hostage.

Alec walked into the courtyard and mounted his horse, the soldiers behind him doing the same. Other than a small troop left behind to guard Fort William, all of the men in his command were arrayed here, waiting patiently in their regimentals for the signal to advance. Nearly half of them were cavalry, the others infantrymen.

This day's ride served another purpose in addition to finding Hamish. It would be his initial inspection of the territory surrounding Fort William and must, therefore, be done with a show of force. Showing the Highlanders the full complement of soldiers would not only prove that the English were here to stay, but it might deter thoughts of rebellion.

"I heard you released the piper," Sedgewick said, mounting and moving to his side. "It came as a great surprise when you exchanged him for a hostage."

"Should I have sought your permission, Major?" Alec asked sharply.

"No, sir. I just congratulate you on your good fortune to select one of the few women within miles with some promise. After you find the piper and release her, I'll have to try her myself." He smiled, an expression of challenge rather than mirth.

Alec faced forward. Damn Hamish and his stiff-necked pride.

Leitis smoothed her hands over her wrinkled skirt, pulled on her shoes, looked around for her hair ribbon, and, finding it on the pillow, tied her hair back. The mundane duties kept her hands busy as her mind whirled with plans to escape.

There was one spot in the window where the glass was shattered, forming a cobweb pattern. Grabbing a length of sheeting and winding it around her hand, she tapped on the glass until a hole appeared.

On the horizon the sky was lighter, as if the earth were an overturned bowl and the rim of it pale blue.

The dawn sun was sending streaks of orange and pink light across the sky. It was a perfect summer morning in Scotland. All her life she had loved this season most. The scent of lush flowers and grass, the screech of an eagle on its morning hunt, brought back the magic of her childhood. She could almost hear her brothers' laughter as she raced with them across the glen or hid in the forest and caves she knew so well. It felt as if something warm bloomed in her chest and she was suddenly aware of a feeling of gratitude for those enchanted days of freedom and joy.

How strange to recall her childhood now. Was it being at Gilmuir after so many years?

A soft knock on the door made her turn. She called out a greeting and Donald peered inside.

"Good morning, miss," he said, grinning broadly.

She could not forestall her own soft smile.

"I've breakfast, miss. Will you eat?"

She nodded. It would be foolish to turn down a meal.

He stepped inside the room, bearing a heavily laden tray. He sat it on the table and began to make a place for her.

Donald was so young and eager to please that she couldn't be cold around him. He reminded her too much of Fergus.

"Doesn't the Butcher eat breakfast?" she asked, staring at the dispatch case.

He frowned at her, but answered all the same. "The colonel was in a lather to be on patrol this morning, miss. I expect he'll eat in the saddle. There have been too many times when we've done that."

She knew, suddenly, that he was going to find Hamish. She hoped her uncle had the good sense to stay hidden. But if he'd had any sense at all, he'd never have played the pipes in the first place.

The place set, the ale poured, Donald moved to straighten the bedcovers, making no comment as to their disarray, as if his colonel slept with a woman every night. Perhaps he did.

Leitis looked away, concentrated on the light streaming in through the window.

"Have you been with him long?"

"Long enough," he said cautiously. "Ever since Flanders."

She glanced at him curiously.

"The War of Austrian Succession," he said. "A strange place, Flanders, miss," he said, bending and tucking in the sheet until it was taut. "I'd much rather have my feet here on English soil." He straightened, smoothed the blanket, and folded it neatly, never realizing what he'd said. Scotland wasn't England, but would there come a day when people could not distinguish one from the other? If the Empire had its way, yes.

"Is he an easy man to serve?"

He glanced over at her, grinning. "He wants what he wants when he wants it. In that, he's no different from any commanding officer, I expect."

Donald retrieved the case and the colonel's other possessions, but it didn't strip the room of his commanding officer's presence. "I'll be back in a while, miss, with warm water for your wash."

She smiled her agreement, waiting until the moment the door closed before she stacked the biscuits, cheese, and ham into a napkin. Cautiously, she opened the door, peered from side to side, and when there was no sign of a guard, raced through the archway to the other side of Gilmuir. There, a series of stunted gorse bushes clung tenaciously to the edge of the cliff. Leitis moved from one to the other, peering over the side.

A moment later she found the entrance to the path. Dropping to her knees, she tucked the parcel of food in her bodice, then lay flat on her stomach. She inched backward toward the sheer drop, her legs flailing in the air before her feet found a foothold. Praying that her memory hadn't failed her, and more importantly that the path hadn't crumbled since she'd used it last, she lowered herself down carefully.

It was nothing more than a shelf of stone encircling Gilmuir, a natural outcropping of the rock that formed the island. It had looked wider as a child, she suddenly realized, staring down at the glittering cream-colored slab of rock.

Slowly, she edged along the path, only once glancing to her right. Far beneath her was the loch, its deep blue water still and ominous. It didn't matter that she had learned to swim as a girl; she doubted if she would survive the fall.

Where once she would have found the journey around Gilmuir daring and even exciting, now it was only harrowing. The path undulated like a stone serpent, sometimes rising high enough that she had to bend over so that the top of her head wasn't seen. Once the track cut so sharply into the face of the cliff that she had to crawl beneath a rocky overhang. When she came to a straighter section, she knew that the land bridge was above her. A few more feet and she could begin the upward climb to the glen.

The idea of solid earth beneath her feet was almost heady. So, too, was the fact that she had escaped the English. And more importantly, the Butcher.

"I beg your pardon, my lady, but a messenger just delivered this."

The Countess of Sherbourne looked up from her needlework curiously.

Hendricks crossed the sitting room floor, handed the message to her with white gloves and an impeccable manner. His livery was dark blue, his wig a glaring white. She suspected that he refurbished it every morning, because wherever he walked the air was laden with a cloud of powder.

She took the message and stared at it curiously. Her late husband's name stared back at her in a black, perfectly executed penmanship.

Brandidge Hall was a serene place, so much so that she could hear the individual footsteps of each person as they walked through the fifty rooms. She rarely heard laughter or conversation, the earl having disliked discourse between his servants. Patricia wondered, sometimes, if they ever smiled at each other or winked in passing.

Her husband had a taste for the French, and even this room, her private retreat, bore signs of his influence. The lady's writing table was a delicate piece, with its curved legs and intricately carved top. She put aside her needlework, walked to it now, and placed the envelope down on its inlaid surface.

"A letter, Mama?" David asked, turning from his position on the settee. The gray cat sitting on his lap glanced up at him in remonstrance, her pale yellow eyes narrowed in annoyance. David smiled down at her and resumed his affectionate petting. Sometimes Patricia thought that animals loved David in a special way. That particular cat, named Ralph in honor of David's first and only tutor, would never have sat on her lap for so long.

"Yes, dearest," she said. "From your brother." If only it had arrived when Gerald had been alive. It would have pleased him so much. Opening the flap, she began to read Alec's words, telling herself that it was necessary to do so, if only to obtain his address.

He must be informed of his father's passing and his own ascension to the earldom.

> *I have been posted to Gilmuir, Father, a command I truly wished to reject. But the army and the Duke of Cumberland do not take into account a man's past or his reluctance. Therefore, I am here, in the very place I wished never to be.*
>
> *Scotland, itself, has suffered greatly from her rebellion. I cannot say that the Scots have learned from it. One of their own proverbs states that twelve men and a set of pipes will spur a rebellion.*
>
> *My command consists of a hundred twelve men, mostly unseasoned. But Scotland ages a man quickly.*

He went on for several pages, the words to his father those of a fond son, not one who had not communicated in so many years. She wondered, now, if she had contributed to the separation between them. She had not fought against his decision to join the regiment when he was eighteen.

Perhaps because it had been increasingly difficult to compare the two brothers. Alec had been a charming boy with a ready smile. He showed a determination to do as he wished, however, despite what his father wanted for him.

Patricia glanced at her son and smiled fondly. She had known ever since he was a small boy that David was different. At first his difficulties were not noticeable to most people, even to her closest friends. But as time passed and David remained immured in a world other boys left behind, it became obvious that he would never advance to adulthood in his mind.

It would have been easier, perhaps, if she had treated him as most of her friends did their children, leaving their intimate needs to be catered to by a variety of paid servants. But from the very beginning he had been dear to her heart.

In those years when her friends had reported glowingly of their own progeny's triumphs, Patricia had smiled politely and ached inside.

David was a kind young man with not a word of dislike for anyone. Instead, he viewed the world with a wide-eyed wonder as if expecting all the best from it. He saw nothing but friends in even the most suspect of places, and would willingly give his last penny to anyone who asked. Because of his innate goodness and innocence, he needed protection and almost constant guidance.

Nature had provided him with good looks in compensation for other deficiencies. Her son was almost perfectly handsome with his dark brown hair and large brown eyes.

"Can I read the letter?" he asked now.

"Certainly," she said, holding it out for him.

He carefully placed the cat on the adjacent cushion and rose, taking the letter. "I remember Alec," he said, smiling.

Although he read the letter carefully, Patricia knew that he would not understand the meaning behind all the words. She repeated to him what Alec had written.

"I wish I could see him," he said, passing the letter back to her. "He was very tall."

"You are his equal now," she said.

"I'm tall," he said proudly.

She nodded and smiled, hiding the spurt of pain at the sweetness and vacancy of his expression. Over the years she'd become accustomed to that ache just as she was her breath and the beat of her blood.

"Perhaps he'll come to see us soon," she said, hoping that it was, indeed, the case. The meeting with the solicitor had frightened her.

"I'm afraid, my lady," he'd said, "that the earl made no provisions for David. Could it be that he wished his son to provide for him?" he added, his voice filled with kindness.

"Yes," she said, folding her gloved hands together on her lap. "He did. I was just hoping that he might have made other arrangements as well."

The solicitor shook his head, his expression one of compassionate gravity.

Every penny was entailed to Alec and could not be touched until he returned to Brandidge Hall. There was some hint he was in Scotland, but the records were so poor that there was no way to determine exactly where. But she'd learned that the Duke of Cumberland himself had been his sponsor, so she had had her solicitor write to him in hopes that the duke would tell her what she needed to know.

Now Patricia knew where Alec was, but the knowledge did not aid her. Even when Alec returned, whenever that might be, there was no guarantee that he would provide for David. Or even for her.

She and her son shared an uncertain future.

"It's important that we see him quickly," she said, speaking the words aloud before she thought them. She didn't like to worry David and withheld most concerns from him.

"Do you love him more?" David asked, frowning.

"No, of course not," she said, folding the letter again. "You are my son," she said. "Alec had a different mother."

At his look, she sighed. She would have to explain it now.

"Alec's mother died," she said, "and his father and I married. You are our son."

"Are you going to die, Mama?"

"No," she said, in order to soothe him. Another worry—what would happen to him when she died?

"Why can't we go to see him?" he said, smiling at her angelically.

She stared at David, the thought so simple that she should have thought of it herself. The rebellion was over; there would be little danger in traveling through Scotland. There she could speak to Alec about the one concern she had over all: David's future.

"Indeed, David," she said, smiling at her son. "Why can't we?"

It was a pleasant thing to have a woman around, Donald Tanner thought as he crossed the distance between the fort and the ruined castle. He held a ewer filled with steaming water with both hands and a pile of clean washing cloths tucked under his arm.

He wished that Fort William was not too new to have attracted wives. In a year or two they'd arrive, perhaps. Flowers would be planted along the perimeter of the fort and soft laughter would be heard as commonly as the rough oaths that rang through the courtyard now.

Women brought something with them that was lacking in the presence of men. Or maybe, he thought, it was simply that with women around men could forget about war for a while. He'd learned to read through the kindness of a barracks wife, a vicar's daughter who'd married an infantryman and now followed the drum.

He stepped through the courtyard, carefully balancing the ewer, knocked on the door, and waited patiently for Leitis to open it. When she didn't answer, he pushed it open, walked inside, and set the ewer down on the table. He frowned when he realized the room was empty, but then he glanced toward the privy door. To give her more privacy, he left the room again.

After a few more moments in which he tapped his foot and occupied himself by counting the rows of bricks in the opposite wall, he knocked on the door again. When there wasn't a response, he entered and crossed the floor, hoping that the sinking feeling in the pit of his stomach was only his breakfast and not a dawning suspicion.

But when he knocked on the privy door and she did not answer, he realized that it was as bad as he had feared. He pulled open the door and walked down the short hallway.

"Miss?" The echo of his voice was the only response.

Leaving the colonel's chamber, he hurried through the archway and around the piles of bricks to gain a clear view of the land bridge and the glen. There was no sign of her.

The colonel wasn't going to be pleased. His commanding officer wasn't angry often, but when he was, every man knew that it was better to avoid him. He had that way about him, of speaking in a low, tight voice with his eyes singeing holes through you. Donald hadn't been reprimanded all that many times, but the experience had left him wishing not to repeat it.

A feeling of presentiment struck him then, not unlike the Sight some of the Scots claimed to have. From the way he'd looked at the woman last night, Donald was certain that her disappearance was going to greatly displease the colonel.

Chapter 10

⁓◦◦⁓

The village of Gilmuir was, in comparison to the rest of Alec's patrol area, well fed and prosperous. It startled him to realize how much the Highlanders had suffered this last year. It was one thing to see the gaunt figures of the men in Inverness, another to see the dirt-streaked face of a young child too weak to cry.

They rode north from Gilmuir into an area that had not been linked by General Wade's roads. No doubt Wade would have thought the area uninhabitable, stark as it was. A purple haze, only occasionally lit by streaks of sunlight across the valleys, shadowed the hills. A lake they passed appeared almost like blue crystal, tranquilly reflecting the forests and high, snow-dusted mountain peaks encircling it.

What clachans remained were tucked into protected areas between the hills, in glens that were gray
with slag or brown with mud. The huts of one small
hamlet cowered on their foundations like abused animals, their inhabitants equally silent and wary.

A woman stood in the doorway, clutching the hand
of a child with a skeletally thin face. The mother wore
a guarded expression as she watched the column of
soldiers pass, but it was the look in the boy's eyes
Alec would forever remember. As if he had witnessed
too much for his tender years and silently waited for
the next misfortune.

That look, he realized as the day progressed, was
common among the people he saw. They were sur-
vivors even as they held on to their humanity with an
almost desperate grip. The shadow of what they had
once been was there in the proud tilt of a chin,
thinned lips, and eyes that glittered with hate.

Another realization came to him as they passed
slowly through the territory that had been given him
to oversee. There was nothing left of the Highlands to
defeat or subdue. If there was resistance, it was in the
thoughts of men like Hamish who lived in another
time, or in the glances of the women who pulled their
children close to their skirts and whispered of the
English devils.

He had yet to meet a hale and hearty man who
might have fought against him.

"A long way from the comforts of England, sir,"
Sedgewick said, looking around him with disdain.
"I'd never thought that anyone could live in this man-
ner until I was posted here."

"Did you never think to feed them?" Alec asked,
turning in his saddle. Fort William was more barnyard than fortress. A few cattle would never have

been missed, but would have made a difference in the lives of these people.

"Why should we, Colonel?" Sedgewick asked, surprised. "The fewer barbaric Scots, the better."

"I believe that wholesale genocide is not the aim here, Major," he said impatiently. The truth, however, was just the opposite. *Do your duty, Colonel.* In his mind, Cumberland's voice echoed. *Subdue them by any means. Kill the beggars if you have to, Colonel. Make them know that England rules them with an iron fist. Starve them, burn their homes, teach them a lesson.*

Sedgewick evidently didn't care that the Highlanders he might have saved were mostly women and children, along with a few old men. He did not see them as individuals, but only as a race of people who had dared to rebel against the might of the Empire and therefore should be punished.

Sedgewick and the Duke of Cumberland thought alike in that regard.

It was almost noon by the time they reached the farthest point of the quadrant, but there was no sign of Hamish. None of the people they met confessed to knowing him or his whereabouts. But then, Alec had doubted from the beginning that they would betray the old fool. He had expected Hamish, however, to be piping on the highest hill in plain sight, in cheerful disregard for the English laws and the danger such action might bring to Leitis.

"We'll stop for the noon meal on the other side of this settlement," he said to Harrison, knowing his adjutant would send the information down the line.

This place was little more than a few mud huts gathered together in the vee of a mountain valley. Grass grew on the roofs of the houses, once a grazing place for sheep. But there were no animals in sight now.

An old woman stood leaning heavily on a whittled cane, unmoving as they approached. Her white hair was neatly braided, her dress tidy, the worn shawl she wore bearing the look of having been lovingly woven. She was painfully thin, her hands gnarled like the root of an old tree, her features drawn and pale. However, there was no fear on her face, only a simple acceptance of their presence.

He slowed his horse and dismounted. Behind him the column of soldiers halted. Walking down the path to where she stood, he bent and spoke to her.

"How can I help you, Mother?" he asked softly in Gaelic. He'd had time since returning to Scotland to refresh his memory of the language. In Inverness the ability to understand the prisoners' conversation had proven disturbing rather than helpful, but this was the first time Gaelic had passed his lips since he was a child.

She didn't look surprised at his knowledge of the language. Her eyes, a soft green and surprisingly young in her lined face, studied his, as if she could see beyond his appearance to the man beneath. Slowly, her gaze moved from his shoulders to his boots, but there was no disdain in her glance. Yet the absence of expression was as telling as anger would have been.

"I need nothing, English," she said, her voice little more than a whisper.

He had the thought, errant and unwelcome, that she was a ghost of this place, left behind to speak for all of them.

"Where are the others?"

"I have a few neighbors, English, but they are hiding from you. Fear makes them cautious."

"But you're not afraid?"

"I'm too old to be afraid," she said, and unexpectedly smiled. The expression made her face younger, hinted at the beauty she had been in her youth and might have been in her old age had near-starvation not made her haggard.

"Have you any food?" he asked.

"I have dirt, English," she said, her smile never fading. "A hill full of that."

He dismissed the unwelcome thought that it might have come to that in the past year and motioned to Harrison. His adjutant dismounted and stepped forward.

"Bring my provisions," Alec said. The loss of one meal would not harm him, but it might well mean the difference between life and death for this woman.

"Is that wise, sir?" Harrison asked, glancing over his shoulder at Sedgewick. He sat impassively waiting, his attention fixed on Alec.

Alec pressed his fingers against the bridge of his nose, closed his eyes, and wished his headache away. Harrison was right. Any act of charity would be construed as aiding the enemy. Information he suspected Sedgewick would not hesitate to use against him.

"I'll not take your food, English," the old woman interjected. She shook her head as if to accentuate her denial, then turned slowly and began to walk toward her cottage. She was so weak that she had to stop a number of times, leaning heavily on her cane. He approached her, held out his arm, and when she would not take it, took hers. A quick sideways frown from her only increased his irritation.

"You would die rather than take my food?" he asked.

"You have taken everything else from me, English. I'll cherish my pride."

"You cannot live on pride," he said.

"Nor can you live without it," she said simply, silencing him.

He walked with her, stood in the doorway of her cottage. He'd expected her to shut the door in his face, but she had no energy left for that. Instead she sat on a chair beside the door, gripping the cane tightly with white fingers and leaning her forehead against the backs of her hands.

The cottage was little more than a mud crofter's hut, round, with a chimney hole cut in the roof. In the center of the earthen floor a small pit had been dug for a fire, both a source of warmth and a place to prepare meals. Now, however, it was cold, the ashes swept clean.

Against one wall were a small table and the mate to the chair in which she sat. On the opposite wall, cut into the stone of the hill, was a bed of sorts, piled high with animal skins. But the most surprising article of furniture in the hut was a loom.

He entered the cottage, ducking his head beneath the lintel. His fingers trailed along the wood of the frame.

"Do you weave?" he asked.

"I used to," she said, her voice whispery thin in this silent place. "Before my hands grew too pained. My daughter took it up."

He glanced at her. "Where is she?"

"Close enough," she answered, her gaze intent on him. "Beneath the cairn stones."

"I'm sorry," he said simply.

She smiled slightly. "I cannot blame you for that death, English. It was a hard birth, and neither she nor the child survived it."

"Would you sell me your loom?" he suddenly asked.

"What would I do with your coin, English?" she asked, amused.

"Then trade," he suggested. "Your loom for food."

She studied him again silently. "Why would you want such a thing?"

"To right a wrong," he said, offering her a truth.

She finally nodded, and he went to the door, motioned for Harrison. The trade was concluded when two men loaded the loom into a rough cart purchased from another villager.

Before they left, Harrison brought not only Alec's provisions, but also his own, piling the food on the old woman's table.

She glanced up at Alec, her smile gone.

"It's a path you'll take. Not an easy one," she said enigmatically, "but one that your heart makes for you."

"A fortune?" he asked kindly.

"A truth," she said, smiling once more. She touched his arm in parting, a gesture that felt, strangely, almost like a benediction.

Chapter 11

Leitis sat in the cave, her back against the rock wall. The sunlight was softening, heralding nightfall. The domed ceiling of the cavern was black from fires lit by long-ago inhabitants. The slate floor, a dark purplish gray, was uneven and pocked. Shadows lingered in the cavities like tiny pools.

She drew up her knees and tucked her skirt around her ankles. It was a fey place, one in which she had sought sanctuary ever since she was a child. Here she had come in times of trouble or simply to escape her brothers.

There was a whisper of air against her cheek, the breeze sighing through the bushes that guarded the entrance.

It wasn't memory that made her suddenly wish

to weep, but the sheer beauty of the scene before her. Gilmuir sparkled in the distance like an ancient lady attired in her best jewels. The golden light of a fading day danced upon the fallen walls. Like a regal matriarch she sat with her tattered garments around her, studiously ignoring the upstart fort at her side.

Leitis could not see the clachan from here, a view that was almost prophetic. If she returned to the village she might bring danger to her clanspeople, since it would be the first place the Butcher would look.

She tipped her head back against the wall, tired in a way she'd rarely been. "What will I do?" she asked of the shadows, but they remained mute.

She couldn't live here. Nor did she have any relatives other than Hamish who might take her in. She wouldn't endanger her friends or the villagers, which meant that she was left with no alternatives.

It would be easy to hate the Butcher for her dilemma, but she knew only too well that Hamish had played his part. He had dared the Butcher of Inverness, and she suspected that the man was just as stubborn as her uncle. But the outcome of their confrontation was not in doubt. The colonel had more than a hundred men under his command, a formidable will, and the determination to carry it out.

For all the threat he posed to her clan and her country, she couldn't quite forget that moment when he'd sighed against her, his lips pressing gently on her brow. He had seemed as lost as she felt at this moment.

The afternoon was well advanced by the time Alec led the way back to Fort William. The waning sun was kind to the ruined castle, bathing it in an amber haze.

When they arrived, he gave the signal and the men behind him began to dismount.

"Have the cart moved to Gilmuir and unloaded," Alec instructed Harrison. His adjutant nodded and began to give orders to the men.

"Welcome back, Colonel," one of the sergeants said, taking the reins of his horse.

Alec dismounted and looked toward Gilmuir. "It was an uneventful day, I trust?" he asked.

"Yes, sir," the sergeant said. "Should I inform the duty officer that you would like his report?"

"No," Alec said. "It will wait until later."

He strode toward Gilmuir, preceding the squeaking cart. From the poor state of the vehicle, it was a miracle it had made the journey back to the fort. It might as well be scrapped for firewood after it was emptied of its contents, he thought wryly. But it had served its purpose, that of conveying the loom to Leitis.

He pushed open the door of his chamber, his words thought out and mentally rehearsed on the way back. He would again apologize for his actions of the previous night before he presented the loom to Leitis.

The only person to greet him, however, was his aide. Donald stood at his entrance, his stance militarily precise. Arms back, shoulders squared, fingers together, thumbs aligned along the seam of his breeches, gaze fixed firmly on the horizon. All executed perfectly, but with such a disconsolate air that Alec instantly knew what happened.

"She escaped?" he asked, glancing around the room.

To his credit, Donald didn't look away. "Yes, sir," he said reluctantly. "I haven't been able to find her, sir.

But I did look. I took a few men with me, sir, and searched the village. I should have guarded her better, sir," he added.

Alec smiled then, the only amusement he felt all day. "If Leitis MacRae wants to do something, Donald, not even God Himself can stop her."

His aide looked surprised at that assessment, and well he might be. Not the words of a man who'd only known a woman for one night. But his knowledge of Leitis had been formed in his childhood. Held within him was an image of the girl she'd been, more alive than anyone he'd ever known, as well as the most stubborn creature on the face of the earth.

He knew, suddenly, where she was.

She'd given the three of them all a scolding one day for the sin of teasing her. A remark he'd made about her hair had been taken up and expanded upon by her brothers. With a look of contempt in her eyes, she'd stomped away, promising dire consequences if anyone followed her. They would have preferred to leave her alone, but Leitis's mother set them to the task of finding her, a chore that had taken all afternoon and given Alec a thorough knowledge of the caverns around Gilmuir.

He left the room now without another word, destined for the stables. Once there, he ordered a fresh horse to be saddled.

"May I accompany you, sir?" Alec turned. Donald had followed him and now stood stiffly beside him, his face a picture of determination.

"No," he said. "This particular mission is best accomplished alone."

Donald nodded once, stiffly.

Alec rode west, past the glen and into the hills that gently rose behind the clachan. A series of caves, hidden by the thick forest, had been Leitis's childhood sanctuary. He did not doubt that she was hiding in one of them now.

Soon the thick undergrowth made it impossible to continue. Dismounting, he tied the reins of his horse to a sapling, continuing the rest of the journey on foot.

The passage of time was erased with each step onto pine needles, each branch bent back to ease his way. As he climbed upward, he was no longer the colonel of the regiment, nor the Butcher of Inverness, but an eleven-year-old boy who felt only freedom in this wondrous place.

One of the Wild MacRaes.

"A strange man, your colonel."

Harrison glanced toward the door. Major Sedgewick stood there surveying the room. He would find nothing amiss here. Harrison's quarters were, as usual, impeccable. He hadn't risen to the position of adjutant to the colonel of the regiment without adhering strictly to rules and regulations.

He finished unpacking the last of Colonel Landers's maps before closing and locking the case. It had been a long day and he was tired, but Sedgewick outranked him. Therefore, this visit, and the curiosity that prompted it, would last as long as the major wished.

Sedgewick stepped into the room, nothing more than a small square box with a window high in the wall overlooking the courtyard. If Harrison stood on tiptoe, he could just glimpse the lake in the distance. But the fortress had been built to impress upon the Scots His Majesty's position in the Highlands, not for the view.

Because of his position as the colonel's adjutant, he was not required to share quarters with another officer. In other, not-so-hospitable surroundings, he and Donald and even Colonel Landers had been grateful for a roof over their heads or a tree or even a haystack, sharing their accommodations without regard to rank or position. But those had been battlefield conditions; and they'd all been used to hardship.

He glanced at Sedgewick. From what he'd seen of the man, the only privations he'd suffered had been here at Fort William. And although the duty could not have been comfortable, it was a damn sight easier than having bullets and cannon aiming for you.

"Is he? Why would you say so, sir?" Harrison asked pleasantly enough. But he did not, for all his surface affability, like the man.

"He takes a hostage then releases the piper, only to spend the day looking for him. Why would he do that?"

"You would have to ask that question of Colonel Landers, sir."

Sedgewick's smile was thin and feral. "Quite a sponsor to have, the Duke of Cumberland. Do you know him?"

Harrison had been in the background of numerous meetings between the colonel and the duke, but he shook his head.

"Pity," Sedgewick said, tapping his foot against one of the colonel's chests. "It might have helped your career as well."

"Colonel Landers was promoted in Flanders for bravery, Major Sedgewick," he said respectfully. "Before he ever made the acquaintance of the duke."

Sedgewick stared at him, his eyes narrowed.

"Is that so? Still, I wonder if Cumberland realizes his predilection for helping the Scots?"

"In what way, sir?" Harrison said stiffly.

"When he arrived. Or do you not agree that he appeared almost as disturbed as the Scots by the village being burned?"

"I believe, sir," Harrison said carefully, "that the colonel wishes no further enmity between the two countries."

"How strange," Sedgewick said mockingly. "I thought he was to subdue the Scots, not make friends of them. Today he gave food to an old woman. An act that interested him more than finding a seditious piper."

Conversation of this sort always made Harrison wary. He'd learned to guard his comments over the years, especially when one of his fellow officers said anything critical about the colonel. Harrison would have followed the man anywhere, especially after Inverness.

"We are going on patrol again tomorrow, sir," he said, bending to straighten the placement of his pillow. "He will find him, sir. Do not doubt that."

Sedgewick nodded, fingering the blanket at the end of Harrison's cot and testing the tightness of the sheet. He'd find nothing lacking there, Harrison thought.

"Protect yourself, Harrison," the other man said unexpectedly. "There are those in command who would not think kindly of the colonel's releasing the piper in the first place. Nor of his actions today. He brought a loom to his hostage. It is not wise to feel such compassion for the enemy."

Sedgewick came closer, ran his fingers over the colonel's dispatch case. "Perhaps you should give some thought to your own career. A transfer might be well timed."

"I'm right where I wish to be, sir," Harrison said coolly.

The major walked to the door, then turned and

smiled at him. A toothy grin, what with all those pointed teeth. A wolf might stare in a similar fashion at a lamb.

Harrison nodded, knowing that he had been warned. He wondered if Sedgewick realized that he would waste no time in repeating his words to the colonel. Or had that been his intent, to threaten his commander? If so, it had been a clumsy move on Sedgewick's part and an unwise one. The colonel had dared Cumberland himself. This major was a puny foe.

Chapter 12

A rustle in front of the cave made Leitis turn her head. An animal? Or a bird swooping down to alight upon a branch? Another sound, that of a footstep, made her stand quickly, back braced against the rock wall.

The English could not have found the cave. It was too well hidden. Tucked among the trees and concealed by the overgrown bushes, it would be almost impossible to find.

She waited breathlessly, telling herself it was Hamish coming to find her. Or one of the villagers who knew the layout of the caves. But her palms were icy, her heart booming so loud it sounded like an English drum. When the bushes parted, she almost sighed in resignation.

The Butcher stood in the entrance to the cave.

Why should it not be him? He'd not done what she'd expected since arriving at Gilmuir.

Half his face was shadowed, the other lit by sunlight. She had the curious thought that he had two identities—the man she expected him to be and the man he truly was.

She'd lived around men all her life, and had become accustomed to her brothers' bursts of temper and her father's bellicose nature. This man, however, held his anger within, all the more powerful for not being voiced.

She would have, perhaps, been wiser to be afraid, to shelter her fears behind a stillness of her own. Instead, she took one step toward him, then another, until her shoes touched the toes of his boots. Tipping back her head, she stared at him.

"How did you find this place?" she asked.

"Perhaps one of your villagers divulged the secret," he countered.

"They would not. Especially not to an Englishman."

"You are defiant and courageous, Leitis, almost dangerously so," he said softly. "Did you treat Sedgewick with such disdain?"

"No," she admitted. She had always tried to avoid notice, the appearance of meekness safer to assume. Sedgewick's cruelty could never be predicted. Yet, for all his fearsome reputation, she felt safer with the Butcher of Inverness than she did with the major. Surely that knowledge should disturb her more than it did?

"How did you leave Fort William?" he asked. "I stationed a sentry on the land bridge, but he never saw you pass."

She smiled. "Another question you cannot expect me to answer."

"It's a matter of curiosity on my part," he said, glancing around the cave. His gaze fell on the shelf in the rear of the cave where something metallic glinted in the waning rays of the sun.

His boot heels clicked loudly on the slate floor as he moved to the back. He stood there silently, picking up first one dirk, then another, passing his hand over the remaining sets of pipes. A few pieces of silver, the weapons that had not been confiscated by the English, and the few objects the villagers had been able to salvage from Gilmuir were all hidden there.

"How do you propose we come to an amicable conclusion to our difficulties, Leitis?" he asked casually, as if he had not just discovered a reason to arrest every one of the people of Gilmuir.

He returned to her side, his face bathed in an errant beam of sunlight. His smile, devoid of mockery or cruelty, startled her. It seemed almost a boyish expression, as if he were genuinely amused by what he'd found. Sedgewick would not have hesitated to round up the villagers, would have been pleased for the excuse to imprison them. But then, Sedgewick had never hidden his true nature, while the more she learned of this man, the less she discovered.

"What are you going to do?" she asked.

His shrug irritated her. So, too, the fact that he seemed to command the space around him. It was uncomfortable to realize that his authority came less from his strength or his role as colonel than from the force of his character.

"Why are you here?" she asked, placing her arms behind her and gripping her hands tightly. "You don't need a hostage now, not when you're going to arrest my uncle. Or do you deny that you've been looking for him all day?"

"Why should I deny the truth?" he said easily.

"And when you find him, you'll hang him."

"It was his choice to disobey the terms of our bargain, Leitis."

"He's an old man with nothing left but dreams of glory. Can you feel no pity for him?"

"Yes, enough to offer you a bargain. Come back with me and I'll spare your uncle."

She stared at him in disbelief. "How? He disobeyed your laws."

"I'll pardon him," he said easily. "Or give out that he's a demented old fool who thinks the world is as it was fifty years ago. No one at Fort William would execute a doddering old man."

"I've no reason to trust your word," she said tightly. "And I've had my share of your hospitality, Colonel. I'll decline."

"Even if it means saving your uncle?"

"Go away, Butcher."

"My name is Alec," he said calmly. "Or Colonel, if you object to that."

"Your name is Englishman," she said, angrily. "Sassenach. Burner of villages. Slaughterer of sheep and cows. You trample crops and accost women. Butcher is a perfect name for you."

His smile nudged her temper up higher.

"Do I amuse you?" she asked testily.

"Yes," he said surprisingly. "It's not often that I've been dressed down as thoroughly."

"Come back with me to the fort, Leitis," he said coaxingly. "If you do, I'll not look for your uncle."

"As your hostage? Or your whore?" she said, stepping away from him.

Not only had she to contend with the very real difficulties of survival this past year, but the loss of those she loved. She and the people he'd seen today were defiant in a way that summoned his admiration.

Even now she glared at him, an expression she'd given him often enough as a child.

His gesture of pardoning Hamish might very well be looked on as aiding the enemy. In addition, the ruse that Hamish was not a crafty, devious, and surly old man would not be easily accepted. But he didn't tell her that, only strode toward her, reached out and stroked the softness of her cheek with the backs of his fingers. He traced the line of her eyebrow, then pressed his thumb gently against her throat to measure the beat of her blood. Her heart felt like a struggling bird.

Swear on all that's holy to the MacRaes that you'll not tell anyone what we're about to show you. He could almost see Fergus's merry face in the fading light, pick out the freckles that dotted the bridge of his nose. Had he grown out of them? And James, serious and somber, with more responsibility than his carefree brother, what had he been like as a man?

Fergus had cut too deep; Alec still had the scar, faint and white on his palm. Beneath the leather of his glove it throbbed now, as it had not in all the intervening years.

"I swear on all that's holy to protect you," he said somberly. The ghosts of his childhood companions nodded, satisfied.

He said nothing to hurry her, knowing that she must come to trust him in this matter of her own accord. It was not a decision that would come with persuasion or force.

"Why won't you leave me alone?" she said finally.

"Because it would be intolerable if anything happened to you," he said honestly.

She looked surprised. "There are other women in the glen, Butcher, who have as much to fear."

But they had not played with him in the forest, nor run a race with him. Not one of them had laughed with him so hard that her face grew red with it, or had brothers he had counted as his truest friends.

Pink clouds, streaking across the sky like claw marks, signaled the final moments of the sunset. A moment of farewell, as if the sun regretted its descent. And still she studied him as if to weigh the truth of his words.

"Why should I bother escaping, only to return with you a few hours later?"

"To protect Hamish," he said simply. "Because if you do not, I'll have to continue looking for him. I'll have no choice but to arrest your uncle and have him hanged," he said softly.

There were so many reasons other than that, but it would, perhaps, be better if he didn't try to explain those to her. He wanted to keep her safe because of the guilt he felt for his actions of the night before, and because Sedgewick made no pretense of disguising his intentions. And there were the specters of his childhood friends, demanding that he guard her. The boy he had been, innocent and trusting, in glorious and youthful love, stood within him, insisting upon her protection.

"And if he plays the pipes again?" she asked, the words so soft they sounded as if they choked her.

"You have little faith in your uncle's honor," he said, threading his fingers through the hair at her temple. She jerked away and stepped back. He smiled as he moved to close the distance between them once again.

"I have the greatest faith in his," she said softly, "but none in yours."

"I wish," he said somberly, "that your uncle cared as much for you, Leitis. He allowed you to be exchanged for him and not once looked back."

Her expression softened almost into a smile. "He's my family," she said quietly. "Whatever his faults, Butcher, he is kin."

"Will you come back with me of your own accord, then?"

"You will not touch me?"

He shook his head and held out his gloved hand for her.

Finally, she nodded once. She didn't take his hand. Instead, she pushed past him, leaving the cave. He followed her and they walked together down the hill. They retrieved his horse, but he didn't mount, content to walk with her the rest of the way to Gilmuir in silence.

At the land bridge, Alec nodded to the sentry on duty.

"Is he here to keep the English at Gilmuir, or keep the Scots from Fort William?" Leitis asked dryly.

"Perhaps his duty is to keep you from running away," he said, turning to her with a smile. "But then I doubt one sentry can keep you somewhere you do not wish to be, Leitis," he said.

She looked irritated at his affable mood.

Donald stood at attention in front of the closed door of the laird's chamber, his expression shadowed by the darkness. At Alec's appearance he snapped rigidly to attention.

"I have placed your meal in your quarters, sir," Donald said stiffly, careful not to look in Leitis's direction before leaving.

"He's still angry over your escape," he said.

"Did you punish him for it?" she asked, glancing at the closed door.

"Does he look punished?" he asked crisply. "Beaten, perhaps? Tortured?"

"There are punishments other than physical ones," she said.

"I can assure you, Leitis, that Donald's own castigation was far greater than anything I could do to him. He has a well-developed sense of duty and felt as if he'd failed me. Even the English are capable of honor, Leitis," he said, irritated.

She said nothing, only walked slowly past him. He realized, then, that her attention was directed to the loom that had been moved into the room during his absence. Harrison had placed it where he would have, near the window so that the light could aid Leitis in her work.

"Where did you get this?" she asked faintly, her hands reaching out but hesitating only inches from the wood. The loom was ugly, constructed to be functional, not attractive. Crossbars of thick, planed wood acted as legs, while the frame was an open square, with pegs pounded into the sides to hold the threads. He didn't presume to understand how it worked.

"I neither stole it nor killed for it," he said sardonically. It had been a foolish impulse to obtain the loom for her, but one that he could not, even now, regret.

He knew little about the skill, only that Leitis's mother could often be found sitting at the loom while she hummed to herself. Her fingers would fly over the two frames as she worked, creating a pattern where there had only been an incomprehensible collection of threads.

It was the only occupation that could coax Leitis inside on a summer day. Sometimes, when he went to fetch Fergus and James, she'd be sitting on the bench nodding earnestly as her mother taught her in a soft and lulling voice, using words he hadn't understood such as *weft* and *warp* and *heddle*.

Leitis said nothing now, trapped in a silence that was alien to her. She wiped her hands on her skirt before placing her fingers gently on the thick frame. The loom was old and there were places where generations of hands must have rested, darkening the wood.

"I've no wool to weave," she said faintly.

An oversight on his part, he realized, and one he'd have to rectify.

"Why did you do this?"

It was easier to speak to her when her voice was filled with derision, not soft wonder. It made him wish to take her into his arms and hold her close, whisper that he would keep her safe.

He had believed that the reasons for bringing her here were complex, rooted in his past and an obligation to a boyhood friendship. But Alec abruptly realized that it was less for Fergus and James than it was for her. He wanted to protect not the child Leitis, but the woman who looked at him with stormy eyes.

Pride was an emotion of the Highlanders, and one she had in abundance. Courage, stubbornness, loyalty, she possessed all those traits that helped these people persevere when others would have been crushed.

The answer he gave her was simplistic, not hinting at the truth beneath.

"For the loss of your home," he said easily.

"Were you at Culloden?" she asked suddenly, her attention riveted on the loom.

"Yes," he admitted, determined to tell her the truth when he could. "Why did you want to know?" he asked when she turned.

Her glance rested on his waistcoat, on the badge he wore more out of protection than pride.

"Because," she said softly, "I cannot ever forget who you are, and what you've done." Her gaze rose to meet his, her eyes deep and unfathomable, as if she wept, but did not allow the tears to fall. "Even if you're capable of an act of kindness."

"Consider it bribery, if you wish," he said. "An incentive to remain here."

"You have my uncle for that," she said quietly.

He nodded.

"Who are you," she asked suddenly, "that you would do such a thing yet threaten to hang Hamish?"

"I'm a soldier," he said simply. "Whatever pity I feel for Hamish will never prevent me from performing my duty."

"Even if you must kill an old man?"

"Do you think that the only ones affected by war are those who wear a uniform, Leitis?" he asked curtly. "The world is not that easily divided." He made a slicing motion in the air with one hand. "On that side the battlefield, while here is sanctuary and peace."

"I know that only too well," she said bitterly. "And yet you seem to take pride in your position, Colonel. Is there nothing about you that makes you better and more noble? Or are you simply content to kill?"

Instead of answering her, he bowed slightly, forcing a smile to his lips before leaving her.

Her words followed him as he left Gilmuir and crossed to the fort. He nodded as he was greeted, scanning the courtyard with the habit of command even as he climbed the stairs to his quarters.

Entering his room, he removed his coat and hung it on a peg. The jacket, stiff with lining and heavy fabric, was too warm for summer wear.

Walking to the window, he stood staring at the expanse of loch before him. This chamber was the only one that boasted a large window. Not necessarily a secure addition to the fort, and one he doubted was in the original architectural plans. But at this moment Alec blessed Sedgewick's pride of place. He could see a glimmer of Gilmuir from here, and the sight of the old castle connected him in an odd way to Leitis.

She saw him, as most people did, as he had wished to be perceived. A man of single-minded determination whose reputation acted as a barrier to further investigation. His ruse was effective, then. Perhaps too much so.

Is there nothing that makes you better and more noble? Her question troubled him.

In the past few months he'd discovered that the horror of war didn't exist solely in battle. Nor did it subsist in the aftermath when women wept and men walked among the carnage to find companions who might be saved. The true horror of war was what it could do to a man's soul. In Inverness Alec had become adept at recognizing the indifference in the eyes of those men who had learned to kill the wounded, the ill, the imprisoned without a shred of remorse.

He had done what he could in Inverness and must do the same now. Could he ignore the MacRaes any more than Cumberland's prisoners?

The answer was simple but not easy, if for no other reason than the fact that the logistics would be difficult. Walking to the table aligned against the wall, he pulled out the map of the territory surrounding Gilmuir. By the light of the candles he carefully noted the locations of all the clachans he'd visited today.

He was going to save the MacRaes. Not to be a better man, or more noble, but to aid those people who so desperately needed it. He could not watch wordlessly as old women were left to starve and children grew gaunt and fearful.

Once again he was going to become a traitor.

Chapter 13

Leitis was awakened by the sound of thunder. No, not thunder, she realized groggily, but wagons.

She stood, pulled her dress over her shift, found her hair ribbon, and donned her shoes.

A watery sun lit the clan hall; the archway was shadowed in the faint light. She passed through the shadows into the brighter courtyard, stood staring at the sight before her.

Three rumbling wagons piled high with foodstuffs led the way over the land bridge. Chickens squawked in their cages, boxes and crates and barrels were piled high and tied with rope to secure them.

A column of soldiers followed, crossing to the glen. Leading them was the colonel, his red coat too much color against the blue of a sky barely past dawn. Another patrol, one more excuse to enforce the English presence on the hapless Scots. Or had he lied and was seeking Hamish again?

He turned his head and stared directly at her as if he'd heard her thoughts. They were too far apart to see each other in detail. But she suspected that on his face was the same studied expression of stillness she'd seen before and in his eyes a watchfulness that no doubt mirrored her own.

What sort of man saves a village and promises death to an old man? Who was he, that he had forced himself upon her yet remembered the loss of her loom? A man of mystery, one who incited both her confusion and curiosity.

A cool morning breeze flattened her skirts against her legs. Grouse, rousted from their nests, flew into the air. An officer called cadence; a horse whinnied in protest at a command from his rider.

But Leitis remained there trapped by his gaze and her own bewilderment. He looked away, giving his horse his head. Horse and rider flew over the land bridge as if they had wings, at one point jumping over the burn that fed into Loch Euliss instead of taking the longer and safer way around.

The MacRaes were the finest riders in Scotland. One of the legends they told was that the first laird had been transformed from a horse for love of a Scottish lass. The Butcher of Inverness could shame them all, she thought, and felt only regret that it should be so.

She turned to find Donald standing there, his face wiped of any expression at all. In his hands he held a tray holding her morning meal and a pitcher filled with water.

"Should I be grateful to be a prisoner?" she asked, annoyed by his reproachful silence. "And never have attempted escape?"

She whirled and walked back into the laird's chamber, Donald following.

"It's not much of a prison," Donald said, glancing around the room. "You've got something to eat other than rats, and you have a bed. You're not naked and cold."

He indicated the loom with a sharp gesture of his chin. "You've got occupations other than counting the days until they come and beat you again." He smiled, but the expression held no humor. "No, miss, it's not much of a prison."

"Did that happen to you?" she asked quietly.

He nodded. "A Jacobite prison, miss. In Inverness."

She sat abruptly on the chair.

"Did you think it was only a Scots thing, to hate?" He smiled again, the corners of his mouth twisted. "We English have reason enough for it. You Scots are good at being jailers, miss. I've the scars on my back to prove it."

She had never considered the point before, never imagined that there would be English prisoners and Scottish prisons. Innocence or naïveté?

"How did you escape?" she asked hesitantly.

He glanced at her. "I didn't," he said. "The war ended and I was released to the colonel's service again."

"Is it true what they say about the Butcher? Did he kill all those men in Inverness?"

Donald studied her, his face oddly expressionless. But in his eyes was a flicker of irritation. As the moment lengthened, she realized that it might not have been the wisest thing to reveal her curiosity.

"People will think what they wish, miss, whether or not it's the truth," he said finally. But he didn't elaborate.

"I'm sorry," she said slowly. "Not for escaping, but for your imprisonment. For the cruelty with which you were treated."

"I don't fault you for it, miss. I've learned that one person cannot be blamed for the whole of a nation."

She felt warmth bathe her cheeks at his words. A chastisement subtly and effectively uttered.

He walked to the loom and stood staring down at it. "Can you figure this out?" he asked, glancing over his shoulder at her.

She came to stand beside him. "It's not that difficult," she said. "I'd show you if I had some wool." Her fingers stroked the wood of the warp pegs.

"What would you weave?" he asked.

"Something to remind me of better times," she said truthfully. "Something bright and cheerful."

He looked around at the room. "Maybe it's this place that makes you sad," he said conversationally. "Some of the men think the castle's haunted." He smiled suddenly. "It wouldn't surprise me if the ghosts here would be pleased at the idea of frightening the English."

"The English have done their share of inducing fear," she said quietly.

"There we go again," he said ruefully, "right back to where we were."

"I don't hate you for being English, Donald," she admitted.

"Nor I, you, for being Scot, miss," he said, grinning at her.

He left the room, closing the door carefully behind him.

Was this a presage of things to come, she wondered, that the loathing she felt for the English was eased one person at a time?

She walked to the center of the room, wondering how to pass the time. She was unaccustomed to inactivity. There had always been chores to be done in her cottage, work that was magnified by the fact that there was only one set of hands to do it. When there was any free time, she occupied herself with her weaving.

But there was no cottage anymore. No home to return to. She pushed the sadness of that thought away as she looked around her.

Donald was no doubt a better aide than he was a chambermaid. Cobwebs still hung from the corners, and the walls looked as though they could do with a good washing. The paper had originally been gold and ivory but appeared mostly gray now.

Doubling over a length of toweling, she wrapped it around her waist to better protect her only dress and, pouring the last of the water into the basin, began to scrub the walls.

When Donald returned, she asked him for a bucket of hot water and soap. He only frowned in mild censure, but brought it and many more after that. By midafternoon, she'd scrubbed the floor, scraped out the fireplace, and had washed all but one of the walls.

The room looked almost as it had in the old laird's day. The pale gold pattern on the walls looked fresh; the soft red of the fireplace brick was cleaned of its soot. Even the oak floorboards beneath her feet, old and pocked and squeaking in a few places, gleamed almost proudly.

Looking at this one room, it was almost possible to believe that Gilmuir was intact after all.

"I don't think the colonel would like it if you wore yourself out, miss," Donald said, bringing her evening meal. She glanced over her shoulder, but continued scrubbing the last wall. It was true that she ached in places, but no more discomfort than sitting at a loom for most of the day.

"I cannot bear inactivity," she said, lowering the cloth. "I'll be doing your mending next."

He grinned at her. "I'd be taking you up on that, miss. I'm not a good hand with a needle. Still," he said, regarding her, "I don't think he'd want you working so hard."

"And above all," she said curtly, "we must keep the colonel pleased."

His glance was softly chiding.

She washed her hands, pushed back her hair, and sat at the table, truly hungry.

"What do you do when the colonel isn't around?" she asked, taking a plate from him.

He looked startled at her question. "I brush his uniforms, and polish his boots, tend to his horses." He hesitated a moment before continuing. "But normally," he said, "I'm always with him."

"Do you have no spare time, Donald? No sweetheart to write?"

His cheeks darkened with color as he shook his head. "There are barracks' occupations, miss, gambling and the like. The colonel has strict rules about it, though, and everyone is careful not to disobey. At least before they know whether or not he's bluster."

"I shouldn't think it would be an easy thing to obey a man like him," she said.

"You have him all wrong, miss," he said, then stopped himself.

She eyed him curiously, then concentrated on her meal.

"I've a notion on how to spend some time, miss, if you'd like to learn a game."

"I'm willing to play dice with the devil himself," she confessed, "if it means having something to do." And if it kept her from thinking about the Butcher.

He left the room, only to return a few minutes later with a deck of cards and a long, rectangular board. Laying them on the table, he explained the rules of the game. "We usually play for money, but I'm saving mine. We can find something else to wager, if you wish."

"A walk in the open air," she said without hesitation.

"I couldn't do that, miss."

"A walk in the open air with you guarding me," she amended. "If I do not leave this room, Donald, I shall scream."

He looked startled. "You're only jesting, aren't you, miss?"

"I'm not," she said firmly. "I'll wager you a walk in the glen. If I lose, I'll shine the Butcher's boots."

"I couldn't, miss," he said, looking stricken. "The fort is nearly empty, but if word gets back to the colonel, I could lose my position."

"Is being his aide so important to you?"

"I'd serve Colonel Landers in hell itself, miss. Begging your pardon," he said.

What kind of man incites such loyalty? She shook her head, determined to dismiss all thoughts of the Butcher of Inverness.

"Then to the clan hall. And the priory," she added quickly. "Only there, and no farther." Just a brush of fresh air across her face and some sight other than these four walls.

"If you promise not to attempt to escape," he said.

She nodded. Not as much a sacrifice as he would believe. She had no place to go.

"Then a shiny pair of boots against a short walk," Donald said, and smiled.

She smiled her agreement and they began to play.

Chapter 14

Alec stood looking at Loch Euliss. They were on the eastern side of the lake, and rolling hills obscured the view to Gilmuir. But he glanced toward the old fortress as if he could see the ruined walls.

"You look disapproving, Harrison," Alec said, turning to his adjutant. The other man glanced quickly at him and then away.

"It is not my place, sir, to approve or disapprove."

"The right answer," Alec said wryly, "but I'd rather have the truth at the moment."

"I think it's a dangerous thing to do, sir," Harrison said reluctantly. "Your life could be in jeopardy. Inverness was bad enough, but this is even more dangerous."

"It's something I have to do," Alec said, turning. "But I understand if you don't wish to help."

"I do, sir. As does every man from Inverness," Harrison said loyally. "But I worry about Sedgewick's men. Armstrong, especially. He seems no more than Sedgewick's toady."

"Then I will have to ensure that his suspicions are not aroused," Alec said, smiling.

He glanced up at the darkening sky. The moon would be nearly full tonight, but he doubted if it would be visible through the oncoming storm. Gray clouds were being chased across the sky by an angry wind. Even the trees rendered it homage as branches shivered beneath the gusts.

"Another storm, Colonel," Harrison said.

"Scotland is angry at us," Alec said, a whimsical answer unlike him.

He wore one of his best shirts and tan breeches, both dyed black by Donald, the better to be unseen on this mission of exploration.

Every military exercise must be carefully planned, and this adventure in treason no less so. His original plan was to slip away from the encampment at night in order to aid the Scots. But that strategy was too limiting. He couldn't be on patrol endlessly. What he needed was a way to enter and leave Fort William without being seen.

It startled him to realize how easily he was becoming one of the Wild MacRaes again. A curious feeling of freedom to experience at that moment.

After all, they could only hang him once.

"If Armstrong wishes to see me," he said, turning to Harrison, "tell him I've left instructions not to be disturbed."

"Gladly," Harrison said.

"As far as the others," Alec added, "I leave it to

your discretion." Which, as they both knew, meant only the men who'd accompanied him from Inverness.

Ian entered the skiff, sat, and tested the knot of the rope that led to the second boat, both Castleton's acquisitions. He had been right to put him in charge of the stores for the fort. The young lieutenant was proving to be adept at procurement.

He lit the lantern only once, as he rowed around the sharp outcropping of rock that led to the hidden cove. But he extinguished the light as soon as he found the opening. The fact that he discovered it on his first attempt was, he hoped, an omen for the rest of this night's investigation.

Beaching the skiff on the rocky shoreline, he untied the second boat and moored it more securely. It was only practical to prepare for any contingency, including a hasty departure from Fort William.

Pebbles crunched beneath his boots as he walked toward the rock face. His memory failed him when it came to finding the cave entrance, before he realized he was using the perspective of a boy of eleven. Consequently, he bent lower, and it was then that he found it. He ducked his head, entered the small opening. Once inside, the ceiling soared and he could stand again. Once more he lit the lantern.

The boy had been fascinated with the colors and the secrecy of this cave, but the man recognized the artist's love for this woman. It shone through so strongly in these portraits that Alec felt like an intruder.

He left the lantern lit at the base of the stairs and began the long climb up to the priory. It was as if time stood still in the intervening years. The sense of danger, coupled with the strong odor of decay, was the same. He pushed up on the two stones guarding the entrance and pulled himself free, slipping into the darkness like a shadow.

"You promise you'll stay within sight, miss?" Donald asked with some degree of trepidation. "And you'll not try to escape?"

Leitis smiled and nodded, stepping into the clan hall, breathing in the slightly dusty air with a feeling of relief.

They had played Donald's game so long and with such equal fervor that night had come. Leitis had been graced with luck, winning finally.

If she peered around the archway to her right, she could see a grassy strip of glen and beyond to where the forest began. At night the trees always appeared larger, silhouetted black against a lighter sky.

She glanced over her shoulder. Donald stood behind her at some distance, as if he knew that his presence was intrusive.

The cool mist against her face, the whipping wind, and the sweet smell that presages rain were all promises of the storm to come.

The thunder was louder at Gilmuir, and the lightning more fierce. Perhaps it was because cliffs encircled the castle and the wind blew with more challenge around the headland.

She closed her eyes and tilted her head back, anticipating the storm. She could almost pretend she was a girl racing with her brothers over the green rolling earth of the glen, laughing at the threat of lightning and thunder.

There was another boy in her memory. Ian, that was his name. His visits promised so many indescribable treats. She'd come to expect his arrival over the years, looked to the heather blooming over the glen and knowing that any day he and his mother would arrive in their fine coach and she would once more be bidden to Gilmuir to be his friend.

She peered through the gloom, but Donald wasn't there. Instead, the chamber door was open and his shadow flickered on the wall. She smiled, grateful for his understanding and unexpected kindness.

You laugh prettier than any girl I know. Ian's words, a confession made in that last year. How strange that the memory should pain her so much. Perhaps it was the realization that he would be her enemy if she met him today. Yet she had said a prayer for one English boy, that he was not involved in the war.

From the shadows Alec watched her as she walked slowly through the priory. The moon was nearly full, lifting the darkness and painting the night with a gray tinge. The storm was moving away, but the hint of it remained in the wild, soughing wind and the taste of rain in the air.

Her head was bent in concentration as she made her way to one of the arches, her arms folded at her waist. A reflective Leitis, a portrait he'd never before seen. What would her eyes reveal, sadness or the barest flicker of anger? Or would there still be a trace of fear in them, hidden well but visible to someone who cared to look deeply enough?

He wanted to speak to her, but there were no words he could say. Reassurance would only be a ploy—he could not guarantee her safety or solace or even that tomorrow would come. Comfort? She would not accept it from him. Companionship? He smiled at his own sophistry.

It disturbed him to watch her stand beneath one of

the arches and stare out to sea. The pose was a lonely one, her air of composure fading, to be replaced by one of sadness.

He stretched out his hand, wanting to place it on her shoulder, hold her hand, touch her in some way. Instead, he remained motionless, a companion of the shadows and his thoughts.

Ever since he'd stepped onto Scottish soil, it had been more and more difficult to forget the years of his youth and the people he'd once loved and admired. But coming to Gilmuir had freed those memories from behind closed and shuttered doors until he was inundated with them.

You're not such a bad swimmer, for an English boy.

Come on, Ian! We'll beat Fergus and James together!

I hate Fergus, truly I do. She'd confided that to him one day, the sound of tears in her voice making him ache in an odd way. He couldn't remember exactly why she and her brother had argued, but the disagreement was soon resolved.

Leitis. He spoke her name in his mind, and for a moment thought she'd heard. She came toward him, but then stopped and picked up a glittering piece of stone from the floor, examined it, then gently, almost reverently, lay it back where she'd found it.

Slowly she walked to the arch closest to him, standing motionless in the center of it, her head tipped back, eyes closed as if to savor the wind blowing the storm away. She looked, in that instant, like a figurehead, tall and proud with flowing locks of auburn hair.

He saw the movement out of the corner of his eye, glanced up to see a thin shower of mortar dust raining down from the top of the arch. An instant later a fragment fell from the keystone.

He reached Leitis, jerked her out of the way, pushing her against the west wall. Her arms covered her head and he shielded her back as the arch disintegrated.

The floor vibrated beneath their feet. He bent, his face close to hers, their breaths in concert as a cloud of dust whirled around them. The rumbling sound of bricks tumbling to the loch below sounded almost like a growl of protest from the old structure.

When Alec looked up a few moments later, he was surprised to find that the destruction had been limited to one end of the chain of arches. Three brick pillars had crumbled, leaving a jagged hole. The priory had weathered the elements for centuries, only to be weakened by a cannon's bombardment.

He released her slowly, his withdrawal done in an odd kind of precision. Remove his hand from the brick as her head came up. Stand straight, distancing himself even though he could still feel the curve of her body against his chest. She turned slowly until they stood close enough for him to hear her ragged breathing.

A moment suspended in time, rendered mysterious by the darkness.

"Are you all right?" he asked, his fingers cupping the curve of her shoulders.

"Yes," she said breathlessly.

"Miss?" Donald called out anxiously.

She moved cautiously away from Alec, away from the shadows and into the gray light. "I'm fine, Donald," she replied, raising her voice so that she might be heard.

She glanced over at the ruin of the arch. Where she had stood a moment earlier was now covered with broken bricks and stone. "I could have been killed," she said, dazed.

"Who are you?" she asked, turning to stare at him.

He smiled, thinking that she had cut to the core of it, asking the most difficult question of them all.

It was so dark that she couldn't see him. But she could still feel the imprint of his hands, the impression of his body as he pressed her against the wall. He'd acted so quickly that she'd no time for fear. Even now she wasn't afraid as much as surprised.

He didn't answer her, but something about the way he moved appeared familiar, so much so that she felt her heart leap to her throat.

"Marcus? Is that you?" she asked, and waited, breathless, for his answer.

"No," he said finally. "I am not him, Leitis," he said, in perfect Gaelic.

"How do you know my name?"

"There is little that goes on at Gilmuir that I don't know," he said.

He slipped into the shadows, his form touched only briefly by moonlight.

"Who are you?" she asked, prudently moving away.

He hesitated for a moment, removed something from his shirt, and extended his hand to her. There on his gloved palm was a MacRae badge. Lit by a beam of moonlight, it appeared shiny and golden.

"It is mine by right of my birth," he said.

"You're a MacRae?" she asked incredulously.

"Yes," he said simply, tucking the badge away.

"There are not many of us left," she said. "Do I know you?"

"I don't think you do," he said somberly, stepping deeper into the shadows.

She looked toward the corners of the room, straining to see him. But there was only the inky darkness.

"Did I imagine you?" she asked.

"I am real enough," he replied, his voice deep and echoing in the partially roofed structure.

"What is your name?"

"Give me one," he challenged.

She turned back to look at Donald, but he was still in the chamber. "Shadow," she suggested.

"It lacks character and sounds too dour," he said, his tone amused. Her own lips curved into a reluctant smile.

"But why do you wear black?"

"To avoid scrutiny, perhaps," he offered. "Especially from the English."

"For what purpose?"

"Are you always filled with questions?" he asked.

"Would you not be, to find a Scot among so many English soldiers?"

"A pigeon among all these cats?" he asked. "Your ability to name me has no poetry, mistress. Are there no heroes you might pull from your memory to call me?"

"Do heroes skulk in the shadows?"

"Those who wish to live another day, perhaps."

"Raven," she offered. "Black as night, yet cunning."

"It has a ring to it," he said agreeably.

"Why are you here, Raven, in an English stronghold?"

He hesitated, and when he finally spoke, she had the impression it was a reluctant truth he offered her.

"To save the MacRaes," he said.

"Then, Raven," she said, smiling, "you are as daft as my uncle, who insists on defying the English single-handedly. What can one man do?"

"The colonel is only one man, Leitis," he softly said. "As is Cumberland. And the prince."

Her cheeks warmed at his words, as if he chastised

her. "All of them have followers. And force of arms. Do you?"

"There is only myself," he said soberly.

"Alone in an English fortress? You're either a brave or a foolhardy man."

"Gilmuir is not English," he said in a clipped tone. "As to being brave or foolhardy, I claim neither."

"Modest as well," she said, smiling.

"Miss? It's time," Donald called out.

"You'd best leave," she said to the Raven, unwilling for him to be caught by the earnest sergeant.

"Why do you protect me?" he whispered.

"You're a MacRae."

"Are all the MacRaes so virtuous that you can stand in isolation with one and fear nothing?" he asked, his voice once more sounding amused.

"Yes," she replied quickly.

"Then I would be a fool not to claim myself a MacRae," he said.

"Miss?" Donald stood at the doorway of the chamber, looking out toward the archway.

"A minute, Donald, please," she called out, then turned to the Raven. "Take care. There is a regiment of soldiers not far from here."

"I understood they were on patrol," he said.

"Most of them, but not everyone, and there are lookouts everywhere."

"Is he one of them?" he asked, looking at Donald standing in the archway, illuminated by the faint light of the candles.

"My jailer," she admitted. "The colonel left him behind."

"Then it's you who should take care," he said.

"Let me help you," she said, surprising herself with the request and the sudden elation that filled her at the prospect. "You want to save the MacRaes and so do I. There must be something I can do."

"This is no adventure, Leitis. It is dangerous and if you're captured by the English they will not be kind simply because you are a woman."

"They have not been kind now," she said, tilting her chin up at him. "Or do you think I'm here willingly?"

"There are those who say the colonel is captivated by you. That he is acting in a way unlike himself. You are safer here than in harm's way."

Her thoughts about the colonel were her own and not to be shared with anyone, even if he was a MacRae.

"I did not have your protection in this last year, Raven," she said quietly, "when we nearly starved. We were rousted from our beds at night and made to assemble in a circle in the middle of the village in our nightclothes. We women didn't know if we were to be raped or left to freeze, and the men were powerless to defend us. Our cattle were slaughtered in front of us, not because the English were hungry but so that we could not eat. But you were never there."

"All the more reason," he said, his voice low, "to guard you now."

"No," she said, quietly assertive. "It's not. I can survive, Raven; I've proven that."

"I don't wish anything to happen to you, Leitis," he said softly.

"Then you should turn back time itself," she said gently. "Because it has."

A moment passed and then another. "Are you faint of heart?" he asked in the silence. "Afraid of horses or shadows or the wind blowing through your hair?"

She smiled, an expression of ridicule for his questions, even as she felt a surge of excitement. She

walked closer to where he stood. "I will be exception-
ally brave," she promised him. "But any MacRae is."

"Even the women?"

"Especially the women," she answered. "We have
more cause."

"Then meet me here," he said. "Tomorrow, just before sunset."

She stepped away from him, moved toward the
open arch. It was lighter here, gray where the shadows of the priory were ebony. He didn't follow her. Instead, he was rooted to the spot, shielded by darkness.

"Can you lose your jailer? I've no wish to have the
English following us."

"I will," she promised. How, she didn't know, but
she would find a way.

She turned, peering into the shadows, but the
Raven had vanished like steam in the wind.

"Miss?" Donald's voice again, closer now, calling
her to captivity.

"I'm coming," she said, and reluctantly left the
priory.

Alec stood in the darkness and watched her. She
squared her shoulders, tilted her chin up, and resolutely returned to the laird's chamber. Her form was
only a soft shadow. But his mind made her hair the
shade of autumn leaves and her face a soft ivory. And
in her lovely eyes he saw the sincerity of pain and the
courage she'd forged from grief.

He walked slowly across the floor of the priory until he stood next to the opening of the staircase, removing the stone and then lowering himself to the
first step.

His plans would have to be reevaluated. It was all
too obvious that he couldn't use the staircase as a way

to enter and leave Fort William now. The chances of being seen by Leitis were too great.

Perhaps it would be better if he sent her back to the village. But it would attract attention if he did so without also seeking out Hamish. The old man would be found, and when he was, Alec would be forced to execute him. Stubborn, yes; irritating in his hatred, yes again; but Hamish's acts did not deserve hanging.

It was, perhaps, foolish to allow Leitis to assist him. Yet he knew what it was like to stand and watch as atrocities occurred and be powerless to prevent them. He would have to plan for more safeguards, be even more circumspect. In addition, he would have to speak to Donald, and ensure that his aide was missing when Leitis left and returned. Not a difficult task, since Alec trusted him with the truth.

But above all, Leitis must not be harmed.

There were no inns to speak of in this stark and wild country, a fact that Patricia Landers, Countess of Sherbourne, had learned to accept.

The journey had been difficult. They'd broken two wheels, the second requiring that they seek out a smithy. Storms had accompanied them from England as if to chase them home.

But through it all, David had remained excited and childlike. A blessing, perhaps, to have his nature.

"Will we get there soon?" he asked, his smile broadening as he stared out at the wild and inhospitable countryside.

Brandidge Hall was in Surrey, a land of gently rolling hills that undulated from horizon to horizon. A familiar and soft beauty against the pale blue English sky. As if nature had created the scene so as not to offend the eye.

Here in Scotland, everything was harsh. The sunsets were garish and bold, as if insisting upon attention. Even the eagles that soared from the stark hills greeted the world with a more raucous cry.

"Soon enough," she said, forcing a smile to her face. Any destination would be acceptable. She felt as if she were permanently affixed to the coach seat.

"Will he remember me?" An expression of worry flitted over David's face and she hurried to reassure him.

"Of course he will," she said fondly. "You're his brother."

The coachman was making their camp on the side of the road. She had chosen to sleep in the carriage rather than beneath a tree. There were no insects on the narrow bench seat, no buzzing bugs, curious frogs, and small, slithering creatures that so captivated David.

She leaned forward and straightened David's stock, pushed his hair behind his ears. David rarely noticed his own appearance. He enjoyed the company of kittens and cats, could stare for hours at the paintings in Brandidge Hall, and was fascinated with every creeping, crawling thing that God had unfortunately created.

In addition, he was agreeably entranced with the scenery they passed day after endless day. It was the same stark sky, ringed about with harsh mountains and green hills. It rarely changed, except to rain upon them or send the glaring sun to heat the interior of the coach.

She admonished herself for her own thoughts. It would do no good to complain. It would not ease the journey, nor make it more quickly done.

"I'll tell him about my cat, shall I?" David asked, stepping down from the carriage. Ralph hunkered down in her basket, ears flattened, her yellow eyes merely slits. She doubted that Alec would want to hear much about the feline, but Patricia nodded to his question anyway.

Most of David's conversation centered on topics that might be suitable to the new Earl of Sherbourne. She didn't know what kind of person Alec had grown to be. A kind one, she hoped, glancing at her son. He stood with Ralph's basket tucked against his chest, transfixed by the site of the campsite and the brightly blazing fire the coachman had just lit. His eyes were open and kind and eternally trusting.

Please don't let him be hurt. A prayer she'd uttered numerous times a day, ever since it was obvious that David could not protect himself.

Ralph made a snarling sound and Patricia suddenly smiled, thinking that she and the cat shared the same feeling about Scotland.

Chapter 15

Leitis waited impatiently until the day passed and she could meet the Raven in the priory. The room was clean, scrubbed until it nearly gleamed. If she had been at home, she would have been occu-pied with a hundred chores and wondering when she'd have the time to finish all of them. Weeding her small garden, searching for berries and wild onions, caring for her one cow, or washing, taking pride in the way her clothes always looked fresh and clean.

Her cottage was gone, her cow slaughtered by the English, and her only clothing this poor excuse for a dress. She smiled at herself. Here she was, about to be a rebel, and she was concerned with her attire.

She would not, however, as much as she joked

about it, offer to mend the garments of the English Therefore, the inactivity made time pass more slowly

She should give more thought to Donald. How could she rid herself of him? Claim a female com plaint? If he was like her brothers, that would speed him from the room, but he would, no doubt, continue to guard the door. State that she was ill and worried that it might be contagious? She doubted he would believe her. Challenge him to another of his games and hope she won? Too uncertain. She could just a well lose. The afternoon passed, each moment ticking by so slowly that it nearly made her daft, and yet she was no closer to an answer.

She opened the door when Donald knocked moved aside for him to place the evening meal on the table. One thing she could not fault about her impris onment: She certainly ate well.

She smiled and thanked him, still no closer to an idea how to banish him and resigning herself to being a prisoner again tonight.

"I need to see to the colonel's clothing, miss," he said, fumbling over the words. "I've other chores tha I've been neglecting as well. I can summon another guard, or extract your promise."

"Which is?" she asked cautiously.

"Not to escape," he said earnestly.

She nodded and smiled. She didn't doubt the Butcher's threat to find and hang Hamish if she es caped. But he'd said nothing of being rebellious.

As soon as Donald left the room, she moved to the door and pressed her ear against it. His footsteps faded as he walked through the archway and into the courtyard. Slowly, she opened the door, slipped out side, and ran to the priory.

The storm had passed them the night before, and

the late afternoon was streaked with purple clouds heralding fair weather.

She stood in the priory, holding her hands tight in front of her in an effort to slow her breathing. Her heart beat so loudly it echoed like thunder.

All her fears and anxiety and anticipation and excitement made the blood rush fast through her body. Was this how a man felt before he went into battle? Knowing that he faced danger and fearing it so much that his knees wobbled?

She heard a sound and turned, a welcoming smile on her face. But it wasn't him, only the brush of something against the floor. A rodent, or an insect, or even the wind swirling through the debris on the floor. She waited for what felt like an eternity, each moment ticking by with increasing slowness, as if giving her time to realize what she was about to do.

The English could capture her. That would be fearsome enough, but what would happen to Hamish? Was she endangering him by her actions?

A strange sound of brick rubbing against brick made her turn her head. She followed the noise, creeping across the rubble-strewn floor of the priory like one of the mice that lived at Gilmuir now.

She halted, startled, as a stone began to move beneath her feet. Quickly she stepped back. It moved again, then was replaced by a head, then a torso, as a body emerged from the floor.

A cloud of black appeared. A ghost? She took one more step back before realizing that he wasn't a spirit after all, but a man. A man garbed in black, a mask obscuring half his face. She had named him aptly, then. The Raven.

He bent down, placed the stone back into position, then straightened slowly.

"I'm not to know who you are, then?"

He turned toward the sound of her voice. "The mask is for your protection," he said easily. "If you are questioned by the English, you can honestly say that you have never seen me."

"I would say that regardless," she promised.

"And I would keep you safe," he countered. "Do not question me on this," he said softly but resolutely.

She nodded, suspecting that if she did not agree, he would leave without her.

"Did you make me wait on purpose?" she asked. "To make me realize what I was doing?"

"Was it a successful ploy?"

"Nearly," she admitted. "I don't like being afraid."

"No one does," he said calmly. "The trick is to hide it well enough that no one realizes what you're feeling."

"What is this place?" she asked, stepping closer to the spot where he'd emerged from the stone floor. "A hidden room?"

"A staircase," he answered. "One of the secrets of Gilmuir."

Her head whipped up and she stared at him. "Secrets?"

"Like myself, perhaps," he said, his voice barely more than a whisper. "Are you prepared to learn secrets, Leitis?"

It was a dare he offered her. She smiled and nodded.

"Then promise," he said, "that you'll never tell what I'm about to show you."

She frowned at him. "I promise," she said, wondering exactly what he wished of her.

He turned and looked back toward the archway. "Is your jailer waiting for you?"

"Not tonight," she said. "Perhaps I should be grateful that the Butcher is such a taskmaster."

He said nothing, only knelt and held out his gloved hand to her. The sunlight streamed in through the arches, creating patterns of light and shadow on the far wall. He was part of these; a man who promised to reveal secrets yet remained encased in his own. His eyes, dark and solemn, measured her. His hand did not waver, remaining in the air between them.

Once again, he reminded her of someone, the memory disturbing in a way she could not understand. Pushing aside that thought, Leitis walked toward him.

"You're trembling," he said after she'd placed her hand in his. "It is not too late to change your mind," he said softly.

"I will not be faint of heart," she said, smiling.

He released her hand, swung his legs over the side, before bracing his forearms on either side of the opening. "It's dark," he warned, "and not pleasant-smelling."

"Neither of which bothers me," she said, kneeling on the stone floor.

He descended into the darkness, with her following slowly. After she'd found the first step, he brushed by her, reaching up to slide the stones back into place.

Her breath hitched as he bent his head, his lips close to her ear. "Forgive me," he said, and she had the oddest feeling that it was for more than this unintentional closeness that he asked her pardon.

She nodded, but he didn't move away. The darkness was absolute, the sensation of being so near to him unnerving. Once again he reminded her of someone.

"What is it, Leitis?"

"Nothing," she said, telling herself that she was foolish to think such a thing.

"Don't be afraid of me, Leitis," he said, his voice low, the Gaelic of it a treat to her ears. Forbidden or not, the villagers spoke it together. But she'd been alone these past days, cut off from those she knew well, a captive in an English world.

"I'm not," she said, but her voice quavered.

He hesitated for a moment, then moved away and began to descend the steps.

"It's helpful if you put both hands on either side of you," he said quietly as if the moment had not just occurred. "The walls are slippery, but a handhold is better than falling."

She followed him, stretching out both arms and touching her fingers to the walls, discovering that he was correct. The walls were moist, what she hoped was only lichen growing on their surfaces. An unpleasant experience, going down the staircase.

"Does this go on for much farther?" she asked after several moments.

"Not much more now," he said.

"It would be helpful to have a lantern," she suggested.

"No," he said, his voice amused, "it wouldn't. I doubt you would want to see what you're touching."

She jerked back her hands and frowned at him. A wasted gesture, since they couldn't see each other. For the remainder of the descent, however, she kept her hands at her sides and carefully away from the walls.

"Have you taken these stairs often?" she asked.

"Not often," he said, and didn't speak further. Evidently he wasn't going to say more than that.

"How did you discover it?"

"Two friends showed me," he said.

"Do you object to my questions?" she asked. "Is that why you never answer them?"

"Have you always been this inquisitive?" he countered.

"Yes," she said honestly.

"You must have been a trial to your parents."

"It was my brothers who were that," she admitted. "Although I had my share of adventures."

"Is that why you're here, Leitis? For an adventure?"

"Yes," she said, the truth surprising her. "And to be a rebel for an hour or two."

"To discover what it's like?"

His perception startled her. "I've often wondered," she confessed. "My brothers and I were close. But as we grew up, we grew apart. They became men, and began to live a life different from mine."

"In what way?" he asked. She could tell from his voice that he'd stopped. Waiting for her answer?

"I was expected to marry, to raise my children, and to occupy myself in those duties that fall to women. James and Fergus were simply themselves. They hunted as they always had, and fished as they always had, and swam in the loch and behaved like idiots from time to time. Boys, still, but grown."

"While you were expected to become a woman?" he asked.

"There were compensations to my role," she admitted. "They were the ones who marched off to war, and paid the price for it while I remained safe at home."

The darkness was oddly intimate. She'd not meant to tell him those things.

"We're almost there. Hold out your hand," he said. She placed a hand in his and felt his gloved fingers curve around hers. He pulled her toward him and she went unprotesting. Perhaps she was bemused by the darkness or by the fact that she felt as if she knew him.

Two more steps downward, and suddenly they were in a small cave illuminated faintly by sunlight. Shadows flickered on the walls as she turned in a slow circle, enchanted by the paintings above her.

"Another secret?" she asked.

"Have you never heard the story of Ionis?"

She shook her head.

"I'll tell it to you the way I heard it," he said. "Once, in a faraway time, there was a man by the name of Ionis. He was greatly revered for his devoutness and love of God. But the devil stepped in and lured him away from sanctity and into sin."

He smiled at her, a strangely boyish expression for a man attired in a mask.

"A woman, of course," she said, understanding.

"When is it not?" he asked. She frowned at him and he held up his hand as if to ward her off. "But God," he continued, "missed the piety of Ionis. One day Ionis's love sickened and died and he was inconsolable."

"Why are all our tales so dour?" she asked.

He shrugged. "But the angels pitied Ionis and petitioned God to forgive him. God agreed, with one condition. Ionis could be reunited with his love for all eternity, but only after the course of his natural life ended. Until then, Ionis would have only one love, that of God. So he came here and became a hermit, his life spent in contemplation and holy thoughts."

"Ionis didn't spend all his time on holy thoughts," she said wryly.

He smiled. "But he became renowned as a pious man, and the island became a place of pilgrimage. Until, of course," he added, "the first MacRae settled here."

She looked at him quizzically. "How do you know that? I've lived here all my life and never heard that story."

"Perhaps my branch of the MacRaes know their history more completely," he teased.

"What branch is that?" she asked.

He only smiled at her before turning and leaving the cave. She followed him out to the shoreline, frowning in puzzlement at the loch. A ring of tall rocks, arranged in a half circle, stretched before her. She glanced up at Gilmuir, wondering why she'd never seen the cove before, only to realize that the overhang of cliffs hid the fortress from view. She looked from the rocks back to the cliffs, then finally at the Raven.

"It's a secret cove," he said, studying her intently.

"Another thing I never knew," she said in amazement. "But then you promised me secrets."

"I have more," he said, smiling again.

He followed a path on the shoreline, one obviously familiar to him. There, in a tiny inlet, was a skiff bobbing in the current. He grabbed the rope, pulling the boat toward him with one hand while he beckoned her with the other. She stepped into the vessel, moved to the seat in the back. He unwound the rope from a boulder, tossed it into the bow.

He picked up the oars and began to row, the paddles slipping into the water without a sound.

"Your identity need not remain secret," Leitis said. "If you remove your mask and reveal yourself, I promise I will not tell anyone."

"What you do not know, you cannot tell," he said infuriatingly.

"So you will not trust me?"

"It is not a matter of trust, but one of protection."

"And your name? Will you not even tell me that?"

"Raven," he said, smiling.

He didn't appear to notice her irritation, only concentrated on their destination, a series of triangular rocks that formed the outer wall of the cove. Glancing up, she finally saw the shadow of Gilmuir high above them.

"Where are we going?" she asked.

He didn't answer and she felt upbraided by his silence. "Have I been too inquisitive again?" she asked.

He glanced over at her, then away. "I was questioning my own impulse just this moment," he admitted.

"Have you changed your mind?"

"I should," he said, "but I haven't. We're going to the English encampment."

"Why?" It was the only word she could manage.

"Where else to find a supply wagon?" he asked, smiling.

"We're going to steal food from the English?" she asked, dazed.

"Do you know a more fitting way to exact revenge?" he asked. "It was the English, after all, who brought starvation to the Highlands."

"It is not even fully dark yet," she said, stunned at his daring.

"If we waited until dark, Leitis," he said with a smile, "the horses would be out of harness and we'd have to carry the wagon on our backs."

She only shook her head, speechless.

He rowed easily around the last tall stone, and it was only then that Leitis realized the chain of rocks wasn't a solid barrier after all.

"It truly is a secret, isn't it?" she asked in amazement. "You can't see the cove from Gilmuir and you can't see the opening unless you know where to look."

He smiled at her as if pleased at her discovery but said nothing in response.

He headed for an embankment, and jumped out to secure the rope before holding out his hand for her.

The grassy bank sloped gently upward. At the top of it stood a horse equipped with a black leather saddle adorned with two silver shields.

She stared, once more surprised at his effrontery. "You've stolen an English horse," she said in amazement.

"They have so many," he said calmly. "They'll never miss the one." He studied the horse carefully, then glanced at her. "What gave him away as English?" he asked.

She slowly mounted the bank and stood beside the animal, pointing at the silver shields. "The symbol of the 11th Regiment," she said.

"You'd studied their insignia?" he asked, surprised.

"They parade in front of the window day and night," she explained. "I can't very well ignore them."

"Then we shall pretend that he is no longer an English horse," the Raven said.

He mounted easily and held out his hand for her. She placed her hand in his, expecting him to help her settle behind him. Instead, she found herself seated crosswise in front of him, his arms around her as if to protect her from falling.

She was so close to him that she could feel his breath on her cheek. His arm seemed too close to her breasts; her knees rested against one of his thighs. But she didn't move, daring herself to remain where she was. A strange excitement seemed to flow through her, partly because of the adventure they were on, and partly because of him.

His eyes were the color of Gilmuir earth, his hair as dark as a moonless night. And his mouth appeared to be made for humor just as his square jaw was formed for a stubborn nature. A man who looked to have his way, create his own destiny. Not something easily accomplished by a Scot in these past years.

"Where have you been all this time?" she asked.

"Too many places to mention," he answered cryptically.

"Yet you survived," she said quietly.

"Do you fault me for that?" he asked.

"No," she said, looking away. "And yes," she added a moment later.

He remained silent, waiting.

"I wish everyone had come back."

"Including this Marcus you spoke of?" he asked softly.

She nodded. "And my brothers, my father, and so many others."

"You loved Marcus very much, didn't you?"

She loved Marcus with sweetness and innocence and friendship. Although she'd never asked, it being a subject not easily ventured to another person, she felt that there should be something more to love. Something elemental and powerful, like the feeling she had when watching the sun set over Loch Euliss. At those times, or when the clouds parted during a rainstorm and thunder shook the hills, she felt a surge of joy and wonder. Love should be like that, spearing your heart like lightning.

She'd not felt that with Marcus, and that secret would remain hers.

The Raven urged his horse onward, following the shoreline of the loch. The horse lengthened its stride until they were racing toward the west. She had never heard the wind's voice before, but the faster they traveled, the louder it whispered in her ears. Not a caution, low and resonant, but a breathless gasp that seemed to praise her sudden and unexpected wildness. Her hair was pulled from its ribbon, tossed against her cheeks.

She'd not been daring for years, nor wild for what felt like a lifetime. She had been sober and responsible, and mired in a grief that had stolen happiness from her. But now, in this moment, with the streaks of cloud tinted orange and pink and gray lingering on the horizon, she felt exhilarated and alive in a way she had not felt for a very long time. She wanted to laugh with sheer joy.

They raced on, the horse's hooves a drumbeat of sound as if to rouse nature itself to their passage.

Occasionally Leitis had accompanied her mother on an errand to another clachan, to trade patterns or dyes. But her travels had never taken her so far from Gilmuir. She could no longer recognize any landmark.

Shadows followed them. In less than an hour, the sun would be behind Loch Euliss and the sky would darken into night.

A rash and audacious adventure, surely, to venture to an English encampment with the intent of thievery. She should be worried, or concerned as to her safety. At the very least, she should be concerned that she felt safe with the Raven despite the fact that she didn't know his name, nor had never seen his face. Instead, he was her accomplice and mentor. Even masked and gloved against recognition, it felt as though she knew him.

Or even more important, she thought, facing the truth, he intrigued her—fascinated her in a way she'd never before been affected. A part of her, young and unafraid and undaunted by the fears that sometimes limited the woman, urged her to tighten her arms around him, lay her cheek against his chest, and glory in this moment without question.

He slowed the horse, riding behind a copse of trees before dismounting and holding out his arms for her. She slid into them easily, and was set on the ground as softly as if she were a priceless parcel. He moved to the saddle, untied a leather pouch, and pulled a scarf from it. Holding the material by opposite corners, he wrapped it around her hair, then tied the scarf at the nape of her neck.

"The color of your hair is very distinctive, Leitis," he said quietly. "The English must not wonder how their hostage escaped."

She patted the kerchief into place, nodding.

"Although," he said, tipping his head and studying her, "your hair is not as bright as when you were a child."

Time abruptly slowed in an odd and disturbing way. Their gaze met and locked before he looked away.

"When did you see me as a child?" she asked, her throat tight and the words themselves barely voiced. There had once been hundreds of MacRaes in the Highlands. His answer might explain, however, why she felt as if she knew him.

"Who could forget even one glimpse of Leitis MacRae, with her bright hair and equally bright laugh?" he said, turning and ducking beneath the horse's head, and winding the reins loosely around a sapling.

He had a habit of reticence that was irritating, but she doubted she could convince him to say more.

In front of them a pit was being dug, and wood lay on the ground beside it. The English had evidently not learned how to use peat. It made for a longer-lasting fire, one that burned steadier.

The encampment was not a quiet place. A man was singing, a rowdy tune that incited laughter and warmed her cheeks upon hearing the words. Not far away, fires were being lit as men stripped the saddles from their horses. Others sat and began to ready their gear for the next day.

She wanted to ask what his plan was, but the Raven turned and placed his finger over his lips. Curiosity, however, was not so easily quelled. What were they going to do now?

Three wagons, each piled high with barrels, wooden boxes, and crates, stood in front of them, and as the Raven had predicted, their horses had not yet been released from their harness.

He crept back to where she stood. "You can't be serious," she whispered. "There must be a hundred men here."

"Not that many," he said calmly. "Whatever their numbers, it gives them a false sense of security. It's best to do something when people are not expecting it."

She only nodded, thinking it was something Fergus might have said. But then, her brother had often been unwise and daring, a disturbing combination of traits. Fergus, she suddenly realized with some humor, would have approved of both his plan and her presence here.

The Raven began to circle the copse, his gaze darting from the men readying for night to the cooks stirring a large cauldron. Just when she thought he might have reconsidered his actions, he untied the reins of his horse until they dangled free.

She looked curiously at him, but he didn't explain.

"Are you a fast runner?" he asked, his grin revealing white, even teeth.

She nodded, thinking of all those races through the glen.

He grabbed her hand then and led her around the copse, toward the cook fires. They began to run, and just when she was certain they would be spotted, he bent over, pulling her down until they were below the side of one wagon.

The chickens began squawking furiously. It sounded as if they realized they were about to be commandeered and loudly objected.

"Hush," she whispered, glaring up at the wagon bed. The Raven glanced back at her, smiling.

"I doubt that works," he said softly. "Chickens are notoriously insubordinate."

She frowned at him, even as the racket increased. "That's because they're English chickens," she whispered, disgusted. He placed his arm around her shoulders and she could feel his silent laughter.

He reached the front of the wagon, pulled himself up to the seat and reached down for her just before releasing the brake. Picking up the whip, he snapped it above the hindquarters of the horses. She was nearly jolted off the seat by the sudden forward movement, but he reached out and wrapped one arm around her.

Someone began to shout, but the Raven didn't look the least worried. They raced down the hill in the lumbering wagon to the accompaniment of angry cries, screeching chickens, and the Raven's laughter.

She glanced behind her. The chicken cages were loosely tied together and bouncing with each rotation of the wheels over the rocky ground. Following them at a canter was the Raven's stolen English horse, reins trailing.

Behind them a man stood staring after them, one of the Butcher's men. He was, she was shocked to see, almost as suffused with merriment as the Raven. He stood in the middle of the track, his hand on his lips, and his head tipped back in laughter.

When she turned and faced forward, the Raven pulled her to him so suddenly that she was startled. And just as quickly bent his head to kiss her.

She pulled back and looked at him in astonishment. "Was that another instance of doing something when it's not expected?"

"Perhaps. If I'm going to be condemned for my actions today, it might as well be for following all my impulses," he said enigmatically.

He drew her to him again, this time so slowly that she could have easily pulled away.

The chickens squawked in dismay, their strident clamor an odd accompaniment to a tender kiss.

A moment later she sat back, putting a few inches between them.

"Forgive me," he said, his voice low. "It was an impulse I should have ignored."

She nodded as if in agreement, but in actuality she was still nonplussed. Her lips tingled. He'd kissed her so sweetly and tenderly that her heart felt as if it tumbled end over end in her chest.

"What are we going to do?" she asked, hoping that her voice didn't sound as tremulous as she felt.

"At the moment," he said with a smile, "we're going to elude the soldiers following us."

She turned, horrified, only to discover that there was nothing behind them but the Raven's horse.

"They'll be coming," he said, and snapped the reins.

"Shall I go after them, sir?" Lieutenant Armstrong asked, his face a stiff mask of disapproval.

Harrison sobered and turned, nodding to the two captains on his right. "That's been taken care of, Lieutenant," he said. He watched as Monroe and Wilmot pursued the thieves. As soon as they were out of sight, the men would slow. They might even find a place to rest for a few moments before returning, unsuccessful, to the encampment.

A pity to lose a whole wagon filled with supplies.

"I would be more than happy to join them, sir," Lieutenant Armstrong said.

A most formidable young man, Harrison thought. Why was it that the older he became, the more he grew intolerant of youth? Armstrong's puppylike eagerness was tiring.

"You're needed here, Lieutenant," he said sharply.

Armstrong nodded and stepped back, his salute formally and perfectly executed.

Harrison waited until Armstrong moved away before glancing back in the direction Colonel Landers had taken. It was a dangerous choice to be a rebel, but the role oddly suited him. Harrison doubted, however, that the colonel would have succeeded without some collusion. The two of them, and the chickens, had made enough noise to alert the men on the other side of camp.

The two of them had looked pleased with themselves. The colonel's hostage was a lovely woman, but not attractive as his Alison.

Her face came before him as it did a hundred times a day. Alison Fulton, a woman as beautiful as any he'd seen. He was too ugly for her, and had made the mistake of telling her that one day. She'd not spoken to him for days, she'd been so angry.

"I'll not be loved for my beauty, Thomas," she'd said. "Because if that's all you care about, you've no real knowing of me at all."

He smiled, the memory of her, as it always was, painful and sharp. They'd met one day at the provost's office, an accidental encounter. She'd brought her father his noon meal and he'd stood like a fool, staring at her openmouthed.

Thinking of Alison was painful when there was no hope for them.

He turned away, resolute. Instead of remembering her, he should be concentrating on allaying Lieutenant Armstrong's suspicions.

Chapter 16

They lost the English patrol with such ease that it surprised Leitis. The soldiers went in one direction as she and the Raven traveled in another.

He stopped at one point and tied the horse to the back of the wagon, then climbed back up beside her.

As the sun set, they followed a well-worn path through the hills, into the very shadows. The night was clear, the stars glittering down at them from a sky rendered a pale gray by the full moon. The chickens kept up their raucous sound, aided from time to time by the call of an empathetic bird from the underbrush.

She lost track of how long they traveled. They halted, finally, before a place so poor and desolate that it looked to not be inhabited at all.

The Raven jumped down from the wagon seat and walked to one of the houses.

An elderly man with a bald head rendered shiny by moonlight peered out of the door. "Who are you and what will you be wanting?" he asked, annoyed.

"My name is not important," said the Raven, "but I've come to bring you food."

The door shut in his face.

Leitis bit back a smile.

He simply stared at the closed door and shrugged. Walking to another cottage, he knocked on the door and was greeted by an old woman clutching a sputtering taper.

"I've brought you food," he said, bowing slightly.

"And who are you?"

"One who cares."

"Then go shoot an Englishman," she said, and slammed the door in his face.

Leitis tried to stifle her laughter, but the Raven heard it nonetheless.

He walked back to the wagon, the moonlight illuminating his frown.

"Why won't they take the food?" he asked.

"Did you expect them to kiss your hand?" she said, smiling. "We're a proud people, Raven. We don't take easily, even from our own."

She jumped down from the wagon seat, went to the first cottage, and rapped loudly on the door.

"We've stolen some English food," she said before the old man could speak. "That man," she said, pointing at him, "is the notorious Raven. Wanted by the English for his sedition and daring."

The man looked curiously at them both.

"We've chickens. And flour," she added, guessing at the contents of one of the barrels. As to the rest, perhaps it would be wise for them to make an inventory of the wagon's contents before she boasted.

The old man grinned, revealing a large gap between his front teeth. "Chickens, is it?" he said, stepping out of the cottage.

"English chickens," she said, smiling and leading the way. "Annoying things. They'd make a fine meal."

The Raven went back to the second cottage and knocked on the door again. When it opened he began to speak. "There are English provisions in the wagon over there. Food we've taken from English soldiers."

"Have you?" the woman asked.

"Would you have some of it?"

She peered beyond him toward the wagon. "Have you any oats?"

"Come and see," he coaxed.

She nodded sharply, but instead of following, walked to the next cottage and summoned her neighbor. Before many minutes had passed, twenty people were gathered around the wagon as barrel lids were lifted and wooden crates examined.

There were two barrels of flour, two of oats, a variety of pickles. There was salted beef and bacon so thick that it looked to be a whole haunch of pork. The turnips produced only laughter, and Leitis could well understand why. The vegetable was now a staple of her diet since the English had slaughtered their livestock.

Most of the chickens went first, and then the other meat. It appeared, after a few moments, as if a plague of locusts had descended on the wagon.

It would have been more satisfying to know that the food would last. But of course it wouldn't, and these people would be hungry again soon enough.

Leitis and the Raven climbed back into the wagon, headed for another village.

"Did you argue for the rebellion?" she asked suddenly.

He looked surprised at the question. "No," he said simply. A moment later he continued. "Reason prevails only when emotion is absent. There was too much emotion and too little reason in favor of the prince."

"What would you have changed?" she asked him curiously.

"There are a hundred easy answers to that question," he said carefully. "None of which matter, because my knowledge is based on what ultimately occurred. But if I had been one of the leaders, I would have equipped my men with more than shovels and pikes with which to go to war. I would have trained them, and outfitted them, and ensured they did not go hungry on the return from England. I would have seen their exhaustion, and known that they needed to rest before they fought."

"You were at Culloden," she said quietly.

"I was there," he confirmed.

"Was it as bad as I think?"

"Worse," he said shortly.

They fell silent. She could not ask him for details, because he might provide them. It was cowardice, perhaps, to want that last vision of her loved ones to be as they were laughing and walking away from Gilmuir. She did not, Leitis discovered, want to know about the suffering they'd endured.

"There will be no food left for Gilmuir," he said. "I thought it would last longer."

"It's not an easy thing to feed a nation," she said softly.

He said nothing, only placed his hand on her arm and squeezed it lightly.

The euphoria she'd experienced earlier had dissipated, and in its place was a feeling of easy companionship. Leitis wanted, suddenly, to lay her head on his shoulder and whisper words that might ease his regret. But there was nothing she could say to offset the truth.

A little while later they halted again at another tiny hamlet.

The Raven descended from the wagon and helped Leitis down. She smiled at this evidence of his gallantry.

He went around to the back of the wagon and took out the remaining two cages of chickens along with a half barrel of flour and one of oats. He made several trips, placing them in front of one small cottage. The door opened as he placed the chickens atop the oats.

An old woman stood in the doorway, her white hair shining as bright as a beam of moonlight.

She stared up into his masked face, unsmiling.

"How are you faring?" he asked.

"Better, for the generosity of a stranger," she said, her voice carrying a lilt of humor. She stretched out her hand, touched the edge of his mask with trembling fingers. "It's not always wise to hide who you are," she said.

"I've brought you some food," he said, carrying the barrels inside the small cottage as Leitis followed with the crates of chickens.

The elderly woman looked bemused, then smiled, sitting heavily in her chair. "It is only fair that we make another trade," she said, pointing to a large basket. "Have you any need for that?" she asked, turning to Leitis.

Her hands rested on the arms of her chair, the

knuckles too large for her fingers. She was little more than bones and skin, too frail, almost birdlike. But there was a brightness to her, almost as if she glowed from within.

Leitis moved across the room, opened the basket, and peered inside. It was filled with skeins of dyed wool, the color uncertain in the light of one taper.

"I have no use for it," the old woman said, her eyes twinkling merrily up at the Raven.

"Did the Butcher of Inverness take your loom?" Leitis asked suddenly.

"I know of no Butcher," the old woman said, smiling. "Can you use the wool?"

Leitis nodded.

"Then take it with my blessings," she said.

"Thank you," Leitis said, picking up the basket.

The old woman's response was to reach up and place one withered hand on Leitis's cheek. "And thank you," she said. "It gives me pleasure to know that it will be used."

"You know her?" Leitis asked as they walked toward the wagon.

"I met her once," he said.

"What did she mean about another trade?"

He shook his head as he helped her up to the wagon seat. Once again Leitis knew he would not answer her.

"I need to hide the wagon someplace where the English can't find it," he said a few moments later.

She nodded, understanding. While it might be useful to the Highlanders, it would also be proof of a deed they had not committed.

They found a deserted village not much farther on, tucked into the side of a hill. The moonlight crafted long shadows around the huts, creating figures where there were none.

Leaving the empty wagon behind one of the vacant cottages, the Raven released the horses, slapping them on the rump.

"They'll eventually be discovered," he explained as he tied the basket to his saddle. "Or find their own way to the encampment."

"We look like peddlers," Leitis said, amused.

"I refuse to gather up pots on my way through the glen," he teased, helping her to mount. Once she was settled, he walked some distance away before returning to her.

"My mother always said that an apology should be accompanied by an act of contrition," he said, extending his hand to her.

Nestled in his palm was a clump of heather, most of the spiky blooms falling victim to the wind. She reached over and took it, held it like a nosegay with both hands.

"Thank you," she said, touched.

"There is a preponderance of heather in Scotland," he said softly. "A hardy plant," he said. "Like its people."

"Even heather needs to be nourished," she said, letting the tiny blooms float free between her fingers.

"It's not enough, is it?" he asked. She knew he spoke of their efforts tonight.

"No," she said, agreeing.

"It will never be enough," he said angrily.

"Perhaps not," she said, "but you alone cannot alter the world."

"I don't care about the world," he said roughly. "But I do care about these people."

"It is as bad throughout Scotland as it is here?" She felt compelled by curiosity to ask.

"It is better here than in most of Scotland," he said.

"The English no doubt, concentrated more on building Fort William than in terrorizing the Scots."

"They did it well enough when they razed Gilmuir," she said. "It made no difference to them that Gilmuir had no cannon or that it posed little threat."

"What happened to all of the people who lived there?"

"Most of them came to the village," she said. "Some left. Some died."

"The English aren't going to leave," he said suddenly.

She glanced at him. "I know," she said.

"Scotland is never going to be the way it was."

She only nodded, having come to that conclusion months ago.

"I wonder if the people of Gilmuir would leave Scotland," he said a few moments later.

She turned and stared at him. "The English would be pleased," she said. "As long as there are no Scots in Scotland, how it's achieved doesn't matter."

"So they endure only to spite the English?" he asked skeptically.

"They endure because this is their home."

"A home is not necessarily a place, Leitis," he said surprisingly. "Instead, it's people. To me, Gilmuir is nothing but an empty shell without Niall MacRae."

"You knew the old laird?"

He nodded but said nothing further.

He didn't like to speak of himself, that was obvious.

"Someone told me recently that you could not live without pride. How long will it be until even that has been taken away? Between the Dress Act and the Disarming Act, there's little identity left for the Scots."

"They do care a great deal about our clothes," she said, bemused.

"The better to keep the Scots from rebelling."

"It would take more than that," she said, unwillingly amused. "Or don't the English know that our men would just as soon fight naked?"

He chuckled, the tense mood eased.

"How would they live? Where would they go?" she asked a few moments later.

"A place where they can be Scots, speak their language, wear their tartans, carry a dirk in both hands if they wish, and play the bagpipes until their ears bleed."

She realized, suddenly, that he was serious.

"You sound like Hamish," she said. "My uncle has a way of believing that which cannot possibly happen."

He smiled at her, the moonlight playing over his mask. "Another secret to divulge, Leitis," he said. "When I want something to happen, it generally does."

The moon was on the horizon by the time they reached the place he'd left the boat. He helped her from the horse, untying the basket of wool and handing it to her as she settled in the skiff.

He unwound the rope and settled into the boat. She watched him, making no pretense that it was his skill at the oars that fascinated her. Nor was it that she wished to peer beyond his mask. It was the man in his entirety that captivated her. A man of laughter and mischief, one who cared for strangers, and kissed her so tenderly that her heart had seemed to stutter.

It was not wise to think of his kisses. But they had felt so oddly right that it had startled her. Would he kiss her again? The night wasn't over, and she was not done with being one of the Wild MacRaes.

It was an enchanted night, the perfect time to be outside of herself. Perhaps she should be wearing a mask, too. Or had she already become someone other than Leitis MacRae?

A silvery shadow flickered just beneath the surface of the water. She reached out her hand and almost touched the back of a fish. She chuckled, amused. "My brothers taught me how to tickle fish," she said.

"And lured you from being ladylike?" he said, smiling.

"I doubt I would have been back then," she said. "The memories of my childhood might be tainted," she admitted. "But everything seemed bigger, more important. Even my feelings. I was never merely content, I was rapturously happy. Never angry when I could be furious. Never simply melancholy when I could be grieving."

His smile revealed even teeth made even brighter against the contrast of the black leather. She leaned forward and touched the mask gently.

"Is this still necessary?" she asked. "I'll not divulge your identity."

His hand covered hers, held there until she could feel the warmth of his skin through his glove.

"Rebellion is compelling," she said. "Or should I confess that?"

"Did tonight meet your expectations, then?"

"I admit there were moments when I was terrified," she said, tipping her head back and studying the sky. Already the eastern horizon was growing light in preparation for dawn.

"But . . . ?"

"I felt powerful," she said, looking at the approaching shoreline. "As if I had some control over what would happen to me."

"The definition of freedom," he said quietly, stowing the oars in the bottom of the boat. "What Scotland has lost."

She shook her head. "There's a difference," she said,

obviously surprising him, "in the freedom of a country and the freedom of one person."

He studied her intently. "How so?" he finally asked.

"If a man fights for his country's freedom," she said, thinking aloud, "it's for an idea. A notion. Scotland's freedom from England wouldn't have changed my life. But if a man struggles for his own freedom, it's a personal thing. The way he lives his life. Whether he chooses to be a carpenter or a smith, a fisherman or a farmer."

He stood, helped her from the boat, and walked with her to the cave opening, still not speaking.

"If you were free, Leitis," he said finally, lighting the lantern, "what would your life be like?"

The flickering light seemed to grant life to the portrait of Ionis's love above them. Leitis looked down at the smooth cave floor and spoke what was in her heart. But then, she realized with a start, she always had, with this man.

"I would not be here, for one," she said abruptly, glancing at the stairs to her left. "I would not be the colonel's prisoner."

"Does he treat you well?"

She looked at him, unwittingly amused. "As well as any jailer," she said. "His aide says my accommodations are luxurious and I should feel myself privileged. But I cannot walk where I will, nor do what I wish."

"What would that be?"

She walked to the cave entrance, looked out at the sparkling water. The loch was never silent, splashing and rolling with its current.

"What would that be?" she repeated, mulling over the question. "I'm not a famous personage," she said quietly. "Nor have I ever wished to be. My family was important to me and I miss them every day. So I would wish for a family, first. I want a simple life, perhaps. And I would wish for a small and cozy place to live, and friends."

"A modest set of wishes," he said kindly.

"And you, Raven?" she asked, glancing at him. "What would you wish for?"

"To kiss a woman in moonlight," he said.

He drew her closer, half expecting her to pull away, to upbraid him for his actions. But she remained silent, the moment rendered so still and extraordinary that Alec knew he would never forget it.

Too much separated them, yet none of it was their doing.

He leaned closer and she placed her hand on his chest. She had ceased speaking and he could not help but wish she felt as bemused as he.

She sighed and he wanted to capture the sound, inhale it. Her lips were soft and sweet, her open-mouthed gasp an invitation to continue. But he didn't deepen the kiss. Instead, he kept it light, teasing them both.

Finally, he pulled back, breathing heavily against her temple. "Leitis," he murmured. Just that, only her name and nothing more.

In the lantern light her eyes deepened, the soul of her open and revealed as never before. Or the thought could be simply whimsy, the ramblings of a man enchanted by a woman's loveliness.

He told himself that his only true bond to her was the shadow of the child she had been and the ghost of what he had once known himself to be. But that thought fell like feathers before a greater truth.

She was not simply the Leitis of his childhood. She was a woman touched by moonlight, a woman who incited his laughter as she shushed chickens, or touched him by placing her hand on his arm in wordless compassion and artless friendship. She had escaped from him, insulted him, and stared fixedly at his nakedness. A woman who fascinated him completely.

He extinguished the lantern, picked up the basket, and slowly turned, extending his hand to her. At the top of the staircase, he pushed up the stone carefully so as not to make any noise. He pulled himself up, then reached down for her, helping her to the priory floor.

He handed her the basket of wool, and she took it wordlessly. Together they stood looking at each other, the moment timeless and trembling.

One last kiss. Wordlessly, he bent his head, touched his lips to hers. He had not known until this moment that a kiss could both hold passion and a myriad of other emotions, friendship and compassion, joy and wonder.

He pulled back finally, cupped her cheek with his gloved hand. Moonlight rendered her a monochrome of beauty; shadows clung to her cheeks and dusted her lips. Her hand rested flat on his chest once more as if she could feel beneath his clothing to the man he was, neither colonel nor Butcher nor Raven. Only Alec.

He felt as if he hung over a precipice, the moment both breathless and frightening. Every thought but one had been stripped from his mind. He left her then, without a word of parting, almost desperate to escape before he divulged another secret to her. Not that of his identity, but of these past moments and a realization that stunned him.

He smiled ruefully, thinking that it was a strange and unwelcome time to fall in love.

"You were unable to capture these miscreants, Harrison?" Alec asked at dawn.

Behind him his tent was being dismantled and what looked to be controlled chaos around him was actually a surprisingly efficient decampment.

Years of being on campaign had made him adept at functioning without much sleep. A fact for which he was grateful, since he'd only returned from Gilmuir a few hours ago. He'd been able to slip into his tent and get what rest he could, only to awake at dawn and perform this dressing-down of his lax adjutant.

He frowned at Harrison, a credible imitation of a glower, Alec thought.

His adjutant hung his head, for all the world like a whipped puppy. He made a mental note to tell Harrison that such abject humility was not necessary in the future. But for now he stifled his smile and scowled at the man.

"You sent men after them, I suppose?"

"Yes, sir," Harrison said, meeting his eyes just for a moment before his gaze slipped past him.

Alec knew from Harrison's sudden stiffening that they were, indeed, being overheard, exactly the reason for this ruse.

"Why wasn't I informed immediately?" he demanded.

"You asked not to be disturbed, sir," Harrison said meekly.

"In the future you will inform me at any time these damn Scots show themselves," he said tightly.

Harrison saluted, turned on his heel, and left him, head hanging like a severely chastised subordinate. The ploy was necessary for a variety of reasons, not the least of which was to insulate Harrison from his own actions. Alec didn't want his men to suffer for the fact that he'd become the Raven.

It wasn't as easy as he'd thought to assume two identities. The past hours had proven him to be neither colonel nor Raven, but instead an amalgam of both.

Armstrong had been commanded to bring up the rear, to assist Lieutenant Castleton in the guarding of the supplies, the remaining two supply wagons, and their horses.

Englishmen had built the only roads in this barren place, but the colonel had avoided those, choosing instead to follow tracks that meandered through the hills. Almost, Armstrong thought, as if he wanted the journey back to Fort William to be one of difficulty.

Lieutenant Armstrong frowned at the wagons in front of him, slow and ponderous even nearly empty. The drivers were evidently in no hurry to return to Fort William. They appeared, instead, to be enjoying the snail's pace.

"Can't you go any faster?" he asked, coming abreast of the second wagon.

"I'm sorry, sir, the wagon is wider than the track and we have to take care. If we fall into one of the ruts we might damage a wheel."

"Well, do what you can," Armstrong said, impatient and irritated.

The wagon ahead of him halted. A problem with a wheel? He rode forward, annoyed.

"What is the matter now, private?" he asked the driver.

"There are two women blocking the track, sir," the man said, pointing ahead to the pair.

"Then tell them to move," he said.

"They don't seem to be listening." Armstrong could see what the man meant; their voices were loud enough to reach Fort William.

He rode forward, stopped beside the two women. One held a cage; the other reached for it.

"It's mine, I was there when he came."

"Can I help it if I sleep at night? I'll not be punished because I didn't see your phantom."

"It's my chicken!"

"And where, Fiona, is your name inscribed on the bird?" the other woman asked, peering into the cage as if to inspect the chicken's beak. "No, I see nothing there."

"You're impeding His Majesty's troops," Armstrong said sternly.

One woman turned to the other, an expression of amusement on her face.

"Did you hear that, Mavis? We're impeding His Majesty's troops."

"Impeding, you say?" the second woman said.

"Take your argument and your chicken somewhere else," Armstrong said, riding closer. "Before I move you myself."

Both women reluctantly stepped aside.

He waved the wagon on, bent low, and jerked the cage from the woman's grip. Hefting it to eye level, he and the chicken glared at each other.

"Where did you get this bird?" he asked, remembering the crates tied to the stolen wagon.

Neither woman spoke. "I'll give the chicken to the first person who tells me," he said.

"A man came to my cottage with it last night," one woman said.

"Who was he?"

She shook her head. "I don't know. I've never seen him before."

"He had a name," the other woman said, stepping forward. "Is that worth the chicken?"

Armstrong eyed the two of them sourly. "What name?"

"You only know that because I told you."

"I've a right to the chicken, same as you."

"No one gets it," Armstrong said, his exasperation mounting, "until I have his name."

"Raven," the two women said at once.

"Raven? What sort of name is that?"

"That's what she called him."

"She? A woman was with him?"

The two of them nodded. "But that's all we know. He came in the night and left as soon as he gave us the food."

Armstrong dropped the crate, uncaring which woman ended up with the stolen chicken.

He removed his journal and made careful notations of the women's words. He'd promised Major Sedgewick to keep him informed of everything that transpired in his absence.

Armstrong folded the book and tucked it into his coat.

It wasn't fair, he thought, that Major Sedgewick had been so summarily exiled. But then, it had not been right that Colonel Landers had assumed command of the fort. A post no doubt due to the identity of his mentor. The man was indeed privileged to have the Duke of Cumberland interested in his career.

Raven? He frowned and rode ahead, catching up with the wagons.

Chapter 17

Alec rode across the land bridge, pleased to see the changes already occurring at Fort William. Nowhere was there a sign of sloth or inactivity. Several men were bathing, the acrid smell of vinegar and soap wafting over the courtyard. Troops not engaged in polishing their insignia or belt buckles were marching on the southern end of the courtyard. Not all of the men at Fort William were cavalry. Most were infantrymen and destined to remain at this post for the length of their military service.

He made a mental note to speak to Harrison about inviting wives to Fort William. The women who would come would be seasoned campaigners, accustomed to the Spartan conditions the fortress offered.

He nodded to a few of the men he passed. Over

the weeks they would grow accustomed to his way of doing things until it became second nature. When not occupied with war and survival, often the only commonality among men was a shared hatred sometimes directed at a commander. Alec was determined, in this case, that the element that bound them together as soldiers would be pride in belonging to the 11th Regiment.

An irony, that he reinforced his position as colonel of Fort William at the same time that he engaged in treason.

Last night had been filled with surprises. An unwise adventure, perhaps, but one that proved that Leitis had not essentially changed. She was like a thistle that bloomed triumphantly in cracks and crannies, its stem filled with spikes, but its flower lovely. He smiled at his own whimsy and the thought that Leitis wouldn't be pleased to be likened to a thistle.

He'd erred with his horse. He'd never realized how observant Leitis was, or that she would note the regimental insignia. A flaw in his masquerade. He would have to ensure that that mistake was not repeated.

Alec dismounted, walked through the courtyard, and strode up the stairs to his quarters.

He entered his chamber, removed his coat, and stood staring out at the courtyard. Leitis was close enough that he could almost feel her. So near that he could be at her side in moments. Touch her if he wished, kiss her, but not as himself, only as the Raven.

A knock announced Harrison. Alec opened the door to find not his adjutant but Lieutenant Armstrong standing smartly at attention. His uniform was resplendent, rows of lace adorning his shirt and cuffs, his lapels large and pinned back with gold buttons.

There were no uniform regulations for officers, and the lieutenant had evidently taken advantage of that fact.

"I believe I have something of importance to report, sir," Armstrong said.

Alec stood aside, sighing inwardly. Armstrong would have been an invaluable reconnaissance officer in battle, but he was proving to be a nuisance now.

"I know the identity of the man who stole the wagonload of provisions, sir," he said.

For a moment Alec couldn't speak. An uncomfortable feeling, to have his heart resting between his ankles. But Armstrong's look was one of eagerness, not accusation.

"And he is . . . ?" Alec said, releasing his death grip on the edge of the door.

"They call him the Raven."

Even that bit of information was disturbing. How in blazes had Armstrong learned it so quickly?

"Raven?" The young man nodded. "And you think this Raven is responsible for stealing the wagon, Armstrong?"

"I have proof, sir, that he's also distributed the food to the Scots."

"A fearsome act of sedition," Alec said dryly, then smiled at the young man to negate his sarcasm. "You were very observant, Armstrong."

"Thank you, sir," Armstrong said, looking pleased. "I would like to volunteer for the patrol to capture him, sir."

"If, indeed, he exists and is not simply a jest of the Scots, then I'll arrest him, Lieutenant. But in my time. And in my way."

Armstrong had the good sense to look abashed.

"There are other duties just as important," Alec said. "Perhaps even more so than capturing your mythical Raven. I have not yet assigned a man to be in charge of the ordnance, Lieutenant. I think you're a capable man for the position."

"The ordnance, sir?" Armstrong asked, his voice sounding choked.

"See Lieutenant Castleton," Alec said. "He'll give you the particulars."

Armstrong wisely remained silent. At that age, Alec remembered, thoughts flowed like water from the mind to the mouth. It was better to keep some kind of plug in place. That is, if Armstrong wished to have a career in the military.

The lieutenant saluted him, executed a perfect about face, and walked down the hallway with his boot heels nearly sparking fire on the floorboards.

"An angry and dangerous young man."

Alec turned at Harrison's approach.

"I intend to keep him fully occupied," Alec said, "so that he'll have less time to observe."

Leitis slept fitfully despite her fatigue, her dreams frightening yet so amorphous that she wasn't able to make sense of them. When she awoke it was as if she'd not slept at all. Rising from the bed, she splashed cold water on her face, kept the toweling over her eyes until they were less swollen. It felt, oddly, as if tears lay just beneath the surface.

Last night she'd been too tired to do more than hang her dress on a peg, and now stared at it in dismay. She picked it up, noticed the scarf, and pulled it free. Pressing it against her cheek, she marveled at the softness of it. It summoned memories of the night before when she'd been a reiver's accomplice. When she'd been kissed in the moonlight and left speechless by the power of it.

She cleaned her dress as well as she was able, wishing that she had something, anything, else to wear.

Once dressed, she peered outside the door. Donald had not, blessedly, been standing guard when she'd returned last night, nor had he appeared yet this morning. Curious, she walked into the archway that connected Gilmuir to the priory.

The archway was tinted a tawny color by the dawn, the early morning sunlight streaming through the latticework of brick and stone and forming a pattern on the opposite wall. The shadows in the corners of the clan hall were darker, as if night were a guest who did not know when to leave.

Leitis returned to the room, leaving the door ajar to savor the early morning breeze. She spent the next few minutes occupied in mundane tasks, straightening the sheets on the bed, dusting the dresser, and rearranging the items on the table before turning to the basket of wool.

She lifted the lid, pulled out the first few skeins. It took time to spin wool and dye it. When she and her mother worked together, one of them would begin sorting the next batch of wool the moment the first threads were laid. There was enough wool in the basket, however, to make several garments or a blanket.

The colors, too, surprised her. She marveled at the delicacy of the shades and the skill of the woman who'd dyed this wool. There was a pale blue, the hue of heather as it began to bloom. And a pink so delicately tinted that it resembled the blush on a baby's cheek. But in the bottom of the basket were several other shades as well, some of which interested her the most—crimson, black, and white, the colors of the MacRae plaid.

It was as if the pattern lay before her, needing only

her fingers to coax it into reality. She took the wool and sat on the bench inspecting the loom. It was well worn and not as intricately designed as her mother's had been, but someone had loved it and cared for it well. Only one of the small pegs of wood around the frame needed to be wedged back into its hole. The wool would be tied to these and then tightened until there was tension in the threads, the warp serving as the foundation for the pattern.

If she were simply weaving an article such as a blanket with a solid color, the work would go swiftly. There wouldn't be a need to pick the threads with such precision. But the MacRae tartan was a complicated pattern and the first few rows were crucial.

Weaving had always been a source of joy to her, a way to envision in wool a creation of beauty. She wondered if God felt the same way upon viewing a flower.

Once her fingers became accustomed to the lay of the threads, and her hands adept at the pattern, she could lose herself in thought. It had been a way to escape the cacophony of her home as a child, and cope with grief as a woman. In the confines of the colonel's chamber, the loom became a way to shorten the passage of time.

The sound of boots on the wooden floor alerted her to his presence. Tensing, she kept at her weaving, pretending the Butcher was not in the room. But he was not content with that, coming to stand at the side of the loom until she raised her eyes to his.

Wordlessly, they stared at each other. He had been gone only a few days and in that time she'd become a rebel.

His gaze alighted on the basket on the floor beside her. She felt a sense of sick horror at his discovery. She should have hidden it.

"You have your wool, I see," he said after bending

and looking inside. "The color of the MacRae plaid," he said softly. "Will you engage in sedition, Leitis, and weave it before my eyes?"

Her stomach fluttered at his question.

"What would you do," she asked curiously, looking up at him, "if you discovered that I had been guilty of it?"

Slowly, he traced his fingers over the first few rows of weaving. Instead of answering her, he asked a question of his own.

"Did you know that the Scots were forced to take an oath swearing that they would be loyal subjects? Do you know it?" he asked somberly.

He didn't need her answer, apparently, because he continued, " 'I swear as I shall answer to God at the great Day of Judgment, I have not, nor shall have in my possession, any gun, sword, pistol, or arm whatsoever, and never to use tartan plaid, or any part of the Highland garb. I promise that I shall not take up arms against the English, or engage in acts of insurrection against the same. If I do so, may I be cursed in my undertakings, family, and property.' "

"You know it well," she replied, the words difficult to say.

"I heard it enough times," he said.

What was she to say to that revelation? Or the fact that it was uttered in a voice lacking any emotion at all?

He glanced at her, his eyes shuttered as if, once again, he meant to be more a mystery than a man. Or perhaps the look she witnessed was a revelation after all. Perhaps the colonel was as tired of war as she was of subjugation.

"I came to see how you were faring," he said softly.

"I am fine," she said. Two people expressing polite sentiments across a gorge of nationalities.

She stood, uncomfortable with his nearness. Walking to the table, she pretended an interest in the grain of the wood beneath her stroking fingers. It was easier than the sight of him standing there, perfectly handsome in his uniform. The crimson hue of his coat seemed to accentuate his sun-bronzed face. His cuffs of lace were perfectly laundered, the boots he wore polished to a sheen. Even his gloves were oiled black leather.

A peculiarity, those gloves. She'd not recalled him wearing them when he'd first come to Gilmuir, and now he was never without them. Another oddity, that she should be so curious about him.

"Have you everything you need?" he asked from beside her.

"Yes, thank you," she said, wishing he would move away.

He stretched out one gloved finger and stroked her cheek. Her lashes shielded her eyes as she gazed at the floor. Her breath was painfully tight. *Please, move away.*

Instead, he took one step closer until his boots slid against her shoes.

He hadn't touched her since that one night. But now he did, so softly that it might have been only a whisper. He bent and pressed his lips to her forehead. Before she could object, before she could step away, he turned her, cupping her face with his hands and then slowly bent his head and kissed her mouth.

Her hand reached up instinctively to push him away.

"Please," he murmured against her lips. Both a soft plea and gentle invitation whispered in a harsh voice. She felt the warmth of his lips, allowed her eyelids to flutter shut. If there was a world beyond her closed lids in those next moments, she was unaware of it. But she felt the racing, booming rhythm of his heart beneath her palm, and knew that hers felt the same. But it was the sensation of being filled with something sweet and intoxicating that startled her. As if the most potent heather ale flowed through her body, luring her to drunkenness.

He was the first to pull away, his breathing harsh as he pressed his lips to her temple. She kept her eyes closed even as her fingers splayed against his coated chest. Even beneath the fabric she could feel the warmth of him, the strength of muscles quiescent and waiting.

His lips pressed against her eyelids, then the bridge of her nose, a gesture rooted in tenderness. She was adrift in confusion and sweetness, and the sudden wish to weep.

Resolutely she stepped away from him, placing her fingers against her lips.

"Do I taste English, Leitis?" he asked softly.

She shook her head, suddenly mute as if the ability to speak had been kissed from her.

He remained motionless, a handsome man with somber brown eyes and a military bearing. He didn't smile, did nothing but watch her, his gaze lingering on her hair, then her features, as if he wished to imprint the sight of her on his mind.

Then, without another word, he turned and left her.

No, she thought, staring at the closed door, he didn't taste English. Instead, he tasted familiar. Known. But he had kissed her once in the throes of a dream. That was all it was. There was no mystery to the colonel.

Yet he had treated her as a cherished guest instead of a hostage. His men were deeply loyal even though he was a strict commander. He was the Butcher of Inverness, but for the first time she wondered if the stories were, indeed, true.

Once when they were children, she and her brothers lay flat on their backs in the middle of the glen, staring up at the pattern of clouds.

"It's a bird," Fergus said, pointing to a fluffy white shape.

"It's not," James countered. "It's a claymore," he added, pointing out all the various angles.

"It's neither," she had said, losing patience with both of them.

Both boys had glanced at her, surprised.

"It's nothing more than a cloud."

Fergus pointed to the cloud again. "See the part on the left? Just that, and nothing more? Tell me what you see."

"Just that?"

He nodded.

She squinted at it, then began to see the shape of it. "A duck," she announced.

Fergus grinned at her. "There you have it. Sometimes the best way to see something, Leitis," he'd said, "is to peek at it. Not try to view the whole thing all at once."

She had the sudden, disturbing thought that the colonel was like that cloud. And another realization occurred to her, one as perplexing. He'd never asked where she'd gotten the wool.

Chapter 18

There was, Alec thought, only one way to accomplish the exodus of the people of Gilmuir, and it would, unfortunately, involve Leitis's participation. He doubted if the villagers would listen to him, masked and mysterious. And they would most certainly not believe anything the Butcher of Inverness would say.

As the evening faded into dusk, Alec mounted and rode from the fort.

"Lieutenant?" Harrison said, coming up behind Armstrong. "Is there a reason you're standing here in the dark?"

Armstrong was half curled around the corner of the courtyard, his gaze fixed on the land bridge.

"No, sir," he said, moving aside. "I thought I saw something, that's all."

"Were you watching the colonel, Armstrong?"

"I was just curious as to where he is going in the dark, sir," the younger man said.

"Are his movements any of your concern, Lieutenant?" Harrison asked.

"No, sir," Armstrong conceded.

Troubled by the lieutenant's behavior, Harrison watched as he walked back to the fort. Something must be done about Armstrong.

Where was the Raven now? He'd left her without a word last night, with no indication that she'd see him again, or when. How did she summon him? By her wishes and her wants?

Leitis stood, pushed the bench neatly under the loom. She stretched, rolled her shoulders, then bent from the waist to ease the ache in her back. She'd worked too long today, but it had been the best way to make the time pass. Occupying herself with the complicated pattern had alleviated both her confusion and her longing.

She left the room, escaping once more to the priory.

A gentle breeze blew through the arches and pulled at her skirts. They danced playfully around her ankles and teased her hair free of its ribbon. It was a night of moon and silver. Her hearing was tuned to the slightest movement, but all she heard was the riff of wind and a splash of waves on the loch below. A night bird sounded, its call echoing her own desperate longing.

The taste of rebellion was heady, but it was not solely for that reason she wished the Raven's presence. She wanted to speak with him about small thoughts and great wishes, laugh with him about nonsensical things. She wanted most to feel what she had the night before, that strange and effortless companionship as if she knew him well and deeply. And another reason as well, she confessed to herself. There was that sense of excitement when she was with him, a feeling she wanted to experience again.

She returned to the room, lit a candle, and walked to the window, listening to the sounds from Fort William. Did they never stop marching? In earlier days, Gilmuir fell quiet at night. Enshrouded in a mist from the loch, the castle became a magical place, one of serenity and safety. No more.

She thought of less dour things, the memory of last night when laughter alternated with fear. And the Raven's kisses. His first kiss had been done quickly, pressing his smiling lips against hers. Then he'd offered her heather in a tender gesture.

He'd seemed so familiar to her, as if she'd known him for a long time.

Her thoughts stuttered to a halt. She began to circle the room in a restless movement, her thoughts on the Raven and last night.

He had known the old laird, the existence of the staircase, the story of Ionis. All secrets he might have known as the laird's grandson. The clan badge he'd shown her appeared to have been made of gold, not a common practice. But a laird's grandson might have been presented with such a gift.

Could he be the boy from her childhood? Ian MacRae, with his English father and his Scots mother, who'd left Gilmuir on that long-ago day and never returned?

Was it possible? She sat abruptly.

Surely she would have recognized him. Or would she?

She recalled that moment at his mother's lykewake, his eyes so filled with pain. There had been anger there, too. She recalled it as well as she did her own hurt when he crushed her gift beneath his boot.

But he'd known her, a revelation he'd made when he'd tied the scarf around her hair and spoken of the brightness of it as a child.

Was he Ian?

Leitis remembered that boy's laughter, the way he and her brothers teased her, the way he had of listening to her so intently that she felt she could tell him anything. And his appearance? A handsome boy with dark hair and eyes that always appeared alight with happiness. But he had been a child when last she saw him, and too many years had passed to be certain.

Was it him? And if it was, why hadn't he said so? Why hide himself behind a mask and claim it was for her protection?

The soft knock startled her but was not unexpected. It was probably Donald, coming to see if she required anything. She walked to the door, opened it to find the man who'd occupied these past moments of thought.

The Raven hesitated on the threshold, filling the doorway. He was even more mysterious in the candlelight, a tall, broad-shouldered man dressed in black. His mask framed his face, accentuated the fullness of his lips, the sharp line of chin and jaw.

"You shouldn't be here," she cautioned. "It's not safe. Donald might come at any moment."

"Still protective," he said, smiling. He entered the room, closing the door behind him.

"Someone should look out after you," she said, looking up at him. "You take foolish chances."

"Perhaps the goal is worth the risk."

"Is it? It depends on your goal."

"I might have more than one," he teased.

"Why are you here?" she asked softly.

He bent closer to her until she could feel his breath on her cheek. "Perhaps I wished to kiss you again," he teased.

"Oh," she said, clasping her hands tightly in front of her. She would have been wiser to run from Gilmuir, from the colonel's touch and the Raven's. But it appeared that she was to be kissed again today, by another man she barely knew.

Or did she?

She tipped her head back and closed her eyes, telling herself that this kiss would be an antidote to the first. His mouth settled over hers with no more invitation than that.

His lips were warm, his breath hot, the intrusion of his tongue against her mouth an astonishing act. Her body warmed as she unclasped her hands in order to grip his arms.

The material of his shirt was soft and smooth to the touch. A last thought before he deepened the kiss and sent her thoughts flying to the stars in a hungry, open-mouthed kiss filled with daring.

She heard a sound, a slight gasp of wonder, then realized it was her own. Should a kiss be this powerful? How strange, that she'd never before equated that word to a simple touch of mouth to mouth.

Her lips fell open as her hands clutched his arms in a talonlike grip. And still he kissed her, as if he'd heard her earlier thought and wished to expunge all other embraces before this one.

Yes. A sigh, a greeting, a prayer. Yes, please. More and more. He'd kissed her before, but it had been calming, soft, and sweet. Not heated and dangerous.

He pulled back finally and she wanted to protest.

Instead, she lay her forehead against his chest, heard the pounding beat of his heart, and knew that her own mimicked it.

Step back, Leitis. Gather your dignity about you and pretend you've felt such a thing before.

But her feet didn't move, and her hands didn't release him. Her dignity had been lost in that first murmur of surprise. Nor had she ever felt anything as delightfully wondrous. Not with Marcus. Certainly not with the Butcher. Not ever before.

Words tripped from her mind, landed on her tongue, and rooted there. *Why did you kiss me like that? Why am I trembling?*

"Should I ask your forgiveness?" he murmured, his breath coming as fast as hers.

A wise woman would have said yes, gathering up the cloak of her pride. She could only shake her head. She lay her cheek against his chest, then placed a kiss on his shirt where his heart beat strong and fast.

Kiss me again. A demand she did not make aloud. But her hand smoothed the material of his shirtsleeve, a gesture as telling as a request.

He placed his fingers beneath her chin, tilted back her head, and kissed her again. A long, slow, drugging kiss that urged her to wickedness and heat. Colors flew across her closed lids, shades of rainbows and harebells and heather.

He was the one to end the kiss, to pull away. He walked to the table and stood there, his back to her. "I came here for your help," he said. "Not to accost you."

"Is that what it was?" she said gently. "Should I be angry, then? Or ashamed?"

He glanced over his shoulder at her.

"For liking it," she added.

His soft laughter startled her. "I can never antici-
pate what you will say."

"A woman should be mysterious, surely," she
teased, feeling absurdly lighthearted at the moment.
How strange, that a kiss should have that effect on her.

She approached him, stretched out her hand, and
brushed her fingers over his back. A touch as delicate
as a butterfly's wings, but it appeared that he felt it
all the same. He stiffened, remaining still. His stance
made her smile, as if the power of a kiss had been
transferred to her touch. She'd never before felt this
way, enchanted in the moment, silent and filled with
expectation.

"How can I help you? What can I do?"

Her hand dropped as he turned and surveyed her,
the candlelight adding shadows to his features. "You
offer so easily," he said. "Why?"

"You stole a wagon," she said, smiling. "And fed
people because you wished to aid them. How could I
do less?"

"I want you to ask the villagers if they wish to
leave," he said abruptly.

She studied him intently in the light of the candles.
"Do you think they will?"

"I think they would be foolish not to," he said can-
didly. "The English presence here will only get
stronger as the months pass. And the conditions will
only get worse."

She moved away, moved to stand beside the loom,
staring out the window. "A sad day, when a Scot must
leave Scotland."

"They can create their country wherever they go,"
he said, an argument he'd begun last night.

She turned and faced him. "Why do you not ask
them?" she asked curiously.

"There are reasons," he said enigmatically.

"Because you don't wish them to know you're Ian MacRae?"

He stared at her, obviously stunned.

"Did you think I couldn't tell?" she asked, amused. "The clues were there all along."

Still he said nothing.

"You'll deny it now," she said, sighing.

"No," he said, and that one simple word sent her heart soaring.

The reason, then, that he had been so familiar to her, that he felt as much a friend as a man capable of making her heart stutter with a kiss. She wanted to turn and disappear with him into darkness, find a soft and safe place and ask him about all the years in between.

She took one step away from him, suddenly stunned by a thought. He'd lived his life in England, the heir to an English nob.

"You're one of them, aren't you, Ian?" She glanced in the direction of Fort William. "You're one of the soldiers there."

"Would a soldier have stolen an English wagon, Leitis?" he asked, coming to her side. "Would a soldier have cared about feeding hungry Scots?"

She shook her head. "Then come with me and talk to the villagers yourself."

"They'll listen to you," he said reasonably. "They'll not remember me, nor do they have a reason to trust me."

"Do I?" she asked. "Take off your mask."

"When I can," he answered.

She felt buffeted by too many emotions. Happiness, confusion, curiosity, and a curious sense of warning that could not be dismissed. But she dismissed it, pushing it away. At the moment, she simply didn't care.

"Then shall we go?" she asked, extending her hand to him. She smiled brightly, then let him lead her to the priory and the staircase. To rebellion and further.

Chapter 19

❦

"Are you certain you'll not come in?" Leitis asked, turning to him at the door of Hamish's cottage.

The journey to the glen had been a circuitous one, made necessary by the fact that they couldn't take the chance of slipping across the land bridge and being seen by the sentry. They'd had to row across the cove, then circle back on the Raven's horse.

"No," he said, "but I'll wait for you. There," he said, pointing to a grove of trees.

She nodded and walked to Hamish's cottage, glancing one more time toward the shadows before she knocked on the door. He was gone from view, his ability to slip into the darkness disconcerting.

When there was no answer, Leitis pushed open the

door and entered the darkened cottage. After lighting the candle on the table, she looked around the room. There was no sign of her uncle. His bed was made; no dishes had been dirtied. Hamish was a tidy man, so it was difficult to know whether or not he'd been absent for a day or more, or simply gone for the moment.

At first she thought the Butcher had arrested him after all, feeling a spike of fear at the thought. Or perhaps he had been wise enough to hide from sight. In that case she would have to gather the clan herself.

But a few moments later she heard the sound of whistling. A merry tune, one she knew as well as the identity of the whistler. Hamish opened the door, only to freeze at the sight of her.

"You'll not be content, will you, Uncle, until the English have hanged you?" she asked, glancing at the pipes on his shoulder.

"A fine MacRae you are, then," he said, grinning, "to have escaped the Butcher."

Hamish set his pipes on the floor, then hesitated. His gaze rested on the stone wall, then the floor. Finally, he studied the ceiling intensely. "Did he use you, Leitis?" he asked finally.

She felt a flush warm her face at his question, followed by irritation. "No more than you," she said abruptly. "Do you care so little, Uncle, about my being hostage to your good behavior?" She stared at the pipes fixedly.

"That's why you're here, then, Leitis? To grumble at me again?" He placed his fists on his hips, his face contorted into a glower.

"I doubt you'll listen," she said, masking her hurt. Strange, that it was the Butcher who pointed out Hamish's selfishness. She pushed the man out of her mind, annoyed that she'd thought of him at all.

"I've come to speak to the clan, Hamish," she said, moving to the door. "Can we meet here?"

"Why, Leitis?"

"I'll say it only once, Uncle. Will you help me gather them?"

He frowned at her, then nodded. "You take the eastern half and I'll take the west. It'll be faster that way. Sooner started, sooner finished."

They each began to knock on doors, announcing the meeting. One by one the members of the clan filtered into the cottage, mothers with children, old men with canes, matrons with cool and watchful eyes, the young ones who had seen too much for their years.

Each of them greeted her, asked after her health and her presence among them. Every query was followed by a quick and condemning look at Hamish, who pretended to ignore everyone.

Leitis waited until they were all assembled in the cottage before beginning.

"I've come to ask the people of Gilmuir a question," she said hesitantly. "If you had a new place to live, somewhere away from Scotland, would you leave?"

"You want the people of Gilmuir to emigrate?" Hamish narrowed his eyes and glared at her. "Why do you ask such a foolish question?" He sat at his table, arms crossed over his chest, the look on his face one of condemnation.

Leitis stared at him, wondering why she'd never seen his bitterness before. Or the tightness about his mouth as if he were determined never to smile again unless it was at an Englishman's expense. She realized as she studied Hamish that it had not been pride that motivated his acts, nor even stubbornness. But a hatred requiring a single-minded determination and diligent practice to keep it deep and strong.

"Because it's the only way we'll survive," she said softly.

"We'll do well enough here," he said, his tone clipped.

She turned to the clan members. "Will we? It is your decision, after all, not Hamish's."

"How would we leave Scotland, Leitis?" Malcolm asked.

"I don't know," she answered honestly. "I only promised to ask you for another, one who wishes you safe."

"Who would that be?" Dora asked.

She glanced over at the other woman. "A man you all once knew," she said. "Ian MacRae."

"Ian MacRae, is it?" Hamish asked, frowning. "Has he come back to Gilmuir to be laird now? Or doesn't he know there's no clan left?"

"That's why he would do this, uncle," she said, turning away from him and addressing the rest of the clan. "He says that the English presence will only get worse here, and I believe him. We cannot live through another winter like the last."

Dora nodded, but said nothing.

"Where would we go?" Mary asked.

"I don't know," Leitis said, "but a safe place. Perhaps we can all agree where."

"Someplace away from the English, though," Ada said.

"A country where we might be Scots and not punished for it?" another woman asked.

Leitis nodded, grateful for the women's support. Were women different because they nurtured the young and cared for the sick? Did it give them an ability to understand bitter truths more quickly? How many women would have counseled for rebellion, if the decision had been left to them? A foolish question to ask, simply because the answer didn't matter.

"It's a sad house where the hen crows louder than the cock," Peter said.

Dora stepped up to him, her hands on her hips. "Better to hide with the rabbits than be eaten by the hounds," she said cuttingly. "Or have you noticed how many of the clan aren't here anymore, Peter?"

"Well, I'm no hen," Malcolm said, "but I agree with the women. We should leave here."

"I'd never thought to hear you speak those words," Hamish said angrily, staring at Malcolm. "It's treason."

"Who am I being a traitor to, Hamish?" Malcolm asked. "Our leaders? They've emigrated to France, sworn allegiance to England, or have died. Our country? Where is Scotland now? It's been swallowed up by England."

"We'll rise up again. We'll be free once more," Hamish said stubbornly.

"Thoughts are free," Alisdair said, stepping forward. "And I'll say them now. I'd leave this place, Hamish, if only to escape the sadness of it." He glanced behind him, where more than one clansman was nodding his head.

"Better fed than dead?" Peter asked mockingly.

"The English won't rest until they've killed us all," Angus said. "It'll get worse now that the Butcher is in command."

"Are you all daft?" Hamish asked incredulously.

"You don't have to come, Uncle," Leitis said quietly. "The English will think it a game to hunt you until you're dead. Then you can haunt them for eternity. It's the only way you'll be at peace."

He stared at her as if amazed at her effrontery. But something had changed within her when she'd seen his pipes tonight. He'd not cared that he endangered her. The hurt of that was so great that she wanted to weep.

"She has you there, Hamish," Peter said, grinning. "I can see you now, merely a shade, marching in front of the English fort with your pipes and daring them to capture you." He wiggled his hands beside his ears and made a ghostly sound.

"You're an old fool," Hamish said, annoyed.

"Who are you calling old?" Peter asked, narrowing his eyes. "I'm two years younger than you and ten years smarter."

Leitis moved to the center of the clan. Everything that they decided, from the election of their laird to this most important decision, was put to the vote. It was time for it and an end to the blather.

"How many are for leaving?" she asked. She counted the hands, realizing that most of the people in this room were prepared to leave Gilmuir. "And for staying?" Hamish and Peter, that was all.

"I'll let you know more when the plans have been made," she told them.

"And where will you be until then? And how did the Butcher let you escape him so easily, Leitis?" Hamish asked bitingly.

The members of the clan stilled, anticipating the answer as well as Hamish.

"Do you begrudge me my momentary freedom, Uncle? I'll be back there soon enough, a guarantee for your obedience. But it's evident that you care little for my being your hostage," she said quietly, staring at the instrument on the floor next to him. "I wonder if the bagpipes will keep you company when we're all gone."

"When you're all seeking to be fools, you mean," Hamish said fiercely, picking up his pipes. He glared at all of them before leaving his cottage.

"I've a sister on the other side of the loch," Mary said, coming forward. "Can she come, too?"

"And my daughter?" Dora asked unexpectedly. "She married a MacLeasch, as you know."

A dozen more names were tossed to her.

"I don't know if we can bring them all," she said helplessly. "But I'll ask."

The reaction from the villagers had surprised her. But perhaps they had already recognized what she was just now realizing. Hope must be nourished by fortune and freedom. There had not been any good fortune in Scotland for years, and there was no longer any freedom.

Are you one of the soldiers at the fort, then? She'd asked him that. His answer had been sliced so finely that Alec could see the outline of the truth behind it. No, he was not one of the soldiers. He commanded them.

She had stunned him. Rendered him speechless and filled with both admiration and trepidation.

The clues were there all along.

Perhaps he had deliberately let her know one identity so as to hide a greater secret. He vowed, as he waited, to tell her that the boy she'd known as Ian was also the colonel who commanded Fort William.

He watched from the cover of trees as the people entered Hamish's cottage. The discussion was fierce, as was the passion of the people who spoke. Leitis's voice appeared to be a cooling influence.

A few minutes later, Hamish left, his bagpipes tucked under his arm. Gradually the rest of the villagers departed. The candles were extinguished and darkness shadowed her as Leitis stepped from the door and headed toward him.

The sound of bagpipes was alluring in the summer night. She stopped and listened for a moment before continuing.

He reached out his arm for her and pulled her close to him. "A fool, your uncle," he said softly. "Doesn't he know that his actions could endanger you?"

She sighed heavily and shook her head. He realized then that she was crying. Leitis MacRae, weeping. Another shock, one that made him wrap his arms around her, pull her close to him.

"What is it, Leitis?" he whispered. "Tell me."

He would make it better, ease her mind. Protect her. He fumbled for words. "It didn't go well?" he asked.

She nodded against his chest. Placing his hand against her cheek, he felt the startling heat of her tears.

"Oh, Leitis," he said, perplexed and frustrated, "tell me."

She sighed again, a gusty sign of exasperation or temper or some other emotion he could not understand at the moment. She shook her head, then pulled back, wiping at her cheeks with the backs of her hands. "They want to leave," she said. "All but Hamish and Peter. They'll stay."

"And you're crying for Hamish?" he asked, trying to comprehend.

She shook her head. "I'm crying for a foolish reason," she admitted. "I don't want to leave," she said. "I understand why I must, but this is my home. And Hamish, however foolish he is, is my last relative."

She looked around her. "Gilmuir has always been free. Whatever happened in Scotland didn't touch us here. Now we'll never be able to avoid it."

He couldn't say the words to ease her, in whatever

guise he wore. The truth, stark and bitter, was that life would never again be the same for the Scots.

"You can be free if you find a place that will allow it," he said, feeling inept and unsure. He placed his arm around her shoulders and pulled her to him.

"There are others who might wish to come," she said, surprising him. "Mary's sister and Dora's daughter and two sons. There's Malcolm's brother's children, and a few others." She hesitated for a moment. "Well, more than a few," she confessed.

"I'll hire a ship. The logistics will be difficult," he admitted, "but a few more people won't matter."

It would be easy enough to afford such a venture. He'd used his paternal grandmother's legacy to purchase his commission, but had never touched the rest of the funds.

"The only difficulty I see," he said, thinking aloud, "is in arranging the exodus. It will have to be done as quickly as possible once the ship arrives."

"Or just the opposite," she offered, smiling up at him. "A ship is more likely to be noticed than the Highlanders are to be missed. What if you moved them into one place?"

"Where do you suggest we hide a few dozen Scots?"

"What better place to hide a lamb than in a flock?" she asked. "Use the empty cottages here in the village."

"On the assumption that the English won't notice the cottages being filled?" he asked. "One Scot looks just like another?"

She nodded.

"Are they so uncaring?" he asked carefully.

"Is it easier being Scot than English?" she asked abruptly, a question so surprising that he pulled back and stared at her.

"It's not easy being either," he said honestly.

"Yet you've lived most of your life as an Englishman."

"Yes," he said simply.

"And now you've become a Scot. What made you change?"

He thought about the question. A series of incidents. Culloden and Inverness, the desperation of the Scots, Cumberland's barbarous decrees. And the most important reason of all, perhaps, the discovery that his mother had been killed by the English. "I never liked a bully," he said finally. "And it occurred to me that Scotland needed a hand up."

"My brothers would have approved of you," she said, startling him.

"Tell me what they were like," he said. They began to walk through the trees, following the upward slope.

"Not that much different from when you knew them. Except in appearance, perhaps. Fergus grew to be a mountain of a man; one my mother swore could not be her son, he was so huge. He had a red beard that he was very fond of, and was forever bragging that the lassies liked it, too."

He could hear the smile in her voice and was grateful for it. "And James?" he asked.

"Less fierce, but then he always was. He grew tall and thin and serious, of course. But it was Fergus who voted not to rebel. His was the lone voice of contention about the war with the English."

"He didn't want to go?" he asked, surprised.

"No, but he did, of course, because of Father and James. And you, Ian?" She glanced up at him. "What was life like for you?"

He smiled, wondering how to condense it into a few sentences. "I went back to England," he said.

"My father married again—too soon, I thought—and had another son. I grew, I learned, I became an adult." Beyond that he couldn't tell her. He'd become a soldier, a man decorated for courage, and yet he was too cowardly to reveal himself wholly to her.

"And have you no wife nor sweetheart?" she asked casually.

He smiled, not convinced of her nonchalant manner.

"Not until now," he said.

Her head jerked up as she stared over at him. The moonlight filtered through the trees, touching upon a curve of her cheek, the curve of her smile.

"There shouldn't be a moon," he said suddenly. "Even one waning."

She said nothing, only continued to smile at him, bemused.

"Because," he said, reaching out and turning her, brushing his lips against hers, "you are even more beautiful in the moonlight."

She sighed into his kiss and he was enchanted.

Chapter 20

⟨ೕೕೕ⟩

"**Y**ou were the most fascinating person in my life," she said, pulling away finally.

"What about Marcus?"

The memory of him was fading, oddly enough, as if not fixed and sure in her mind. But she still could see Fergus and James and their parents as clear as if they stood before her now. Still, it felt disloyal to speak of him when he was not here to defend himself. Silence was a better recourse.

"Where did you meet him?" he asked a few moments later.

"He was Fergus's friend," she said, amused at his curiosity. But then, she felt the same about him.

They began to walk, hand in hand, until they came

to the foot of the caves where she'd always found refuge. She smiled.

"I used to come here and think about you," she confessed. In fact, after he'd kissed her, she'd gone to her hiding place in the cave and stared at Gilmuir for hours. The confusion and delight she felt had been equal to her shame. She could still recall that look of astonishment on his face when she'd slapped him. She'd returned to Gilmuir to apologize, only to learn of the tragedy.

"Did you?" he asked, sounding surprised.

The words were muted in the forest, overcome by the sound of the wind sighing through the leaves, the crunch of brush beneath their feet. Even the forest creatures, accustomed to night for cover, were louder than her confession.

It was time to reveal another secret. "The kiss you gave me didn't really disgust me," she said, focusing her attention on the tips of the trees. In the moonlight they looked like arrows pointed at the sky.

"Shall I kiss you again?" he said, his lips curving into a smile, "just to test that fact?"

She glanced up at him, amused. "Haven't you already?"

"I would hate to be wrong," he teased.

He kissed her again, and long moments later, she pulled back. "No," she said weakly, "it doesn't disgust me."

Above them the moon was a pendulous globe in the sky, illuminating the edges of the surrounding clouds with pale blue light.

Turning, she took his hand once again, pulling him up the incline.

"Where are you taking me?" he asked, his voice laced with humor.

"To my secret hideaway," she admitted.

He pushed back the bushes, following her into the cave.

"We should have brought a candle," he said, turning slowly. "Or a lantern."

"The better to illuminate the changes," she said, smiling. "You would no doubt find the space a disappointment."

"A comparison between my childhood memories and my adult perceptions?"

"There is often a difference," she said.

"Not so far," he said, turning to her. He found her in the darkness, extending his arms around her. He stood close, speaking near her ear. "I recall everything about you, Leitis," he said. "From the shape of your ears to the way you laugh. Nothing disappoints me."

She was stunned by his words. Not that he felt the way that he did, but that he could be so unhesitant in voicing his feelings.

The past year had altered her. She was no longer the confident woman she'd thought herself to be all her life. Instead, she was a person wary of others. Experience had taught her that she had more to fear than to trust.

She had lost so much, how could she bear to lose him? It was wiser to hold herself aloof than to drown in his words.

"And you, Leitis? Does the man pale beneath the boy?"

She answered him with the truth, unable to do less with Ian. "The boy charmed me," she said hesitantly. "The man frightens me."

He fell silent, the next few moments filled with tension.

She placed her hands on his upper arms, tightened

her grip. She wanted to keep him close even as her words would probably induce him to leave her.

But he surprised her by threading his fingers through her hair, his palms resting on her cheeks. "Is it so hard to love, Leitis?"

She nodded, tears coming to her eyes with his tender words.

"It is easy enough," he said softly, moving his hands until they were on her shoulders. "At least it was for me."

She held herself still, waiting.

"All you need do is accept it. I love you, Leitis."

She bowed her head, leaning her forehead against his chest. She could not breathe, and her heart was beating too loudly. The words of caution would not come, the warning not to spend his emotion too lavishly, make himself too vulnerable. Because she needed to hear his declaration just as she needed to feel him close.

"When did I begin to fall in love with you?" he continued. "Was it when you stood in the priory and insisted upon protecting me? Or when you laughed at my inability to give away a chicken?" he added, his voice amused. "Or could it have been all those many years ago when you handed me something from your heart and I crushed it?"

"You gave me heather," she said softly, the words tinged with tears.

"I'd give you a country if I could," he said. "All these long years you've been in my mind waiting."

A sound escaped him when he bent and kissed her, finding her lips damp with tears.

"Leitis," he murmured against her lips. He made of her name a word of wonder and solace. Winding her arms around her neck, she stood on tiptoe to return the kiss, deepen it, enchanted by the tenderness that led so quickly to heat.

"I never knew a kiss could be like yours," she said a few moments later.

"How are mine different?" he asked teasingly. He bent and brushed a kiss over her lips. Softly, like the touch of a butterfly wing.

"As if birds flew in my chest," she murmured.

He deepened the kiss, her lips falling open as she sighed into his mouth.

"Like my blood is too hot," she confessed.

He smiled against her lips, then kissed her again. Cupping his hands on either side of her face, he traced the curve of her mouth with the tip of his tongue.

She was selfish in her need, wanting him to love her. Yet at the same time she recognized that love was a dangerous emotion. It sliced with invisible wounds and wrapped around her heart and strangled it with grief. She could not bear to feel the same anguish again. To love was to lose.

"Would you lay with me?" she asked. She could not give the words back to him, but she could give him herself.

"No," he said unexpectedly.

Startled by his refusal, she could only stare at him. "Why?"

"Because you might have a child from it, Leitis," he said gently.

She wanted to argue with him, decry his protectiveness, but at the same time she appreciated the fact that he wished to shield her. Hamish had done the opposite, willing to sacrifice her for his own hatred.

"Please," she said.

He placed his hands on his arms, drew her closer.

His breath was warm against her cheek. "It is my dearest desire, Leitis, but it might bring danger to you."

He felt her tremble beneath his fingers, suddenly awed by her courage. Her comment about stallions and mares that first night in the lairds' chamber indicated well enough her opinions of loving. Her experiences must have been unpleasant for her, yet she offered herself to him.

But he would not bind her to him with a child.

Slowly, he stepped back, facing the direction of the cave opening. He felt her behind him and sensed the confusion of her thoughts.

"I cannot," he said, wondering if she knew that refusing her was one of the most difficult tasks he'd ever set for himself.

He wanted her to know that coupling could be done in sweetness and passion. He wanted to hear her sob in his arms at the pleasure of it. But most of all, he wanted her safe.

"Please," she said again.

"It would not be wise, Leitis," he said.

"We have not been wise in our deeds thus far," she said.

"But those acts would not leave you with a child," he argued.

"No," she said, moving away from him. "But have you ever regretted the things you've not done, Ian? I have. I wish I had told my brothers that I loved them, and hugged my father one more time. I wish I had been kinder to those friends I lost. I have regrets, Ian, enough to fill the whole of this cave, but I would not regret this."

She walked around until she stood in front of him. "Lay with me, Ian."

"I am no saint, Leitis," he said, his tone filled with

rueful humor. His greater honor was being swamped by his wishes and wants.

"Please," she said, extending her hand to touch his chest. He felt the burning imprint of each of her fingers.

He removed his gloves slowly, giving her time to change her mind. He reached out and placed his hand on her bodice, tracing the curve of her neckline. His mind counseled restraint, but his fingers fumbled in their haste to untie the bow.

He wanted, almost desperately, to touch her. To cup her breasts in his hands and place his mouth on her nipples. She had vanished his battlefield dreams and replaced them with visions of her. And each of them led to this moment.

Spreading her bodice open, he pushed her shift downward. He heard her gasp as he touched a finger to the inward curve of her breast.

His fingers followed, greedy and impatient, smoothing over her skin, feeling the warmth and silkiness of it. Her breasts were full, filling his hands. She made a little start of surprise when his palms brushed over her nipples, gently abrading them.

She was an innocent despite her claims of experience. She knew nothing of seduction, of passion that could range from tenderness to lust. He wasn't surprised to feel both for Leitis.

He bent and kissed her throat, alert to her in a way he'd never before been. As if he could see her in the darkness, breathed in a matching rhythm, even joined his heartbeat with hers.

Delicately, he touched her skin with the tip of his tongue. He pulled back, knowing as he did so that one taste would never be enough. He wanted to love her until the memories of any other man were banished.

Gently, he pushed the bodice of her dress downward, trailing a necklace of kisses from shoulder to shoulder. He pulled her sleeves down to her wrists, felt her hands clenched into fists.

Another indication of her innocence, one that angered him. The man she had loved had used her, leaving her with memories of pain instead of pleasure.

Removing his shirt, he let it fall to the floor, then followed that with his boots.

"Are you undressing?" she asked faintly.

He smiled, unfastened his breeches, and lowered them. "Yes," he said, "and then you."

She remained silent, but he heard her indrawn breath.

He bent and grabbed the hem of her skirt, pulling it over her head along with her shift. He lay the garments down on the floor next to his clothing. Not a suitable bower, but it would have to do. He bent and removed her shoes, sliding them from her feet as if she were a princess and he her manservant. One by one he removed her stockings, rolling them down her legs slowly. He warned himself about haste again, even as he stroked his hands from her ankles to her knees.

There were times in his life when he'd been awed by the spectacles around him. The majesty of a mounted regiment, the beauty of the sea as it changed colors and moods. But nothing had ever affected him as deeply as Leitis trembling in the darkness, waiting to be ravished.

He stood and, taking one of her hands, placed it flat on his chest.

"Touch me," he said softly. "I want to feel your hands on me."

Her fingers drew up until her fist rested against his

skin. Then, hesitantly, she spread her fingers again, moving her palm across his skin, mapping him. He took her other hand and, curling her fingers with his, brushed a kiss against her knuckles. "Leitis," he said. Just that, her name as an endearment.

He reached up and untied his mask, letting it fall to the floor. On this occasion, on this night, there would be nothing separating them.

Something landed on the floor and she reached up and touched his face, hoping it was his mask. His face was bare, revealed as it had never before been. She wished for a shaft of moonlight, the dawn sun, something that would illuminate his features.

"Are you certain you've been protecting me?" she teased. "Or have you grown ugly in all these years?"

"Would you care?" he asked, his voice somber.

"No," she answered truthfully. But she couldn't imagine the boy had grown to be anything but handsome.

The darkness offered her concealment for her daring. Her hands reached up and traced the line of his nose, his cheeks, and his jaw. Her thumbs brushed against his closed lids, feeling the feathery-soft spike of lashes. There was no deformity to be found beneath her fingers, no scar to mar the perfection of his features.

"Will I do?" he asked, standing quiescent beneath her touch.

"Yes," she whispered before standing on tiptoe again to kiss him. The most audacious act of all, and one she'd never before done, to kiss a man because she wished it. To place her lips on his in wonder, hoping that he would show her how to render him as enchanted as she felt.

Suddenly he bent and, placing an arm beneath her legs, bore her up into his arms.

"It's a strange experience," she said, "to be carried about like this in the dark. It makes me feel as if I'm floating in the air."

"I thought you were an angel once," he said teasingly. "Perhaps you are in this moment."

She laughed, the sound reverberating throughout the cave. "I cannot claim any angelic virtues," she admitted.

The kiss he gave her then was sweet and deep. She surfaced from it with a delectable dizziness. As if she'd twirled and twirled on the top of Hamish's hill until she was left reeling.

He lay her down on their bed of clothes, then knelt beside her, kissing each of her fingers delicately and slowly, as if they were precious things and not callused on their tips and sides from years of working the loom.

But he did not move to mount her.

She lay there quietly, waiting. "I'm not frightened," she said, "if that's why you're taking your time."

"You wish me to hurry?" he asked, the amusement in his voice causing her to frown.

"Only if you wish to," she said. "I don't mind either way."

"You don't mind?" he asked in a whisper as dark as the cave.

She shook her head, then realized he couldn't see her. "No."

"That's very gracious of you," he said dryly. "If it is all the same to you, I'll be long at it. I like to touch your skin, you see."

The strangest tingle ran up the back of her neck at his words. Or it could have been the fact that he kissed her throat again. She pushed her hair out of the way so that he might do it again.

"You like that," he said, murmuring against her skin.

"I do," she admitted, the words coaxed from her by delight.

His hands were slow, his fingers soft upon her skin, dusting where they touched as if to leave only a hint of their passage. The darkness both hid his intent and absolved her ignorance.

He brushed his cheek against her temple, his night beard gently abrading her skin.

Her sole experience with a man had been a furtive coupling in the forest where the trees had acted as sentinel. The ground had been cold, and the day wet, as if nature itself knew of the parting to come and wept for it. This dark cave was not a better trysting spot, but it did not seem to matter at the moment.

"Kiss me again," she demanded, startled to hear her own words.

"My pleasure," he murmured.

He kissed her until her blood felt heated. His hands learned her in the darkness, trailing from her shoulders to her ankles.

She reached out her hands and did the same, remembering his words. *Touch me.*

His skin was warm, almost hot. The muscles of his arms bunched beneath her exploring touch. She wrapped each palm around his shoulder, then gasped as he stroked his fingers across the tips of her breasts. Her nipples tightened, the tingling sensation his touch evoked spreading outward to her toes and fingertips.

He bent and touched his lips to her breast, startling her. Then he placed his mouth upon the tip of it, his lips capturing her, gently moistening before suckling tenderly. The spike of pleasure she felt muted her protest. He was as adept at this type of kissing as the other.

She had thought the act would be swift and painful. But he did not hurry in his possession of her, seemingly content to touch every inch of her skin. His fingers trailed from her waist to her hips and back up again to rest beneath her arms, inciting small shivers. His hands cupped her knees, the bulb of her heels. One hand moved to rest against her stomach, the heat of his palm seeping into her body.

She moved restlessly, a stranger to the feeling that flamed within her, a need as elemental as the requirement for food and drink.

"Slowly," he whispered, placing a gentle kiss against her lips.

She had never been explored this way, never felt as if her breasts were swelling and heating, their tips both puckering and elongating at the touch of his tongue.

At the base of his throat his blood beat heavy and strong, and so quickly that it mimicked hers. Her thumb rested there as her fingers spread over his neck.

His hands suddenly fisted in her hair as he kissed her deeply, inhaling her sigh. She felt like a supplicant, a neophyte, a virgin trapped in wonder and delight.

"I've dreamed of this," he confessed in a whisper. "But it was daylight and you were lying in the glen, your arms outstretched to welcome me. Your hair sparkled like fire, and even here was lit by sunlight," he said shockingly, trailing his fingers through the curls between her legs.

Reaching up, she cupped his cheek with her hand.

He turned his head and kissed her palm, a gesture so filled with tenderness that she felt the spike of tears.

This night would be forever etched into her mind like the leaves she'd sometimes found embedded in rock.

She felt him heavy and hard against her thigh. She was no maiden, but at this moment she felt as untried as one, as ignorant of the deed as if it had never before happened to her. Tentatively, she reached out and touched him, a gesture that elicited his gasp. Another touch, less timid and more fascinated, had her placing her palm upon the length of him. She noted with fascination that he was larger than the distance from her wrist to the tip of her middle finger.

"You're very big," she whispered, both intrigued and anxious.

He laughed again, and pulled her to him, until she was draped over his chest like a warm and living blanket.

"I never thought to spice my loving with humor, Leitis," he said tenderly.

"Is it a foolish thing I've said?" she asked, embarrassed.

"No," he said tenderly, placing his hand on the back of her head. He pulled her gently toward him for another kiss.

Yes, please—a last cogent thought for several moments.

Gently he turned, leaning above her, but instead of kissing her again, he bent and pressed his lips against her waist. His hair, clubbed at his nape, fell loose, spreading over her skin like a delicate fan. A whisper of touch as he tasted her with mouth and tongue, kisses that anointed her skin and warmed it.

He taught her more about herself than she'd known before. The inner curve of her knee proved to be as exquisitely sensitive as the front of her ankles and the area above her heels.

"You shiver when I touch you," he said, his voice a dark whisper.

She nodded in agreement. "I can't help it," she confessed.

His thumbs brushed against the inside of her wrists tenderly, then moved to her elbows. "Your arms," he said, as if to mark the place with his words and his touch. Bending his head, he bestowed the most tender of kisses on each nipple. "Your breasts."

He leaned over her. "I want to know everything about you," he declared softly. Her hands gripped his upper arms. "What you wish for most in your life. What causes the sad look in your eyes. What your dreams and nightmares are made of."

She pressed her fingers against his lips. "Stop," she said. "Please." It was too much. Her heart hurt with his words.

He kissed her fingers, then removed them. "What sound you make when you find your pleasure," he said purposely.

He flattened his palm against her stomach, his fingers splayed. Slowly, so slowly, he moved his hand, touching her again. Her breath felt too tight. She closed her eyes, wrapped her arms around his neck, feeling a curious mixture of embarrassment and a new achy sensation.

His thumb stroked through her softness, circled slowly. She bit her lip, raised her hips instinctively. But he didn't hurry. Instead, he kissed her deeply, his tongue and his fingertips in tandem at exploration.

She'd never known that her body might be overcome by such sensations, as if it were separate from her will. Captivated by his hands and mouth and softly whispered words.

"I want to know what it feels like to be inside you, Leitis," he said, his words oddly breathless.

"Please, Ian," she said. A welcome in his name, an invitation in the slow widening of her legs.

He entered her slowly, filled her completely, and stretched her gently. His possession of her wasn't painful or rushed. Instead, she bowed beneath him, astonished by the sensation. She bit her lip and arched farther toward him as if to deepen the feeling. But he would not move. Instead, he remained perfectly still, his breathing harsh and rapid.

She lay with eyes closed, savoring the pleasure.

Slowly, excruciatingly slow, so that it felt as if time itself halted, he withdrew from her. Her sound of protest changed abruptly to delight when he entered her again.

Her openmouthed gasp was inhaled by his mouth, transformed into a moan as he withdrew and entered her again. This time her hips arched higher, meeting him in an instinctive dance. Her hands gripped his arms, rubbed from elbow to shoulder in wordless encouragement.

She had thought to keep herself invulnerable, yet now she welcomed her surrender. Her bare heels pressed against the slate floor as she lifted herself to him again. Her eyes closed, her fingers splayed almost into talons.

She was almost there, to a place she'd never been before, the destination as much a mystery as the journey itself.

"Leitis," he said, his voice a guttural rasp. A sound escaped her, a sob of delight.

"Please," she said, ignorant of what she wanted. But he seemed to know, because he plunged into her again. His kiss was an accompaniment, deep and ardent, stealing her breath and emptying her mind.

All that remained was sensation.

A waterfall traveled through her body, carrying with it heat and a breathless joy. It was simple and pure and wondrous and eternal.

Something was happening to her. It felt as if she were being torn in two, but the rending was accomplished in excruciatingly slow degrees.

She wound her arms around his neck, pressed up into his kiss, seeking succor and safety within his embrace. The darkness of the cave was suddenly altered by the sparkling light behind her eyelids.

A moan escaped him, a sound that echoed her own body's bowing delight. She cradled him, rocked him, and held him tight to her.

Suddenly she cried aloud, the sound echoing through the cave. She was insensate, clutching him, lost in the sensation and him, helpless and humbled.

An eternity later, she reached up and cupped his face with her palms, suddenly overcome by a feeling so acute that it stole her breath. This was not simple mating, but a joining in a way she'd never known before, never suspected might exist.

It felt like love.

Chapter 21

He had not intended to lay with her, Alec thought, as he stood and searched for his mask. But all temptations could not be so easily avoided. Kissing Leitis was one of those. Loving her in the darkness was another.

He tied the strings of his mask, then returned to her side, stubbing his toe on an outcropping of rock. He cursed softly and cradled his foot in his hands.

"I was beginning to believe you had eyes in the dark," she said, her voice laced with amusement.

"You are supposed to feel pity for my injury," he said, amused, "not ridicule me for the manner of it."

"Is this the same Ian who laughed at me when I sprained my ankle jumping down from a tree?"

"You retaliated by putting spiders in my bed, as I recall," he said, sitting beside her again.

"You knew about that?" she asked, surprised.

"Of course. Who else would dare?"

She laughed, and the sound of it encouraged his smile.

It was strange to help a woman on with her clothing in the dark. But he accomplished the duty slowly. He cupped his hands beneath her breasts, anointing them with gentle kisses as her shift slid down to cover them. He kissed each of her shoulders before shielding them from view with her dress.

"Was it something English that you did to me?" she asked abruptly.

He sat silent, feeling a sharp spike of tenderness for her. She was so bold in some of her adventures and so innocent in others, a fascinating juxtaposition.

"No," he said, kissing her temple, brushing back her hair with his fingers.

"Are you very experienced?" she asked hesitantly.

"Very," he said, finding the task of lacing her back into her bodice filled with possibilities.

"You said that very quickly," she accused.

"It's always better to state a point than to whittle around it."

She pulled back as if affronted, but he extended his arms around her.

"If the world were perfect and kind," he said gently, "then we would be the first for each other. But we're not."

"No," she whispered.

"All we can do is take what we have and be grateful for it."

"I've never felt that way before," she confessed, extending her arms around his neck.

"Then all the experience was worth it," he said, nuzzling her throat.

It had never occurred to him that he might feel blinding passion interspersed with humor. The combination was intoxicating. Or perhaps it was simply Leitis who enthralled him.

Trailing her fingers from his shoulders to his wrists occupied her attention while his hands slowed in lacing her bodice.

"Where did you get this?" she asked, tracing the pattern of an X-shaped scar on his hand.

He chuckled. "From Fergus," he admitted. "When he and James showed me the secret of the staircase."

"They knew?" she asked. "They never told me."

"My grandfather made them promise," he explained.

She held out her hand to him, reached for his fingers, and helped him trace a path around a similar scar on her own hand.

"Fergus?" he asked, surprised that he had never noticed it before. "What great secret did he impart to you?"

"No secret," she sighed. "But I was sworn not to tell Father that he was the one who broke Mother's prized blue plate."

They held their hands together, palm to palm.

He placed both hands on either side of her face, his thumbs brushing the corners of her mouth. Now was the time to tell her of his other secret.

She stood, stepping away from him, brushing down her skirt.

"I should return," she said, "before Donald misses me."

"Does he treat you well?" he asked, smiling.

"I can tolerate him," she said firmly. "It's the Butcher's presence that I find intolerable."

"Do you?" he asked carefully.

"I hate him," she said coolly. "Everything that he represents, everything that he is."

"Surely he's just a man?"

She bent, searching on the floor of the cave for her shoes.

"You've always called him Butcher," he said, the words pushed past the sudden constriction in his throat.

She glanced over at him in the darkness. "And you never have," she said. "Why?"

"Rumors are not always to be believed," he said. "The tales of his exploits at Inverness are not necessarily true."

"Do you believe that?"

He shrugged. "Things are not always as they seem," he said, walking to her. "But you're right," he said, before she could speak. "We should return you to the fort." He held out her hair ribbon and she took the end of it, the two of them linked by that crimson strip.

"I wish I didn't have to go," she confessed, looking up at him. "But if I don't return, he'll arrest Hamish."

"You have a great deal of loyalty for your uncle," he said.

"He's my only family. Sometimes he makes it difficult to love him," she confessed. "But then, love isn't always easy."

No, he thought, it wasn't. Especially when it was obscured by secrets.

She straightened, squared her shoulders. A hard-won resolve that almost pulled the truth from him. But he remained silent, escorting her from the cave and toward Fort William and the Butcher.

They mounted and circled the glen, following the line of the loch. A circuitous journey, made necessary by the sentry on the land bridge. The moments were spent in silence and reflection, each of them trapped in private thoughts.

As they neared the loch and the boat moored there, he glanced down at her. Her body was cradled against his, her head turned so that her cheek lay against his chest. The moonlight illuminated her face, cast shadows, and highlighted features. Her hands were in her lap, palms and fingers curling upward as if demanding from the world even in her dreams.

Leitis.

His heart thudded like a drum, a strange tattoo measuring the depth of his wonder.

He wished he could transport her to Gilmuir without her waking. But he was not a sorcerer, and if he were, he would choose another task, that of softening her toward the Butcher of Inverness.

She blinked open her eyes and looked around her, awareness coming in stages as she smiled sleepily up at him. He kissed her, the need he had for her surprising him. A physical response and one of the spirit. She made him feel fresh and clean, untainted by the last few years.

He helped her into the boat, the journey made in companionable silence.

Leitis stepped out of the boat once they reached the shore. Together they mounted the hidden staircase.

Once back in the priory, she would have spoken, had he not stepped close to her, pressing his fingers to her lips. He didn't want to hear her words of regret, or hatred, or longing. Instead, he bent, replaced his fingers with his lips, and captured her breath on a sigh.

His duty, stolid, unchanging, rooted in honor and

responsibility, awaited him, yet he could not move. Nor could he command his feet to take another step or even his chest to expand with a breath.

"Come with me tomorrow," he said. Dangerous words. Being with her was more threatening than the treason in which he engaged. Because, sooner or later, she would discover who he was, and would hate him for it.

One more time, Alec decided. Only one more incarnation, and the Raven would be no more. There would be no more reason for him to exist. There would be no trysts in caves and moonlit rides, no more shadowed meetings in the priory or the forest.

She nodded, and he left with no further words of farewell. He could not speak in case he revealed the emptiness of his own regret.

Harrison entered his room later that day, obeying his summons with the punctuality that Alec had come to expect. His adjutant closed the door behind him and strode to the map table, where Alec stood.

"I need you to go to Inverness," Alec said.

"Inverness, sir?"

Alec nodded. "To hire a ship."

Harrison remained silent, but the question was there on his face.

"I won't be stationed at Fort William forever. In a year or two another commander will replace me and there's no guarantee that the man won't be exactly like Sedgewick. The safest thing for the people of Gilmuir is to find another place to live."

Harrison looked surprised. "The Highlanders are leaving?"

"They are," Alec said, reaching beneath a stack of maps until he found one of the lake. He'd drawn it from memory of his recent travels around Loch Euliss.

"Here's Gilmuir," he said, pointing to a well-marked promontory. "And this," he said, indicating the recent addition to the plan, "is the hidden cove."

"Hidden cove?" Harrison asked, bending to study the map more intently.

Alec explained the layout, including the necklace of rocks guarding it. "It should be deep enough for a ship," he added.

He had kept this secret for years, but felt no hesitation in divulging it to his adjutant. Harrison knew about his heritage and his activities in Inverness and had never betrayed him.

Harrison looked at him curiously. "Where will the Scots go, sir?"

"To the colonies, or to France, or to some other place they choose."

His adjutant began to roll up the map, tucking it under his arm.

"I have another duty for you as well," Alec said, explaining what he needed.

Harrison flushed, but nodded his head.

"Will you be seeing her?" Alec asked nonchalantly as his adjutant moved toward the door.

Harrison glanced over his shoulder, surprised.

"Doesn't a certain Miss Fulton still live in Inverness?"

"I doubt she'll be wanting to see me, sir," he said. "She's no doubt engaged. Or married by this time."

"Don't you think you should find out for certain, Harrison?" Alec asked with a smile. "What was the difficulty between you?"

"There was no difficulty between us, sir. It was her father who objected to my suit."

"He was the provost, wasn't he?" Alec asked. A mean-spirited man, one who toadied to Cumberland; but then, he'd have to be self-effacing for his own survival. The duke had ordered the man who'd previously held the post thrown down the stairs.

"Be careful," he cautioned Harrison. "I'll not have you on my conscience. It's full enough."

"I would urge the same caution, sir. I think we have an informant among us," he added, describing Armstrong's recent activities. "He's too curious about your movements."

Alec nodded, the information coming as no surprise.

He gave Harrison a bank draft, the funds easily accessible in Inverness, since the English presence was so great in Scotland. He didn't doubt that the other man would be able to hire a ship, money being an excellent inducement for a ship captain's compassion.

It occurred to Alec as he watched him leave that Harrison looked almost happy at that moment. Was it the possibility of seeing Miss Fulton again? Or simply being away from Fort William?

As for his own happiness, it did not seem possible. He was caught in a web of deception. Being Ian allowed him to be near Leitis, spend time with her as himself. Yet all the time he was cautious of his words, of accidentally divulging something that would betray him.

He should never have loved Leitis. Now he couldn't forget their time together. He recalled every moment with her, the sweetness of her wonder, her awed delight. He'd felt that same delight, catapulted to a place where love mixed with passion and was topped off with tenderness.

In weeks she would be gone, and where would he be? In his role of loyal colonel? The thought was distasteful, but not as much as the notion of never seeing Leitis again.

Lieutenant Armstrong's grin did not quite reach his eyes, Donald thought, and the smile itself appeared forced. As if he thought he should take on an air of affability, the better to mix with the lower ranks.

Donald might only be a sergeant, but he knew when he was being cozened all the same. He hefted the tray on one hand, opened the door of the kitchen with the other.

Another irritating thing about lieutenants: They thought themselves above doing anything. The colonel didn't find it demeaning to clean his own boots when necessary, or even sweep out his own lodgings. But lieutenants were so filled with their own importance that it was almost comical. They strutted around the courtyard like roosters, with their puffed-up chests and their spotless uniforms and their white gloves that looked to have never seen a day's worth of work. Even Lieutenant Castleton, one of the most bearable of officers, had his lieutenant-like moments in which he looked down his nose at good honest labor. A few more months in the colonel's command would take care of that.

Donald suspected, however, that Armstrong was one of those people who accomplished what he wished by tricking other people into doing it for him. Which is why Donald grinned like a mad dog back at the lieutenant so as not to appear unfriendly, but pushed past him all the same.

Armstrong followed him out of the smoke-filled room. An indication that he wanted something. Donald ignored him, began to cross the courtyard.

"Sergeant!"

It was easy enough to pretend that he didn't hear

him, what with all the clamor and racket going on. The soldiers were marching again. Not in order to learn to walk in formation, Donald decided. They did that well enough now. It seemed that this duty was a way of keeping all the soldiers at Fort William occupied when they weren't out on patrol. He himself had spent too many hours in such worthless occupation. Sometimes, he thought, the aim of the army was to keep men on their feet, whether or not it made any sense.

"Sergeant!"

He sighed and halted, an affable smile on his face. "Sorry, sir, I didn't hear you," he lied.

Armstrong looked decidedly unhappy at the moment, Donald thought. His cheeks were red—not from exertion, he suspected as much as from irritation. Another thing about lieutenants: They didn't like to be ignored.

"Where is Harrison going?" Armstrong asked bluntly, all pretense of civility gone.

Donald only wished his own feigning of respect could be as easily dismissed. "I don't know, sir." *I'm the colonel's aide, you skinny little barnyard runt, and if you think I'd tell you, then you're an idiot.*

Tilting his head in the direction of the tray, he continued, "Will you be asking me more questions, sir? If so, then I'd just as soon put this down. It's heavy."

Armstrong glanced at the covered meal, then beyond to Gilmuir. "He treats his hostage with great care," he said.

Donald remained silent.

"An attractive woman."

The hair on the back of Donald's neck stood at attention. "Will that be all, sir?"

Armstrong looked as if he'd like to say something, but clicked his heels together, executing a perfect about face. Donald watched his departing figure, frowning.

The more he watched and learned, William Armstrong thought, the more concerned he became. The colonel had made no attempt to capture the man known as Raven, nor had the search for the piper been continued.

The fact that Armstrong had been relegated to inventorying ordnance was another indication that something wasn't quite right. Colonel Landers had removed Major Sedgewick from the fort, sending him to patrol the outlying quadrant. Why? Because the major disapproved of his actions in saving the Scottish village, or because Landers deemed him a threat?

Had Colonel Landers felt the same about him? Was there something he had done to warrant this duty? He slipped into the ordnance room and pulled out his journal.

He leafed through it and decided that it was time to send the information he'd collected to Major Sedgewick.

At dusk Leitis stood up from the bench and stretched. She was proud of the work she'd done so far, but she had a more pressing engagement at the moment. She smiled, anticipating seeing Ian.

Where did he stay all this time? There had been no talk of strangers in the glen. She looked in the direction of the fort. He had denied being one of the soldiers. Where, though, did he remain during the day?

She walked to the dresser and combed her hair, tying it back with her ribbon. She smoothed her hands over her skirt, brushed her shoes clean, and washed her face and hands.

Her mother had saved a bottle of precious scent, a gift from the Countess of Sherbourne. It was French and only worn on special occasions. Leitis would have used it tonight, had it not been destroyed in the fire. Or she might put flowers in her hair, but she doubted that Donald would allow her to wander through the glen, searching for the perfect harebell blossom.

She entered the priory slowly, trying to hide her anticipation and eagerness. What should she say to him? Her abandon the night before didn't feel shameful, encouraged as it was by love.

Loving was not something to suffer through, but to enjoy. Her fingers touched her lips, then stroked over her jaw to her throat. Her breasts felt heavy, tender. When he touched her, it was alchemy, as if her entire body were charmed.

She wanted to tell him how grateful she was for understanding her grief about leaving Gilmuir. And for bringing her memories of laughter and sunshine, of joy not easily summoned to this place and this time. For being a man who would help those in need, and for his kindness to an old woman, for his anger against injustice and cruelty.

What would happen now? A question she had not dared to ask. Would he come with them or remain behind? Would he leave Gilmuir once more or would he vanish, as he had all those many years ago?

The answers would either give her joy or sorrow. Perhaps it was better not to know, to only accept what she'd learned in this past year. No one was guaranteed a future, especially not in these turbulent times. Today was all they had and today must be enough.

Once, in this very place, she'd spied on him, later feeling only shame for the act. He and his mother had talked together and he'd confided in her. She had answered him with wisdom Leitis had never forgotten.

"It is good to have someone better than you," his mother had said.

"But I would like to be better at something," he had complained. "Fergus is better at fishing and James better at climbing, and Leitis can do everything else."

"How will you ever get better if you do not find yourself challenged?"

He'd not looked pleased at that remark. "So often?" he asked, and the countess had laughed. The sound trickled through the room like water falling over rocks. Leitis could not help but smile herself.

The countess' hand cupped her son's face and she bent down to place a kiss on his forehead. "You must simply try your best. That's all that matters. Comparing yourself to others does no good. Measure yourself against your own vision."

He'd gone on to be better at fishing than Fergus, and climbed as well as James. But she could always outrun him, she thought with a smile.

Her heart leapt when she saw a shadow. Ian leaned against one of the pillars that supported the arches, his gaze on the oncoming storm. The recent bad weather had passed them by last night, only to return with a vengeance.

To her disappointment, he still wore his mask. But she said nothing, knowing that he would dispense with it when he was ready, and not before.

"It looks to be fierce weather," he said, turning and smiling at her.

Sheets of rain drew a curtain between the glen and the loch. Gusts blew the storm closer to Gilmuir and Fort William, showering English fortress and Scottish castle alike.

She smiled, thinking that he had eased their meeting with such commonplace words.

"I'm used to the rain," she said.

"You would have to be, living at Gilmuir," he said, glancing at her. She stepped closer, placing her hand on his arm, needing to touch him.

"Where are we going tonight?"

"We're going to play highwaymen," he said, smiling. "Come with me and we'll ride through the Highlands, offering succor and safety to those who would come with us."

"And fetch Mary's sister?"

"And Dora's daughter," he said, nodding. "We'll pluck the brightest and the best and take them with us."

"And the old and the infirm," she added.

"The young and the weak," he said.

"Lead on," she said, "and I'll be your partner in revolt."

"Not revolt," he corrected, "but rescue."

She followed him to the center of the priory and to the entrance to the staircase. Soundlessly, he pulled the stone away, revealing a set of stairs just as black, just as steep as they had been a day earlier. But the journey was made easier both by practice and his presence and seemed to take no time at all.

At the base of the stairs, he bent and lit the lantern.

They stood at the cave entrance staring out at the storm. The cove acted as a chamber of echoes, so that the drumming sound of the rain beating against the loch was almost deafening. The black sky was pierced by a silvered bolt of lightning, a low and rumbling roll of thunder growling in approval of its display.

"It sounds as if God is English," she said, pulling back from the entrance, "and angry at us for what we're about to do."

He smiled, studying the storm.

"It's not wise to be on the water when there's lightning," she said. Her hand reached out and touched his arm, feeling the muscles beneath the fabric of his shirt.

"Have you another way of getting to the glen?" he asked, turning to her. "One that will not alert the troops at Fort William?"

She nodded. "I do," she confessed, "but I wouldn't use it today."

He stared at her, obviously surprised.

She pointed above them. "There's a track all around the island," she said. "I used it to escape from the Butcher once."

"A track? Where?"

"Around the cliffs," she said, and smiled at the look on his face. "It's wide enough not to be dangerous," she said. "If you're careful."

He shook his head, murmuring something she suspected wasn't the least complimentary.

She moved away slightly, leaning against the curved wall. Above her was the final portrait of Ionis's love. "I merely meant," she said, smiling back at the woman immortalized by a man's devotion, "that we should wait. Perhaps there is a way that we could occupy ourselves," she suggested. She closed her eyes. It was one thing to be daring in the darkness, quite another when he was looking at her with such interest.

"How?" he asked quietly, his voice low and slumberous.

She felt her cheeks warming. "Donald taught me a game," she said, "but I've no cards here."

"Nor am I in the mood for one of the games we played as children," he said.

She blinked open her eyes, looked at him. He was smiling, but the expression in his eyes was oddly wicked.

"Perhaps there is something else we could do," she said, studying the portraits above her. "Only to while away the time, of course." She felt absurdly breathless, as if she'd run the length of the glen. Her cheeks were heated; her heart beat so fiercely that it sounded louder than the rain.

He bent and extinguished the lantern, plunging them into darkness.

"I have an occupation in mind," he said. "A game of another sort."

"Do you?"

"It's a game in which there are two winners," he softly said.

"Are there?" she teased. "How can you be so certain?"

"I shall be very careful to ensure it," he said softly.

"Is it not necessary, first, to come closer?"

"In a moment," he said. She could tell by the sound of his voice that he hadn't moved.

"What did you like about last night, Leitis? What was the one thing that pleased you the most?"

Her body grew heated, embarrassment traveling from the top of her head to her feet. "Don't you know?" she asked, hedging.

"I want to hear it from you," he said, inflexible.

"There's more than one thing," she said, her hands fluttering in the air.

"Only one."

"When you kissed me," she said, then decided that was wrong. "No," she corrected, "when you held me." There was the other, too. "When you touched me," she whispered, the words difficult to speak. It was one thing to dream about him, or to recall those moments in the privacy of her mind, another to tell him.

"Only one," he said, moving closer. "When I touched you? You were shocked by it."

She nodded. "It was a very shocking thing."

"When I entered you?"

She nearly choked on her gasp. "Should you be saying such things, Ian?"

"Let me be the Raven tonight," he said. "A man of mystery. I could be anyone," he said. He reached out his hand and gently touched her face, found her lips, and traced them with one finger. "I could be your worst enemy, your most dreaded foe, a stranger," he whispered.

She turned toward his shadow. The storm raged above them, disapproval and censure in the sound of thunder. Despite herself, she felt a thrill of anticipation, something abandoned that curled inside her and stretched with new life.

"Would I want you to touch me?" she asked breathlessly.

"You couldn't help it," he said, his fingers brushing down her throat.

"I dislike feeling weak," she said.

He chuckled. "You never could be, Leitis. You love like you live, with ferocity and joy and complete abandon."

"Is that a bad thing?" she whispered.

"It's dangerous," he said, his voice deep. "It incites passion in a man who might wish to taste that life, experience it."

"Does it incite you? Even being a stranger? An enemy?"

He whispered against her lips. "An enemy who cannot help himself."

"I should weaken you somehow," she said. "If you were truly my adversary."

"Touch me," he urged. "That should accomplish your aim."

She smiled, charmed, amused, and a little anxious by his game. But she'd never resisted a dare in her life. Her hand reached out and flattened on his chest, crept lower until it hesitated at his waist. A streak of lightning flashed, illuminating the cave, and Ian. He wasn't smiling, nor were his eyes amused. Instead, his look pinned her in place, as if he were truly a stranger, an enemy, the Raven.

She pulled back her hand, but he retrieved it again, placing it on his chest.

"Shall I tell you what I liked?"

She said nothing. An assent would plunge her into wickedness, but she was too curious to deny him.

"When you screamed," he said. "I heard the sound in my dreams last night and woke hard with the thought of you."

She stepped back against the wall, her hand still held to his chest.

"I want to taste your nipples, Leitis. Feel them against my lips; stroke the softness of you as you grow wet for me. I want all of these things as anyone you deem me to be, friend or foe, lover or stranger."

She began to tremble. Not in fear, which might be more acceptable, but in some other emotion she'd never before felt, something dark and dangerous and abandoned.

"Then I've won," she said, her voice sounding hoarse.

"Not yet," he said, and pressed against her. She could feel the length of him, the firmness of his muscles, his strength.

She closed her eyes again, an act of surrender. "I remember how you felt," she said, placing her other hand on his chest. The tips of her fingers pressed against his shirt, traced the placket, and burrowed beneath to his skin. A sigh escaped her as she touched his bare skin, as if she had waited all this time for just this.

"And when you entered me," she admitted, the words a whisper as she stood on tiptoe to brush a kiss against his lips. His mouth was hot and hungry. His hands were suddenly everywhere, unlacing her dress, fumbling beneath her skirts, baring her in a wild flurry of fabric.

He smoothed his hands over her shoulders, down her arms, pushing her bodice open so quickly that she heard the stitches rip.

She didn't care. She had become someone frenzied, a person she barely recognized. She wanted to touch him, feel him, hold him in her arms, and kiss him so deeply that he couldn't speak. Render him as unsettled as she felt.

Passion required no tutelage, she discovered. No slow gaining of knowledge, no practice, nothing was necessary but the moment and the craving.

Her fingers unfastened his breeches, reached within them as if she'd done this before, as if she'd always been decadent. He was hard against her palms and so hot that he almost scorched her. A sound escaped him, a gasp, a moan, some note that echoed her own excitement.

He bent his head to kiss her, then followed that kiss with another. His mouth closed over her nipple and tugged gently. She clenched her fingers on his shoulders and arched her head back, captivated by the sensation that flowed through her.

More, please, more.

A thought she found herself whispering.

"Yes," he said, his voice guttural. He pushed aside her bodice, revealing her other breast, then kissed her as sweetly there. His fingers clutched at her skirts, burrowed beneath them. She felt his hand flatten on her thigh, then his fingers intruding between her thighs.

"More?" he asked roughly.

She nodded, but all he did was bend and kiss her throat, the tip of his tongue tracing a pattern against her pulse. She nodded again, but his hand remained where it was, cupping her gently but unmoving.

"Please," she finally said, turning her head, her hands reaching out to flatten against his cheeks. "Please," she whispered against his lips.

His thumb circled her softness, tenderly boring against a spot that made her gasp in surprise.

"Kiss me, Leitis," he said, and she did, infusing into that kiss heat and exhilaration, and all the various emotions she was experiencing at this moment.

Her pulse raced, her heartbeat so loud it vied with the thunder. She found herself being lowered to the sandy floor of the cave, her cushion the Raven.

He kissed her again and again until her lips learned his, until every one of his breaths felt like hers. Fingers flew in desperation, only at peace once they rested in curves and hollows. The planes of his chest, the hard length of him beneath a questing finger, the curve of his shoulders, his muscled arms, all of these places felt with the tips of her fingers and the tactile surface of her palms.

She bent and whispered against his lips. "Should an enemy be able to bring me such delight?" she asked faintly.

"Only if he loves you," he replied softly.

He pulled her atop him more firmly, slid slowly inside her, each movement he made making her wish to stretch this second further until it reached to infinity itself.

"My enemy," she gasped as he surged inside her.

"My love," he whispered.

The joy she felt was applauded by the roaring thunder, punctuated by flashes of lightning that illuminated the cave. The storm and his kiss muted her sounds of delight.

Long moments later, she roused and leaned up on her elbows. She wished she could see him, but the lightning had moved away with the thunder, now threatening the far hills.

"You have a great deal of experience in loving, Ian," she said.

He didn't speak for the longest time. "You were the first girl I kissed, Leitis MacRae," he finally said. "I've learned a bit since then."

She leaned down and kissed him tenderly. "I'd be just as pleased," she said softly, "if you don't learn any more."

"I've not yet shown you all I know, Leitis," he teased.

She sighed, only half joking. "I'll no doubt die of pleasure," she said.

"Better that than be hanged for sedition," he said soberly, sitting up. He folded his arms around her, helped her lace her dress in the dark. He did it quite well, she thought sourly, and wished his experience were not quite so extensive.

"Have you noticed that we have an affinity for caves?"

"I never notice anything," she said artlessly, "when you're around."

He bent and kissed her lightly.

"We should leave," he said, "now that the storm has passed. Both the one inside the cave and outside."

She smiled and reached up to cradle his face between her palms. "Ah, but Highland storms are never to be trusted, Raven. They'll come again soon enough."

Chapter 22

Her words were, unfortunately, prophetic. The storm had not moved on, only abated for the moment. He rowed across the cove to the shore, where his horse stood beneath a tree, patiently waiting in the drizzle.

Ian mounted and held out his arm for her. This time, however, he placed her behind him. She gripped his waist with both hands and laid her cheek against the middle of his back.

They traveled to the farthest place first, where Mary's sister lived. She was a sweet-faced woman with three boys, all below the age of ten. After Ian and Leitis explained that the people of Gilmuir were leaving, she asked only one question.

"Is it true that Mary's going with you?"

"It's true," Leitis said.

With that, the woman gathered up her belongings and left the cottage without looking back. The two youngest children were mounted on the stallion, while the oldest walked beside his mother, Leitis, and Ian.

The procession grew as they traveled back to Gilmuir.

The distance of the journey would be no great hardship to the young and able-bodied, but Leitis wondered how the older people would fare. Ian answered that question by striding to the summit of the tallest hill and breaking off a clump of heather. A moment later it was ablaze and he waved the smoky torch in an arc before stamping it out and returning to where they stood waiting.

A few moments later Leitis heard the sound of a vehicle approaching. She watched as a wagon, pulled by four sturdy-looking horses, passed between the rolling hills. The driver wore a mask similar to Ian's.

"Borrowed from the English, I presume?" she asked, amused.

Ian turned in her direction. "They were not using it," he said, his voice tinged with humor.

She didn't ask about the man who accompanied him, nor about the mask he wore. There were some things, perhaps, that she should not know, and he would not tell her.

The younger children, silent in their bemusement, clambered into the back of the wagon, as the older people were helped up. Grown women, some of childbearing years, some older, all of them aged by the harshness of the previous year, walked beside the wagon. There were only two men at an age to have been in the rebellion. One was blinded in one eye and the other had lost an arm. But they both refused the wagon and walked beside the women.

A ragtag group of refugees, armed with only their will and their courage. She had never felt more proud to be a Scot than at this moment.

They stopped at a clachan Leitis recognized. Ian lit a lantern stored in the back of the wagon, closing all but one of its shutters, then walked to the cottage and knocked softly on the door.

The old woman who had given Leitis the wool answered, her braid draped over one shoulder.

"I've come to offer you a new home," Ian said. "A place to live where you'll be safe," he said.

"I am safe enough here," she said calmly.

"You're not safe where there are English," Leitis said, walking to stand at Ian's side.

"The English can do nothing further to hurt me, child," she said, smiling gently.

"They can starve you out," Leitis said. "Or burn your village."

"Whatever will happen will happen," she said quietly. "I have lived here all my life; I'll not leave now. Who would tend to the graves of my loved ones? The English?" She smiled at both of them. "There must be a sentinel," she said, "for the past."

"There is the ship coming," Ian said in an effort to persuade her. "It will take you wherever you wish to go."

She smiled at him gently. "Unless it can fly to heaven, young sir, I'm content enough here. There are many here and in the neighboring glens who will leave. Enough to fill your ship. Take them."

She tilted back her head and surveyed him with kind eyes. "You do as you must," she said. "And may God go with you. But not I."

She reached up and touched his face, where the mask ended at the curve of his cheek.

Leitis thought for a moment that he would argue further, but the old woman placed her fingers against his lips, silencing any subsequent protest.

"We should be going," Leitis said, but Ian only nodded. She had a feeling that the older woman's decision disturbed him greatly.

He leaned over and placed a gentle kiss upon her withered cheek, inducing a smile of delight.

"Be well," he said.

She looked up at him with suddenly somber eyes. "You are the one who should be on guard," she said.

Ian was quiet as they left her cottage. He studied the crofters' huts, lost in thought.

"If she does not wish to come," Leitis said gently, "there is nothing you can do to persuade her."

"Yes, I know," he said. "But I do not think her long for the world."

"You cannot save them all."

"I know," he said somberly. "But it does not mean I shouldn't try."

"Do you suppose that people will wonder one day what happened to us?" she asked, looking around her. There was a mist forming over the ground, as if the clouds rose from the grass itself. Far away, a night bird called, and the echo of its voice was oddly plaintive.

This land, harsh and wild and unearthly beautiful, would always be inhabited by dreams and wishes and memories of the people who had lived here.

"Will our lives be better?" she asked, almost desperate that it would be so.

"Yes," Ian said shortly. "Life is always preferable to death."

Their procession now numbered twenty, and as

they passed through clachan after clachan, the word spread.

"Are you leaving, then?" one old man asked, peering out of his cottage.

Another man seated in the back of the wagon answered him. "We're leaving the English behind before they can do to us what they've done to Scotland."

Before they'd passed through the village, they'd acquired another émigré.

The journey back to Gilmuir took them three times as long as it would have on horseback. The wagon needed to follow a well-worn track. Otherwise, it would have sunk into the grass due to its weight.

The storm, undaunted by its earlier display of bravado, returned, its arrival announced by a grumble of thunder.

A child began to cry in fright even as his mother shushed him.

There was no place to seek sanctuary, and the forest was a more dangerous refuge than being out in the open.

Leitis and the others followed silently behind the wagon in pairs. It was a few minutes later when she realized something was wrong. The wagon, filled with people, was becoming mired in the mud.

She walked to where Ian stood inspecting one wheel. She couldn't see what he was looking at, but she knew well enough that a wagon wheel could snap under this pressure.

"What should we do?"

"We can carry the children and leave the older people to ride," Ian said, moving around to the rear of the wagon.

The rain came in earnest then, a torrent that soaked

through their clothes quickly and muted speech with its sound.

Leitis joined Ian at the rear of the wagon, holding out her arms for a small girl no more than five. The child shied away, then changed her mind a second later when lightning struck nearby. She nearly catapulted herself into Leitis's arms. She set the little girl down gently before helping Ian lift another child to the ground. Only when the wagon was nearly empty, its only occupants an elderly man and a woman of similar age, could they push the wagon free of the mud.

Leitis reached out her arms for the little girl once more, wishing she had a shawl to shield her from the rain. They were all drenched, miserable, and chilled by the wind that accompanied the storm.

They began to walk, to slog through the mud as best they could, each adult holding a child. Ian carried a small boy in each arm, both children winding an arm around his neck, instantly companionable.

It could be that some of the sons and daughters of Scotland had not seen a grown man in a while, their homes being isolated and their kin not returning from the war with England. The twin boys he held might well have never felt the touch of a father's hand or heard a man's voice speak to them in a low and comforting tone.

The sound of the thunder was a blessing in a peculiar way. There was no danger of the soldiers at Fort William hearing them. Nothing could vie with the storm, not even the children's startled cries when lightning came too close.

A sizzling sound preceded the boom of thunder as a tree was struck by lightning. In seconds it became an arrow of white flame from its roots to the top branches, and seemed to shudder before crashing to the ground.

The storm was ominously quiet for a moment as if in homage to its own destruction.

Leitis clapped a hand over the little girl's ear, pressed her closer to her chest, and continued to walk.

Gilmuir suddenly emerged from the darkness, a darker cloud on the horizon. A mile, then, no more than that, and they would be warm and dry. A thought she held on to with determination, since the remainder of the journey was uphill.

Her legs ached with the effort of walking through the mud. The little girl, who had tearfully confided that her name was Annie, had long since wrapped her arms around her neck and pressed her face against Leitis's throat, her soft breathing an oddly comforting counterpart to the rain and thunder.

Leitis's skirts were sodden, mud dragging at the hem. She had never felt as wet or as tired.

When she had thought of spiting the English, of engaging in feats of rebellion, she'd imagined something other than this. The courage needed now was simply that of endurance. All she needed to do was place one foot in front of the other, and ignore the mud clinging to her ankles and shoes, wipe her face of the rain, and murmur reassuring words to the frightened child in her arms. Not great deeds, only forbearance.

Was that the true meaning of courage, then? Knowing that she could not take another step but somehow finding the fortitude to do it? Small acts strung together. If that was what courage was, then the Scots had it in abundance. Tenacity, too. The sheer will to live, and to prosper despite the circumstances.

She knew then that they would do well, wherever they chose to live, because the will was in them to do so. But it made her ache for her country that its people were leaving. This was the greatest sin to lay at the feet of the English. Not that they had won, or even that they acted as victors, but that the nature of their conquering would alter a nation.

As if they heard them coming through the storm, the village of Gilmuir began to awaken. One by one the cottage doors opened to reveal a soft spill of welcoming light. Dora cried out and reached for the little girl in Leitis's arms. Leitis surrendered the child to the older woman, averting her eyes when Dora began to cry in relief.

Leitis went back into the night, guided the child's mother and brother into Dora's cottage.

The other villagers were standing at their doorways, each welcoming a family group. Ian had relinquished the two little boys in his arms to their mother, who was being tearfully welcomed to Ada's home.

An old woman approached Ian, reached up, and patted his chest. He looked startled, even more so when she gestured him to come closer. He bent low and she kissed him smartly on the mouth.

Leitis thought the sight of Ian surprised into smiling was a memory to recall forever.

He'd had love and protection all his life, and even in his darkest hour, when he learned of his mother's death, Ian had a home and a parent to welcome him. The children he surrendered to their aunt had only an uncertain future and no father.

He turned and walked back to Leitis. His approach was all it took for her to smile up at him, welcome in her look.

Ian wished, in a purely selfish way, that there were

limits to her character. But she had wordlessly held
out her arms for a frightened child, and uncomplain-
ingly traveled back to Gilmuir on foot.

She'd overwhelmed him with her passion and
humbled him with her courage. She made him laugh,
yet had the capacity to irritate and infuriate him. A
woman of fascinating dimensions.

He should have told her from the beginning who
he was. Another thought countered that one. If he
had told her, she never would have believed he was
sincere in wishing to help the people of Gilmuir. She
would have repudiated him based on his reputation
alone.

Once he had been glad of his sobriquet. It had
aided him to be called the Butcher of Inverness. Now
he cursed the name and the rumors that accompanied it.

He had fallen in love with Leitis as a boy, held her
in his arms, and loved her. If he told her the truth, he
might lose her. Not an inducement for honesty, he
thought wryly.

In one way he was the young boy tied to Gilmuir by
bonds of memory and blood. Yet, at the same time, he
was an English colonel trained in obedience and duty.

Time was running out for him, both in his masquerade and in this venture. The ship should be here
soon, and with it another choice to make.

"We should be heading back," he said.

Leitis said nothing, only placed her hand on his
arm and walked with him to his horse.

Hamish MacRae stood in his doorway, looking out
at the scene before him. You'd think all these people
would have a notion of the time, he thought. A body
wished to rest at night and not have to use his pillow
to muffle shouts and cries and the sound of tears.

Dora was crying, and that fool Malcolm was bouncing up and down like a thistle in a brisk wind. And Mary, with her soft smiles, was weeping so hard her face was red with it.

And his niece? She was the worst of all, looking after a man with her heart in her eyes, smiling in that soft way that a woman does when she is in love. A masked man, at that.

If he was Ian MacRae, why didn't he bare his face like an honest man?

And why was she here at all? It didn't make sense that the Butcher would choose her to be his hostage and then allow her to slip from Gilmuir so easily.

He narrowed his eyes and studied the man in the mask.

The storm, having vented its fury for the last time, moved away, the lightning darting from cloud to cloud to occasionally touch the summit of a hill. The world was gray and black with flashes of light, an ethereal scene and one strangely muted.

Ian and Leitis climbed the stairs in the same serenity, the moment hushed and almost sad.

"Will you come for me tomorrow?" she asked, when they stood in the priory once more.

"No," he said shortly.

She stepped closer to him, placed her hand on his arm. "When will I see you again?"

He covered her hand with his before stepping back into the shadows. "I'll get word to you when the ship arrives," he said, and slipped into the staircase.

Clutching her arms around her waist, she watched as he disappeared. As the moments lengthened, she remained there, feeling a sense of loss so strong that her chest felt hollow. She didn't wish to return to the laird's chamber. Instead, she wanted to stand here where the memory of him lingered even now. Here, where there was a hint of him.

Please don't go. The plea was in vain, because he'd already left her.

Chapter 23

Leitis slept heavily, waking with a question. When would she see him again?

Hours? Days? The waiting would be endless; the delay would feel interminable.

She would simply have to endure it.

Rising from the bed, she dressed. Her dress was still damp from the storm, but her shoes were in worse condition. Scraping the mud from them was no easy task.

The maneuvers of the soldiers captured her attention for a few moments, the sound of booted feet on packed earth so routine that it was almost lulling. They were, she thought, watching them march to the land bridge and back, a sight to inspire caution. All those red-coated men marching in a precise line, looking neither right nor left.

She moved to the loom, began to work, grateful for the occupation. The movements of her fingers were accompanied by errant thoughts. A black thread represented Ian as the Raven, a crimson one for the Butcher. And she was the white thread, all of them as entwined as the MacRae plaid. An odd thought, one that stilled her, the heels of her hands resting on the frame of the loom, her gaze pinned to the pattern beneath her fingers. The Butcher and the Raven? Where had that thought come from?

The colonel knew about the cave and Donald had been conveniently absent when she needed him to be. In addition, the English soldiers had been almost comically inept in following the provision wagon, allowing them to easily escape.

All things could be explained away. Coincidences, only that. The Butcher of Inverness would have been pleased to kill a Scot, not aid one.

Then why had he looked so stricken that night when he'd kissed her in his dream?

She shook her head, pushing those troubling thoughts away, and sat looking at the tartan, inspecting her work critically. The quality of the wool was important, as was the type of weather when the initial threads were tightened. Too much rain and the weave looked almost swollen, with gaps through the finished material. If the air was too dry, the wool felt almost scratchy to the touch.

Donald announced his appearance with a knock and a sneeze.

She glanced at him as he walked into the room. He didn't look well, she thought, with his flushed cheeks and glittering eyes. He placed the tray containing her noon meal on the table and backed away.

"Are you ill, Donald?"

He shook his head at the same time he sneezed again.

Ever since he'd been attending to the colonel's duties he'd been more reticent with her, their earlier camaraderie tucked beneath a newfound formality.

At the door he turned, his hand on the latch. "Would you like a bath, miss? The tub's just sitting there and I don't mind fetching the water."

"You should be in bed, Donald, not offering to make yourself more work."

"I'd just as soon be on my feet, miss," he said with a half smile.

"It's a bother," she said, shaking her head.

"I'd be pleased to do it," he answered.

She hesitated. "Then I'd be pleased, too," she said, capitulating. It was too much of a temptation.

He left, only to return a little while later with his contingent of helpers and the copper tub. Once it was filled, she took the precaution of placing a chair in front of the door to ensure her privacy before undressing.

Why did it feel, she wondered as she slipped into the tub, as if all the problems in the world could be solved with a little hot water? She smiled at herself, began to use the soap Donald had brought. It stung her skin, but it was a petty annoyance against the greater pleasure of being clean.

She leaned her head against the back of the tub, closed her eyes, and simply enjoyed the hot water. The small moments in life are just as important as the tragedies and blessings, she thought. The completion of a complicated pattern on her loom, the pleasure of eating until she was full, this private moment in a deep bath, they were all to be savored in their way.

She tried not to think of Ian or remember the loving that they'd shared. Those moments would be remembered a little at a time like a bit of rare sweetness.

Would he come with her? He'd never said, and she had not asked. There was a sense of reserve about him still, as if he held parts of himself aloof.

What about Hamish? Was he going to change his mind or continue to be stubborn until the day they sailed away, leaving him behind?

Instead of asking questions that could not be answered at the moment, she occupied herself with washing her hair and rinsing it with the clean water Donald had provided.

Standing, she sluiced water over her body, then stepped carefully from the tub, reaching for the toweling. Frowning, she looked at her dress. She couldn't bear to don such a filthy garment after her bath. She knelt before the tub, used the barracks soap, and began to scrub her dress and her shift.

She moved the chair, stretched her shift across it, and covered it with her dress. Moving to the dresser, she picked up a comb Donald had found for her and sat on the bed.

When the knock came, she pulled the coverlet up to her neck, ensuring that she was modest. She called out a greeting to Donald and heard his boots sounding hollow on the wooden floor.

She bent and began to comb through the tangles, wishing she had some of Dora's sweet flowery oil for her hair.

"I regret I timed my visit too late to view you in your bath."

Her head jerked up, the comb snared as she stared at the colonel. He was impeccably attired, his crimson coat almost too bright in this room filled with sunlight. The brilliant white of the ruffles of his shirt was a testament to Donald's perseverance, as was the shine of his tan boots. He wore the uniform of his country well, and assumed the power of it equally successfully.

She held on to the edge of the coverlet with one hand while she disentangled the comb with the other.

Her cheeks warmed as he continued to stare at her. "Then perhaps the timing favored me," she said.

He smiled but said nothing. She wished he wouldn't smile so, or study her so directly with that unflinching gaze of his. It felt, sometimes, as if he knew all her secrets, divined her thoughts.

If only he looked like Sedgewick. But he was so handsome that sometimes it took her breath away just to see him.

She looked away from him, uncomfortable with her thoughts.

"I need nothing," she said. "If that is why you're here."

"No," he said soberly, "you do not."

She glanced at him, startled.

He strode toward her, and before she realized what he would do, touched the base of her neck, so tenderly that it startled her. She looked down, the sight of his gloved hand against her skin disturbing. His fingers traced the pattern of a red mark where Ian's beard had scraped her. She'd not noticed at the time, but now it seemed a brand.

She jerked up the coverlet, pushing his hand away.

"You've been injured," he said in a low voice.

Only by passion, a confession she would not utter to him.

He said nothing further, only walked toward the door.

"Why do they call you Butcher?" she asked suddenly.

He spun around and stared at her. The question obviously startled him as much as it had her.

"It is easier to label one man," he answered, "than to fault the many."

She remained silent, wondering if he would continue.

"There were five judges in Inverness," he said finally. "Each of whom was given the task of adjudicating the fates of the men who came before them."

"Were you one of them?"

He shook his head. "I was given the responsibility of seeing that their orders were carried out."

"The Crown's executioner," she said faintly. It was, if anything, worse than she'd imagined.

"If you wish," he said, placing his hand on the latch. He stared at the door as if the iron-banded oak held a scene of some great interest. "There were those who showed compassion, Leitis," he said soberly. "But it was dangerous to do so. Cumberland executed nearly forty English soldiers for the sin of showing kindness."

"But not you, of course."

He turned and faced her. "Be careful, Leitis, or your loathing of the English will become as strong as Cumberland's hatred of the Scots," he said.

Her stomach clenched at the near insult.

"You will become as blinded as he by it," he added.

She did not hate him. The English, yes. But not the man standing in front of her, his brown eyes never leaving hers. From the very beginning he'd been different.

She stood, clutching the coverlet around her. "I don't know who you are," she said. "But I do know what you've done, at least since you've been at Gilmuir. You saved my village and protected me. What I don't know is why." A confession. She was confused by him, intrigued in a way she felt was dangerous.

"Have you become so cynical that you must find a reason behind every action, Leitis?"

"Perhaps," she admitted. Or her curiosity might have been born of her dawning respect for him, and the feeling that they knew each other better than their new civility indicated.

He came and stood in front of her, reaching out one hand to touch her damp hair. It curled riotously after it had been washed and seemed to trap his fingers.

"What should I tell you?" he said in a voice barely above a whisper. "That you fascinated me from the beginning? That a beautiful woman with a core of strength and an awesome courage altered me? I would have protected you if you'd been an old tooth-less hag. But I would not have, perhaps, begun to dream of you at night instead of the nightmares I've had for months."

He had dreamed of her. She swallowed heavily, gripping the coverlet with trembling fingers.

The voice of her conscience whispered a harsh chastisement. What sort of woman loves one man and grows warm at the words of another?

She moved away from him, disturbed. Was this sudden interest in him because she was new to passion? Had something dormant and dangerous in her nature been awakened since she discovered that the touch of a man's hands on her could make her body bow in delight?

He came and stood behind her, placing his hands on her shoulders, pushing the coverlet aside until she felt the leather of his gloves on her skin.

He bent and whispered against her neck. "See me as who I am, Leitis. Not as you think I should be."

"Who are you?" she asked, hearing the quavering of her voice and wondering at it. She had asked the same question of Ian that first night in the priory. But neither he nor the colonel answered her.

Instead he slowly turned her, looked down at her face, before pulling her closer. "Please don't kiss me," she said, almost desperately.

He wrapped his arms around her, placing his hand on the back of her head, holding her gently against his chest. She felt as if she might weep, so poignant was this moment, so charged with unspoken emotion. She wanted his kiss and feared it. Wanted to know him while loathing her own duplicity. With her eyes closed, she could almost pretend he was Ian. And it was ridiculously easy to do so.

Both of the men in her life had a capacity for tenderness, were of the same height, spoke in a voice that was similar.

She pulled the coverlet closer, abruptly conscious that it alone covered her nakedness. Stepping back, she moved away from him, the thoughts coming fast one on the other.

He spoke a different language, but his voice was the same. Ian knew English as well as Gaelic. He wore a mask, yet his smile was identical to the colonel's. So, too, the look in his eyes. He commanded with ease, and formulated battle strategy even in the exodus of the villagers.

A foolishness, to think them alike. She loved Ian with a breathless wonder, while this man only made her cautious.

Her hands felt cold, her lips dry. She was wrong. She had to be. The two men could not be the same. She could not love the Butcher of Inverness.

"Who are you?" she asked again, taking another step away from him.

"Whoever you wish me to be," he said enigmatically. His face changed, falling into more severe lines, as if he wore a mask of flesh.

"Please leave," she said, the words sounding choked.

His smile looked oddly sad, but he left the room, leaving her to stare at the closed door.

Captain Thomas Henry Harrison stood before the home of Alison Fulton, experiencing a fear greater than any he'd ever felt. Even before a battle he'd not been this uncertain. War, in fact, seemed easier than the task he'd given himself.

He flicked a piece of lint from his sleeve, pulled at his tunic, arched his neck until his collar felt as if it weren't strangling him.

He lifted his hand to the brass knocker, then dropped it again, stepping back.

The house was square-built of red brick on a crowded Inverness street. Four small windows faced him, their panes of thick watery glass set in white frames. There were flowers in the tiny beds on either side of the front door. A sign of occupation, as was the gray smoke that curled against the night sky.

He forced himself to take the step again, raising his hand and gripping the knocker. It struck the brass plate hollowly, surely not loud enough to be heard. His next knock was much harder, but was still left unanswered.

Stepping back, he straightened his tunic again, bent, and brushed a speck of imaginary dust from his boots. He told himself that it would be best to leave now, return to Fort William. His errand was done, the ship hired. There was nothing to keep him in Inverness.

He flattened his palm against the painted white door in farewell. It opened, and for a moment he wondered if he'd pushed it ajar. But no, there was her beloved face, looking as startled as he felt.

"Alison?" he asked, standing at attention.

"Thomas?" she whispered, a smile coming to her face.

"You look well," he said. An understatement, he thought. She was still unearthly beautiful, with her golden hair and light green eyes.

"It's been months, Thomas," she said, frowning at him. "Months, Thomas," she admonished him again. "And no word. Not a letter, nothing. You might have come sooner."

He blinked at her, stunned.

She reached out and gripped his arm. The top of her head only came to his shoulder, but she was strong enough to pull him to her. Standing on tiptoe, she fixed an irritated look on him.

"You'll not get away again, dearest Thomas," she said.

And to his utter and stunned delight proceeded to kiss him.

Chapter 24

There was no reason to see Leitis. A warning that Alec gave himself during the next two weeks, his resolve weakening as each day passed.

He was, he thought with some amusement, no wiser than a young boy experiencing his first love, uncertain and delighted, terrified and joyous.

There wasn't one remark she'd made or one laugh she'd uttered that he didn't recall with perfect clarity. And every moment of those times they'd loved lingered in his mind in the moments before sleep, before waking, and the seconds between each task and each duty.

He had marked her, the memory of the discovery vivid and fresh in his mind. She'd sat wrapped in her cocoon of coverlet and he'd touched her with a delicate stroke of his finger. The look on her face, startled and reproving, was a caution to him as strong as words. It was all too evident that she might love the Raven, but she still hated the Butcher.

And it was just as clear that she was refusing to accept his identity. The clues were there, but his masquerade functioned only because she wished it to remain in place. The denial was a bulwark against a greater truth—that he was English and a soldier and a man rumored to be a monster.

For the most part, he was able to occupy himself with those mundane and necessary tasks that fell to the colonel of the regiment. He inspected Lieutenant Castleton's alterations in the stores and approved the changes, sent Captains Wilmot and Monroe out on patrol if, for no other reason than to give them experience in command.

Today he'd had the task of a tribunal, adjudicating those offenses that required his attention.

"Have you anything to say for yourself?" he asked the two men who stood before the table.

"No, sir," the first one said.

"I wouldn't have struck him with the bottle, sir, if he'd not said something about my Sally," the second one responded.

"It's a good thing you chose not to demonstrate your irritation on duty," Alec said sternly. "The punishment for such a lapse is flogging."

Both men looked suitably chastised, even more so at the amount of the fine he levied on them.

A second miscreant had been discovered cheating at dice. Honor was important in a military institution. Even more important was the fact that a man's companions needed to trust him. In battle, teamwork was not only necessary, it might mean survival.

"Is this accusation correct?" he asked the man. To his credit, the soldier did not deny it.

"You'll surrender your next month's wages to your companions in the game," he said. "In addition, your ration of rum is forfeited for that time."

A lesson the man was sure to remember the next time he was tempted to cheat. Military discipline was not an assumption; it was a requirement.

An irony, that the man who levied punishment on these men was guilty of more heinous crimes.

Harrison entered the room at that moment, his hands wrapped around a parcel. Alec listened with half an ear to other infractions, impatient to speak with his adjutant. The journey had been accomplished faster than he'd expected, but there was a look on Harrison's face that concerned him.

Alec rendered judgment and stood, signaling an end to the tribunal. He strode through the officers and men to where Harrison stood.

"Walk with me," he said.

Harrison nodded, followed him out of Fort William, around the courtyard, and into the open space between the fortress and the ruins of Gilmuir. A place where they were certain not to be overheard. Especially by Lieutenant Armstrong, whose endless toadying concealed too intrusive a nature.

Glancing toward the old building had become second nature to him these past days, especially his study of the abutment that housed the laird's chamber. Did Leitis spend the time weaving? An occupation not dissimilar to his duties, in that it kept the hands occupied while the mind roamed free.

He wanted to be with her, either as Ian or the colonel. And if that were not enough a clue to his insanity, he wanted to confess all his sins to her. Have her look at him in that cool, measured way of hers. Even her disapproval was preferable to her absence.

"The ship is here, sir," Harrison said in the silence.

Alec glanced at him, surprised. "So soon?"

"The bonus I promised the captain was an inducement to his haste," Harrison said, his face somber. He handed him the parcel in his hands. "I hope you approve, sir. Alison had it made by her dressmaker." Harrison had only been gone a week.

Alec smiled. "So you did see her?"

Harrison nodded, then grinned. "I did. I need to talk to you about that. But first there's a small difficulty, Colonel. The captain refuses to travel through the rocks without a pilot."

"I'm the only one who's made the journey, Harrison," Alec said.

The other man nodded.

"We have time enough before dark," Alec said, scanning the sky. "If Armstrong asks, make the story you tell him plausible. I agree with your assessment. The man is forever watching me."

"He's too loyal to Sedgewick," Harrison said roughly.

Alec smiled. "However inconvenient that is, I cannot fault the man for it. Loyalty is what has kept me alive."

Ardersier was a barren promontory that reminded Matthew Sedgewick of Gilmuir. The land jutted out into the Moray Firth, and was overshadowed by hills a short distance away. The lie of the land here provided for both sea and landward defenses, similar to the location on which he'd built Fort William.

The proposed new fort was in Sedgewick's patrol area, almost an omen for this errand since he'd discovered that General Wescott was in attendance, overseeing the architect's work.

He'd never visited Fort William before, but then that structure was dwarfed beneath the proposed fortification that would employ over nine hundred men in its construction. Sedgewick glanced down at the plans in front of him, amazed at the size of Fort George.

The general would be covered in glory for this task while his own efforts had never been remarked upon, nor rewarded. He had built Fort William in less than a year, using the talent of only one architect and a handful of men with building skills. In the main the fortress had been constructed with inexperienced troops. But not one person had commended him on his accomplishment. Instead, the army had turned Fort William over to Colonel Landers.

The general's temporary quarters were not sumptuous, but neither were they ascetic. The room boasted two windows, one facing the firth and the other the landward side. The large bed pushed against the wall looked too substantial to be a campaigner's. Sedgewick doubted if it disassembled quickly for ease of transport. Nor did the other furniture in the room have the look of having been carried in a wagon from post to post.

Stalks of heather were arranged in a tall blue vase on the bureau, and stretched across a chair was a length of plaid, one patterned in blocks of blue and green.

It appeared as if the general had gone native.

"I was informed that this visit was of an urgent nature, Major Sedgewick," the general said, entering the room.

Sedgewick spun around, facing the general and standing at attention. Wescott was an older man, but one with a robust physique. His hair had whitened, but only at the temples, the rest of it thickly brown and tied at the back of his neck. His face was clean-shaven, his hazel eyes deeply wrinkled at their corners.

"State your business, Major Sedgewick, but most importantly why you felt it necessary to jump the chain of command so summarily." Wescott sat behind his desk frowning up at him.

"I have reason to believe, sir, that Colonel Landers might be harboring a traitor."

"That is quite a charge you are leveling against your commanding officer, Sedgewick." General Wescott sat back in his chair, steepled his fingers, and studied him intently. His expression was dispassionate, but his eyes held irritation. Moments passed, each one measured by the icy shivers down Sedgewick's back.

"I understand that, sir," he said finally. "But I feel very strongly that Colonel Landers's actions should be investigated further."

He bent forward and placed Armstrong's journal on the general's desk.

"I took the precaution, sir, of leaving a trusted man with the colonel and asking him to impart to me anything of a suspicious nature."

"Why would you do that, Major?" Wescott asked.

"On the first day of his command, sir," Sedgewick said stiffly, "Colonel Landers showed his partiality to the Scots. He interrupted my efforts to find a piper in the area, a man known for flaunting both the Dress and Disarming Acts."

"Go on," Wescott said slowly.

Sedgewick pushed the journal across the desk before resuming his stance. "I believe, sir, that Lieutenant Armstrong's notations might be of interest to you."

General Wescott motioned for him to continue.

"There are rumors throughout the glen, sir, of a man calling himself the Raven. He has stolen from our troops in order to supply the Scots and acted in a way that can only be called rebellious. Colonel Landers has made no attempt to capture this man."

"Is this all your information?" Wescott asked sharply.

"No, sir," Sedgewick said. "He's taken a Scots woman as his whore and treats her very well, according to my sources."

"Have you ever seen combat on a foreign shore, Major Sedgewick?" Wescott asked. He tapped his fingers on the surface of his desk, his gaze fixed purposely on him.

"I have not had that privilege, sir," he answered.

"Then you will understand when you do . . . if you do . . . that soldiers take comfort where they can find it. I cannot fault the colonel for that sin." A moment later, he continued, "Cumberland himself has taken an interest in Colonel Landers, Major. You've not chosen your target wisely. Did you know that Landers is the heir to an earldom?"

Sedgewick shook his head. "No, sir, I didn't."

"I suggest, Major," General Wescott said sternly, "that you investigate a little further before you are so quick to accuse. You have an exemplary record, and I would hate to see it tarnished because of your envy."

Wescott stood. "However, because there are certain aspects to your report that I find troubling, my men and I will accompany you back to Fort William. But only to investigate your claims."

Major Sedgewick nodded, pleased. It was exactly what he'd wanted.

* * *

Alec dismounted, studied the left rear hoof of his horse and swore softly. The stallion was one of his favorites, even though he'd vowed not to become attached to the horses that served him. He'd lost too many animals in battle to deliberately establish a bond, which is why he never named his mounts.

It was all too clear, however, that this animal was lame. Alec stared ahead, knowing from his previous patrols that the lake was not far.

"A foolish idea to delay. Don't you think?" he asked his horse.

The stallion tossed his head as if amused.

"You'll have to take him back to the fort," Alec said, turning to Harrison.

"Why not take my horse, sir?"

"Because it would hardly be fair to make you walk all the way back to Fort William, Harrison. And I cannot postpone moving the ship into the cove until tomorrow."

"Are you certain, sir?" Harrison asked, his face creased with worry.

Alec nodded, smiling. "Emphatically so, Harrison." Once the ship was in the cove he would simply use the secret staircase to return to Fort William.

Harrison said nothing further as Alec turned and began walking toward Loch Euliss.

When her shoulders began to ache, Leitis halted her work on the tartan, stood, and stretched.

She straightened the room, although it had not been mussed, and settled the chairs around the table differently. She trimmed the wicks of the candles, then counted the floorboards, amusing herself with the silliness of that occupation.

The MacRae plaid, as difficult as it was, had captured her attention these last few days. She'd vowed not to think of the colonel or Ian, or the impending departure from Gilmuir. But when she wasn't working, her mind flooded with thoughts and questions.

Was she as guilty as Cumberland of undiscerning hatred? She wished to be nothing like the duke, but to accomplish that, she would have to show compassion, pity, and kindness. She had grudgingly become fond of Donald, but had no other contact with the soldiers. Except the colonel.

Had she wronged him? It felt, somehow, as if she had. That look he'd given her the last time she'd seen him reflected a strange disappointment, as if he'd expected more of her.

He'd killed her countrymen.

And saved a village.

He'd promised he would not seek out Hamish.

And kept that vow.

The knock of the door was a welcome reprieve from her thoughts. She opened it to find Donald standing there, his arms filled with a package wrapped in paper and string.

"I've a present for you, miss," he said, smiling. "From the colonel. He thought as how you might like another dress to wear."

She could only stare at Donald, taking the package from him in a daze. He walked away, whistling.

The colonel had given her a dress.

Placing the parcel on the table, she untied the string carefully, parted the paper. Inside was a soft blue garment, the bodice adorned with embroidered flowers in shades of yellow.

She'd never seen anything so lovely.

Closing the door, she removed her dress and replaced it with the colonel's gift. It fit almost perfectly, being only a little loose in the waist. She twirled, watching as the skirt billowed up around her.

A few weeks ago she would have returned the gift. Today, however, she was more practical than prideful.

He'd given her a dress. Smiling, she shook her head. Once again he had confused her.

Leaving the door open behind her, she walked into the courtyard, staring up at the sky. The afternoon was waning, the blue sky darkening in slow degrees.

She wrapped her arms around her waist, staring out at the land encircling Gilmuir. A faint blue mist hung over the landscape, darkening the green grass of the glen and making the mountain crags appear veiled.

She missed Ian. She wanted to touch him again, to assure herself he was real and not someone she'd imagined.

She walked through the archway to the priory. How many times had she done this in the last few days? A vigil she kept as if to lure Ian to her.

The breeze blew through the structure, an oddly sad sound. She'd never noticed it before. Why did she do so now? Was it because she was beginning to bid this place farewell in her heart? Or because she wasn't certain who, exactly, she loved?

She brushed a spot on the floor clean and sat against the west wall, staring out at the loch.

Alec had no more than a mile to walk before coming to the lake. Nor was the ship difficult to find. It sat close to shore like a fat duck in full plumage, its wings ivory-colored sails.

He signaled and a short time later a small boat was lowered, the man inside it rowing toward him with long, casual strokes.

Alec stood on the shoreline, waiting. The fading sun tinted the water silver and made the lake a curious mirror in which to view himself.

He was tall, the better to be seen upon a horse, Cumberland always said. His eyes were brown, his hair black, and his features unremarkable. A man like so many others, nothing glaring about his appearance, no clue as to his attributes or flaws.

His tailor had fashioned his uniform so that it fit well. Cumberland had ordered that none of his troops should have short hair. Consequently, Alec tied his back in a ribbon. He wore the insignia of his regiment and the special badge on his waistcoat that indicated that he'd been decorated by the Duke of Cumberland. An irritation, to be forced to wear a memento from a man he so despised, but it might have caused comment if he had discarded it.

There was nothing about him to indicate that he, Alec John Landers, was different from the men he commanded. Nor was there a hint that the man outfitted in the garb of soldier was engaged in acts of treason. Or that he didn't regret what he'd done either at Inverness or here.

The boat approached the shoreline. "Signore Landers?" the man at the oars asked, his voice heavily accented.

Alec nodded, stepping into the skiff.

"The captain expected you much earlier," the sailor said with a grin.

"I expected to be here much earlier," Alec conceded.

Reaching the ship, he climbed the rope ladder, thinking that he had been wise, indeed, as a youth to choose to purchase a commission in the army rather than to serve in His Majesty's Navy. Everything about a ship appeared insubstantial to him, and this vessel was no different, bobbing in the strong lake current like a cork.

Captain Braddock was a short, stout man with a clean-shaven round face accented by pink cheeks and a tightly pursed mouth. His attire, while unremarkable, was immaculate; a deep blue coat with wide cuffs, a white shirt with few frills, and buff breeches. The fact that his clothing was orderly, as was the deck of the ship, was a welcome sign. A man who was lax in his habits and his discipline was not a good companion in secrecy.

"We've a little light left," the captain said in greeting. "And you've practice in navigating this cove?" he asked with some reservation.

"I've traversed the necklace of rocks a few times, Captain," he said honestly. "But never in a vessel of this size."

Captain Braddock stared at him as if measuring his worth. "Do you think we can make it?"

"I do," Alec said.

"And if my ship goes aground?"

"Then I'll pay to have it repaired," Alec said. The captain only raised one eyebrow, but nodded to the man who'd brought Alec here.

The Italian sailor stood beside Alec as they neared the rocks, thrusting the pole through the water to measure the depth. It had not touched the bottom of the lake, a good sign, since the merchant ship was bottom-heavy and tended to ride low in the water.

The sails were stowed so as not to give the ship any forward impetus. It wasn't easy to turn a vessel this size, and the cove was too small to allow for much navigation. Consequently, the journey was made slowly and with such care that Alec worried they might not enter the cove before nightfall after all.

They finally rounded the farthest point on the necklace and slipped through the opening with ease. The sailor beside him kept plunging the pole into the water, but so far their luck held. The ship crept into the cove like a badger going to ground.

Alec blew out a breath, unclenched his fists, relaxing for the first time in an hour.

"I'll not stay here long," Braddock said.

Alec couldn't fault the other man for his caution.

"I'm taking a chance as well as you," the captain added, his gaze level.

"A day," Alec said. "Or two. That's all."

The captain reluctantly nodded.

Alec left the ship, the Italian sailor rowing him to shore. The *Stalwart*, as the ship was named, dwarfed the small cove, sitting like a brooding bird upon a watery nest.

It was a risky thing to do, to use the staircase in daylight, especially attired as he was in his regimentals. But Donald had assured him that Leitis sat at her loom most days, and no one else would be in that vicinity to spot him.

On his return, he would have to send a supply of food to the village and ensure that Armstrong was kept occupied. A dozen other details flew into his mind as he pushed up the stone on the floor of the priory.

Climbing up to the slate floor, Alec brushed off his breeches, then turned and replaced the stone. Only then did he see Leitis sitting there, touched by the fading light.

The moment had come, both expected and

dreaded. He stood before her, knowing that he would lose her in the next moments.

"I'm Alec John Landers," he said. "Colonel of the 11th Regiment, decorated soldier of the Crown. And the man you know as Raven."

Chapter 25

◦◦◦

Her mind refused to embrace the truth even as she continued to stare at him, stunned.

Crimson and glaring, his uniform marked him as the colonel of the regiment. His mask was gone and in its place the colonel's face. Ian. His beloved face, which she'd touched in passion and wonder. Whose lips she'd kissed and tongued. She'd placed her hands on that jaw, and kissed that throat, and traced her fingers across his body in a delicate exploration of wonder.

My enemy, my love.

She sat immobile in the dress he'd given her, refusing to believe the truth. Slowly he came forward, moving toward her with caution. Standing in front of her, silently, he removed his gloves.

Leitis glanced down at his hands. There, on the

heel of one palm, was the mark Fergus had given him, the mirror to the one on her own hand.

She felt herself crumple inside. A perfect moment, so horrifying and still that she would recall it all her life. Here were the answers to all her questions.

Words would not come. Nor could she seem to do anything but stare at him. Her fingers felt numb, her breath had stopped, and even her heart seemed to slow to an extended beat before speeding to catch up.

Slowly she got to her knees, feeling elderly and frail. Standing, she braced her hand against the brick wall for support, welcoming the abrasion on her palm because it proved that she could still feel.

She had loved him, found pleasure in his arms. Laughed with him and let him see her tears. And all this time he was the Butcher of Inverness.

You knew, Leitis.

The thought suddenly flew into her mind. Just as quickly she refuted it, only for it to be reborn a second later. *You knew. How else could you leave Gilmuir so easily? Why would Ian have worn a mask? You knew, Leitis. Or you would have sought the answers to difficult questions instead of turning away from them. You knew. You knew. All this time, you knew.* It was a refrain that repeated itself over and over, slicing at her.

A keening sound escaped her lips, an acknowledgment of a terrible truth. She began to run, through the priory to the archway, to the courtyard and beyond. She grabbed her skirts in her hands, running as she had as a child, late and anxious to be home, frightened and needing her mother's embrace. She wanted to be anywhere but here, anywhere but forced to see him. The Butcher of Inverness and the man she loved.

He followed her, the look of horror on her face acting as an impetus. She ran as fast as she had as a child, but he was faster. As he reached her, gripped her arm, she turned and kicked at him, her fists flying. This was the Leitis of his childhood, the obstinate, rash girl who never let anyone best her.

Her foot connected with his booted shin, the impact unexpectedly painful. So, too, was the blow to his chin. Leitis pulled back her fist, shaking it and glaring at him.

When she started to run again, he lunged for her, pinning her to the earth in a sudden tackle that had them both gasping for breath.

"Let me up," she spat, wiping the dirt from her mouth with the back of her hand. He fared little better. His leg ached where she'd kicked him, and his chin hurt.

He held her to the ground with both hands on her wrists. She glared up at him, as angry as he'd ever seen her. But then, he'd given her reason enough for rage.

"Let me go, Ian!"

"Will you listen to me, Leitis?"

"To another lie? I thought you were a man of honor," she said. "And all this time you were the Butcher of Inverness."

"You've always used the name," he said, exasperated. "But not once have you asked whether or not I deserved it."

He abruptly released her and stood. She lay still on the ground, staring up at him.

"What do you mean?" she asked finally.

He stared down at her, held his hand out to help her up. She refused it and scrambled to her feet, deliberately distancing herself by taking a few steps backward.

"Cumberland wanted results," he said, his voice

constrained. His commander's bloodlust sickened him even now. "He wanted the names of men who went to the gallows or died in imprisonment, and proof that the Highlanders were well and truly quelled. So I gave him what he wanted."

She said nothing, only continued to stare at him.

"The gallows were built in a secluded area of the prison, so there were no witnesses to my acts. Every hour of every day for weeks, a cart would be dispatched to the cemetery bearing the body of a prisoner. Every day, they passed Cumberland's headquarters in the provost's office. And every day, Cumberland would take note of the numbers of Scots who'd gone to their maker."

"Butcher is a name that suits you well, then," she said between thinned lips.

He frowned at her, annoyed by her stubbornness. "The duke never thought to notice that the wagon merely got to the end of the street, circled around, and passed by him again. And the prisoners that I supposedly executed were English soldiers who had died of influenza or their wounds."

She still didn't speak, but neither did she look so horrified.

"Over a period of weeks, my reputation grew. I became Cumberland's most efficient executioner. Day in, day out, hour by hour, he saw my handiwork. But for every body he saw, another man slipped away to return to his home."

He faced the land bridge, looking at the hills that bracketed the glen. A realization came to him then, as all great revelations do, without warning or fanfare. He loved this place; its memories and mountains, the twilight that lowered over Gilmuir like a soft blue-gray blanket.

"Why?" she asked. "Why did you let them go? Why did you even care? They were Scots; you should have been pleased."

"When a man is lying in his grave, he cannot boast of his nationality," he said, turning and walking toward her. "I've found the same to be true of prisoners." He reached out and brushed a smudge of dirt from her cheek. Surprisingly, she didn't flinch from his touch.

"It was war, Leitis," he said somberly. "Men die in war. But they shouldn't have to die to satisfy someone's bloodlust."

"Why didn't you tell me before?" she asked angrily.

"Would you have believed me?" he asked curiously.

"No," she said, and he almost smiled at her reluctant honesty.

"Do you believe me now?"

She studied him for several moments. The time ticked by in interminable seconds. Did she realize the words she would say were possibly the most important in his life? What she said would decree whether or not they had a future together.

"Yes," she said, finally. "Because you're Ian."

He couldn't answer her; his mind halted at her words. *Because he was Ian.* Had it always been that simple?

"You deliberately let people call you the Butcher of Inverness, didn't you?"

He smiled ruefully. "How else to convince the Duke of Cumberland that I was carrying out his orders?"

"Donald knows," she said suddenly. "And Harrison. How many more of your men know what you did?"

"My actions are mine, Leitis," he said. "The men in my command are loyal English soldiers."

"But they aren't," she said, a statement that had him looking at her in surprise. "They're loyal to you."

"They're good men," he said. "They hated what they saw as much as I did."

"Is that why you played the part of Raven?" she asked faintly. "Because you were afraid I wouldn't believe you?"

"Partly," he admitted. "But I also wanted to do something more to help the people of Gilmuir. Not because of you, Leitis, or even because of me. But because they also suffered because of Cumberland's rules."

A sound interrupted what she might have said then. They both glanced toward the glen. There, swaying heavily in the sea of lush green grass like a full-masted schooner, was a coach. A driver outfitted in a dark blue livery controlled the four matched grays as they careened across the land bridge. Tied to the back was enough baggage to outfit the villagers of Gilmuir.

The vehicle slowed gradually to a stop. The driver jumped down from his perch, opened the door, and unfurled the steps, standing back to assist the occupants in descending.

From this distance, Alec couldn't make out the woman's features. But her hair was so golden that it gleamed in the sunlight. The young man with her stood behind her slightly, surveying his surroundings. Alec wasn't certain of their identity until he saw the Sherbourne coat of arms on the door of the coach.

"Who is that?" Leitis said from beside him.

"I think it's my stepmother," he said, amazed.

"What is she doing here at Gilmuir?"

He didn't answer her, reluctant to voice his sudden thought. He hoped he was wrong, but the woman standing beside the carriage was dressed in deep mourning.

He glanced at Leitis. "We need to talk, you and I," he said softly. "Unfortunately, now is not the time." He left her then, walking toward the coach and his stepmother.

"Is this where he used to live, Mama?" David asked. He looked around him in fascination as Patricia exited the coach with a feeling of blessed relief. For a few days, at least, she would rest in a place that did not rock and sway. If it were possible to have a bed wider than a bench she would be doubly blessed.

"Yes, dear, it is," she said, looking toward the ruin of the castle. "But I don't believe it looked this way when he came to spend his summers here."

"Madam?"

Patricia glanced over her shoulder to see a young man standing there attired in a bright uniform of blue and red. He snapped to attention, startling a smile from her.

"May I assist you, madam?" he asked, his gaze on the coach rather than her face.

"I am looking for my stepson," she said. "Alec Landers."

The young man's face changed. The studied indifference softened, became curiosity.

"I shall have him attend you with all possible speed, madam," the young man said.

"I am already attending, Armstrong."

Patricia turned and Alec was there, as handsome as she remembered. But the years had changed him. He was taller and broader, his face leaner. His eyes had lost their innocence and in its place was a cool, almost wary expression.

Extending her arms, she enfolded him in a quick

embrace, then stepped back and pulled David for-ward.

He shook his head, gripped Ralph's cage with both hands, and refused to budge. As much as David had anticipated the journey, he also feared his reception. He knew enough of the world to sense that he was different from most of it.

"This is David," she said, forcing a smile to her face. "Your brother."

She would forever love her stepson for what he did next. Instead of acting in a superior manner or a con-descending one, he stepped closer to David and bent down to look into the cat's basket. "It looks to be a fearsome creature," he said kindly.

"Her name is Ralph," David said.

Alec stuck his finger in the cage, wiggled it be-tween the cat's ears, and quickly withdrew it when Ralph decided it might be a meal.

"A most formidable mouser," he said, grinning at David.

"She eats roast beef," David said, shaking his head.

"And anything else she can find," Patricia con-tributed. "She eschews mice, I'm afraid," she said, smiling up at Alec. "She feels they're beneath her, I think."

"Ralph?" Alec asked softly.

"Gender does not matter to David," she explained in a whisper.

"Would you like to hold her?" David offered, fum-bling with the cat's basket.

Alec looked from him to Patricia.

"Not everyone is offered that privilege," she said, hoping that he would understand. But it appeared as if he knew how easily David could be hurt. He re-mained still when the basket was unfastened and Ralph lay in his arms.

The two of them, cat and colonel, eyed each other with vigilant respect.

A moment passed, then another. Finally, Alec passed the cat back to David. "I think she likes you best," he said, smiling.

"I think so, too," David agreed with an angelic smile. "But you can hold her whenever you like. It's easy to go to sleep with her when she's purring. And sometimes when I wake up in the middle of the night I talk to her."

Alec put his arm around David's shoulders and steered him toward the fort. Patricia, her maid, and the coachman followed in silence. It was, she thought, the very best of signs.

"He's dead?" Alec asked, unable to wait until she spoke the words. He anticipated the sudden heaviness of grief and it came with her solemn nod.

"I'm sorry," she said. "It was a sickness of the lungs. It took him suddenly."

"Did he get my letter?" he asked.

She shook her head, the look of compassion on her face genuine and appreciated.

She smiled a watery smile, reached into her reticule, and retrieved a ring. Stepping forward, she handed it to him. "I believe this is a ceremony the Landers observe," she said.

"I doubt it's many generations old," he said, staring at the silver and onyx signet ring. "It belonged to my grandfather, and then to my father."

"And now to you," she said softly. "The fourteenth Earl of Sherbourne."

He nodded, feeling oddly detached from the realization. It did not seem possible that his father was dead. Or that he'd unexpectedly ascended to an earldom he'd ignored all these years.

Still, there were other things more pressing at this moment than a new title.

He felt as if his world were caving in, and in the center of it was Leitis. She'd looked at him as if he were the most loathsome creature in the world. And when he'd parted from her, she'd only stared at him, bemused.

Had he deliberately let her discover his identity? Had he simply wanted the masquerade over?

Time was running out. He had to get the villagers to the ship before another day passed. But more importantly, he had to determine his own future. Would Leitis want him with her?

Would he give up his heritage for her? Or surrender his commission? Yes, he realized, he would.

All he had to do was convince Leitis that he loved her. And hope she loved him.

Chapter 26

Leitis stared at the scene, her mind still reeling. There he stood, the Butcher of Inverness, Ian, holding a cat tenderly in his arms.

The woman beside him wore a tricorne hat not unlike the officers at Fort William. Attached to it was a long black lace veil. Her ebony dress declared her a widow and boasted a fitted bodice, tight sleeves, and a skirt split to reveal a black underskirt. Even though she was wearing deep mourning, she was smiling brightly.

Leitis shook her head as if to empty it of all the contradictions she faced. She walked back into Gilmuir's courtyard, resisting the urge to limp. Her foot ached from where she'd kicked Ian.

Entering the archway, she walked into the clan hall. Sunlight bathed the interior, even as shadows

316

clung to the corners. She stood in the middle of the once-impressive room, staring up at the clear blue of the sky. One night the Butcher—no, Ian—had done the same, desperate with confusion. Or burdened with his secrets?

In places the floor had been demolished and the stone ribs of the foundation could be seen. She had the feeling that her life was like Gilmuir in that the core of her was being revealed.

He had once warned her of being too like Cumberland. Had she truly been so blinded by hatred?

The English were not the only ones responsible for what had happened to her country, to Gilmuir. The Scots leaders held their share of responsibility. So did every man who left for battle with the thought of rebellion in his heart and every woman who watched them go with pride.

They had not considered what could happen if they lost. They had wanted something so fiercely that they refused to think of the alternative.

Just as she had.

She had not wanted Ian to be the colonel, so she had pretended it wasn't so. She'd ignored her intuition and even her intelligence.

How had she fooled herself so completely? By ignoring all the signs. All along she'd been reminded of someone by the way he walked, by his bearing. She'd thought it was Marcus, or had that been simply another pretense she'd offered herself?

She walked through the archway; the path dappled by sunlight, and entered the priory.

How strange that this place had never seemed filled with ghosts. The only spirits lingering here were those still alive.

Are you faint of heart? Afraid of horses or shadows or the wind blowing through your hair?

What had the past years been like for him? Had he been as conflicted as she felt now? A Scots mother, an English father. The Scots would hate him; the English would suspect him.

She went to one of the middle arches, staring out over the loch and beyond. A land she loved. But a country is more than the earth and the hills, the lake and the forests. It is the people that make it alive. Men of great deeds and petty tyrannies. Women of courage and selfishness. People frail and strong, brave and fearful. Not gods, not saints, only people.

And the colonel of the regiment? A person as well. A man wedded to his duty until the obligation proved too onerous. Wasn't that what had happened to her own country? The people had accepted what they could until the breaking point. Good or ill, wise or foolish, they had rebelled.

As had Ian.

Alec summoned Lieutenant Castleton to his side.

"Do we have two available chambers for the countess and my brother, Castleton?" he asked.

The other man's expression could only be construed as worried, but then he was a conscientious soldier, one who hated to disappoint him.

"There are no empty chambers, sir. But we could clear out the ordnance rooms, move the gunpowder."

"Then see that it's done," he said.

The lieutenant raised his arm, motioning to Armstrong. The other man glanced over at him, then wisely smoothed his face of its momentary irritation.

David occupied himself by talking to his cat, tapping gently on the sides of the basket.

"I don't remember him being this way," Alec said carefully in an aside to Patricia.

"He was a child when you left. Others grew, he didn't," she said simply.

"There are those who would have chosen to keep him hidden," he said, voicing a truth that she surely knew. It was easier to keep a dotty aunt, a deformed child, a senile father locked away. Society pretended that it was perfect. David would banish that notion with his very presence. Only the very rich or the ennobled were allowed to be eccentric or different.

"Yes," she said, agreeing. "But then they would never have had the joy I have." She looked at her son. "David loves with his whole heart and never looks at life as evil or sad or lonely."

"I remember that about you," he said smiling. "You were always very protective of those you loved. My father was very fortunate."

"You're very like him," she said, studying him. "I'd never realized it before."

David was smiling brightly, greeting each of the soldiers who passed him. Inappropriate behavior, perhaps, for a young man, but not for a child.

"We didn't quarrel," he said absently, watching David. "We simply lost interest in each other."

"I think your presence was difficult for him. He loved your mother so very much."

"And seeing me brought her back?" he asked skeptically, glancing at her.

"No. It only emphasized the futility of longing for her," she said surprisingly. "Without you around, he could pretend. That she was away for the summer, perhaps. Or visiting relatives in France. A place from which she could return. I think it's why he distanced himself from me as well," she added.

"Then he was foolish," Alec said. "It's not often that a man has two remarkable women in his life."

The sound of a rider approaching captured his attention. Harrison drew up, a look of concern on his face. He dismounted quickly, approached the group, and nodded in wordless apology for disturbing him.

"Sir, Major Sedgewick is approaching," Harrison said, his face creased with worry. "I saw him on my way back."

"It was too good to last, Harrison," Alec said, annoyed at the major's appearance. He resigned himself to Sedgewick's presence at Fort William for a few days before he could send him out on another patrol.

"That's not all, sir," Harrison said. "It looks as if General Wescott is accompanying him. And quite a large force of men, Colonel."

Alec stepped away from his stepmother, a dozen thoughts flying through his head.

His routine letters to Wescott kept the general informed of the status of Fort William. There was more than one reason why the general would be accompanying Sedgewick, but he couldn't afford to ignore the most dangerous one.

"Everything that could associate me with the Raven needs to be destroyed, Harrison. And anything that can link you to my activities," he said, concerned for the other man's welfare.

Harrison nodded. "What are you going to do, Colonel?" he asked, worried.

"Get to Leitis," Alec said quickly.

Chapter 27

"**I** knew I would find you here," he said, his voice low and somber.

She turned, slowly, to see him standing in the doorway leading to the archway. "It felt right to come to the place where it all began."

He smiled. "I think it began in the glen," he said, "with the sight of you running so fast your feet seemed to fly over the grass. And the cloud of your hair behind you."

"That soon?"

"From the beginning," he said, striding forward until he stood close to her. He reached out his hand and wrapped his finger around a lock of her hair. "It looks as bright as fire in the sun. Like that faraway time."

He dropped his hand, his smile evaporating. "General Wescott will be arriving soon. Before he gets here, I want you to leave."

She frowned, confused.

"Why should his arrival concern me?"

"Because it's possible that I will be arrested," he said, "and either you will be turned over to Sedgewick's care or imprisoned also."

"Do they know about the Raven?" she asked, shocked.

He shrugged, a gesture meant to be nonchalant, she was sure. But it failed at convincing her that he was calm about the possibility of being arrested. His jaw was too squared; a muscle in it twitched with tension. His hands, resting at his sides, were clenched into fists. "If not now, I'm sure they'll find out soon enough."

"If he doesn't know, then what is the danger?" she asked, confused.

"I've performed more than one act of insurrection, Leitis," he said, his lips curving in a crooked smile that was absolutely charming. "There is Inverness, for one. And Sedgewick has never forgiven me for saving the village."

"Why did you?" she asked, discounting the answer he'd first given her. Something to the effect of it being easier to save the village than to rebuild it.

"Because the people of Gilmuir lived there," he said, reaching out and tucking an errant tendril of her hair behind her ear before letting his hand drop. "Because it was your home."

"If it had been any other place, would you have done the same?"

"I like to think I would," he said. "But I might not have," he added, the words stark in their honesty. "I can't say what I might have done, Leitis. I can only be accountable for those actions I've committed."

He glanced up at the ceiling, still mostly intact, even after the English bombardment.

"I served my country as well as I could," he said. "The Scots would think me a traitor for it, while the English will consider my ruse as Raven equally treasonous."

She wasn't certain what was real or imaginary at this moment. The Butcher of Inverness was no longer a man to be feared for his cruelty. The colonel was a rebel whose self-imposed mission was to protect the Scots. Ian was Alec, and they were both the man she loved.

"Whatever my faults, however they're measured, regardless of who judges me, I want you to know that I never meant to hurt you, Leitis."

"The only way you've hurt me is by being English," she said honestly.

His glance was gently chiding. "I cannot change that for you, Leitis. Did you never think that it would have been easier for me to love a woman who didn't see me as her enemy? One who wasn't stubborn and heedless?" he added.

"Who watched her tongue?" she asked, moving away from him. She faced the loch, but heard him come to stand behind her. "Who didn't take you to task?"

"Or didn't weep when she was touched too much for words," he said softly.

"Or love you in a cave," she said quietly. A proper and virtuous woman would have felt shame in uttering that truth. Wanton as she was, she couldn't help but flush at the memory of her abandon.

He reached out and gently turned her in his arms.

"You see," he said earnestly, "I've no choice in loving you. You've been in my heart since I was a boy and I cannot pry you loose."

She stepped away. "I accept that you're not the Butcher I thought you, but I cannot wrap my mind around the fact that you've taken up arms against my country. Am I to forgive that with such ease?"

"Your countrymen did the same, Leitis," he said. "There are some things that cannot be wiped clean, Leitis, however much we wish it. I spent years hating the Scots because they had killed my mother."

"General Wade's troops were responsible," she said, confused.

"I didn't know that at the time," he answered. "I didn't know any different until you told me."

"Yet it didn't stop you from saving the men in Inverness," she said slowly.

"The men were kept naked, cold, and starving. It was difficult to see them as Scots, and easier to see them as people who needed help. I would truly have been a monster if I had ignored their plight. Besides, Leitis, sometimes you have to stop hating."

She folded her hands in front of her, tipped her head back, and looked steadily at him. Ribbons of sunlight streaming in through the arches bathed his face. He returned her look, unmasked, his face handsome and strong, his eyes direct and unflinching. He stood before her naked in spirit. Revealed as who he was, not as she had thought him to be. Not a monster, nor a rebel, but a man of contradictions and frailties, a man who had earned both her respect and her love.

Her sigh felt tinged with tears. Inside her chest was this great hollow place that echoed the sound of her fast-beating heart. "I tried not to love you," she confessed. "I told myself that it would be safer not to. For a time I even believed it; but then, I seem to be adept at delusions."

Slowly, giving her time to pull away, he bent and kissed her, a soft and hesitant kiss like the one he'd once given her as a boy. She placed her hand on his cheek, her palm abraded by the afternoon growth of his beard.

She pulled her hand away, looked at the X-shaped scar. Slowly, he placed his hand over hers. A meeting of scars, a meeting of minds. And hearts, she admitted.

She shook her head, confused, uncertain, overwhelmed. Love, she discovered in that moment, existed whether or not it was convenient or proper. And love flourished in unexpected places like the harebells she loved, strong and hardy, growing in rocky fissures or deep soil.

"I'm a poor Scot," she admitted, "to concede so quickly to an Englishman. But I do," she said. "I love you, Colonel or Raven, Ian or Alec."

"Perhaps you can console yourself with the thought that you brought me to my knees."

She pulled back and smiled at him. His own smile faded as he looked at her.

"I once thought that if I could stare long enough into your eyes," he confessed, "I could see your soul."

"Can you?" she asked, entranced by his words.

"I see your heart," he softly said. "And your courage. You will need it for what might come."

The sense of dread she began to feel was so overpowering that it made her stomach lurch.

"You must leave now, Leitis," he said softly.

"What are you going to do?" she asked, biting back her fear.

"At this moment? I'm going to return to Fort William," he said.

She didn't fool herself that the general would be compassionate or kind or even understanding. The English would punish Alec for his actions; he had done more than disobey Cumberland's orders. He had dared to feel kindness.

"You might be hanged," she said.

His fingers dusted a path from the lobe of her ear to her chin. The expression on his face was intent, as if he memorized the look of her, this moment, for all the time to come. "I sincerely hope not," he said. "I've plans for my life."

"Don't make me leave you," she said, blinking back tears. "Please."

He shook his head slowly. "Don't you know that they can't hurt me unless they hurt you? I couldn't bear it if something happened to you. I'll come when I can. I promise you that."

"I've heard those promises before," she said, pulling away from him. " 'I'll return, Leitis. I'll be safe enough. There's nothing to worry about. It will be an adventure, Leitis, and you'll be sick with envy to hear of it.' I've heard it all," she said fiercely. "From my father and Fergus and James and Marcus."

"I swear on all that's holy to the MacRaes that I'll come when I can, Leitis."

He bent and kissed her sweetly, and she allowed her eyes to flutter shut, captured between grief and delight in that moment.

Please, keep him safe. She had not prayed in so long that it felt uncomfortable to do so. In those months after Culloden she had felt no great accord with the Almighty. She had, instead, experienced only anger. This prayer was different, unselfish. *Keep him safe, not because I love him, but because he deserves to be saved.*

Again he kissed her, and for the length of the kiss she forgot about English troops, divided loyalties, and even danger.

Patricia waited patiently in the courtyard, David beside her softly crooning to his cat. The vista was spectacular, pulling from her a reluctant admiration. The deep azure of the sea and the brilliant hue of a storm-free sky were a backdrop for the green rolling hills to either side of Fort William. Even the sharp peaks in the distance, all jutting angles and black and gray shale, could not spoil the scenery. It was not calm in the way an English landscape often was, but it was quiescent at the moment. There was no rain, no bristling wind, and even the waves on the water seemed tranquil.

The warm breeze was a gentle brush against her cheek. Nature's caress, as if it approved of her presence here.

She glanced over at the ruin of Gilmuir. Moira's childhood home. The place where she'd died. She'd expected to feel a host of emotions on viewing this place. Instead, she felt only sadness for the other woman. No envy, no anger.

"My lady?"

The young man Alec had summoned stood there waiting patiently. Castleton, that was his name.

He stood stiffly at attention, then inclined his head. Almost, she thought, as if he couldn't quite decide whether to bow or salute her.

She smiled to ease him.

"The chambers are ready, Your Ladyship," he said, his expression earnest. "If you would accompany me." He extended his arm.

The thundering approach of what looked to be a hundred troops drowned out his next words. A column of men, riding in pairs, galloped over the narrow strip of earth that joined the island to the meadow, their horses' hooves throwing up clods of earth and chunks of grass.

They slowed to a canter between the two structures before filing into the courtyard. Between the sound of the horses and the orders being shouted, the enclosed space was suddenly a scene of pandemonium.

She stepped back from one particularly intrusive horse that appeared determined to eat the top of her hat. She almost batted at him with her reticule before his rider turned him away.

The troops parted soundlessly and an imposing-looking man of rugged features rode through them. His horse was white, his saddle dotted with silver medallions. Was he the leader of this rude group?

He glanced in her direction before looking away. Then, in a thoroughly affronting manner, he slowly glanced at her again. A scrutiny, she thought irately, that took in the tips of her black shoes to the top of her silk hat and spared little in between, including the curve of her bodice. The fact that she was in mourning did not seem to matter to him at all.

She drew herself up and frowned at him, her mouth pursed in a moue of disapproval. The insufferable man simply smiled at her, a most rapacious gesture that made her want to hit him with her reticule as well.

He dismounted with ease, giving orders to the men around him as he did so. One particular man appeared as interested in her presence as the general, but he soon tired of his inspection of her and sought out another soldier.

The general, however, was not finished with his effrontery.

He strode to where she stood, unaffected by her glare. His bow was as slow and as arrogant as his look.

"Madam," he said, "I never expected to see a woman of your beauty in this desolate place."

She blinked at him, surprised. She hadn't been called a beauty since before her marriage to Gerald. But that fact did not soften her toward him. In fact, she should be even more insulted. Her appearance was not a topic of conversation, especially from a stranger.

"Allow me to present General Wescott to you, Countess," Castleton said as if he'd heard her thoughts.

"Countess?" The odious general looked surprised.

"General," Castleton continued, "the Countess of Sherbourne."

"A relation to Alec Landers?" the general asked. "His wife?"

She was determined that this man would not startle her further.

"Of course I am not his wife," she said annoyed. "I am his mother. His stepmother."

"Which accounts for the disparity in age, my lady," he said, bowing once more. "You are still too young to be his stepmother. Did your husband pluck you from the cradle?"

Was there no end to his temerity?

"I am a widow, sir," she said frostily. "A fact that you would soon glean if you directed your attention at the shade of my attire and nothing else."

"A fact to my advantage," he said equally as coolly. But there was a twinkle in his hazel eyes. "I am a widower, my lady."

She simply stared at him for a moment, flummoxed.

"I am a very recent widow, sir," she said finally, frowning at him.

He reached out and took her gloved hand, bowed over it, and in the manner of the French kissed the air above the back of it. "My condolences, my lady," he said smoothly, his voice entirely too intimate. So, too, was the warmth of his hand. Her palm felt singed even through her gloves.

"Will you take refreshments with me?" he asked, that irritating twinkle back in his eyes. "I will endeavor to make you forget my earlier boorishness."

She jerked her hand back. "Certainly not," she said, annoyed.

"Will you partake of the evening meal with me, then?"

"Are there no boundaries to your effrontery, sir?"

He smiled, an expression, she was certain, that had been practiced many times. It was effective, rendering his rugged face almost boyish. For a moment they simply stared at each other, until she remembered her true reason for being here.

She shook her head, looked in the direction Alec had gone. She needed to pose the question she'd come to Scotland to ask before military matters intruded, before he was commanded by this . . . general to do something else or go somewhere else.

It was vital that David's future was assured.

Her maid sighed heavily behind her, the sound both a hint and an impetus to action.

She turned to the other woman. "Go with the lieutenant, Florie, and rest if you wish." She smiled a dismissal, and looked at the general once more.

An entirely irritating man, she thought.

"Have I offended you again?" he asked, his smile having a tinge of wickedness about it.

She shook her head. It would be best if she didn't respond to his words or speak to him at all.

"If you will excuse me, sir," she said, beckoning to David.

She began to walk toward the ruined castle with David at her side, Ralph meowing with every step.

"Where are we going, Mama?" David asked.

"To find your brother," she said, determined.

"I like him," he said, smiling. "Ralph likes him, too."

She glanced toward the cat's basket. She doubted that the ill-tempered feline liked anyone other than David, but she didn't say that to her son.

She had rehearsed the words countless times on the journey through Scotland, Patricia thought. Why, then, were they so fleeting now? Everything she'd thought to say was gone, flown from her mind as if they were bubbles on a gusty day. That odious general's fault, no doubt.

She glanced over her shoulder at him. He was still watching her with that enigmatic smile on her face. Her anger was the reason for the sudden feeling of heat on her cheeks. That was all. It had nothing to do with his crude manner or his words.

He thought her beautiful. She halted, the rocky ground biting into her slippers. What did it matter to her if a stranger found her attractive? Or was so crass as to comment upon it? She looked at him again. Another man was addressing him and he nodded from time to time, evidently immersed in thought.

It was absurd for her to feel so disappointed.

Matthew Sedgewick dismounted, handed the reins over to one of the privates assigned to stable duties, and looked around for Armstrong. He found him directing the placement of a wooden box filled with gunpowder next to one of the cannon portals.

"I beg your pardon, sir," Armstrong said, straightening, "but the colonel has me clearing out the ordnance rooms for his mother and brother."

The presence of the colonel's relatives was an irritation. But their being here would not delay the outcome of his investigation, nor render his accusations inappropriate. Armstrong had furnished enough information to cast doubt on Landers's loyalty.

"I've brought General Wescott with me," he said curtly. "Before we begin to question Colonel Landers, are there any changes you wish to make in your journal? Any omissions or additions?"

"Yes," Armstrong said, smiling faintly. "I overheard a conversation between the countess and her son. Evidently, the colonel is familiar with this place. He used to spend his summers here."

Sedgewick frowned, trying to make sense of Armstrong's latest revelation.

"Have you considered, sir, that Colonel Landers might be a Scot?"

The idea was intriguing. A nail in Landers's coffin. Even if Wescott did nothing, Cumberland would be furious.

"Where is he?"

"I believe, sir, that he's at the Scottish castle. He has an affinity for that place."

"Or his hostage," Sedgewick said abruptly, turning and crossing the open space between the fort and the ruins of the castle.

He was going to enjoy telling Landers he was under investigation, he thought, entering the ruins of the castle from the side.

Two people were talking, their voices echoing in

the stone chamber. One speaker he recognized instantly. The other was female. The hostage?

"What about the villagers? Is there no way to get them to the ship?"

"None that can escape detection at the moment."

A possibility occurred to Sedgewick, one that was almost exhilarating to contemplate. What if Colonel Landers's sin was greater than simply ignoring the Raven's presence in his territory? What if Landers himself was the traitor?

Realizing what he was hearing, Sedgewick smiled, and pulled out the pistol he'd tucked into his waistcoat.

This strange place was a labyrinth, Patricia thought, and every single brick of it interested David. He entered the archway, stared above him at the partially intact roof.

The sunlight cast delicate shadows on the walls. "Pretty," he said, holding Ralph's basket close.

"Yes, dear," she said patiently, "but we must find Alec."

They entered one room that showed some sign of habitation, but it was empty at the moment. Another larger space was open to the elements. It seemed an oddly sad place, as if it had once known joy and now only felt sorrow. Even David did not want to enter it.

She stepped over fallen stones and walked down a hallway that led nowhere, as a wall had collapsed upon it. Each path she took led to nothing. Finally, they retraced their steps to the archway and began to follow it through the ruins.

"A tender scene, Colonel," Sedgewick said, slipping out of the shadows.

His uniform was coated with dust, his blond hair

in disarray, and the look on his face one of fatigue. But that wasn't what held Alec's attention. It was the gun in his hand. The pistol boasted a walnut stock and checkered grip, and was obviously well kept, from the shine of the brass on its six-inch barrel.

"It's a formidable offense to pull a weapon on a superior officer, Sedgewick," Alec said, very conscious of the fact that Leitis was standing beside him. He stepped in front of her.

"Not if the officer is guilty of treason. As I suspect of you. Sir," Sedgewick added, bowing slightly in a mockery of respect.

"Even stronger words," Alec said dryly.

"Do you deny that you're the man known as Raven? Do you deny that you attempted to aid and abet the Scots?"

"Most emphatically," Alec said. There were times when bluster and bravado were helpful attributes. When a battalion was outnumbered, when the odds were enormous, and at this particular moment. "How do you come to that fanciful conclusion, Sedgewick?" he asked cuttingly.

"Armstrong has kept me informed of your movements," the other man said, the pistol steady and pointed at him.

"Then Armstrong is an idiot," Alec said dryly.

"General Wescott doesn't think so," Sedgewick said. "Else he would not have accompanied me here."

"And you felt it necessary to escort me to him at the point of a gun?"

"I wouldn't care, Landers, if you tried to escape and I had to shoot you."

Alec smiled mirthlessly. "Is that your ploy?" he asked, attempting to look unaffected by the other man's threats. "I think it would be best if you returned to Fort William now, Major. I will join you shortly and together we'll hear General Wescott's judgment as to your imaginative findings."

"I think now would be a better time," Sedgewick said. The gun barrel wavered in the air, pointing in the direction of the archway, then back at his chest.

"Are you threatening me, Sedgewick?" Alec asked in a clipped voice.

"I believe I am, sir. Would you like to try to escape?" he asked, smiling. "When you're dead, sir, I'll sample your whore and see if she's worth keeping alive."

"I hope," Alec said, enraged, "that you have proof beyond any doubt, Sedgewick. Because when I'm exonerated, I'm going to make every effort to see that you spend the rest of your life in the gaol. I suggest that you begin to formulate your explanation to General Wescott. I know exactly what I'll say to him."

Alec stepped forward, hoping that Leitis would take advantage of the diversion he was about to create and slip from view.

"The gun is ready to fire, Colonel," he said. "I've taken the precaution of being prepared for your refusal. If you're dead, it won't matter if you're the Raven or not," Sedgewick said, smiling. "The general will be satisfied. I will probably be commended on my courage, and another traitor will be dead."

He raised the pistol and aimed it at Alec's chest.

"Let her go," Alec said, glancing at Leitis, "and I'll come with you. Without a struggle."

"But you see, I don't want you to come with me," Sedgewick said, still smiling. "The more I think about it, the more the idea of your death pleases me."

He sighted the gun carefully.

"Mama? Is he going to hurt my brother?" David asked fearfully.

Both men turned at the sound of the voice, startled.

Patricia and David stood in the door of the archway staring at Sedgewick.

Alec took advantage of the moment and lunged for the major, grabbing his legs with both arms and pulling him off balance. The pistol fell with a metallic thud to the stone floor.

Sedgewick kicked at him, rolled, and grabbed the gun. The major rose to his knees, then stood, all the while pointing the barrel at him. It was only then that Alec realized the major was standing directly beneath the fallen arch.

Sedgewick glanced down at his feet, a look of horror on his face as the earth began to crumble beneath him. In a moment oddly slowed in time, Alec watched as Sedgewick flew backward, his arms and legs flailing as a look of stark terror crossed his face. There was nothing but air, no firm ground, no handhold as he continued to fall. The sound of his scream gradually faded into silence.

Alec stood and moved to the neighboring arch, looked down. There was no hope that Sedgewick would have survived the drop to the loch below. He felt arms extend around his waist as Leitis pulled him back from the edge.

He enfolded his arms around her, resting his cheek against her hair. She was trembling or he was, but it didn't seem to matter at the moment.

"He fell, Mama," David said.

"Yes, dearest," Patricia said softly, extending her arms around her frightened son.

"I don't like this place," he said, burying his head against her shoulder.

Patricia met Alec's gaze across the room. "I'm not sure I do, either, dearest."

Chapter 28

L eitis stood clutching Ian, filled with a quiet kind of terror, and not because a man had died in front of her. She was trembling because she knew these moments were the ones on which her happiness rested.

"I won't leave without you," she said fiercely. "I won't let you be brave or daring or noble. Not now."

"I could convince them that it was Sedgewick's jealousy of me that was the reason for his charges, that his suspicions were entirely unfounded," he said, stroking his hands over her back.

"And his death? They'll think you guilty of it."

"I am still the colonel of the 11th Regiment," he said, smiling wryly. "My word has some weight." He pulled back and traced his thumb over her features. Nose, lips, chin were all subject to that soft touch.

"There's another way," she said, desperate to convince him. "You could come with me. Remember the path around the cliff? We could both get the villagers to the ship."

"And who will occupy the general in the meantime?" he asked with a smile.

Patricia walked over to where they stood. "I admit to not knowing what you're discussing," she said. "But it's evident that you need a distraction. Someone who would keep General Wescott occupied in some way."

She glanced toward David, then back at both of them. "The boor seems to have taken an interest in me," she said, her cheeks flushing. "Perhaps I can have wine with the general. Or dine with him."

"I couldn't ask you to do that, Patricia," he said. "It would be too dangerous for you."

"Why, because you're my stepson?" She drew herself up haughtily and glared at him. "I shall simply tell them that you're an odious disappointment to me. That you were estranged from your father for the same reason and that my only purpose for visiting you was to inform you of your succession to the earldom." The arrogant air she assumed was ruined by her quick smile.

"Earldom?" Leitis said helplessly. "You're an earl now?"

"My father is dead," he said softly.

Her hands pressed against his arm. "I'm sorry," she said, wishing that she could spare him the pain of his grief. There were some journeys, however, that each person had to make alone.

He pulled off a ring, handed it to Patricia, then unfastened the badge he wore on his waistcoat. "This is inscribed with my name and was a present from Cumberland. Tell the solicitor I was killed in Scotland," he said. "He'll believe it easily enough with this as proof."

Patricia stared at him in disbelief. "I can't take this," she said, staring down at the two items on her palm. "I wanted to ask you to provide for David, but this is too much. You can't give up your birthright, Alec," she remonstrated. She glanced over at her son. "David cannot be earl," she said softly.

"With you at his side, Patricia, I've no doubt that he can be an apt one." He smiled. "You'll find that society will forgive a great deal if a man has power."

She looked bemused, turning the ring and the badge over and over in her hand.

"You can't do this, Ian. . . ." Leitis halted, threw up her hands in frustration. "Who will you be now?" she asked. "What shall I call you? Ian or Alec?"

"Ian, I think," he said, considering it. "Ian MacRae."

"Then, Ian MacRae," she said firmly, "you cannot give up your future."

"Would you care to be an English countess, Leitis?" he asked.

"No," she answered, so quickly that he smiled.

"I didn't think so," he said. "I haven't given up my future, my love. I've simply changed one title for another."

She merely shook her head at him, confused.

"That of husband, Leitis. I prefer it to earl."

That he would give up his legacy to be with her stunned her. She tipped back her head and stared at him, suddenly realizing what he'd said.

"Are you asking me to marry you, Ian? You might be a bit more forthright."

He began to laugh, bending down to kiss her smartly right in front of his stepmother. She pushed at him, but he released her when he was done, and not a moment before.

She pulled away finally, dazed.

"Will you marry me, Leitis?" he asked, smiling. "Is that forthright enough?"

She nodded, smiling.

He wrapped his arm around her shoulders, turned to Patricia. "Two hours should be enough of a delay," he said.

"I shall play the flirty female," the older woman said. "A role that should be interesting to assume."

He bent and kissed her on the cheek. "Thank you," he said simply.

She pressed her palm against his face. "Be well," she said tenderly. "Be happy. Something tells me you will be," she added, her glance including Leitis. "She's the match for your stubbornness."

He looked startled. "My stubbornness?"

"He always wanted his own way as a young man, my dear," Patricia said in an aside to Leitis. "His charm was the only reason he was not unbearable."

"I am not stubborn," he countered.

Patricia glanced at Leitis once again, as if to say, *See, did I not tell you?*

Ian only shook his head and turned to his brother. "I have to leave now, David," he said.

"Will I see you soon?" his brother asked.

"Perhaps," he said, a vague answer. David, however, looked content enough with it.

Leitis led him through the priory, to the small shelf of land on the side of Gilmuir. Here a collection of gorse bushes grew in a scraggly line.

At the fourth bush, she nodded, then turned and smiled at him. "This is it," she said, sitting beside the bush, her legs dangling over the edge.

A moment later, he stared in horror as she disappeared from sight. He threw himself flat on the ground, his heart in his throat, his arms grabbing for her, only to have her pop her head up a moment later, smiling at him.

"At the risk of offending you, Leitis," Ian said, his heart still pounding wildly, "were you part goat as a child?"

"It's not so terrible once you're used to it," she said in an attempt to reassure him. "Although," she admitted, "I wouldn't attempt it at night or in a storm."

His glance at her was accompanied by a faint smile. He had no doubt that if the provocation were enough, she'd dare that, too.

He dropped down beside her on the path, uttering a curse as he stared at the sheer drop below. "You weren't a goat," he said, frowning, "but an eagle."

War was tedium mixed with horror. Hours were spent waiting for a signal to advance, but those moments just before a battle began were filled with a stomach-clenching fear. He was disconcerted to experience that same feeling now.

Slowly, Leitis began to follow the path around the cliffs. He stayed close behind her, one hand, like hers, flattened on the side of the cliff for balance.

The face of the rock was striated, bands of brown and black interspersed occasionally with a layer of pure white glittering stone. The path itself was a shelf of beige granite littered with small pebbles. He made the mistake of watching one of them fall to the loch below, his stomach squeezing even tighter. It was not the opportune moment to recall Sedgewick's descent.

"I can't believe you used this path," he said incredulously.

"Did you never wonder how I escaped all of you so easily?" she asked, amused.

"I thought it was because you could outrun us," he confessed.

"I could," she said smugly.

"I'm not sure all of the villagers are going to be able to navigate it, Leitis," he said, concerned. "Does it get much narrower?"

"No," she answered, glancing over her shoulder at him. He wished, fervently, that she would pay more attention to the path. "It is bound to be frightening to some of them," she admitted. "But we are Scots and we can do anything."

He smiled, amused.

Halfway around the island the track abruptly rose higher for about five feet. Unless they bent over, they could be seen. Once the path dipped slightly again, Leitis stopped and motioned to Ian. Together, they peered over the edge of the cliff.

There was a sense of cacophony about Fort William now. The order and regimentation that had once marked the fortress wasn't in evidence. Men and horses milled about, camp had been made, and fires lit in preparation for night.

Ian glanced up at the sky, wondered if they had enough time to get the villagers back to the priory and to the ship before nightfall.

"Will your stepmother be all right?" Leitis whispered.

"Against Wescott?" he said, smiling. "I have no doubt."

"I never had a chance to visit with her," she said regretfully.

"The better to learn my secrets? Then I should be grateful the meeting never transpired," he said dryly.

"I know all your secrets," she said, smiling. "Don't I?"

"I don't feel at all comfortable discussing my frailties when I'm perched on a ledge like a bird."

"You're not comfortable with heights," she said, looking as if the discovery amazed her.

He braced his hand against the rock, the glittering stone abrasive against his palm. "Up until this moment," he said, "I've had few opportunities to test my affinity for cliff-walking."

She began to smile, obviously amused. He bent down and kissed her, captivated by the moment and the woman.

"Have you no other secrets?" she asked a moment later.

He thought about it for a moment, then shook his head. "I don't like the taste of mutton," he said, "although you'll need sheep for your wool. And I have no ability to sing."

She smiled at him before turning and following the path. It didn't get easier, he noted, but as long as he concentrated on the cliff face and not the sheer drop to his right, it was bearable enough.

They reached the land bridge, finally, the path rising steeply upward.

"We have to cross the glen," she said, gesturing to a narrow neck of land.

He glanced from it back to the fort, measuring the distance. The soldiers didn't appear particularly vigilant, but it was never good to underestimate an adversary. With a start of surprise, he realized that's exactly what the English were now.

Slowly, he slipped off his coat, folded it inside out, and tossed it over the side of the cliff.

"It would be seen too easily," he said at her questioning glance.

She stretched out her hand. "It's a race," she said, smiling. "I've always been better at running than you," she boasted.

"I caught you in the courtyard," he reminded her as he took her hand.

She grabbed her skirt in her fist and together they

ran across the strip of grass, Leitis muting her laughter with effort.

"I won," she announced on the other side, a bit of sophistry he allowed her. Her laughing face was flushed, her hair lit by a fading sun until it was tinted red-gold. In her lovely eyes was joy, so pure and unalloyed that his heart seemed to swell in gratitude for it.

"Don't do this now, Ian," she said, glancing up at him, her lovely eyes clear and deep. "Not at this moment."

"Do what?" he asked, confused.

"Look at me in that way. It makes me want to kiss you."

She sighed as he caught her up in his arms and kissed her anyway.

"We should get to the village," he said moments later.

She nodded, clutching at his waistcoat with possessive fingers.

"It doesn't seem quite right," she said, gazing up at him. "We are fleeing for our lives, responsible for getting almost fifty people to safety, and any moment we might be pursued by hundreds of English troops. I shouldn't be so happy, should I?"

"Happiness is fleeting enough. Hold it tight when it comes and don't let it go." To mark that thought, he pulled her to him again, spiraling down into their kiss with a jubilant delight.

Slowly they parted, each looking at the other. A moment of discovery and acknowledgment, he thought, that what was between them was greater than nationality or country.

They turned, finally, walking toward the village hand in hand. But when she would have veered onto the well-worn path through the glen, he pulled her into the cover of the forest.

"It's shorter this way," she protested.

"But we don't know whether or not Wescott has posted troops there," he said. She looked startled by the possibility.

But when they emerged from the forest a few minutes later, there was no sign of the general's troops.

The village was unearthly quiet, as if the inhabitants had already left. There was no smoke from the chimneys, no sign of life.

Leitis knocked on the first door and an old man answered. "It's time," she said. "I'm sorry we couldn't give you any warning," she added.

"We're ready," he said.

Ian strode to a cottage banded with flowers. An older woman answered, her gnarled hands clutching the doorframe tightly. "It's time to leave," he said gently.

Her only response was a tight-lipped nod.

One by one the cottage doors opened and people emerged, gathering in the middle of the village.

"We have to leave Gilmuir quickly," he said, addressing them. He didn't wish to alarm them, but neither did he want them kept in ignorance. It was better if they understood the need for haste. "The English might well be searching for us soon." Their faces each wore varying degrees of fear.

"You'll not be able to take more than you can carry, and even that should be limited. We'll be taking the path around the cliffs."

"I know of no path around the cliffs," a voice said. Ian turned to see Hamish standing a short distance away, his feet braced apart. One hand gripped his pipes, while the other was bunched in a fist and braced on his hip. For all the world, Ian thought, like a banty rooster defending his barnyard.

They stared at each other, Ian knowing the exact moment when Hamish recognized him.

"So, it's the Butcher himself," Hamish said, "come to lead those foolish enough to go. Where does an English colonel hope to take the MacRaes? To hell? Or just to prison?"

Ian heard the collective gasp of the people surrounding him.

Leitis came to his side, placed her hand on his arm in wordless support. "The reason the English will be searching," she told the clan, "is because he's Ian MacRae."

Hamish looked startled, then his eyes narrowed as he stared at them both. "He's the Butcher of Inverness."

"He's also the man who's put his own life in jeopardy," she said. "Not for his pride, Uncle," she said, staring fixedly at the pipes. "But for others."

"O-ho," Hamish said, frowning at her. "It's like that, is it?"

She nodded. "It's like that," she said firmly.

"Your grandfather would be spinning in his grave to see you now, Ian MacRae," Hamish said, turning to him.

Ian took one step closer to the old man. "You dare to talk to me about what my grandfather would have thought?" he asked incredulously. "Your own actions have been nothing but selfish, Hamish. You allowed Leitis to be your hostage, never caring what might happen to her."

He was so close that he could reach out and pick up the old fool and fling him away like so much rubbish. The fact that he wanted to made Ian clench his hands into fists.

"I don't intend to allow anyone else to suffer for

your pride, Hamish. Not Leitis, not any of these people."

He looked out over the crowd. "It's true I'm half English," he said, "but those at Fort William would punish me for being half Scot."

Leitis spoke beside him. "Some of you know him as the Raven," she said. "He helped you all."

"You gave me food," a man said, pushing his way to the front of the crowd.

"And me." An older woman spoke the words. People parted as she came forward.

"And brought us here in safety," another woman said. He recognized her as the mother of the boys he'd carried through the storm.

Ian heard a chorus of responses, all of them gratifying and obviously irritating to Hamish, who stood in the same place looking mulish.

"There's not much time," Ian said. "You can either trust me or you can stay here. Either way, there's uncertainty and peril. I'll not lie to you about that. All I can offer you is freedom."

"You're going, then, Leitis?" a young woman asked.

Leitis folded her hand into Ian's, then looked up at him. "I am," she said.

An old man stepped forward. His look was as sharp as Hamish's had been.

"You're the old laird's grandson?"

"Yes," Ian said.

"That's good enough for me," he said. "No English blood can dilute a true Scot." He turned to address the crowd. "We should be going, then," he said sharply.

One by one the villagers began to nod.

The procession out of the village was a muted one.

There was no time spent in glancing over the structures, whole or burned. And other than a few softly spoken regrets, there was no grief expressed about those possessions that had to be left behind. A lesson in their cheerful acceptance, Ian thought. The people of Gilmuir recognized that memories could be held within and needed no tangible reminders.

The cloudless sky was a whitish blue as they retraced their steps through the forest. The late afternoon sun created long shadows over the landscape. A breeze from the north set the branches of the trees to dancing, as if nature bade them a farewell with a wave of leafy fingers.

Hamish MacRae stood watching them, his pipes on his shoulder. The MacRae Lament was perfect for this moment as he witnessed the loss of his clansmen. Yet he couldn't play it for fear of endangering them.

He had never before felt as old or as useless as he did now. Worse, he felt shamed. The Butcher's words had sliced deep. He had endangered Leitis and done so without thought. And he'd lost her for it. She'd walked out of the village without a look in his direction, without even a farewell. As if he'd ceased to exist in her mind.

There was promise in that stony look he'd received from the Butcher. Ian, he corrected. A born leader of men, he thought.

Turning, he looked around him. He had lived his life with each day passing, one into the other, never noticing how much had changed. Until this moment, when he felt the world was not quite the same, but something altogether unfamiliar.

He didn't feel as if he belonged here anymore. But neither was he glad to be quit of Gilmuir. It was not an easy thing, after all, to begin a new life when he was almost at the age to be passing from this one.

But he wasn't about to be left behind.

He walked through the village to Peter's cottage, rapped hard on the door.

"Who is it?" Peter asked peevishly.

"The English come to call," Hamish said sarcastically. "Who do you think it is?"

The door flew open; Peter frowned down at him. "Dora, with the meal she promised. Something other than turnips, for a change. Or Mary, come to give me a bit of smelly cream for my knee. Anyone but you."

"The rest of them are leaving," Hamish said, pushing back his irritation at Peter for another, more important task.

"Now?" Peter asked.

"We'll be the only ones here," Hamish said. "And I've no wish to spend the rest of my life with only you as a companion, you old fool."

"Why don't you go piping in Gilmuir's courtyard, idiot?" Peter said. "The span of your life is bound to be shortened then."

"I'm going with them," Hamish said.

"You're going with them?" Peter repeated, surprised.

"If you don't hurry, you'll be the only one here," Hamish warned, then gave him back one of his eternal sayings. "A wise man wavers, a fool is fixed."

"I don't think so, old man," Peter said suddenly, squinting at him. "I'll not be a hermit." He left the doorway and Hamish walked inside. Peter was busy spreading out a sheet and piling things inside it.

"You would make yourself daft," Hamish agreed. "Besides, you need someone to point out the errors of your ways."

Peter stood, tied the sheet into a neat bundle. "My

errors?" he said incredulously. "I'm not a fool with the pipes. You've got the pride of a gaggle of clergy, Hamish MacRae."

Hamish grinned and preceded him out the door.

Chapter 29

I an and Leitis led the way through the forest, the journey a soundless one. Individually each of the Scots crossed the small stretch of glen. Some, like the children, thought it a great game and had to be coaxed to silence. Others walked more slowly, their pace causing Ian to look toward the land bridge and hope that the soldiers' preparations for night would distract them from looking toward the glen.

"If the children can walk," Ian said, addressing each of the women, "it would be safer if you did not carry them." He didn't add that it was because they would need to keep one hand free for balance along the more difficult parts of the path. Children generally had less fear, probably because they didn't fully understand the danger.

It was the older people who worried him. As they crossed the glen, he led them gently down to the beginning of the path and paired them with a younger person. That way, they could have the assistance they needed as well as the vocal support to get through the harrowing journey.

Leitis led the way back to Gilmuir, Ian following, the last person on the snakelike procession. He was halfway to the land bridge when he heard muttered whispers behind him.

He glanced around to find Hamish and another man arguing as they made their way across the glen. Hamish carried only his bagpipes, while the other man held a knotted pack.

"Your tongue wags like a lamb's tail, you old fool."

Hamish frowned at that insult. "At least I've the wit to wag it, you dried-up old acorn."

"Better half an egg than empty shells," the other man replied.

Ian stared at them. "If you're coming with us," he said in a much quieter voice than they were using, "it would be better to do so without calling attention to ourselves."

"See what I mean? Keep your tongue within your teeth," the other man said, glaring at Hamish.

Hamish stepped up to Ian. "I'm coming to keep an eye on my niece," he said belligerently. "I've no wish for her to be shamed."

"She'll not be," he said calmly.

Hamish frowned at him. "Is this the magical path? The secret . . ." His words trailed to a halt as he stared to his left and viewed the sheer drop to the loch.

It appeared that the cliff path was the one thing that could silence the old man. Ian felt a similar aversion, but he wasn't about to confess it to Hamish MacRae.

A rock fell ahead of them, and for one eternal moment Ian held himself still, waiting for the accompanying scream of terror. But there was no further sound.

It was a journey made in slow, measured steps marked not with fear but an occasional soft murmur or a child's giggle.

"There was never a height that didn't have a hole at the bottom of it," the man behind Hamish muttered.

"Give your tongue a rest, Peter," Hamish growled. "Or I'll put it to sleep for you."

"You and what English army?"

Ian halted, only to have Hamish bump into his back. Bracing his hand on the rock, Ian was determined not to think of Sedgewick once more. "I'll ask you again to be quiet," he said, as calmly as he could.

"I'll be inoffensive," Peter said curtly. "Not like the fool in front of me."

"If you'd only shut up," Hamish answered, "I'd be pleased."

Ian still didn't move, wondering why he was saddled with the two of them. They might have white hair, lined faces, and bodies bent with age, but they quarreled like tired children.

Finally, they fell silent and Ian began to walk again, not attempting to catch up with the others.

He wished there were a way to get word to Harrison and Donald as to his plans. The rest of the men who had followed him from Inverness were safe, not having been made conspirators in his acts as the Raven. But the fate of his adjutant and aide disturbed him.

They finally neared the entrance to the priory,

reaching the other villagers, who patiently waited to be lifted to safety. He glanced up and saw two of the older men helping Leitis and hoped that their strength lasted for a few more people.

He climbed up by gripping one tenacious root. Behind him, Hamish and Peter began to argue again, and he exchanged a look with a surprised Leitis. "They decided to join us," he explained, "but I'm not sure we're all that fortunate to have them."

He helped Hamish up to solid earth.

"I'd have you forgive me for putting you in danger," Hamish said, addressing Leitis. "For making you my hostage," he added, before glancing over at Ian. "Although I'm thinking you should thank me for that."

Ian just shook his head, extended his hand to help the other man.

"Better beyond the fear of danger than in it," Peter said, finally reaching the top.

"Do you never stop, man?" Hamish asked. "I wish I'd left you behind."

"Leave me behind?" Peter said, disgruntled. "I had already decided to leave."

"You're lying," Hamish said, frowning at the other man.

"Two cats and one mouse, two mice in one house," Peter said dolefully.

Hamish threw his hands up in the air. "What does that mean, you old daft idiot?"

"Will you two be quiet?" Ian said, irritated. "We're in even greater danger here. We don't need you quarrelling."

Hamish glanced over at him, surprised. "We're not quarrelling," he said. "We're talking."

"Then keep your talking to a whisper," Ian said,

and wished a moment later that he'd not suggested it.
Their bickering was annoying at any tone.

Ian strode to the middle of the priory, bent, and
pulled up the stone that hid the iron ring from view.
Leitis came to his side, the villagers trailing after her,
all of them silenced by what he revealed. Evidently,
Fergus and James had guarded the secret well all
these years.

He stood, leaning closer to Leitis so that the echo of
their voices would not carry to the others.

"Will you get them to the ship? There is something
I must do before I can follow you."

She surveyed him in the fading light, as if to measure his intentions. "You're not going back to the fort,
Ian?" she asked in a worried voice.

He cupped his hand around her cheek, smiling
down at her. "No," he said, "I've no wish to be a martyr." He kissed her quickly.

Leitis nodded and sat beside the opening to the
staircase, dangling her feet into the darkness. Another
difficult journey for the villagers, but it could not be
helped.

One by one, he helped them descend to the staircase. "The first step is lower than you expect," he
warned each of them.

A little girl stood against her mother's skirts, her
arms wrapped around one leg. Her mother's hand was
gently pressed against her cheek in wordless reassurance.

The other children seemed to look upon the descent into the staircase like a great and grand adventure, even as the older members of the clan simply
looked resolved.

Ian wished he could tell them that it would be easier from this point on, but he wasn't certain it would

be. The path to freedom was sometimes difficult, but then they already knew that.

The journey down the stairs was laden with both memory and illusion. Leitis could almost hear Fergus as a boy, his excited whispers filling the stairwell. James, always so cautious, would have counseled him to be careful. How odd that it had been James who had been so set on rebellion and Fergus who had argued for calm, wishing to remain at Gilmuir.

What would have happened if they had returned from Culloden? Their presence would not have affected the outcome of Gilmuir. The English were here to stay, even if she was taking their commander with her, a thought that prompted a smile.

Behind her she could hear the muffled groans as a few arthritic knees rebelled at the steep descent. They had all been so brave. The only complaining voices were those of Peter and Hamish, and they were more intent on each other's failings.

Now, at least, there was some measure of safety that had not been there before. The English knew nothing of the hidden stairwell, and of the ship that waited in the cove.

The journey, however, felt endless as she led the way. Before, Ian had always been with her, comforting her with a jest or simply holding her hand. The responsibility she felt for the people behind her should have taken her mind from another worry, that of his safety. But it didn't.

What was he doing? What errand was so important that he had to stay behind?

His courage was greater than hers, she realized. He had had so much more to lose by his actions, his position and his rank.

She had already been under suspicion by the English simply because she was Scot. They had burned her home to the ground, killed her family. There was nothing more they could take from her.

She learned a lesson in those moments. Courage was easy when there was nothing remaining to lose. But when she might have to learn to live without Ian, it became incredibly difficult to be brave.

Finally, she reached the bottom of the steps. In the faint light she lifted the lantern and lit it with the tinderbox Ian had left behind. She moved back into the staircase and removed the lantern's four shields, holding it high to illuminate the blackness.

It was just as Ian had predicted, better to take the stairs in the darkness. The walls were coated with pale green algae that glistened in the lantern's light. More than one person jerked his hand back, green being cited by superstition as the color of calamity and sorrow.

The steps themselves were shiny black stone, the chisel marks still visible. Leitis couldn't help but wonder how long the stairs had been here. Had Ionis the Saint carved them in all those years he'd lived on the island? Or did they predate him?

One by one, the villagers emerged into the cave, expressions of relief being silenced by awe as they gazed up at the ceiling. Another unexpected surprise, that of Ionis's lady faintly illuminated by the light from the lantern.

The villagers huddled together, the hardship of the past hour etched into their faces. Leitis wished there was time to rest, but it was important to get them to the ship.

She moved into the cave, glanced back once more at the staircase. *Please hurry,* she whispered in her mind and her heart. Another prayer to God would not be amiss, either.

She pushed her way through the crowd to the cave entrance and out to the rocky shoreline. She was surprised by the size of the merchant ship; it dwarfed the cove. Holding the lantern aloft, she moved it into an arc above her head, hoping to be seen by someone on board.

Immediately a boat was lowered and two seamen began to row to the shore.

"Can you forgive me, Leitis?" Hamish asked from behind her. "You've not spoken yet."

She faced her uncle determinedly. "I have nothing to say to you, Uncle," she said calmly. "Perhaps in time I will."

"Was it easier to forgive the Butcher his deeds?" Hamish asked curtly.

She began to smile, amused that even now he would be arrogant.

"He was never unkind to me," she said.

"I should have protected you better, Niece," Hamish admitted.

She said nothing in response.

"So, you'll make me pay for my foolishness until my dying day." He frowned at her and she wondered if he was going to choose this moment to lecture her. The boat approached, nudged the shoreline, and the two seamen got out, began to hand the passengers in one by one.

"Can you row a boat, Uncle?" she asked.

He nodded curtly.

She gestured to Ian's skiff tied not far away. "If we send two boats at a time to the ship," she said, "it will make the ferrying faster."

"So that's to be my punishment, then, to be a beast of burden for the villagers of Gilmuir."

His irritation startled a laugh from her. She embraced him swiftly, the gesture unexpected, from the surprised look on his face.

"You'll never change, Uncle," she said, certain of it. "Yes," she added, smiling at him, "that's your punishment."

He didn't say a word, but he began to smile, an expression she didn't often see on his lined face.

"Fair enough," he said. He turned to Peter, smiling tightly. "You'll be my first passenger, then, you old goat."

"He's a wise man that can take care of himself," Peter answered.

"Are you going to swim, then? How wise is that?"

The two of them walked to the boat and stood aside as Martha and her daughter climbed in to sit in the bow.

Leitis would remember this exodus for the rest of her life. The sky was marked by long, thin wisps of clouds lit from beneath by an orange glow. The necklace of rocks appeared almost amber in the fading sunlight. She heard the sound of the water lapping up against the rocks of the shoreline, the sighs of those who did not wish to leave Gilmuir but realized only too well the futility of remaining behind. The excited questions from the braver children reminded her of Fergus and James and Ian and herself, feckless and daring.

The breeze blew her hair back from her face, carrying with it a faint chill. A hint of winter, a promise of seasons changing.

She wanted to be with Ian in winter, when ice formed on the branches of the trees and the wind grew wild and harsh. She wanted a fire in a cozy cottage, and to have him enter, slapping his arms against his chest and grinning, red-faced, at her. He'd scrape his shoes at the door and tell her what he'd done that day. She would feed him well and listen intently and show him the plaid she'd woven. A new pattern, an amalgam of the MacRae tartan and something new. When it was time for bed, they would hold each other and gift each other with laughter or passion or fierce need.

Please, God, let it happen.

Chapter 30

When the last of the villagers entered the staircase, Ian closed the entrance to the stairs and walked quickly to the laird's chamber.

He went to the loom and slipped the pattern from it. Folding it under his waistcoat, he left again, entering the archway that led to the clan hall.

A sneeze alerted him.

"I've looked all over the fort, sir," a nasally voice said, "but he isn't there, either."

"He's got to be here somewhere," Harrison said. "We need to find that staircase of his."

Ian waited a moment in order to ascertain whether any other men were with them. When it was obvious they were alone, he stepped out of the shadows to face his adjutant and aide.

"I was trying to find a way to get word to both of you," he said, the feeling of relief he experienced staggering. "It's not safe you for you to be here, especially since I will soon be labeled a deserter in addition to being a mere traitor."

"You don't think we'd leave you, sir?" Harrison asked.

"You've both been loyal to me. More than any man could expect. But now you must protect yourselves."

"Begging your pardon, sir, but where are you going?" Donald asked nasally.

"Anywhere but Scotland or England," he said. "The destination has not been chosen."

"Don't you want us to come with you, sir?"

"I'd be pleased to have you come with me, both of you. But it's not a decision you can make without consideration. The army doesn't treat deserters lightly."

"They can't hang us if they can't catch us, sir," Donald said, grinning.

Harrison looked up at the sky, the ground, then pulled himself up into a rigid stance. "Sir, I feel it necessary to confess something to you."

"Other than turning me over to Cumberland," Ian said dryly, "what else would account for that look on your face, Harrison?"

"She's aboard ship, sir. Alison, that is."

Ian glanced at his adjutant. "I take it Miss Fulton challenged her father's dictate?" he asked, smiling.

Harrison glanced at him, grinning. The expression, while rendering his face plainer, was almost contagious. "She said that she wouldn't let me leave without her, sir. We were married in Inverness, sir."

"I take it you were going to resign your commission? Wouldn't that be wiser than being a deserter?"

"At the moment, I'd much rather leave than take my chances with Sedgewick," Harrison said.

"He would pose no problem to you," Ian said dryly, and explained what had happened.

"Still, sir," Harrison said, "it wouldn't be the wisest thing to remain in Scotland once her father learns of our marriage."

"I've never been away from England except for Flanders and Scotland, sir," Donald interjected, "but I'd like to see a part of the world that's a bit more pleasant than this. One where there's no war."

Ian's glance encompassed both of them. "Then, if you're certain, you're welcome to come. But as of this moment I'm no longer your colonel, and you should not address me as such," Ian said. He'd explain the change of names later.

He walked to the priory, both men following him, and pulled up the stone. Donald descended to the steps, Harrison close on his heels.

Ian once again sat on the edge, surveying the priory one last time. Shadows draped from the ancient walls like silk panels. In the distance of his memory he could almost hear a ceremony here, an imploration to God before battle. Perhaps he should make a similar plea, but he could not help but think that the outcome of this adventure had already been decided. Good fortune attended them, he was certain of it.

In an odd twist of imagination, he envisioned his grandfather standing against the west wall, nodding in approval. His parents were there, too, his father's arm around his mother, both of them smiling at him. James and Fergus stood alongside, grown men now, attired in their kilts and daring him with their grins.

He nodded in farewell and slipped into the staircase.

Pulling the two stones over him, Ian couldn't help but wonder if this place would ever be discovered again.

Hamish returned to the shore, his passengers having climbed the *Stalwart*'s rope ladder. He stepped from the boat and approached her, his boots crunching over the rocky shoreline.

"And when will you leave, Leitis?" he asked, frowning.

"When Ian arrives," she said firmly.

"Stubborn to the end, my love," Ian said from behind her.

She spun around and he was there, whole and safe, his smile gently teasing. She nearly leapt into his arms, she was so glad to see him. Ignoring the presence of the others, she pulled his head down for a kiss.

"You took long enough," she said when the kiss ended. Her complaint was ended on a sigh as he wrapped his arms around her. She was truly not given to tears, but she felt like weeping now. She hated the idea of leaving Gilmuir, but at the same time she was happier than she'd ever been in her life. Sadness and joy were odd companions.

"I had to arrange for more baggage," he said in a low and intimate voice.

She pulled back, looked up at him curiously. His smile was still anchored in place. Peering behind him, she saw both Harrison and Donald standing there. Both of them were smiling.

"You're coming with us?" she asked, surprised.

Harrison nodded. Donald sneezed.

He grinned at her, looked at Ian, and sneezed again.

She frowned, suddenly realizing how he'd become

sick. "Your cold has gotten worse," she scolded. "You should have known something like this would happen if you go driving a wagon in the midst of a storm."

She glanced over her shoulder at Ian. His grin was confirmation enough.

Donald looked away, sneezed again.

"What about you?" she asked Harrison. "Were you one of us?"

"I wasn't part of that, miss," he said, smiling. "I was in Inverness."

"Hiring a ship?"

He glanced at Ian and then nodded.

"You should be tending that cold," she said, turning back to Donald. She felt his forehead. "You're as foolish as my brother Fergus," she said, slightly alarmed at the heat of his brow.

"So, you'll be crooning to the English now, Leitis," Hamish snapped.

She heard Ian sigh, then watched in amazement as he strode to where Hamish stood. He gripped her uncle by both arms, lifted him effortlessly until his feet dangled a few inches above the shore and their eyes were at a level.

"You'll not speak to Leitis in that tone, Hamish," Ian said firmly. "Not now, not aboard ship, not when we land, not ever."

Hamish nodded, his frown suddenly replaced by a grin.

"You sound just like your grandfather, Ian," he said, pleased. "It's laird you'll be, then. The clan needs a leader."

Ian simply stared at him, before lowering Hamish to the ground. He spun around, walking toward her again.

"Tell me I was right to let him come along," Ian said, reaching her. "Tell me I wasn't a fool."

"You were right," she said, amused. "But Hamish is, too." She squinted at him as if measuring him. "You would make a fine laird."

A pronouncement that had him shaking his head.

Lieutenant Armstrong knocked on the door with some trepidation. The general had taken over the colonel's quarters and for the past hour a procession of aides had entered and left, bearing bottles of wine and crates of crystal. The general evidently had a taste for the finer things in life.

Wescott opened the door himself. In his hand was a glass of wine, the mate to the one held by the Countess of Sherbourne. Beside her sat her son, and on the end of the table lay a cat curled in a ball in front of an empty basket. It was a thoroughly respectable scene, but it had the tinge of assignation, what with the flush on the countess's face and General Wescott's pleased countenance.

"What is it, Lieutenant?" the general asked, his affability quickly changing to irritation. "I thought I left orders that I wasn't to be disturbed."

"I beg your pardon, sir, but Major Sedgewick is nowhere to be found."

"I'm sure Sedgewick is capable enough not to get lost, Lieutenant," Wescott said dryly.

"But he was last seen heading toward the castle, sir, and he has not returned."

"I saw him not too long ago," the countess said unexpectedly. She smiled sweetly at him. "The dear man mentioned that he had duties to perform. But, of course, I did not inquire further."

Armstrong stared at her, their gaze locking. She set

her glass on the table, then smiled at the general.

"Shall I leave, Nigel?" she asked softly.

Wescott glanced at her, then turned and glared at Armstrong. "No, Patricia, I think not. If Sedgewick does not return by morning, Lieutenant, then I will concern myself. Until then, don't bother me."

Armstrong had the curious feeling that the Countess of Sherbourne had just outmaneuvered him. He nodded and stepped back quickly as General Wescott closed the door in his face.

The *Stalwart* looked low in the water, a brooding hen with touches of brown and tan about her. The journey to her side was made slower than Ian wished. He waited impatiently as Harrison and then Donald scaled the rope ladder.

Finally it was Leitis's turn.

"I'll not climb that thing with you staring up my skirt," she said, annoyed.

"Why do you think I let the other two go first?" he asked. "As to what's under your skirt . . ." he began, only to be silenced by her look.

"I'll not look," he promised, and when she frowned at him, he smiled. "Very well, only a little." When she still hesitated, he held her aloft so that she had no choice but to grab the ladder for support.

"You can be as arrogant as Hamish, you know," she said, glancing behind her.

He only smiled in response.

It was not an easy ascent, agility with a rope ladder something that needed to be practiced. But a few moments later Leitis was aboard the *Stalwart*. He followed, Captain Braddock greeting him the moment his boots touched the deck.

"I'm very pleased to see you," the captain said

with obvious relief. "If we hurry, we can make it around the rocks before full night." He stared out at the cove warily. "I must confess that I'm eager to be gone from this place."

Ian turned back to the rail, looked over the side.

Only one more boatload remained, and that carried no passengers, only the villagers' belongings.

"We should be gone in a matter of moments," he reassured the captain.

After the boat had been unloaded and all the packs and cases tied to ropes and hauled aboard, Ian moved to the bow. The same Italian sailor he'd met earlier stood beside him, once again marking the depth. They were entrusting their lives to this captain and his caution was a good sign.

After they passed slowly around the necklace of rocks, the captain gave the order for full sail. As they left the cove, Ian glanced behind him, grateful to discover that the villagers of Gilmuir, Leitis included, were huddled in a tight group. They would not see what he had just noticed, Sedgewick's broken body lying on the far side of the tallest rock.

Once past the barrier, the danger lessened. Even if they were seen by the troops at Fort William, there was no likelihood that they could be overtaken. In less than an hour they would be at Coneagh Firth and quickly out to sea.

He stepped away from the bow, only to be approached by the captain.

"Sir, if you could accompany me for a moment, I think I have a solution to your destination."

He glanced in Leitis's direction. The group was still talking, and from the looks of it, it was an impassioned gathering. But then, anything involving Hamish was destined to be fiery.

Curious, Ian followed the captain to his quarters in

the forecastle, and watched as the man pulled a large rolled map from its case. He spread it open on a small square table, placing a prism on either side of the map to prevent it from curling.

"Here, sir," Captain Braddock said, pointing to an area on the coast of the colonies. "It's a place called Maryland. I've taken passengers there before."

But a small spot far to the north captured Ian's attention, instead. He traced his fingers across the shape of it. The coastline, jagged with inlets and firths, reminded him, oddly enough, of Scotland.

"No," Ian said, beginning to smile. There it was, written right on the map. A sign, an omen, if he believed in such things. "There," he said, pointing to the place. "That will be our home."

"Are you certain?" Captain Braddock asked, frowning.

"I am," he said.

A moment later he left the captain's quarters. Hamish stood in the hatchway, both hands fixed on the bulkhead on either side of him.

"You've been elected laird," Hamish said bluntly, a grin deepening the lines on his face.

"What?" Ian asked, dumbfounded.

"You're laird now, Ian," Hamish said, grinning and following him to the forecastle.

Leitis stepped out of the crowd and came to his side. They linked their fingers, content at the moment for only that. And the space between them was acceptable, too, as long as he could touch her in some manner, look in her eyes and see both the past and the future.

"He can't be serious," Ian said, glancing warily at Hamish.

"I'm afraid he is," she said, reaching out her hands to him. "The people of Gilmuir think it fitting that the grandson of Niall MacRae should lead them."

He wished he knew what to say at this moment. But words were puny things, incapable of holding thoughts of such importance.

"I don't know anything about being a laird," he said, the confession an awkward one.

"Yes, you do," she gently chided. "Everything you've done, every lesson in command has led to this moment."

"And if I fail them?" he asked, looking at the milling people.

"Did you fail your troops? Or the men you rescued from Inverness? Or me?" she asked, smiling.

"Did you vote for me, Leitis?"

"I did," she said, smiling. "It was nearly unanimous."

"Let me guess," he said sardonically. "Hamish disagreed."

She shook her head. "He was the one who suggested it," she said. "Peter was the lone dissenting vote. He said you were too bossy."

"Does that amuse you?" he asked.

"Yes," she answered. "For you to make an impression on Peter, it must have been a fierce scolding you gave him."

"I don't remember even speaking to the man."

"That's even worse," she said, laughing.

He glanced back at the ruins of Gilmuir, shielded by the advancing darkness. "Do you think my grandfather would have approved of my being laird?" he asked her, thinking of the ghosts he'd imagined.

"Yes," she said emphatically. "And he would have been the first to leave," she added, surprising him. "He believed in people more than places."

Ian knew that he would always remember her just as she was at this moment. She was smiling, her face relaxed and beautiful, the breeze over the loch gently stirring her hair. It felt as if he'd been traveling for years to come to this one place, this one woman.

The image of her as a child was replaced with the woman's face. Leitis, laughing, or smiling tenderly at him. Or with her beautiful eyes flashing her irritation. Leitis, with her hair blowing in the wind, her hand clenching her skirt as she raced across the glen.

He turned to address the people on deck, raising his voice so that he could be heard.

"There's a place across the ocean called Nova Scotia," he said, telling them what he'd discovered. "New Scotland."

"I like the name," Malcolm said, and several other voices agreed.

"Near it is an island," Ian added. "A place not unlike Gilmuir. I think we should go there, but it is not my decision alone. We must all agree. Who's for New Scotland?"

"Wherever you decide, sir," Donald said from the rear. Standing beside him were Harrison and his new bride, each of them holding the other. Harrison only smiled his approval.

The vote, including Peter's grudging assent, was unanimous.

Ian glanced down at Leitis. "And you, my love? What do you say?"

Leitis studied the far horizon. "I think," she said, finally, her smile luminous, "that wherever you are is home."

Epilogue

An hour later, Leitis and Ian were married by Scots law, an agreement binding by the sincere, mutual consent of the participants. The words were simple, each spoken by one to the other.

"I will have you as my husband, to live with as long as God decrees," she said. "Before my clan I promise this."

"I will have you as my wife, to live with as long as God decrees," Ian said. He turned and looked around him. Those on deck were, in varying degrees, smiling back at him. An act of welcome and approval that he seemed to understand. "Before my clan, I promise this," he finished.

He opened his arms and she walked into his embrace. But a moment later, he pulled back. Reaching inside his waistcoat, he withdrew a length of plaid.

"You took it from the loom," she said, surprised. She clasped it in her hand, the wool still warm from his body.

"I'm afraid I did so with less care than you would have shown," he admitted, "but I wanted you to have it."

Her arms reached up and encircled his neck. They kissed through most of the journey through Loch Euliss.

Finally, she lay her cheek against his chest, hearing the thudding beat of his heart and feeling a dazed delight. A month ago she had no future and the only emotion she could feel was grief.

Now she stood with the man she loved and her clan. The world seemed a special place now, one in which they could write their own destiny.

Above them in the rigging men shouted at each other, while the first mate bellowed orders from the forecastle. Children laughed, a woman asked a question, a mother's soothing voice calmed a querulous complaint.

The day bade farewell in hues of purple and indigo, a riotous display of color as if fearing the sun would never come again.

The sound of the pipes came faintly at first, then grew louder until it swelled through the air. Not a defiant tune, but a call of forever and home and the soul's longing for itself.

Leitis sighed, lay her cheek on Ian's chest, feeling the spike of tears.

It wouldn't be the last time she heard the pipes, but never would it again be with Scotland echoing the sound back from craggy hills and thickly green glens. Shadows draped the earth as if to gradually hide it from their view and ease the parting.

It was a farewell Hamish played, the twilight mist adding a soft and sweet benediction as if the notes comprised a hymn. The world fell silent around them. Not one person on deck spoke, but more than a few wiped their eyes.

Ian's arms were around her, holding her tight as Leitis recalled the MacRae Lament. The words were oddly fitting for this moment, and this place.

Here is our island, here is our pride.
We are a past never to die.
In good times or bad we'll always endure
In the home of our hearts—Gilmuir

Afterword

William Augustus, Duke of Cumberland, was actually known as Butcher Cumberland because of his cruelty following the Battle of Culloden. Cumberland's decree that a soldier could be hanged for aiding the Scots is, regrettably, historical fact.

Gilmuir and the island that housed it are loosely based on a location governed by the MacRaes. It was fascinating to discover, after I had imagined Ionis the Saint, that the real island had also once been a site of pilgrimage.

Fort William was similar in fashion to other English fortifications built in Scotland at the time. Fort George was actually constructed between 1748 and 1769 and was one of the largest building projects in the Highlands. Ironically, none of its impressive cannon were ever fired.

The Scottish emigration to Nova Scotia began in earnest around 1750, when the ship *Hector* arrived from Scotland.

If you loved *THE HUSBAND LIST*
and *THE WEDDING BARGAIN*
Then don't miss the latest delicious love story from
USA Today bestselling author

VICTORIA ALEXANDER

THE MARRIAGE LESSON

Lady Marianne Shelton has set the members of London's *ton* on their ears by anonymously penning the scandalous *The Absolutely True Adventures of a Country Miss in London* . . . based on the real-life exploits of nobleman Thomas Effington. Now, Thomas is going to teach this impertinent miss a lesson or two about love that she'll never forget!

Coming in May
An Avon Romantic Treasure
Don't miss it!

Avon Romantic Treasures

*Unforgettable, enthralling love stories,
sparkling with passion and adventure
from Romance's bestselling authors*